THE
DUTCH
ORPHAN

Also by Ellen Keith

The Dutch Wife

THE
DUTCH
ORPHAN

ELLEN KEITH

PARK
ROW
BOOKS

PARK™
ROW
BOOKS™

Recycling programs
for this product may
not exist in your area.

ISBN-13: 978-0-7783-3430-9

The Dutch Orphan

This edition published by arrangement with Harlequin Books S.A.

Park Row Books
22 Adelaide St. West, 41st Floor
Toronto, Ontario M5H 4E3, Canada
ParkRowBooks.com
BookClubbish.com

Printed in U.S.A.

To Hannie and Han:

For showing me a new meaning of home

THE
DUTCH
ORPHAN

PROLOGUE

Johanna Vos
May 10, 1940
Zierikzee, the Netherlands

They say that if a stork flies overhead on your wedding day, you'll be blessed with a child within the year. On the day of her wedding, my younger sister rose with the birds and turned her gaze skyward. It was a crisp, spring morning, the type that scatters dew across the dikes. A heavy stillness filled the dawn. Liesbeth perched in the alcove of our childhood bedroom, trying to summon shapes from shadows as the dusty pink glow gave way to sunlight. The neighbor's cows still crowded in the barn, waiting to be milked, and the sky was empty.

I watched her crane her neck until her nose was pressed to the windowpane. "Let's hope Maurits isn't relying on a bird to fill your house with children," I teased.

Liesbeth blushed. "Any luck helps."

She stood up and we started to get ready, dusting our cheeks with rouge and molding our chestnut hair into soft waves. While she pinned her barrette, I opened the wardrobe and retrieved the hanger with the wedding dress, lifting the hem and twirling around with it in a circle. "Well, Lies, are you ready?"

The dress was gorgeous, Liesbeth's own creation. I traced a finger over the folds of satin, the gathers that tapered to a fitted waist. "You've outdone yourself. Nobody in Zeeland has had a dress like this. It's as if you stole it straight from the pages of *Libelle* magazine!"

"Maybe I ought to parade around town first to make all the other girls a tad jealous," she said. I knew she'd sat in the back room of the tailor's shop for evenings on end, sewing on the gown's covered buttons one by one, fantasizing about the day she would give up the job to become Maurits's wife.

I paused, listening to the comforting sounds of our aunt, *tante* Rika, making breakfast downstairs. It felt like it had throughout all those years we'd lived with our aunt and uncle, up until I'd moved to Amsterdam with my husband, Willem. And now, here was Liesbeth, following in my footsteps.

"Are you sure you're ready to leave Zierikzee?" I asked. "It's not too late to find a strong farmer who would keep you nice and plump."

Liesbeth laughed and shimmied out of her nightgown. "I'll happily trade in this dull life for parties and dress shops and nights at the cinema with the man of my dreams."

I didn't respond—I didn't have to. While I'd tried to bite my tongue in the weeks leading up to their wedding, she could read me better than anyone. And although Willem had known Maurits since their early days at university, a part of me regretted introducing her. In the two years I'd known him, Maurits had changed—he seemed intent on climbing his way up in the world two rungs at a time, regardless of where that ladder was leading. I'd even heard him praise Hitler's policies in Germany, as if he'd forgotten the dictator was busy terrorizing Poland and silencing his own people. Maurits preached of nationalism and economic prosperity like that rat-faced Goebbels was sitting on his shoulder.

Liesbeth looked down at the floor. "You'll give him a proper chance, won't you?"

I nodded, because what else could I do? I didn't want to dash my sister's hopes on her wedding day. I forced a smile and pointed to the girdle she was putting on. "Maurits might send you right back if you try to seduce him in that prissy old thing. Tell me that's not what you're planning on wearing tonight!"

Her cheeks flushed scarlet. I reached into the bottom drawer of the wardrobe and produced a package wrapped in colored paper. Inside was a light peach chemise that seemed to be made of air. I winked. "Don't tell *tante* Rika."

She thanked me and slipped it over her head. Then I helped her into the dress, looping button after button through the tiny holes. I'd missed this ritual of getting ready together, the coolness of my sister's skin when I fastened her necklace or adjusted a hatpin. During my first months in Amsterdam, Liesbeth had visited often enough that her absence had felt temporary. I tried to imagine what it would be like to have her there in the city, living only a few minutes away by bicycle.

"Look at you," I said, guiding her to the mirror. The dress hugged her body in a way that suited her: equally flattering and modest. Lies had always been the girlish one. Perhaps my features were more defined, my cheekbones higher, my hair more eager to curl, but, today, with our mother's lily-shaped ear baubles and those layers of satin, she looked like a true lady. "You're radiant," I said.

Soon, someone knocked at the door. Our brother, Gerrit, poked his head in. "Your beau has arrived." He looked Liesbeth up and down. "Sorry, I guess I have the wrong room. I'm looking for my sister—lanky as a flagpole, likes to tip cows at night and dumb as a pig's rear end. You seen her?"

Liesbeth slapped him playfully on the sleeve and took one

last look in the mirror to fix her hair. "No more cow tipping for me. From now on, it's the big-city life."

He grinned. "I'm proud of you. Maurits is a lucky man."

When we went downstairs, Maurits was waiting in the entrance. His outfit looked overpriced, with gold links adorning his French cuffs, and every hair on his head was sculpted into place with a perfection that was almost disconcerting. But when he saw Liesbeth, he beamed with such love, so I hoped with everything in my being that I had misjudged him.

Our relatives arrived at the front gate in a cacophony of bicycle bells. They cheered and whooped and called Liesbeth's name. A crunch of tires on gravel followed as Maurits's family pulled up to the house in a shiny automobile.

"City folk," *oom* Cor mumbled. He straightened his tie and went to greet the guests. Our uncle was a strange sight in his old suit, the one he normally saved for funerals. It hung long in the sleeves, dwarfing his hands, but perhaps he liked it that way, so the new in-laws couldn't see the deep lines of yard work that creased his palms.

The wedding ceremony at the town hall was short and simple. We sat on plush chairs in a room with rococo paneling and gilded portraits of Zeeland's forefathers. Liesbeth clutched her bouquet of pink peonies, and when she said her *I do*'s, Willem passed me his handkerchief before I knew I needed it. A warm feeling overcame me, but I was also conscious that a small part of me had split off and was floating away.

We returned to the house, where the long table in the garden had been set and reset so many times, soupspoons repolished and the vases of tulips rearranged, that even the cows had begun to stare. They peered wide-eyed over the neighbor's fence, while *tante* Rika clanged pans together to chase them away.

Everyone sat down for lunch: roast with buns, a cheese platter, herring from the fisherman down the road. Maurits's family kept remarking how "lovely" and "quaint" everything was, how it felt like "a departure from reality." *Oom* Cor bristled and stared at his shoes.

The sky began to cloud over, and a flock of swallows flew by. Liesbeth's head shot up, so I winked at her from down the table. No stork, not yet.

Maurits rose, clearing his throat. "I'd like to make a toast," he said, "to my beautiful bride. I have no doubt we'll grow old and wise together, with a charming brood of children nestled on our laps." He raised his glass. "There are great forces at work in the world. May today mark the beginning of a prosperous new stage in our lives together."

At the behest of the guests, the married couple kissed. Willem pushed up the brim of his horn-rimmed glasses with his middle finger and leaned over to whisper in my ear. "He had to slip in the word *prosperous*, didn't he?"

"Let's hope he puts Liesbeth's happiness above all that," I said.

When the toasts finished and the dishes were cleared, my turn came. I felt that familiar prickle of nerves when I pushed back my chair. Willem gave me a kiss for good luck, and I got up to join the trio of musician friends I'd invited as a surprise. We gathered in the corner by the magnolia tree.

Liesbeth clasped her hands together. "Please tell me you're going to perform."

The bassist tuned his instrument and counted us in. I breathed deep into my diaphragm and started to sing. The musicians played beautifully, the sounds carrying on the breeze that rustled the fields. Liesbeth's eyes brimmed with tears of joy, which gave me a rush of sisterly love. Even if her heart now belonged to someone else, I knew she would always be there for me.

The song came to an end, and Liesbeth jumped to her feet, calling for an encore. We launched into another number.

Then, in the distance, something rumbled, low and loud, like a hornet. My brother looked up, and I followed his gaze. An airplane crossed the sky, heading out over the sea. Another followed, and then another. Liesbeth signaled for the musicians to play louder, unwilling to permit any intrusions on her perfect wedding day. Maurits leaned in to stroke her cheek.

The rumbling grew louder, until I stumbled over the lyrics and the musicians fell out of tune.

"Look!" Gerrit said. One by one, we turned our heads to where he was pointing. There, on the horizon, were those same threatening aircraft, flying in formation. But they were no longer traveling westward, toward the English Channel. No, the planes had turned around. That V that guided their approach pointed eastward, back inland. Straight toward us.

A feeling passed across the garden, like we could see our whole world falling apart. Guests got up from the table, voices raised in alarm. Maurits was the only one who stayed seated, appearing strangely calm. I locked eyes with Lies and moved to stand beside her. The planes roared louder, before passing overhead, black marks against the cloudy sky.

PART ONE

The Velvet Glove
February 1941–October 1942

ONE

Johanna Vos
February 9, 1941
Amsterdam, the Netherlands

Café Alcazar was full for a Sunday, a crowd with energy that fizzed like a freshly popped soft drink. All the tables were occupied, laughter and flirty remarks bouncing back and forth over *fluitjes* of beer. I watched from backstage as we got ready for our gig, my nerves feeling equally bouncy.

I turned to my dear friend Jakob Cohen, the bassist who had performed at my sister's wedding. "Thanks for taking a chance on me," I said. Jakob had fled Germany with his parents eight years earlier in fear of the changing politics and growing anti-Semitism. Sharp as a razor blade, he spoke perfect Dutch and was a riot. His dark features, with his Groucho eyebrows and slicked-back hair, were the only things that prevented him from seamlessly blending in.

I'd agreed to fill in for the singer in the Rovers, the band Jakob played with when he wasn't rehearsing with the local orchestra. Their gigs had slowed down in the past month. The Nazis had banned Jews from performing in non-Jewish venues, which would eliminate half the band. Lucky for us, Café Alcazar's owner was one of the few barmen in Amsterdam who still welcomed all performers.

Willem appeared beside us and squeezed my waist affectionately. "She's been wearing out her lungs all week for this."

"Oh, hush, you." I swatted at him and took a big sip of water to soothe the tickle in my throat. I probably had overdone it with the practicing.

"I'm proud of you, sweetheart," Willem said. "Just don't make it too good." His gaze swept across the bar.

Jakob came over and wrapped his arms around both of us. "Don't worry—no Nazis yet, but if they come, they come. I know you won't let us down, Jo."

"Aren't you two a pair of good-luck charms? Don't make me more nervous than I already am."

"I'm teasing," Willem replied. "You'll be front and center. You always are." He gave me a kiss. "Good luck. I'm going to check if Lies and Maurits have turned up."

I took a second to admire my Wim's retreating back, his easy confidence, his shoulders broad and masculine despite his slim frame. Then, Jakob assembled the rest of the band to warm up. I ran through a few vocal exercises with the backup singer until the butterflies settled down.

"It's time," Jakob said. "Feeling ready?"

Before I could reply, the bar owner called us up. We filed on stage, the lights bright and blinding. I squinted and saw Willem sitting next to Liesbeth and Maurits. I wondered how Liesbeth had convinced Maurits to tag along. If he found out half the band was Jewish, he would think twice about coming to watch me again.

Jakob started playing, and then the pianist kicked in. That was my cue. The second I began to sing, my nerves disappeared. I took it all in. The lights. The jaunty kick of the trumpet. The sparkle of my sapphire-blue gown and my long white gloves.

Everything felt bright, like my lungs were bursting with joy. The feeling washed away everything else, everything that was happening in the world outside that bar.

We finished the number to wild applause. In the audience, several couples rose to dance as we started the next song. I twirled, turning to flirt with the crowd. Willem winked at me, and I blew him a kiss. Behind me, the saxophonist bobbed and twisted while he played.

During the third song, the door to the bar swung open with the rowdy noise of drunken men. A trio of German soldiers settled at a table at the front, next to the bar. Jakob caught my eye. We were both thinking the same thing: trouble.

"Beers! Now!" one of the soldiers called. He looked around and spotted Jakob. "Oi!"

The soldier to his right nudged him. "Sit down, Helmut."

"We're not in Hamburg anymore. I'll do what I want."

The third soldier interrupted. "Boys. Do you smell pork in here?" He pointed to the stage. "I smell sweat."

"Stink, don't they? Oink! Oink!"

I watched them in disgust, forgetting my place in the song and stumbling on the lyrics. Jakob leaned toward me, his voice barely audible above the music and their shouting. "Keep going."

The oinking soldier, his hair white as clotted cream, sat up straighter. "Play something for the Führer, you useless fucks!"

On stage, we turned to one another, trying to improvise. I waited for some cue from Jakob, but he stood there, looking half his size. I hesitated only a second. Then, grabbing the microphone, I gestured for the others to follow my lead and broke into a German cabaret number Marlene Dietrich performed, one of the few I knew by heart.

I kept singing, determined not to let the soldiers see the cracks in my confidence, not even when Maurits stood up and guided Liesbeth toward the exit. Behind me, Jakob and the others picked up the notes and joined in. I focused on the crowd, and when the ruckus died down, I turned to face the soldiers. They were quiet. As the song came to a close, I prepared to transition into another, but Jakob signaled to me. The owner of the bar was standing at the side of the stage. I moved aside to give him the microphone. "A big thank-you to the Rovers, thank you."

"But we had another twenty minutes," I whispered to Jakob. He shook his head. "Better for us and him we don't."

Sure enough, the soldiers waved the barman over for another round, slapping a handful of coins on the table.

The owner addressed us in a low voice. "Let's give it a half hour. You're welcome to go back on once the fog has lifted."

By the bar, the white-blond soldier was making a commotion. "Who's the pretty one?" He pointed with his chin toward the stage, toward me.

The barman tried to give the soldier his change and move on, but the soldier wouldn't let him leave. "I'm talking to you," he said. He made a grab for the barman and missed, his two mates hauling him back to his seat.

"Let's go," said another soldier.

"Lady. Lady!"

Jakob lay a protective hand on my arm. I didn't dare look across the bar at Willem. Hopefully he had the sense to stay out of it.

The soldier pulled out a fistful of bills and slapped them on the table. "I'd give you all this for…ten minutes."

"This is a music hall not a whorehouse," I said.

The other loud one chimed in. "Dame's got a fine mouth on her."

"Out!" The third soldier grabbed his two companions by the scruff of their uniforms and marched them toward the exit.

"We'll be back, little pigs!" one called on the way out.

I glared at their backs, looking away when the door slammed behind them. A hush had fallen over the crowd. Willem was on his feet, moving toward us.

"We ought to call it a night," Jakob said, guiding me off stage.

"No, we should keep playing," I replied, although it wasn't my decision to make. Then Willem was there next to me.

"How are you holding up?"

"Fine."

"And you, Jakob?"

"Tough crowd, but Jo did well."

Willem kissed my forehead. "You were a star, sweetheart, a real natural up there. I'm proud of you."

"Where are Liesbeth and Maurits?" I asked.

"Probably outside cozying up to the *moffen*," he said, meaning the Nazis. "Liesbeth muttered something about an early start for Maurits."

Before I had a chance to reply, people began yelling at the entrance to the bar. I turned, expecting the drunken soldiers again. But instead, I saw the doorman struggling with the door, trying to hold it shut. The owner rushed over to see what was going on.

"NSBers," someone warned. "A huge group of them!"

I glanced at Willem. NSBers were members of the NSB, the Dutch National Socialist Party. What had started as a regular political party was becoming more radical and hate fueled by the day. Hitler's proud messengers, spreading fascism in the Netherlands.

"We need to get out of here," Willem said. Before we could react, a window broke. People jumped up and out of the way while glass rained down on the tables.

Outside, men shouted, "Let us in!"

Inside, men shouted, "Take cover!"

Another windowpane smashed. Somebody shrieked. A bicycle came tumbling through another window.

The doorman couldn't hold them back any longer. NSBers in black uniforms—the paramilitary branch—rushed the entrance, piling into the bar. "Where are the Jews?" they yelled as they began to push and shove.

"Jo!" Willem called. He was leading Jakob and his bandmates toward the back of the bar.

It was chaos. One giant bar fight. Men brawling, NSBers tossing chairs, throwing half-empty beer glasses at innocent customers. I felt a hand on my wrist, Willem, tugging me. I followed him into the back, and he pulled me through a short corridor to the service exit, then out into the alley, where Jakob and the other band members were waiting.

"Your instruments," Willem said, glancing back the way we'd come.

"We'll get them later," Jakob said, but he looked doubtful. Everything was changing, and, frankly, I didn't think we could be sure of anything anymore.

TWO

Liesbeth de Wit
February 15, 1941
Amsterdam, the Netherlands

Snow fell, dusting the city's bicycles and bridges like sugared *poffertjes*. Every morning, Liesbeth ventured out to check the ice, and by Saturday, the fissures and air bubbles had vanished, hardening into a thick layer. She brewed a pot of mulled wine, and then she and Maurits sharpened their skates and bundled up to meet Johanna and Willem out on the frozen canals.

Outside, the haze that had painted Amsterdam in shades of gray all week had cleared, and the February sun hung low in the bright sky. It seemed everyone had spilled out onto the canals: toddlers leaning on chairs, flocks of schoolgirls, fathers towing little ones on sleds. Liesbeth and Johanna dashed out onto the ice ahead of their husbands, laughing as they flailed to catch their balance. Together, they skated loops and figure eights in the shadow of a windmill, their blades etching white lines into the dark ice. They linked arms and called out to Maurits and Willem, "Slowpokes!"

Willem grinned. "You'd better hope we don't catch you."

He and Maurits hunched down low, until their hands almost grazed the ice, and broke away at a racing speed. They quickly encircled the sisters. Maurits pulled Liesbeth away, spinning her around, clapping his gloved hands against her rosy cheeks, the wool warm and scratchy against her skin.

She looked up at him, puffs of her frosty breath meeting his. Although she kept sniffling and her lips felt chapped from the cold, he tweaked her nose with his thumb and leaned back to admire her. "You're the prettiest little snow fox I've ever seen."

She pecked him on the cheek before taking off, sneaking a peek back at him, watching him move in long, powerful strokes. Sometimes she still had to pinch herself—what luck she'd had to marry him. She sighed and let herself get lost in the crisp winter air, the sound of her blades like scattering marbles. If only it could always be like this, the pure innocent fun of a winter's day, your only foe the elements.

The four of them made their way along the canals, criss-crossing the city, stopping once or twice when the ice ended and they had to skitter across planks that had been laid over the cobblestones for protection. Johanna and Willem skated hand in hand, as did Liesbeth and Maurits, but when they turned onto the Brouwersgracht, Maurits slowed down, a flicker of tension in his grip. She looked at him, but he said nothing.

Willem pointed to his satchel, which contained the food and mulled wine. "How about a pit stop?"

"A little farther ahead," Maurits said, waving vaguely into the distance.

"Here looks perfect," Jo replied. "A bench right in the sun."

Liesbeth agreed and slowed to a stop. Maurits looked like he aimed to protest, but she didn't want him to be difficult. "Come on," she said as she clambered onto the embankment. "Jo's right; this is perfect."

The four of them crowded onto the bench. Willem unscrewed the lid of the thermos, releasing the inviting aroma of cinnamon and cloves, and, one by one, they helped themselves to the mulled wine. Maurits took more than a healthy share, polishing it off.

"More?" Willem asked, amused.

"Don't mind if I do." Maurits took the second thermos and took another swig. It went around again, as did the buns with their meager slice of rationed cheese. Maurits stared out at the canal and grimaced. Then he reached for the thermos again.

"Trying to turn back the clock to our student days?" Willem joked. "You'll need more than a few sips of mulled wine for that, I'm afraid."

Liesbeth blushed. The two men had met while Maurits was studying pharmacy and Willem was training to be a veterinarian, but Maurits normally drank in moderation—what had gotten into him? She nudged him. "Why don't you let Wim finish off the rest?"

Willem rejected the offer, and they sat there talking about the cold snap, the prospect of the snow staying. However, Johanna changed the subject to her recent performance at Café Alcazar, the one Maurits had insisted on ducking out from when he sensed trouble.

"How come you left early the other night?" Johanna asked Maurits.

"I had a headache," he said.

She raised an eyebrow. "Isn't that supposed to be your wife's excuse?"

Maurits shrugged. He withdrew the cigarette case from the inner pocket of his coat and turned it over and over against his knee. Whatever thoughts were occupying him had taken him far away from Jo's questions.

"It was stuffy in there," Liesbeth said, "too crowded. We both felt a little under the weather."

"Things got messy," Willem said. "Be glad you weren't there for it."

"That seems to be the growing pattern," Liesbeth said. All week, they'd been hearing stories of clashes between the Jews and the Nazis, the Jews and the NSB. Tension was rising, and everyone had taken notice.

Maurits let out a puff of air, like he meant to interject, but instead he popped open the silver case and lit up a cigarette. The smoke tickled Liesbeth's lungs and she turned away. A long pause followed, while they listened to the scratching of skate blades and happier conversations.

"Maurits," Willem said. "Is something bothering you?"

Maurits took another drag of his cigarette. When he replied, he spoke slowly, staring out at the canal. "On my twelfth birthday, my father promised to take me to see the automobile race that was passing through town."

Liesbeth turned to him in surprise. He seldom spoke of his childhood, preferring to lean forward into his grand dreams rather than back into his past.

"Alfa Romeos, Bugattis, Mercedes-Benz, all built for speed. Ma had packed a lunch for the two of us, and I sat there on the front steps with the picnic basket on my lap, waiting for him to come home. Only he didn't come. At first, I thought he was out buying me a present, the pocket watch he'd promised me once I was man enough. Then I considered the possibility that he'd gotten held up, sweet-talking the woman who owned the flower stand next to the tobacco shop. I'd seen the way he eyed her skirt, the compliments he paid her instead of my mother. But lunchtime passed and he still wasn't home and I had to listen to the roar of the automobiles in the distance."

Liesbeth stiffened, realizing now why he didn't want to stop along this stretch of canal. She didn't understand why he felt the need to share the story when the conversation was already on edge, but Jo leaned in, intrigued.

"Eventually Ma went out looking for him. She found him here, by this canal." He pointed to a boarded-up jeweler's shop, with a sign that bore the markings of many coats of paint. "This used to be a pawnshop. She found my father out front, like she had on many occasions before. This time, he'd lost the money for my birthday present in a wager, and he was too drunk and ashamed to return home empty-handed."

Willem patted him on the back. "I'm sorry. He never made things easy on your family, did he?"

"For a while, Ma made him hand over all his pay, so he wouldn't be tempted, but it didn't take him long to figure out that she kept it hidden in the jam pot. I lost count of the times we went without any meat or fish on our plates because my father had pocketed the guilders she'd left out for her errands.

"My father played the part all right, convinced the neighbors that we still fit in, that we still belonged, that we weren't slipping. But at a certain point, he stopped caring. He took off to Belgium once or twice a year, to the casino in Spa. We knew that meant a month of bread and potatoes for dinner."

Liesbeth glanced at Jo out of the corner of her eye. She'd told her sister about Maurits's troubled family, and she knew Maurits had done everything he could to distance himself from his father's reputation since his father's death, but the idea still made her uncomfortable. After all, her Calvinist aunt and uncle had raised them with the belief that casinos were the house of the devil. If they'd known about Maurits's father, they might never have approved of her marriage.

"I can't imagine how difficult that must have been," Jo said, but Liesbeth couldn't tell if her sister's sympathy was sincere.

"He had no shame," Maurits said, "no shame at all. I dare say we would have been a lot happier if he'd left us and not come back. My mother was probably relieved when his liver did him in."

Liesbeth winced, thinking of her own parents and the ferry accident that had claimed their lives when she was seven. Her sister was thinking the same thing. "At least you got a chance to really know your father," Johanna said. "Lies and I would give anything for that chance."

"Everything has a different shade in retrospect," Liesbeth said, "but there's no use dwelling on it, is there?"

"All I'm trying to say," Maurits said, "is that you might think people will be there for you, but at the end of the day, it's all up to you." He held up the cigarette case so Johanna and Willem could see the engraved initials. "I took this when my father died, one of the only things of value he never tried to pawn. A reminder of all the things he stole from my mother, my brothers and me, and my promise to do better."

Liesbeth reached over and squeezed his hand, but she knew he hadn't won over the others with his little speech. Couldn't he see that her sister believed the very opposite, that everyone had to band together to get ahead, that this was the only way to stand a fighting chance against an enemy?

She pushed herself up off the bench and gestured to Johanna, eager to pull her away from her husband's gloomy stories. "Come on, I'm getting too cold sitting around. Race you to the next corner?"

At eleven the next morning, Liesbeth carried a hamper of clean laundry into the bedroom and discovered an array of items arranged in a row on the bed: a tie, Maurits's best hat, and his NSB membership card.

She returned to the sitting room, where Maurits sat hunched in an armchair, inspecting his right shoe for scuffs. He had polished his shoes three times that morning. She knew this because she'd placed the box of polish and brushes back in the cupboard after he'd gone out to fetch a newspaper, only to have it reappear again on the table after breakfast, and again now.

"Going somewhere?" she asked.

He came over to her holding his shoes, which gleamed in the dim light of their apartment. She caught the sharp smell of the polish when he wrapped her in his arms. "I have an NSB meeting at four o'clock, with a dinner afterward. A lot of the wives are coming. Why don't you join?"

She gestured to the pile of potatoes on the kitchen counter. "I've already started on dinner."

"I know you'd trade those tasteless lumps for a good cut of meat any day. Come on, you'd like it."

This wasn't the first time Maurits had tried to coax her into making an appearance at one of his NSB functions. She hadn't let on to anyone how involved he was in the political party. What had started out as a mere vote on a ballot had grown into something much bigger. First a membership card and the occasional meeting, and now his weekends were filling up with functions with dour men who spoke of Hitler like he was some chum from school, the popular boy, the star athlete.

"You know what I think about all this party nonsense. I wish you'd take a step back from it. It feels like you're cheering for the wrong side."

Maurits flopped down at the kitchen table and squeezed his right foot into its shoe. "I'm not against our people at all, completely the opposite. Look around, darling. We're at the cusp of a new era, the industrial age of our generation. With Hitler at the helm, the Nazis are becoming the greatest world power. And as their Germanic brothers, we, too, can look forward to greatness, provided we get on board while the gangplank is extended."

The words sounded strange coming from her husband's mouth, almost rehearsed. She sat down beside him and frowned as she tugged at the wool of the Turkish rug that served as a tablecloth. "All we've seen so far is food shortages and gas cuts and far too many swastikas."

"That's war, Liesbeth. That's not indicative of what we can look forward to. Once it's all over, things will change, if we cooperate now. And if we play things right, we'll come out of this occupation all the stronger."

"So what does that mean for us?"

Maurits picked up his other shoe. "This war will be over in no time, you'll see. And later, when this is over, you'll understand why this is the right move. For both of us—for our children."

"That's easy to say now, but in the meantime, I walk around wondering how many of our neighbors have noticed the men in uniform dropping by, who has seen you leaving an NSB meeting. And worse, how am I supposed to explain your activities to Jo?"

"If it bothers you so much, don't tell her. It might do you some good to have a little space from her and Willem anyway." He stood up. "The incident at Café Alcazar was only a preview of what's to come. I hear the Nazis plan to clear out some of the rabble-rousers who have been causing problems around town."

"Rabble-rousers? If you mean the Jews, they've done nothing wrong."

"Haven't you seen the headlines? They beat an NSBer to death this week."

"It sounded like self-defense."

"Regardless, knowing the lot Johanna hangs around with and her inability to bite her tongue, she's going to find her way into trouble. You can't make the same mistake as her." Maurits gave her a stern look. "I want you to stay safe, that's all. You know I'm only ever thinking of you." He leaned over to kiss her cheek and then went to the bedroom to gather his things, leaving Liesbeth alone to consider his words, wondering if he was asking her to choose between him and her sister, an impossible choice to make.

THREE

Johanna Vos
February 25, 1941
Amsterdam, the Netherlands

I was queuing at the butcher's when I noticed something unusual. Outside, on the corner of the Kinkerstraat, fifteen or twenty people stood waiting for the tram. The line kept growing, but the tram didn't arrive. Ever since the invasion, public transport had run with perfect precision, proud as the Germans were of their efficiency. Across the intersection, other people checked their watches at the opposite stop. At first, I thought little of it, except that I was glad I'd decided to run my errands by bicycle.

I wanted to surprise Willem with a nice dinner. Although I'd saved enough ration coupons for a piece of chicken, most meat had long disappeared from the display cases, and from what I could see, only a few chunks of bacon remained. The Germans got first pick, and they were anything but modest in their selections.

As I reached the front of the long line, a commotion began outside. Men hollering, gathering in the middle of the road, ignoring the honks from passing automobiles and the flustered signals of the traffic cop. Inside the shop, we all shuffled toward the window for a better look. A group of men carrying signs marched toward the city center, but I couldn't make out what the text said. A student hurried by on the sidewalk, and someone in line called out, "You, there—what's going on?"

"Haven't you heard?" the student said. "They've called a general strike. Time to take a stand for the Jews!"

The news landed with a punch. The other customers murmured with excitement while the student took off at a jog. A few days earlier, the German Order Police had swooped into the Jewish quarter and rounded up men, loading them onto trucks and taking them away. In a matter of an hour, they erased hundreds of good, innocent men from the neighborhood. When we heard the news, Willem and I sat at the dinner table, praying for those men, praying for Jakob's friends and family, for the other Jews in our circle. I hadn't attended church since I'd left Zierikzee, but it felt like the only thing we could do. We'd sat there, heads bowed over our peas and potatoes, growing angrier by the minute.

But now, something was happening, something tangible, something that could make a difference. The customers in the shop thinned out as they poured into the streets to join the throng. The noise outside grew. I remembered the ration coupons in my hand and turned back to the butcher. He wrapped up my order, pausing every few seconds to glance out the window.

He handed me the package, and while I rushed to leave, he called out, "Turn the sign to Closed, won't you?" He, too, would join the strike.

I abandoned the rest of my errands and grabbed my bicycle. On all sides, people filed out of their businesses and houses. Leaflets littered the pavement. I caught the bold headline: "Strike, Strike! Shut Down the City!" Everyone would gather in one of the main squares, but the soldiers would be patrolling the city center, desperate to get things under control, and the thought of what they might do when faced with a sea of protesters... I shuddered. Until now, they'd viewed us Dutch as their Aryan siblings. But something darker was underneath it all, waiting to be provoked. We had yet to test them.

If only my Wim were with me. Had word reached him already? I followed everyone toward the city center. It became harder to proceed as the crowds thickened. People were marching, running, cycling. I split off from the group and headed toward my sister's house. The sight of workers ringing doorbells along the way gave me a thrill, their eagerness to spread the news. I passed a group of soldiers on foot, heading the way I'd come. They gripped the Lugers at their belts, while their eyes darted around. I couldn't wait to tell Lies.

Liesbeth and Maurits lived near the southern end of Museumplein, the square that housed the great Dutch masterpieces, works by Rembrandt, Vermeer, and countless other artists I couldn't name. Since the start of the war, Museumplein had transformed. The mansion on the corner by the Concertgebouw had been sold to the Nazis and was now the German embassy. Soldiers filled the grassy square, some off duty, others patrolling.

When I approached Liesbeth's building, she was standing at her third-floor window, squinting down at the street, trying to see what was happening. I cut across the intersection, waving, and she opened the window and called down a hello.

"Lies, come outside!"

"What's going on?"

"I'll explain when you're downstairs."

While she got ready, I paced the sidewalk, impatient to join the excitement. A strike—finally—our city had found its voice. The Nazis were bound to get upset, but we had safety in numbers. Liesbeth opened the front door and stepped outside. In her fur coat and boots, she looked like she was headed out to the Amstel Hotel for dinner, but I didn't want to wait for her to change.

"Let's hurry," I said, "we're missing out."

"What's going on?"

We set off in the direction of the city center, while I filled her in, pointing to the traffic that slowed to a jam as more and more people congregated up ahead. "We have a chance to show those damn *moffen* where we draw the line."

The square in front of us teemed with people: men in suits, tram conductors, factory girls, everyone mingling. I wanted to plunge into the thick of it, where we could shout in protest until our voices grew hoarse. Liesbeth spotted a pair of soldiers surveying the scene from the far end of the intersection. "Are you sure it's safe?"

"Yes, it is."

I continued on with her dawdling a half step behind me. We stopped at the corner, waiting to cross. "This will be a day for the books," I said. "You don't want to miss it."

"I find it hard to believe the Nazis will let this unfold. There will be consequences."

Maybe she was right; maybe we had yet to learn the true meaning of fear. "What are they going to do? Keep us locked up inside all day?"

"All right, what is your plan?"

"We'll stick around here, for starters. From there, who knows, but I'm sure people will be full of ideas."

"Dangerous ideas. Surely it's the communists who distributed all those pamphlets." Her voice trailed off as she tilted her head. She seemed to be watching someone, a lone man carrying a briefcase.

"Since when did you become such a chicken? If we don't defend the Jews, it's only going to get worse for them. Doesn't that mean anything to you?"

Her expression softened. "Of course it does."

"If we don't stand up for them, we hand those bullies another level of power. They may control our laws, but they can't silence us."

The man crossing the square grew closer. He moved like Maurits, and I sensed her worrying. I stepped off the curb. "Are you coming?"

The man stopped to tie his shoelace. As soon as Liesbeth registered that it wasn't Maurits, she nodded, and we crossed the street. We slipped into the fiery crowd, following it westward across the city. Someone tugged at my wrist. I spun around, startled. A group of young men. The one who had grabbed ahold of me raised my arm into the air with a cheer. "Damn the *moffen*! Who do they think they are, messing with our Jews?"

The others joined him in a round of hoorahs, and before I could reply, he had twirled me around in a circle. "Atta girl! You two will join us, won't you?"

I shook myself free, and Liesbeth and I took in their caps and heavy work boots. "Who's us?" she asked.

"Why, the boys from the dry docks. I'm betting not a soul showed up to the shipyard today."

"Glad to see this city still has a backbone," I said, allowing myself to be swept up in it all: the crowd of grocers and bakers and factory workers, the boisterous singing of the dockworkers. I tugged at Lies to follow along, and we walked arm in arm with those men. "Strike, strike," we chanted, "protect our people!"

"Isn't this grand?" I said. She grinned back and began to chant louder.

Then the tanks rolled in. Cautiously, at first, as a soldier with a megaphone poked his head out of the vehicle, commanding the crowds to disperse. Nobody listened. People jeered and tossed pamphlets at them. Several students ran into the path of the leading tank, pumping their fists. "Justice!" they shouted. "Bring our people home!"

A shot fired, sending the students scattering. The soldier

aimed his Luger and fired again. One student dropped to the ground, followed by screams and panic. Another young man ran over to his friend, hollering as he bent over the body. I stood still, unable to move. Was this really happening? Liesbeth clutched my hand, squeezing my fingers between hers. The soldier in the tank gaped at the fallen boy, turning his head to watch while the tank rolled by without slowing. He picked up the megaphone, before putting it back down. But the crowds filled the void, the cheers turning into a furious roar.

"Ladies, are you all right?" One of the dockworkers grasped Liesbeth by the elbow, steadying her. "Fuck those brutes!"

"That poor boy," Lies said, her voice shaking.

Blood pooled around his head, and when I forced myself to look away, the spectral image of his body remained. I'd never seen someone killed before. Somehow, I knew this wouldn't be the last time.

The silence of the dockworkers gave me a chill. They, too, were watching. But as I scanned the crowd, it started moving again. People picked up their signs and pressed forward, gathering in the market square. I turned to my sister. "We'll keep protesting, won't we?" She looked hesitant, but I answered the question myself. "We have to, I don't see any other way."

FOUR

Liesbeth de Wit
February 25, 1941
Amsterdam, the Netherlands

The moment that boy collapsed on the ground, something changed. The crowd heaved forward, furious, and the tanks pressed onward, breaking a path through the masses, but Liesbeth stood there, unable to speak, struggling to make sense of what she was witnessing.

The occupation was no longer planes and soldiers milling around the department stores like tourists in uniform. She was right there in the middle of it.

Jo was saying something, a promise to keep fighting, but the words didn't register. All Liesbeth could think about was that boy and the menacing guns of the tanks. She was shaking, and she looked down to see that she was gripping Jo's hand again with such force that the skin was turning white.

"Lies," Jo said, "talk to me. Are you all right?"

Liesbeth nodded, but inside, she was not. How did her sister look so calm, so determined? Around them, the tanks were rolling farther down the street. The dockworkers called out to the sisters, urging them to carry on.

Johanna touched her shoulder. "You don't have to do this if you don't want to. It's your choice, but I'm going to keep going. I have to."

The dockworkers had given up on them now, and they were pushing ahead with everyone else. Liesbeth couldn't see the fallen boy anymore; the crowds had thickened and closed in around her. Even the clouds hung low overhead. She thought of Maurits, his sharp warning to stay away from trouble, to stay safe. She felt a sudden need for air, for space.

"Lies?"

"I'm sorry. I can't."

Her sister hugged her, holding her close, before moving to catch up to the dockworkers. "I understand," she said, but Liesbeth wasn't sure she did.

A few weeks later, Liesbeth spread her sewing patterns and seam rippers across Johanna's dining table. It was mid-March, and she had to put something together for her second piece for *Libelle*, a women's magazine. "With all these fabric shortages," she said, "we need to get a little more creative with our clothing. I've taken the liberty of hacking apart one of Maurits's old suits. See how worn it was in the knees?"

Johanna fingered the fabric of the suit jacket. "What will you turn this into? A bolero?"

"Yes, but think bigger—we have all the ingredients here for a dress suit. Look, we can turn his old shirt into a short-sleeved blouse, and the pants will become a skirt. Then we'll have enough fabric left over to fashion a bolero from the jacket."

"Smart thinking. Wim ripped a big hole in one of his suits last week. If I can't fix it, maybe I can look forward to a new outfit myself. You'll make a lot of women happy with this pattern."

Liesbeth smiled. When she'd responded to an advertisement

for a columnist with a creative eye for "fashion on the ration," her sister hadn't said much at all. Jo had never had any interest in sewing—too domestic, perhaps. But the first article had been a "grand success," as she'd put it when she'd shown up on Liesbeth's doorstep waving a copy. She'd heard women at the newsstand gushing over it, saying it was about time someone offered some practical advice on how to stretch their worn clothes through another season. Writing the articles gave Liesbeth a sense of purpose to fill her days, reminding her of the job at the tailor's shop that she sorely missed.

Johanna stood up to close the window and make some coffee. She lived in an area of Amsterdam West that was too bustling for Liesbeth's taste, but the apartment had its charm. In the summer months, ivy crawled up the facade of the building, covering everything but the windows and the rosebush that grew in the back. Inside, the furniture was modest and practical, with few embellishments, aside from a big gramophone that served as the centerpiece of the room and an embroidered image of Zierikzee Liesbeth had given her.

Johanna poured them both a cup of imitation coffee. "It's a new brand," she explained. "They claim they're mixing in some real coffee with the chicory, but it's bland, don't you think?"

Like everything those days, the new coffee would take some getting used to. "Coffee substitute, meat substitute, margarine substitute," Liesbeth said. "I've never done such a good job pretending as I have these past months. Even the fabric we're getting into the shops is fake. All those pretty silk gowns the Nazis' wives are wearing? They're made of wood pulp or hay."

Johanna smirked. "They think they're so much better than the rest of us, but they're wearing cow feed. Serves them right."

The clock on the side table clicked as the hour hand fell into place. Liesbeth felt her sister watching her.

"What does Maurits make of all this?" Johanna asked.

"What do you mean?"

"Is he still upset with you for joining the strike? I assume he was, since you haven't said a word about what happened that day. You're acting like an ostrich."

Liesbeth shrugged. Maybe she did have her head in the sand—but for the past two weeks, it was all anyone else had talked about. The roundups—known as *razzias*—of the Jewish men, the strikes, and everything that had followed. A new word had entered the ever-expanding vocabulary of the occupation: reprisals. When the strike began to spread to other cities, the Nazis had struck back with brute force, quashing the protests, throwing hand grenades into the crowds. They'd declared a state of emergency, taken over the police force, and replaced the local mayor with someone who would sing their praises. Then they'd set about arresting the organizers of the strike.

"Eighteen executions," Liesbeth said, in a brittle voice. "Eighteen men lined up before a firing squad in the sand dunes." She stared at the suit jacket on the table, imagining a spot of blood blooming across the lapel. Innocent civilians, killed for standing up for their friends and neighbors. A heavy sadness fell over them both.

"I saw some of those men speaking at the strike," Johanna said. "Ordinary men, could have been anyone. One resembled Wim a bit."

"Maurits says the Nazis had no choice but to respond with force, that a leader is not a leader if he can't command respect. He thinks we need to cooperate if we want to come out of this in one piece."

"A leader? They're our enemy—they're tyrants!"

"Of course," Liesbeth said, "but where has this gotten us? Hundreds of arrests, violence—what's the point in sticking your neck out if it comes at this cost?"

"Don't you remember the story of David and Goliath?" Johanna sighed and poured more coffee. "You're right about one thing: most people are afraid now, and for good reason."

Liesbeth picked up the sewing patterns again and laid them out in the proper order. How quickly the afternoon had soured. Whether they liked it or not, the Germans had beaten their little Dutch army in a matter of days, and she didn't see what they could do about it unless the Allied armies and the powers that be were to gain control. The strikes had proved that your very life was on the line if you tried to resist.

She tried to change the subject. "We haven't done anything as a foursome lately. Maurits has a reservation for dinner this weekend. Why don't the two of you join us?"

"Oh, I don't know. We should save our money."

"A romantic restaurant, overlooking a canal—come on, won't you consider it?"

"I'll think about it," she said. Her voice softened. "Are the two of you still trying for a baby?"

"We are," she said. "I know it's impractical to want more mouths to feed at a time like this, but we'll find a way to make it work. He's so resourceful." Every day, Maurits bent over the newspapers with a scrupulous eye, following the latest updates in the war, tracking the developments and their potential impact. He had so many ambitions: of owning his own pharmacy, of buying a holiday home, of raising their children in a vibrant, well-educated sphere. Whenever he attended an NSB function, he came home glowing with energy. As much as this still bothered her, he promised a shift in the current was headed their way, a very good shift.

"I don't doubt that," Johanna said.

"And you know what? I'm two days late again this month. So maybe this will be it."

Johanna placed a hand on Liesbeth's shoulder. "I hope so. I can't think of anyone who would make a better mother."

FIVE

Johanna Vos
June 8, 1941
Amsterdam, the Netherlands

"Behold the world of the beautiful and affluent," Willem said, sweeping out his arm while we sank into our velvet chairs. The main hall of the Royal Concertgebouw burst with color, hues of raspberries and cream caught in the glitter of the chandeliers. The organ mesmerized me most of all. The instrument seemed to pierce through the stage like an enormous silver trident.

I clutched the tickets Jakob had gifted us for the evening's benefit concert, a performance of Beethoven's Eighth and Ninth Symphonies. Around us sat rows of people with lorgnettes and waxed mustaches, jewels and mink stoles. Maurits would have felt right at home, but the display of opulence grated at me when I thought of all the struggling fishermen and farmers back in Zeeland who had to toil to make ends meet.

By the time the lights dimmed, every seat was full. The crowd hushed as the orchestra entered from the wings, Jakob positioning himself with his contrabass on the right side of the stage. The conductor took his place and raised his baton. Then the hall filled with sound, a jubilant outburst. I closed my eyes and let the music seep in. The first movement of Beethoven's Eighth Symphony danced across my vision, the sonata curling into shapes. These shapes took on tints, red and orange—a fox chasing a hare, a mad dash across sleepy pastures. As the music built, the melody shifted, growing rambunctious, triumphant.

Willem squeezed my hand and my eyes fluttered open. A thick strand of hair fell across his glasses. I reached out to tuck it back into place. He looked completely absorbed by the music, which I loved about him, the way he could be knee-deep in manure one day and in a smart bow tie the next, bending and flexing to whatever life threw at him. I got caught up in my admiration for him while the symphony transitioned into the final movement. During the intermission, we ordered drinks in the grand foyer while everyone milled about.

"Have you noticed how many Jewish couples are here tonight?" Willem asked.

"What's remarkable about that? They're such patrons of the arts."

"I don't think that's quite it." He cocked his head, indicating for me to listen. I caught whispers, hushed warnings, dubious glances at the handful of German officers that sipped champagne by the bar.

"You're right. Something is brewing."

I spotted Jakob's wife at the other end of the room, standing with a group of girlfriends. Unlike Jakob, Ida was a Protestant. She was a startlingly tall woman, with the elongated neck and long face of the gray herons that stalked the parks. I tried to catch her attention, but she was engaged in what appeared to be a serious conversation, so Willem and I nursed our drinks and debated what had sparked the unsettling mood.

The bell rang, summoning us back to our seats for Beethoven's Ninth. When the lights dimmed once more and the musicians positioned their bows, we leaned forward in our seats, rapt with anticipation. Again, the hall filled with music. On stage, Jakob curved his shoulders against his contrabass, his face furrowed. He'd invited us to this concert for a reason; he knew something.

I glanced at the Nazis in the front row, the hard lines of their uniforms a blemish against all the elegance. One of them nudged the officer next to him and pointed. A series of cartouches lined the concert hall, each bearing the name of a famous composer. There, beneath the balcony, was Mahler. Farther down, Mendelssohn and Rubinstein. All of them Jewish. Yes, that was it, the reason for the overflowing hall, the energy of the crowd, why Jakob had insisted we take the tickets. For some of these musicians, this would be their final curtain call.

Willem must have registered this at the same time, for his face reflected my thoughts. I leaned back in my chair, feeling deflated. It hadn't been so long since our disastrous Sunday at Café Alcazar—how would Jakob cope if he lost this, too?

However, the music grew again, enveloping us all, swallowing my thoughts. The musicians played with a ferocity like I'd never seen and the audience responded in kind, enraptured. The choir burst into song, their "Ode to Joy," their voices magnificent, with the power of a tempest.

Willem whispered into my ear, "Transports you to another world, doesn't it?"

If there were such a thing as magic, it was right there, suspended in that hall. One minute, I was floating, the next, soaring. Jakob played on, his concentration matched by a fierce passion. The strings built and the timpani boomed, driving the movement to crescendo. Then, with a final, dramatic flourish, the music ceased.

The musicians bowed and the conductor moved like he was about to make a speech, but then he stepped back and gestured to the musicians. We were all on our feet, the enthusiasm deafening. People whistled, waved handkerchiefs, and fell into each other's embraces, weeping. The noise rose up like a protest. I turned to Willem, my eyes welling with tears. I didn't know whether to feel elated or utterly discouraged and powerless on behalf of the Jewish musicians. We clapped and we clapped, until the Nazis slunk out of view, the conductor gave up on bowing, and the musicians stepped out of formation. Jakob threw an arm around the cellist next to him, and they stood looking out at all of us, their expressions bewildered, overwhelmed. Grateful.

SIX

Liesbeth de Wit
June 14, 1941
Amsterdam, the Netherlands

Summer arrived early but without its promised treasures. Like the year before, there would be no holidaying in Belgium with Maurits's family's car, driving from château to château, stopping at pubs along the way. There would be no weekend trips to a beach house on the coast, none of the things they had fantasized about on their wedding day. Even visits to Zierikzee were becoming difficult, the trains running less often and on unpredictable schedules.

Liesbeth didn't mind. Vacations were an extravagance her family had hardly known. Sometimes they had gone cycling and camped somewhere overnight, and once or twice each year they'd visited The Hague, strolling the promenade on the Scheveningen pier, eating lunch on the bustling terraces in the main square. Their grandfather had made a great game of "discovering" peppermints in the children's ears, and Liesbeth would suck on her mint slowly, savoring the flavor and every moment of those afternoons.

So while Maurits's talk of travels had enchanted her, she stowed away those dreams for another year. *After the war*, she thought, as she did with most things. More serious matters filled her days: how to make a meal on the last of the week's ration coupons, the threat of air strikes at night.

Yet summer was bursting at the seams, and Maurits was determined to celebrate this. On a beautiful Saturday in June, he glanced up from the newspaper as she entered the sitting room. "The weather is expected to turn next week. Let's make the most of today." He gave her bottom a squeeze. "Put on that pretty green sundress of yours. I intend to show you off a little."

Liesbeth did as he told, taking care to style her curls the way he liked and put on his favorite necklace, a slender, teardrop pendant. Then she combed the shelves of the pantry for anything she could dress up as a picnic lunch—the perfect aperitif for a night of romance, the type of night she hoped might lead to a baby.

When she met him in the hallway, he took the basket from her. "Well, what do we have here? The loveliest woman in town, and I have the good fortune to take her out."

She wrapped her arms around his neck and they swayed together side to side. "Oh, can't we just hole up here, forget everything that's going on outside for a bit?"

He laughed and ruffled her hair. "Darling, don't talk nonsense. Let's go, the sunshine's waiting."

The sun was indeed waiting, the sidewalks scorching, but Maurits had taken the heat into consideration and had borrowed a boat from someone he knew. He opened the storage compartment under the seats, retrieving a bottle of white wine from an ice bucket. "Only the best for you, milady."

Liesbeth beamed at him. It felt like the early weeks of their courtship, when Maurits had been full of surprises. But when she pulled the cushions from the compartment, she spotted a copy of the *VoVa—People and Fatherland*—the weekly newsletter of the NSB. It was true what Johanna said, that Maurits had an unconventional group of friends, but they were powerful, successful men. If Hitler hadn't come to power, their political leanings might have gone on unnoticed. The type of men Maurits said would restore Amsterdam to a prime spot on the European map. The type of men who would find a way to provide for their families, no matter the circumstances.

She picked up the newsletter and flipped through it. It contained an article about the pitfalls of modern architecture, a mocking caricature of Stalin, and an advertisement for a new teahouse, some sort of intellectual clubhouse. All relatively harmless, but then there was the section at the end, "A Chapter from the History of Jews," a critical take on the spread of Jewish influence across the country. Liesbeth folded the newsletter and tucked it away, upset by the words that had popped out at her: *infectious, greedy, predatory.* She tried not to dwell on it, not on such a beautiful day.

Maurits handed her the bottle of wine while he got the engine running. "You trust me with this?" she asked. "It might be all gone before you've turned around!" He chuckled, knowing how clumsy she was with a corkscrew, and sure enough, when he pushed off the quay, she teetered sideways and lost a third of the wine to the bottom of the boat.

"I should have left this to the expert," she said.

He brushed the dribble of wine from her hand, lifting it to kiss the pulse of her wrist. "At least we'll never have to worry about you becoming a lush." His smile hid a seriousness, which made Liesbeth wonder how he would react if she ever did manage to embarrass him. He always dressed his best and knew what to say, so she couldn't picture him ever losing face. He was like the men she'd seen in Mercedes ads, posing behind the wheel, proud and self-assured.

They exchanged another kiss and Maurits turned the boat down the Prinsengracht. The wooden hull gleamed with a fresh coat of white paint. Around them, gabled houses squished to-gether like paperbacks on a bookshelf. When she'd first visited Amsterdam, the crowded houses had looked different. In the evenings, everyone had left their blinds open, beckoning the world to peer into the rooms of their homes. She'd cycled along the illuminated canals, each window a diorama of a life she'd never know. But now, blackout paper obscured everything after dusk. Even during the day there was a sobriety to the window-sills, fewer plants and ornaments, as if people had removed any-thing that could make them stand out.

Maurits steered through the maze of canals, past the Seven Bridges and the swans that floated between moored vessels. As he turned the boat out onto the Amstel River, he squinted into the sun, the wind teasing his hair, whipping it back to reveal his rising hairline. The muscles in his forearm flexed while he gripped the tiller. A flicker of heat rose inside her, longing. The only thing that could make the day better would be if there were three or four children between them in the boat, begging their father for a chance to steer.

Fuel was precious, so they only boated a half hour before Maurits found a quiet spot for lunch along a grassy embankment where the river turned. Church bells pealed from the village farther down. Liesbeth pulled out the bread she had packed, the hunk of cheese, an old tin of pâté, and carrot sticks. At the sight of the bread, a flock of ducks came swimming over.

"It isn't much," she said. "If I'd known, I could have saved up for something special."

Maurits poured her a generous glass of wine. "We need to be more resourceful. Plenty of tables in this city are still filled with steaks and champagne."

"What do you mean?"

"My job is to take care of you, darling. We were supposed to travel and dine like bon vivants, but none of that has happened."

"This is already a far different life than I knew in Zierikzee."

He cut a thin slice of cheese and placed it over his bread. "It's not enough."

Liesbeth studied him, trying to figure out what was on his mind. "I couldn't ask anything more of you," she said, "and I know you'll be equally good to our children."

"I want to raise our children in a respectable household. The De Wit name should mean something at the schools they attend."

Placing her glass on the thwart, Liesbeth drew him toward her. Her lips brushed across his jaw—clean-shaven, like always—and found his mouth. She skimmed her tongue over his teeth, tasting the wine and salted butter on his lips. His hand slid up to grasp the back of her head, to clench her hair, desire in his touch.

He pulled back to look at her. "Let's go swimming."

"You know I'm not much of a swimmer. Besides, I don't have my swimsuit."

"It's shallow." He reached for the buttons at her dress collar. "Nobody is around."

She held back, in no hurry to get in. Still, she didn't want to ruin the mood, so she gave him a wicked grin. "As long as my personal lifeguard stays within reach."

He unbuttoned his trousers and pulled his shirt over his head before diving in. Liesbeth undressed piece by piece, her breasts glowing white under the bright sun. She checked to see if anyone was around before shimmying off the side of the boat. The cold water sent a rush of goose pimples up her thighs.

"How's this for refreshing?" Maurits said.

Liesbeth bit her lip to keep from shivering. "Just what the doctor ordered."

"Don't be cheeky!" He swam toward her with practiced strokes and made a move to grab her. She shrieked, trying to wriggle from his grasp as he tickled her.

"Uh-oh." He pointed to the bend in the river ahead. "Better watch out, we've got company!"

She dived for cover between the reeds, but there was no boat in sight.

"I don't think I've ever seen you move that fast," Maurits said.

"You think you're pretty funny, don't you?" She cupped her hand to flick some water at him.

"Watch now," he said, "or you might find yourself stranded here, all alone in the reeds." He pulled her close and she wrapped her legs around his waist. They floated there together, intertwined in the shallows. For once, she wasn't nervous in the water. She traced a finger over the droplets that trickled down his cheek, admiring the defined angles of his face, the way his chin protruded to form a little ledge. She kissed that spot, and he kissed her back hard. His hands found her breasts. Then, a sailboat glided by. Liesbeth broke away from him and dipped down until the water reached her neck, but the pair of men on board barely looked up while they prepared to tack. Once they were gone, Liesbeth reached for Maurits again, and they began to make love.

Afterward, they lay on the thwart boards, drying off in the sun. Overhead, fluffy clouds drifted into shapes: a horse, a tiger, a woman in a gown—all the makings of a circus.

"Imagine," Liesbeth said, "when all of this is over, we can take the little ones out when the circus comes to town. Wouldn't they love it?"

"Of course they would. Popcorn, twinkling lights, a spectacle they'd never forget." He straightened up. "I have something to tell you, some news."

"What sort of news?"

"Good news. Good for us and our future children." He paused for effect, like he'd been waiting all day to make the announcement.

She sat up. "Go on."

"I've been granted a business opportunity, the chance to take over the pharmacy."

"What? That's brilliant!" she said. "Starting when? How did this come about?"

Maurits squeezed her hand. "You needn't concern yourself with the details. What it means is a big jump up and a secure income for the coming years. No need to pinch those ration coupons anymore."

An uncomfortable feeling settled in her gut, but she didn't know why. "How did you manage to keep that in all afternoon? Is there any more wine? We should be celebrating your success!"

Maurits topped them both up with the last of the bottle. She kissed him on the cheek as they raised their glasses. "Here's to you, my love, and your new pharmacy."

After a few sips, curiosity got the better of her. She ran her finger over the rim of the glass and looked at him. "So *meneer* Katz has decided to retire? I wouldn't have pegged him for a day over fifty."

SEVEN

Johanna Vos
June 28, 1941
Amsterdam, the Netherlands

"You're doing it again," Liesbeth said, tugging at the quilt we'd slung over our shoulders while we curled up on my bed.

I laughed. "Old habits." For most of our lives, we had slept side by side in the bedroom we shared with our brother, Gerrit, he in one bed and she and I in the other, and she'd often complained of me stealing the blankets at night. Lately, it was Willem who accused me of this, but he was visiting the zoo in Rotterdam for a couple of days, so I'd invited Lies to sleep over, a night for us to catch up on sisterly things.

I offered up more of the blanket and started flipping through the latest edition of *Libelle*. I found Lies's latest article and held it up. She'd written a piece on how to fashion a raincoat out of old bedsheets, including instructions on what mixture to soak the sheets in to make them waterproof.

She perked up. "Have you read it?"

"It was brilliant. Come autumn, your raincoats will be popping up all over Amsterdam."

She blushed, but I could tell she was pleased. "For my next piece, I thought I'd come up with a way to fashion a baby romper from a worn apron."

"Are you trying to tell me something?"

"No," she said. "Not yet. We keep trying, but still no luck." She sighed. Then she pointed to my fingernails. "You know, if you plan to perform more often, you ought to take better care of yourself. These are hardly the hands of a star." She began filing my nails with an emery board from her handbag, trying to smooth the ragged, chewed ends into a suitable shape.

"I have no intentions of becoming a star," I said.

"You could if you wanted to. I'd listen to you sing all day long."

"Thanks, but if I get some smiles or a smattering of applause from the odd show, that's enough for me."

"That shouldn't be hard. Everyone is looking for a reason to smile these days." She held out my left hand for inspection. "Beautiful."

"Some people are finding that more difficult than others," I said. "You know my friend Jakob? The orchestra fired him, along with all the other Jews."

"Oh no. How will he and his wife get by?" Liesbeth stared at my nails, but she didn't pick up the emery board again. Instead she fiddled with the fabric of the quilt, pleating it between her fingers.

"What's eating at you?" I asked.

"Maurits has been promoted."

"What do you mean?"

"He's been granted ownership of the pharmacy," she said, still avoiding my gaze.

I thought of the owner, who I'd seen on the few visits I'd paid to the pharmacy—a cheerful man who greeted every customer by name and kept his shop counter polished to a shine. "So, another Jew gets his livelihood stolen for the benefit of a fine Aryan specimen." I pulled my hand away from her. "That's horrible. I hope you told him that."

"It is awful, but he couldn't have stopped it from happening."

I shrugged off the quilt, feeling hot and uncomfortable. It wasn't her fault any more than Jakob losing his job was the fault of the orchestra conductor, but her news was more kindling for the fire. I wished I could do something, anything.

"He should have refused the offer," I said.

"If he had, they would have shut down the pharmacy. At least this way, *meneer* Katz might have something to come back to once the war ends."

"We both know Maurits would never step down from anything out of his own free will."

"That's true, but are we supposed to turn down opportunities that will help us survive, only to make a point? Costs keep going up, and God knows we can't afford anything on the black market without some extra help."

"War is sacrifice. At least, it is if we want to come out as decent people on the other end. Isn't Maurits still parading around with those NSBers?"

"Yes, as much as it shames me to admit it."

"How can he live with himself, knowing what those men stand for?"

Liesbeth wrapped the quilt more tightly around her. "Not everyone is as strong as you. Maybe you believe we're all fighters, but we're not. We're just trying to get by."

"I know, but the world is not going to change if we sit back and watch it spin. We must make our voices heard."

"I'll try," she said, leaning into me. We sat there together, arms around one another, thinking about the war, and for the first time, I didn't know if my sister and I were truly on the same side.

One sweltering night in the middle of July, I awoke to a terrible wail. I shook Willem. He jolted, fumbling for his glasses and the bag we kept packed before leading me out of the dark room. The electricity was out, so I gripped his shoulder and we felt our way to the narrow staircase.

"Hurry," he said, or perhaps it was me who said it, the word bouncing around my head with the pounding of our footsteps and that long, grating blare of the air raid siren. Willem paused at the ground floor, where our elderly landlord lived. "I'll help him down. You go on."

I didn't waste any time. Outside, the sky was black. The noise of airplanes rose over the sirens, but the nearest air raid shelter was ten minutes away. I ran to the neighbors, three houses over, who had a cellar. I banged on the door with the flat of my palm. "It's Johanna, please, let me in!" The hairs on the back of my neck stood up in the cold while an explosion boomed in the distance. I banged harder, cried out again. Long, ghostly fingers of light scoured the night sky, searching for the bombers.

Our neighbor let me in, his eyes stark white against his shadowy face. He ushered me inside, and I tried to tell him that Willem and our landlord were still on their way, but he had already disappeared. I followed him, scrambling down the ladder into the musty dampness of the cellar. When I'd adjusted to the candlelight, I greeted the others: the neighbor's wife and the family next door. The women wore fur coats and pearls over their nightgowns, clutching handbags with their valued possessions. The little boy hugged a one-eyed stuffed bear. For the second time that week, I took a seat on a stool in the corner and counted the seconds until the trapdoor opened again and Willem's slippers appeared on the top rungs of the ladder.

We huddled in the cellar for several hours. I counted the cans of string beans on the shelves, estimated the weight of the potato sack, clutched Wim's hand. Somehow, he managed to retain the calm composure of a man enjoying his morning tea. I hoped he would never leave my side.

Overhead, the city rumbled. Bombs dropped. Antiaircraft

guns clattered. When the boy began to cry, I sang softly, until his sobs subsided and we all sat there again, listening to our city fending off the attack.

"Strange, don't you think?" Willem said. "Who should we be cheering for—the Brits who are bombing us, or the *moffen* who are trying to both defend and control us?"

I thought about this before replying, "The Allies have strategic targets, away from houses and innocent lives. They'll strike the Germans where it hurts."

"It's easier to believe that, isn't it? Good swooping in to protect us against the forces of evil?"

"I have no doubts about it. 'We shall not flag or fail. We shall go on to the end.'"

The others in the cellar turned to listen. Willem stroked a thumb over the nape of my neck. "My little Churchill." His tone was teasing, but we both knew this was something we could hold on to, the promise of justice.

Soon the boy drifted off, his toy bear locked in a choke hold. Around the cramped cellar, our heads sagged, but we were too afraid to sleep. When the sky had been still for some time, the silence heavy with uncertainty, we waited and listened. Then, the all-clear alarm sounded. And as we emerged one by one into the night, I looked around, wondering what destruction the light of dawn would reveal.

Initially, the trepidation of the night sank beneath the comforting sounds of the morning. We woke to the warbles and trills of the finches and sparrows outside our window, the clopping of hooves as the milk wagon made its way down the street. Willem headed to the newspaper stand, and I queued at the bakery, and while everyone spoke of those tense, sleepless hours, nobody knew what had been hit.

After breakfast, Willem cycled to work. My first instinct was to stop by Liesbeth's, knowing how shaken the air raid would've left her. Yet something inside me resisted, and I recalled our conversation about the pharmacy. Why should I rush to soothe her, when she and Maurits were making selfish decisions, decisions that coincided with the loss and suffering of others? Maybe she didn't support her husband's allegiances, but she wasn't doing much to change his mind.

I decided to give myself some space from her, time to let my frustration subside. I set about the housework and sang my way through the laundry, practicing the vocal exercises I'd learned in the Zierikzee church choir. On Sundays, we had sung during the services, but the hymns were somber, simple enough for every grandmother to follow. Thursday evenings offered a release, when we stacked the hymnbooks on the shelf and wound up the gramophone—cabaret, swing, jazz, anything we could get our hands on. Once, someone brought some records they'd received from an American relative, and we'd spent the entire evening listening to Billie Holiday's haunting crooning in "Strange Fruit."

By the time I hung the last of Willem's shirts in the wardrobe, it was past two, and without any sign of him. Something at work must have been holding him up. However, the sun was shining, and after that nerve-frying night underground, I knew fresh air would do me good, so I decided to cycle across town with his lunch.

As I approached the Artis Zoo, everything became clearer. A smoky, metallic smell hung in the air. One of the nearby houses had lost its roof, and bricks spilled across the road like toy blocks in a nursery. A racket of sledgehammers and squawking birds echoed from inside the zoo. Workers filed out with wheelbarrows filled with rubble, which they unloaded into a truck bed, while soldiers and police supervised the cleanup. They had blocked off the main entrance, preventing onlookers from getting too close.

A Dutch policeman saw me observing everything. "Fire bombs," he said, "a real close call."

"Why the zoo?"

"They missed their target." He pointed toward the nearby railway yard. "Anyway, the zoo is closed until further notice. You go along now. This is no place for a lady."

I debated asking the policeman if he could pass on Willem's lunch, but the tin lunchbox would cost too much to replace if he decided to keep the sandwiches for himself. I thanked him and turned back. Instead of heading home, I cycled along the perimeter of the zoo, where the exit gate had been propped open to allow the stream of workers in and out. I parked my bicycle, and, when nobody was paying attention, slipped inside.

Debris was scattered everywhere: charred timber, chicken wire, mortar. And what a state the animals were in! The mountain goats bucked in their compound, and the camels huddled together, pawing the ground in agitation. I wandered around, searching for a familiar face. Part of the giraffe enclosure had caved in and was cordoned off, the giraffes nowhere in sight. The roof of the hippo house was scorched black. And with so much screeching and howling and chirping, you almost forgot there were no visitors.

I called out to one of the monkey handlers, asking if they'd seen Willem, and the man indicated a building near the petting zoo. Willem stood inside, bent over an examination table. The lines on his face softened as he turned toward me. "Sweetheart."

"How are you managing?" I moved over to rub his back and saw a furry mass on the examination table in front of him—a rabbit.

"A lot better than this little fellow." He gestured to the rabbit's back leg, which hung crooked.

"I couldn't believe my eyes when I got here. How did everyone make it through the night? Were there any casualties?"

"You saw the enclosures that were hit? Well, the smoke was so thick that the director had to let some of the animals out so they wouldn't suffocate."

"The tame ones, I hope." I noticed the sweat glimmering on his dust-caked brow and dabbed at it with my handkerchief.

"That's the best bit. When the fire brigade showed up, a tiger, giraffe, and some hippos were on the loose, and the zoo director was standing there in his nightclothes, armed with a rifle, in case the puma spooked. Those poor firefighters were scared to douse the flames near the cages."

"Don't tell me you were chasing after wild cats all morning?"

"No, no, they'd rounded them all up by the time I got in. We've spent today sedating the animals, trying to gauge the damage. It must be at least fifty thousand guilders."

"A fortune. And here the Brits probably flew home thinking they'd done some good. Maybe I should take back what I said last night."

"We can still count our blessings, all things considered."

I could tell he was trying to be positive, but these sudden costs would mean the zoo would have to cut corners, that it would be harder to feed the animals, to pay the staff.

Between us, the rabbit twitched, its eyes glazing over. "Poor thing," I said.

"This little guy suffered the worst of it. He broke his foot trying to wriggle out of his cage." Willem stroked his fur, trying to comfort him while he bundled him in a blanket. "This here is Robbie."

"What are you going to do with him?"

He gave me a pained look. Then, he held up a needle and asked me to hold the animal still while he found a vein on a shaved patch of fur and gave it an injection. The rabbit lay there on the table, staring up at us, its front paw twitching, until that, too, stopped.

EIGHT

Liesbeth de Wit
August 29, 1941
Amsterdam, the Netherlands

Liesbeth stood behind the counter of the pharmacy, trying to make sense of the various packages in front of her. Maurits's assistant was ill and there was no one to handle the cash register, so she'd stepped in to help. Her husband greeted a customer as he pulled medicine jars down from the shelves.

"Good afternoon," the woman said, "I'm picking up a prescription for my husband. He was in this morning."

"Oh yes," he said. "Liesbeth, please fetch the order with the capsules and the cough syrup."

Liesbeth smiled and tried to make chitchat with the woman, who watched her with a hint of snobbery. As she rang up the order, Maurits came up beside her and checked the paper bag. "This is the wrong one. I said the package that also contains the cough syrup. This dosage could be detrimental for someone with her husband's condition. You can't let distraction get the better of you."

"I'm so sorry," Liesbeth said, mortified. "I'm still finding my way among all these bottles and labels."

Maurits laughed and winked at the customer, as if the two of them were in on a joke. "Not to worry, darling. There's a reason you can't don this white jacket without years of schooling."

As the woman left the pharmacy, Liesbeth turned bright red. "I'll tidy up and leave you to the customers. At least there's no chance of me poisoning the broom."

Maurits nodded and finished some of the bookkeeping before turning his attention back to a white powder he'd been measuring to press into pills. In the back room, Liesbeth swept a pile of crumbs from his lunch into the dustpan, still reeling with embarrassment. This wasn't how she'd pictured her new life in Amsterdam, the constant feeling of being judged, of inadequacy. How was it possible to be in the middle of so many people and feel so increasingly alone?

Maurits's own social circle was growing and had shifted. He carried his NSB membership card in his wallet, tucked next to a love note she'd given him on their wedding day, and she couldn't say for sure which he pulled out more often to admire. He'd stopped socializing with Willem or his other friends from university. More and more, he went out for drinks and meetings, and the men they entertained for dinner often showed up in uniform. German soldiers, fellow members of the NSB. They drank expensive liquor and ate more than Liesbeth and Maurits could afford, but he instructed her to bring out the best for them. Sometimes, she skimped on her own meals for a week after those dinners, trying to think of creative recipes on ration coupons while her stomach growled. All of this would be more tolerable if she could commiserate with someone, but Jo showed little interest in spending time with her.

Liesbeth passed the afternoon helping with odd jobs until the stream of customers had quieted down. Shortly before closing time, the door opened, and three soldiers walked in. She tensed up, but Maurits gave them a casual hello. One of them walked straight up to the counter, and, without another word, Maurits slipped him a package wrapped in brown paper. The soldier nodded before gesturing to his comrades. "Make it an extra dose. These two are on night shift this week."

"You two have a prescription?"

The soldiers laughed but said nothing.

Maurits turned to Liesbeth. "I need four of the orange-and-blue boxes from the cabinet in the back room."

Liesbeth went to get them, examining the cheery text on the label: Pervitin. Outside, another customer approached the pharmacy but turned around at the sight of the soldiers joking with Maurits. She handed over the boxes and shuffled back, away from the soldiers' curious gaze.

"Here you go," Maurits said. "This one's on me." He held up the Pervitin. "Start gradually. Otherwise, you'll complain of headaches. I'll throw in some aspirin just in case."

Once the soldiers had left, Liesbeth asked about the Pervitin, what it was.

Maurits flipped around the shop sign, signaling the end of the workday. "It's something called methamphetamine, the Germans are hooked on it." At her blank expression, he pulled a package out of the cupboard, opening the box to reveal a tube. "It helps you stay awake, keeps you sharp. Happiness in a tube."

"Is it dangerous?"

He grabbed a flyer from a drawer under the cash register. The photo showed a woman eating from a box of chocolates. "Perfectly safe. Look, they even come in praline form. The ideal performance enhancer for the tired housewife."

"Is that a hint?"

He ruffled her hair. "Never! You could teach those old housewives a lot of things."

They finished putting everything away, and the warmth of his compliment stayed with her as they went to a dinner hosted by one of Maurits's NSB friends. The discussion at dinner revolved around politics, and the hostess kept darting off to check on things in the kitchen whenever Liesbeth tried to engage her in conversation. At least, Liesbeth told herself, the war would end soon. Then things would go back to normal, and she and Maurits would have their own little family at the center of their world.

When they left the dinner, Liesbeth realized her purse was missing. She recalled having set it on the counter in the pharmacy while Maurits counted the till. They decided to drop by and pick it up on the way home. The evening was still, the streets quiet. As they approached the pharmacy, something felt off. "What's that?" she asked, pointing. The shop window seemed to vanish into jagged darkness.

They got closer. Sure enough, the window was broken. A shiny rock lay on the tiled floor inside.

Maurits's face hardened. "Stay here," he said, pulling the *knijpkat* from his pocket and squeezing it to activate the light. He flashed the beam in all directions before entering the pharmacy. When he emerged a minute later, he came over to wrap an arm around her shoulder. "Whoever it was, they've gone."

"Well, they made sure to leave their calling card." She indicated the lettering on the window. A single word was scrawled in big block letters over the sign for De Wit Pharmacy. TRAITOR.

Maurits clenched his jaw. She waited for his response, expecting a fiery eruption, but he said nothing, which bothered her more. She fumbled for something to fill the silence. "Who would do this?"

Maybe the Resistance, but more likely someone who lived nearby. She peered down the street. Some of the neighbors stood at the windows, disappearing behind the sheaths of blackout paper they were smoothing out across the glass.

"Bastards," he muttered.

Liesbeth turned to her husband. His face was as stormy as the North Sea in the depths of winter. "Sweetheart?"

He shook his head. "Probably some bored hooligans. You cycle on home. I'll take care of this."

She stared past him at the bridges and tram stops, which were collapsing into shadows and silhouettes as the sky darkened. "You don't think they'll be back?"

"They've had their entertainment. They've probably run home to their mothers by now."

"I'll wait for you." She found her purse where she'd left it and fetched a broom to tidy up the glass and the dirt that had blown in with the wind. While she swept, she recalled the newspaper headlines she'd seen three years earlier, about the Jewish shops that had been vandalized across Germany. The Night of Broken Glass, they'd called it. And now, *meneer* Katz's pharmacy had become a target, only for a very different reason.

Maurits came out of the back room with a piece of plywood and some tools to board up the broken part of the window. "My brother got into this type of mischief when we were younger," he said, setting to work. "I stayed at home in the evenings while he barreled around with his friends, lighting trash piles on fire, dumping bicycles into the canals. He mocked me when I refused to join in."

"And now look where you've landed in comparison."

He paused, the hammer poised midair. "Well, I wasn't going to say it, but that's a valid point. De Wit Pharmacy is one of the most respected in the city. My father would have been proud, wouldn't he?"

"Of course, dear."

Once they had cleaned the place and secured the drugs, they headed out, exhausted and ready for the comfort of their bed. As they got back on their bicycles, Liesbeth took another look down the dark street, where another couple walked, two murky figures who seemed to be watching them. She pedaled to catch up to Maurits.

She was proud of him, too, wasn't she?

★ ★ ★

Liesbeth realized it wasn't her role to challenge him. After all, he was earning more money than ever before. Some families relied on charitable donations of clothing and blankets from the Winterhulp, and others searched the grocer's waste bin after hours, but she and Maurits always made ends meet, even if she had to cut some corners. And they were climbing upward, constantly climbing. However, one thing was still missing—a child. Whatever hope Liesbeth had maintained about timing things right disappeared month after month. She tried to conceal her dismay, but Maurits kept good track of her cycle and knew when to ask. He insisted he could tell when she was most fertile, that she became more radiant, her creamy skin taking on a peachy glow. Yet despite their best planning, every month was the same.

As the September moon ripened, Liesbeth woke to more disappointment. Tears of frustration dripped into the sink while she rinsed her stained undergarments. Was she selfish for wanting to bring a child into the midst of a war? She would have given anything to start a family, to make her life complete.

That evening, Maurits came out of the bathroom with her panties dangling from his pinched fingers. She'd forgotten to remove them from the drying rack. He frowned. "Again?" He sat on the bed beside her but didn't reach out to comfort her like he had before. "How many months has this been now?"

She'd lost count. All those years growing up, she'd assumed it would be easy, that these things came naturally. He picked up his cigarette case from the side table and opened it, lighting up his cigarette with strained movements. "You know how important this is. How do you expect to raise children together if you won't be up front with me?"

"I wasn't quite ready to face it this time."

"Maybe you should visit the doctor again. If something is broken, we ought to find out."

There was no ignoring the accusation in his tone. Was it her?

Perhaps her womb had become as cold and desolate as the city around her. It hadn't seemed to cross his mind that the problem could lie with him.

"Perhaps we both should," she said softly.

He inhaled a deep drag of his cigarette and rubbed a hand over his brow. "Darling, I'm from a large family, twice as many siblings as you have. My side is not the issue."

She turned away to conceal her irritation. He reached out, finally embracing her, but this, too, felt distant. "I'm sorry," he said. "I don't mean to hurt you, but you know how much I want this."

"So do I."

"People are starting to wonder."

She looked at him in surprise. "Wonder? Surely nobody can gossip over that right now. Most couples are waiting until this all ends. Look at Jo and Wim."

"We're not most couples." He offered her his handkerchief to dry the wet patches on her cheeks. "If I am going to build a future for this family, we need to have someone to pass it on to—a brood of charming children, remember?"

The words from his wedding speech, words that seemed so distant now, vows for another life. "Isn't surviving enough right now?"

"The Führer says motherhood is a woman's highest purpose. That comes above war, above everything else."

Liesbeth swallowed and smoothed the wrinkles from her nightgown before getting up off the bed. "Who says I give a damn what the Führer says?"

"Don't act all haughty. This war will be over in no time, and when it is, you'll be glad one of us had the foresight to make the right alliances." He stubbed out his cigarette and pulled back the bedsheets before reaching for the light. "I'll call the doctor first thing tomorrow. You'll see him sometime this week."

NINE

Johanna Vos
September 15, 1941
Amsterdam, the Netherlands

In the weeks after the air strike, repairs began at the zoo, and Willem returned home each evening eager to tell me all about the construction work and how the animals explored their new enclosures, digging and snorting as they pranced around and tossed up dirt. Meanwhile, summer matured like an overripe fruit, softening to rot at its edges as the effects of war set in. We'd had days and months when life carried on with few disturbances, and the Germans claimed to treat us Dutch with a velvet glove. But under the surface, a very different reality was breeding. And the people who felt this at their very core, the first to lie awake at night fearing what was to come, were the Jews.

I'd been worrying about this since the night of Jakob's last performance with the orchestra. Almost every week, another ordinance appeared in the newspapers, banning Jews from owning businesses, from attending public school. One thing after another. And while Jakob could still earn a little playing with the Rovers, there were hardly enough opportunities to suffice. Willem and I planned an afternoon out to help lift his spirits.

I was on my bicycle a few blocks from the zoo when Jakob appeared, cycling from the right. He let out a whistle. "Why, he-llo there, look at you—I bet that husband of yours is afraid to let you out of his sight."

Some girls might have thought him too bold, but he often good-naturedly teased his friends and was devoted to Ida. "Oh, you can bet he's on high alert for any ruffians," I said. "Whenever the milkman comes around with his cart, Willem perks to attention like a German shepherd."

We laughed and slowed to a halt in front of the zoo. When Jakob bent to lock his bicycle, his expression shifted, his mask of cheeriness slipping off. But before I had a chance to question him, the mask reappeared, and he ushered me forward onto the sidewalk. "Finally, a visit to Artis after all these years, and with my own personal guides."

We greeted the man at the ticket booth. "Dr. Vos has set aside some family passes," I said, waving at Willem, who was making his way through the entrance gardens toward us.

The ticket booth attendant nodded to let me pass before leaning forward to get a better look at Jakob.

"Something in my teeth?" Jakob asked, his joke landing flat.

"You're Jewish?"

"Does that matter?" I asked.

"I'm obliged to ask." The attendant pointed to something hanging on the front gate. Jakob and I took a few steps back to examine it. A new white sign, stamped with the words *Voor Joden Verboden*—Jews forbidden.

Another rule. I looked helplessly at Jakob and then at Willem, who had reached the ticket booth.

"Why, hello, hello," Willem said, "everything all right over here? You both look positively anemic."

I guided Willem's attention to the sign. People were starting to line up behind us.

"I'd heard rumors," Jakob said, "restaurants, libraries, markets, everything now."

Willem turned to the attendant, who shrugged. "Sorry," the man said, "they put it up this morning."

"Surely you can make an exception," Willem said. "He's here with me, not as a visitor."

"Rules are rules."

"Let's see what the director has to say about this," Willem said. "Jakob, Jo, you two wait here. I'll get this sorted out."

At the café across the road, a German officer rested his boots on the edge of a flowerpot while he enjoyed a cup of tea.

"I can assure you the director is aware of these regulations," the attendant said.

"I can assure *you*—" Willem began.

Jakob raised a hand to stop him. "Don't bother. I'm not up for it anymore."

The officer at the café had looked up from his tea to observe us. I tugged at Willem's wrist. "Let's go. We'll get a drink instead; I know a nice spot a few blocks from here." I led them away from the ticket booth.

"Going for a drink is also out of the question," Jakob said. "They've succeeded in separating us, stripping us from public life, like lepers."

"What, then? I'd say a stroll in the park, but we can't do that, either." I let out a string of curses I'd picked up from the striking dockworkers. The two of them looked at me in surprise. "What?" I said. "This is utter nonsense. It's absurd. What's next?"

Jakob's stare hardened. "Yellow stars."

"Stars?"

"They've just announced it in Germany. Branding our people, easier to pick out in a crowd. It won't be long until they start that here, you'll see." The acrid coating on his words gave me a chill. Once more, I looked toward the soldier, wanting nothing more than to go over and dump his tea all over his lap.

"There's a grassy spot along the water where we can sit. I doubt that counts as a park," Willem said.

We agreed and stopped to purchase some beer and bread. The baker gave us the newspaper he'd finished with, so we could read the new regulations. No Jews allowed in libraries, restaurants, museums, theaters, hotels—the list went on.

"'Banned from cabarets and bars,'" Jakob read. "Well, there you have it. Another job officially down the drain!"

I wanted to ask if we could find a way around it, some flexibility in the rules, but the Nazis didn't make exceptions.

"What will you do now?" Willem asked.

"No idea," Jakob replied. "With the orchestra and nightclubs off limits, the only option is to perform at a Jewish venue, but countless musicians will compete for those gigs. For now, I'll see if I can help my pa out with some clerical work."

"I wish there was another way," I said. "I can't picture you cooped up in an office all day."

"*C'est la vie,*" he said bitterly.

We sat along the edge of a canal, watching the odd boat pass by as we digested the news. It was infuriating how the damn *moffen* toyed with people's lives. They pretended to be acting for the betterment of society, but who would want to be robbed of their city's artists? I thought back to Jakob's final performance with the orchestra—how huge the crowd had been, how it'd swelled with energy. And it wasn't just Jews supporting their own, either. I was sure of that.

"Jakob, didn't you say that the conductor of the orchestra received a letter in support of the Jewish musicians after your final performance?"

He nodded. "That's the rumor, anyway. It got passed around the remaining members. Apparently it was a goodbye letter to us, an 'ode to joy' of sorts, lauding music."

"Oh?" Willem said. "Who sent it?"

"It was anonymous, 'loyal concert visitors.'"

"But that's precisely it, isn't it?" I said. "You have Amsterdam's support. People out there want to hear you, to hear these other musicians. There's no better time than now to have music in our lives." An idea came to me. "What if you had another way to perform, somewhere different, where the Nazis couldn't interfere?"

Jakob shook his head. "Whatever you're suggesting, I'm sure it's one ordinance away from being forbidden."

"You mean something secret," Willem said, "something we could keep under wraps."

"Exactly." The idea was germinating, my excitement building. "Perhaps the Nazis can stop the audience from coming to you musicians, but what if it were the other way around? What if you brought the music to them?"

Jakob scratched his chin. "Like a private concert. But where?"

"Private *house* concerts," I said. "Think about it. Which one of those wealthy families wouldn't want to have the best Dutch musicians performing in the comfort of their own home?"

Willem grinned. "That's it. They host, and together their guests will pay your wages. It's brilliant, Johanna."

Jakob took a swig of beer. "You really think this might work, that people would be willing to take the risk?"

"Think about the letter," I said. "You have your supporters. We just need to find them."

Jakob gave a doubtful smile. "I suppose it doesn't hurt to try. I could ask around. Maybe someone at the musical society knows a person or two who might be interested."

I poked him in the ribs. "A person or two? They'll be clamoring to have you!"

His smile broke into something wider, that lopsided grin I knew him for. "Well, if you insist."

I raised my beer in a toast. "Screw the *moffen*. Long live music, long live Amsterdam!"

TEN

Liesbeth de Wit
September 18, 1941
Zierikzee, the Netherlands

Liesbeth understood she'd been foolish to assume her sister would still be there for her when she needed advice. If the unanswered letters were any indication, the notes slipped through her mail slot, her sister had shrugged and turned away. Liesbeth waited a week, wondering what was occupying Johanna, wondering if she hadn't been clear enough in her messages, why Jo didn't respond to her distress. She sat at home while Maurits came and went with his NSB friends, while he rolled over in bed without a good-night kiss, without so much as an arm draped over her waist. She lay on her side of the mattress and stared up at the ceiling, thinking about doctor's appointments and monthly cycles, about the life that refused to take seed.

After a week without a reply, she got on a train and headed home to Zierikzee.

While she stood in the family garden in the rain, the gray sky hanging low overhead, Liesbeth understood how much she'd missed it there. There was no clattering of the tram, no exhaust from passing vehicles, only the patter of raindrops against the leaves and the earthy smell of upturned soil.

Her brother nudged her, pulling her from her daydreams. "Hello? Do I need to send out an SOS or something?"

"What?"

Gerrit scrunched up his snub nose and indicated the umbrella, which was dripping all over his shoes. Raindrops streamed down his brow, darkening the thick splatter of freckles that covered his face. She laughed and tried to hold the umbrella upright while he opened the gate to the chicken coop to spread the feed.

"Let me get this straight," he said. "Jo hasn't reached out to you in weeks? What'd you do this time?"

"No idea." She looked at him. "I mean it."

"Did you try to trick her into going to church or something?"

"No."

"You got sloshed when she was sober?"

"Don't be silly."

"So, it's about Maurits then."

Liesbeth tried to whack him with the umbrella, but he seized the end of it, snatching it from her. She frowned. "It's all so distant when I'm here."

"To be honest, I don't blame her. He's one *'Hou Zee!'* away from groveling before Hitler."

"I don't disagree with you."

"This situation with the Germans is much more than Maurits and his schemes. It's an invasion, an occupation."

"Yes." She sighed. "Maybe I'm still pretending things aren't as bad as they are."

"Something tells me things are only going to get worse. Our family has been through tough times before, though, and we'll make it through now."

She turned away, but not before the memory returned, the cemetery down the road, her aunt trying to explain that their parents would live there for the rest of time, under those big stones that bore Ma's and Pa's names.

"I'm sorry," Gerrit said, "I know how much it bothers you."

Liesbeth tried to block out her feelings of guilt, that persistent awareness that her parents might never have died if it hadn't been for her childish selfishness. She looked around the yard to anchor herself with happier thoughts. "I remember us so well here. The three of us." She pointed to the magnolia tree. "I would be there in the shade, you and Johanna larking around on the lawn."

"Are you still drawing?"

She hesitated. "It was never just drawing. You know that."

Gerrit ran through the rain toward the back door, calling over his shoulder. "Let's go inside. I have something to show you. And there's fresh cream in the ice box!"

Inside, they shook off the umbrella, stepped out of their wet boots and slipped into long woolen socks. *Oom* Cor was reading the Bible at the table. In the kitchen, Liesbeth planted a kiss on her aunt's ruddy cheek before sneaking the jar of cream from the ice box. She poured it over a bowl of berries and joined her brother and Bram, the family sheepdog, on some cushions by the fire. The flames crackled in their hypnotic dance. As excited as she'd been to move away from Zierikzee, her heart needed this visit, far away from the worries of the city.

She noticed Gerrit watching her while she ate.

"Let's go upstairs?" he said.

"For what?"

"I told you; I have something to show you."

She followed him upstairs into the room the siblings had shared growing up. He reached deep into a cabinet and produced a worn file folder. Liesbeth rifled through it, finding all her favorite sketches from throughout the years: an ochre crepe evening dress; a navy jacket with pockets that gathered at the front; drawings she'd made by candlelight, imagining she was Coco Chanel or Elsa Schiaparelli, hunched at an easel in a Parisian atelier.

"I can't believe it," she said.

Gerrit bent over her shoulder to admire them. "I argued against throwing them away." He looked at her. "You've changed, sis. You've lost something. A lightness you had."

Liesbeth sat down on the bed and told him about the argument she'd had with Maurits, their difficulties conceiving a child. Her brother was quiet.

"What do you see in him?" he asked at last.

"He's all I've ever dreamed of."

"Look." He sat down beside her and pointed to her sketches. "That's not true."

"Well, he's handsome, clever, ambitious. He works very hard, and he takes care of me. What more could I ask for?"

"Fine, if that's what you think." He reached over and shut the folder.

"If you mean refusing to see the doctor—"

"Where are your dreams, Lies? Where's the Paris catwalk in Maurits? He's a dealer in little pills."

"Every couple has their spats, don't they?"

"You're missing the point. Maybe his little NSB pantomime wasn't serious at first, but look what it's turned into. You need to think hard about the life you want, and whether Maurits is prepared to give it to you. He's chosen his side and it's not where Jo is standing, or me, or most of the country, for that matter."

They sank into silence, focused on the folder on her lap. After a moment, Liesbeth said, "You always made fun of my wanting to go to Paris."

"Find something you believe in and stick to it. That's all I know. The rest will follow." He got up, shaking his head.

Liesbeth sat there for a minute longer, tracing her fingers over the quilt, following the thread's curved pattern. She opened the folder once more and admired the sketches, lost in recollections of the worlds she'd dreamed up for each of them. Gerrit was right: she needed to change her life, but she was afraid it might take some time.

ELEVEN

Johanna Vos
June 6, 1942
Amsterdam, the Netherlands

It took months for Jakob and me to refine our plan, but once it took shape, the pieces swiftly fell into place. In the spring of 1942, the Nazis ordered Dutch artists to register with the Kultuurkamer, the new Chamber of Culture. Painters, sketchers, dramatists, poets, violinists, sopranos—everyone except the Jews, who weren't even allowed on a stage. It was a bureaucratic scheme to scrape our country dry of its artists, anyone who might dare to make a statement. When the order came, I, like many others, refused to join. Jakob warned me against it, knowing I would lose any chance to perform legally, to earn a few extra guilders to help out at home. However, the decision to register was a matter of loyalties, and I knew exactly where mine lay.

In the end, the Kultuurkamer is what inspired us to action. We all had to choose a side. Were you merely voicing solidarity with the Jewish artists, or did you actually stand behind them? Within weeks, the registrations came in, a long list of names green-lighted by the Nazis. We found our alliances among the names missing from that list. Jakob and I followed the trickle of rumors to other like-minded artists who echoed our calls for resistance. And it was in one of these meetings, held in a cramped attic room, that our initial idea turned into something real.

The plan was for secret house concerts, unmarked and unadvertised. We would spread the news in trusted circles, giving Jewish artists a chance to perform and earn a living on the sly. Our own hidden music salon: a choral "fuck you" to the *moffen*.

We held the first house concert at the home of a Jewish surgeon whose wife was a keen patron of the arts. They lived in a beautiful turreted mansion that overlooked one of the ponds of the Vondelpark, with all its lily pads and weeping willows.

For weeks leading up to the concert, the preparations had commanded my full attention: organizing the venue, the performers, the guest list. Ensuring we had enough ration coupons to provide hors d'oeuvres for everyone and feed the musicians. When the evening arrived, I was so preoccupied that I forgot to jot down the address for Willem, and he was forced to wander the neighborhood until I spotted him from the window and brought him inside.

"There you are," I said. "The guests are due any minute."

"Is that all the hello I get?" he joked. "I've worn my soles thin trying to find this place."

"I'm sorry, dear." He didn't deserve a curt response, but I had to focus. I surveyed the drawing room, running through my mental checklist. Jakob's wife, Ida, was stationed in the front hall to collect the entrance fee, one and a half guilders per person, although donations were more than welcome. Blackout paper hung on the street-side windows with the green velvet drapes closed. The seats were arranged in neat rows in front of the grand piano, with chairs brought in from all corners of the house; the glasses for refreshments were polished to sparkling, and the marble busts on the hearth dusted. Everything was spotless. I'd never seen such an elegant house, but the couple's wealth felt like an afterthought. All that mattered was that the surgeon and his wife were generous and discreet hosts—the first of many, I hoped.

Willem tapped me on the shoulder. "Why don't you introduce me, and then I'll find a way to make myself useful." I obliged, grateful when he swept up the couple in conversation so I could check on things in the kitchen. With his wit and charm, Willem could secure a year's worth of benefactors in a single pass of a room.

Once I had checked on the food and drinks—the surgeon had pulled several bottles of wine from his cellar, a luxury sure to entice the guests to return—I searched for Jakob. I found him in a side room, going over the schedule with the two Jewish performers.

"What if the Order Police catch wind of this?" I asked quietly, the one question we kept circling around. Gatherings of more than twenty people were prohibited, and while the surgeon had composed the guest list with care, we had to count on their neighbors not to pick up the phone and snitch. In times of conflict, trust is like a gilded egg: precious, rare, and easily shattered.

"Well," Jakob said, "I hope the guests all ran track in school." He raked a hand through his curls. "Some of them will come in through the back door, right?"

"Provided they remember the instructions."

"Good. We won't always be lucky enough to have two entrances."

"Let's focus on making it through tonight."

The doorbell chimed. I squeezed Jakob's hand and we moved to greet the first guests. Everyone filed in in cautious silence, removing unseasonably long coats to reveal the gowns and fine suits hidden underneath. Many of them had pinned the new yellow stars to their clothes, a sight that infuriated me.

The concert started at seven thirty sharp. I sat down in the back row between Willem and Ida while our hosts opened with a speech. "I bet the surgeon gets his bed custom-made," Willem whispered, "and do you see how they've raised the height of all the doorframes in here?"

I suppressed a smile. Of course Willem would notice such a thing, tall as he was himself. It wasn't the surgeon's height that I noticed but his balding head, which gleamed under the chandelier like a polished apple.

When the surgeon finished speaking, he raised his glass in a toast to Jakob and me and the others who had helped string things together. I fidgeted as rows of faces turned toward me. These guests knew the risk they were taking in showing up, the Jews above all.

When Jakob took the stage to introduce the musicians, I managed to relax. He was a natural in front of a crowd. Beside me, Ida beamed in adoration, reminding me of my sister. She was intuitive and fiercely protective of the man she loved and, by extension, the people and things he cared about. I felt a sliver of guilt for not letting Liesbeth into our plan but brushed this away. A clandestine concert was no place for the wife of an NSBer.

"Here we go," Willem whispered, as the musicians bowed and took their places. He laced his fingers through mine. The pianist sat down, and the violinist adjusted a string on his instrument. In that long, pregnant moment, the crowd was still. Every sound from the street—a cawing bird, the purr of a car engine—pervaded the room. The pianist let her hands hover over the piano keys. I held my breath. At any moment, a knock could come at the door. We could be fined, arrested, or worse. But then, the pianist's hands fluttered into motion, and the violinist began to play.

As the room filled with music, I focused on the piece. Mozart's Sonata in E Minor, K. 304. The allegro began sternly, with a somber tone. It brought me back to Zierikzee: age nine, following my aunt and sister through the streets as they stopped to buy white lilies from the flower cart. Liesbeth clutching the bouquet as she crouched in the cemetery, laying the flowers one by one across my parents' graves. I closed my eyes and let the sorrow come back to me.

When the second movement came to a close, we all breathed in a collective, wistful sigh. Then, we began to clap, hesitantly at first, as if we were trying to gauge the weight of the noise, whether it would breach the walls and alert someone outside. The applause grew warmer, more assured, and something shifted. The tension disappeared, smiles spreading across the room like sunflowers turning to meet the sun.

That feeling lingered the rest of the evening. We broke for an intermission, and the hosts brought out their trays of canapés. For the first few minutes, people clung to their own circles, but when the wine came around, they started to mingle, talking and laughing and sharing toasts with strangers: nurses with lawyers, Jews with Calvinists. In the corner, the editor of the Catholic newspaper threw his arm around the man next to him in raucous laughter. Willem leaned in. "That man he's talking to is a socialist." I watched, astonished as people crossed the lines of their own segregated worlds, as a sense of camaraderie filled the room.

The surgeon and his wife came over to me with an extra glass of wine. "Thank you," the surgeon said. "It feels wonderful to have the house filled with laughter again. It's good of you to want to help."

"Regardless of our beliefs," I said, "we share this city as neighbors."

The hostess smiled. "Tonight's been a reminder of the beauty that still surrounds us." She leaned in and my attention fell to her necklace, which glimmered in the light. It was such an eye-catching piece of jewelry, a deep red stone cut in a hexagon and set in a gold pendant, the corners decorated with flowers.

"What a gorgeous necklace," I said. "It suits you."

"Thank you. My grandfather was a jeweler. He made it for my grandmother with her birthstone, but she found it too modern for her taste." The hostess then excused herself to gather everyone back to the drawing room for the rest of the program.

The musicians carried on, playing Debussy and Rachmaninoff and Mendelssohn—names the Nazis had banned for being too French, too Russian, too Jewish. I thought back to the night at the Concertgebouw, Jakob's final performance with the orchestra. All those engraved cartouches lining the hall. Surely by now the Nazis had removed the plaques with Jewish composers, like they intended to rename the city's Jewish street names. Erasing an entire people. At least within the walls of private homes, these people remained safe.

Jakob and I exchanged relieved smiles; the night was a success. All these people, Jews, gentiles—all Amsterdammers, all uncertain of where the war would lead them. But for those few cherished hours, we were all there together under one roof, free to think and laugh as we pleased. Free of the Nazis' grip. Free of their cruelty and terror. There was only the music.

Before I knew it, the performances had drawn to a close. The audience called out for an encore. But that, too, had its end, and I found myself rising to usher the guests toward the study that had served as a cloakroom, ensuring everyone had a good excuse to be outdoors as I saw them out the door. And when it was all over and the room was empty and the hired help had cleared the empty glasses and trays, and the violinist had packed his violin, and the surgeon was beginning to doze off in the corner armchair, I found my way into Willem's arms.

"We did it," I said, nuzzling my cheek into his lapel.

"You did it," he replied.

After the success of that first evening, news of the house concerts began to spread, and our artists' Resistance network grew as more and more people opened their homes to the performers. Yet the Nazis continued to impose new rules, tightening the tethers on Jewish life. First, the Jews were forced to "deposit" their valuables at a special new bank. Then they had to give up their automobiles and bicycles. And when summer set in and the days grew longer, the Nazis forbade the Jews from using the telephone, from being outside after 8:00 p.m. We struggled to work around this curfew. Sometimes we held our house concerts on Sunday afternoons, but otherwise they had to run through the night until the curfew ended at dawn, so we began to call them our *zwarte avonden*, black evenings.

We needed to make it easier for people trying to find the concerts, since it was too risky for them to bring along the written address. I suggested a code to be left on the windowsill of the house in question, a vase containing a silk black tulip—silk, because there was no such thing as a true black tulip. A black tulip to mark the music in the shadows, under the cover of night.

Content as I was to stay backstage, recruiting and organizing, those nights of music stirred something in me. I watched while the music swelled to fill the small sitting rooms, enchanting the audiences. It was so unlike the grand hall of the Concertgebouw, with its acoustics that amplified and echoed, with musicians on a far-off stage. Here, you could see the perspiration on the performers' foreheads, see their muscles quiver at the stroke of their bows.

In early October, an opportunity fell into my hands. I had vowed not to take up anyone's spot to perform, least of all a Jewish artist's. However, a poet from Rotterdam had stopped replying to the letters about his upcoming performance. People believed he had gone into hiding. On hearing this, I had the sinking feeling that this would be the first of many of our performers who would be forced to disappear, to leave their houses and belongings and loved ones behind at a moment's notice. How much worse could things get?

Jakob took the news with a grim nod. He had been immersed in such stories for months now, since the deportation summons began appearing in his neighbors' mailboxes. His mixed marriage with Ida kept him safe for the time being, but he struggled with that fact while his friends and family tried to gauge their chances for survival.

Still, it was Jakob who tried to see the spot of sunshine amid it all, urging me to step up and perform. "We have a ballerina performing, Edda van Heemstra, but it won't look good to have a gap in the program. Donate your earnings, if you wish, but give yourself something for once."

"The other singers have been opera sopranos. I'd need an accompanist."

"How about a contrabass?" Jakob asked, and that settled it.

We prepared several numbers together, renditions of popular songs. Every day for a week, I put "I'm Gonna Lock My Heart" on the gramophone, trying to mimic every shift and trill in the music and memorize the English lyrics. I was no Billie Holiday, but I tried to pour something of myself into the song. When my voice was hoarse and Willem arrived home from the zoo, I changed the record to "And the Angels Sing." We belted out the lines over top of Martha Tilton while dancing around the room. When the record crackled to its end, we collapsed on our bed and made love like we hadn't in ages.

On the day of the house concert, I felt more than ready. I'd even started dreaming in English. But that morning, I woke up blurry eyed and exhausted after a troubled sleep. It was the third day in a row I'd woken up like that, my stomach tied in knots. A heightened bout of stage fright. Here I could walk around giving instructions and reaching out to strangers, but I knew if I was in front of an audience, I could be wobblier than a bowl of velvet pudding. After Willem left for work, I ran to the bathroom, and my breakfast came tumbling back up. I tried to coach myself in the mirror—*pull yourself together!*

Jakob and Ida and I had agreed to meet at the patron's house to set up. The country estate lay on the Amstel River at the outskirts of Amsterdam. It took me the better part of an hour to cycle there with my outfit and good heels in my bicycle saddlebags. I arrived flushed and breathless.

Ida took one look at me and told me to sit down.

"Clearly," I said, "I've been spoiled living in the city center."

We met the lady of the house and helped the maids position the chairs, while the hostess fretted over the details. I struggled to remember everything that had to happen. Ida put down what she was doing and came over. "I'll take it from here. Why don't you and Jakob rehearse before it's time to meet the other performers?"

I glanced at Jakob, who nodded in agreement. "Thank you," I said. He set up his contrabass while I conducted my vocal warmups. I felt faint and reached into my satchel for the sandwich I'd packed, but the smell of it turned my stomach so I tucked it away again. In the future, I'd stick to organizing the concerts.

"Ready?" Jakob asked.

He counted us in and started plucking away at his bass until the notes signaled my cue. I began to sing. A few lines in, the room went blurry: the art on the wall melting like a Dalí painting, the herringbone floorboards multiplying. When I tried to bring everything back into focus, I felt myself sway.

The next thing I knew, I was on the floor, staring up at the ceiling. Something cushioned my head. Ida's fuzzy face appeared in my vision, a look of concern. She cradled me on her lap. "You fainted," she said. A cool, damp cloth brushed my wrists.

I peered up at Jakob as he dabbed my forehead with the washing mitt. "I did?"

"Out cold as a pickled herring," Jakob said.

I made a move to get up, but Ida urged me to rest. "Go easy on yourself," she said. "You have a big night ahead."

I took a few deep breaths to satisfy Ida and then tried again to stand. A wave of nausea rolled in. "A little stage fright," I said, but a thought came to me. How many weeks had it been since my last period? With all the excitement of the Resistance work, I'd lost track. I thought of Willem, of the measures we'd taken to be careful. But lately...

"Unless," I began.

Ida gave me a knowing smile. "You need to see a doctor. You'll want to know sooner rather than later."

PART TWO

The Noose Tightens
October 1942–May 1943

TWELVE

Liesbeth de Wit
October 26, 1942
Amsterdam, the Netherlands

The sun shone through the Vondelpark, the trees shedding their red leaves like a lady slinking out of her coat after a long night out. Liesbeth tried not to shiver when the breeze caught her skirt. She hadn't managed to buy a fresh pair of stockings in weeks, and, like many women, she'd taken to tinting her legs and painting a thin seam down the back with her brow pencil to create the illusion of stockings.

She found Johanna by the teahouse in the center of the park. Although the two of them lived only ten minutes apart by bicycle, Liesbeth could count on one hand the number of times she'd seen her sister in the past six months. Every visit had felt stiff, afternoon strolls or a quick cup of tea, none of the games or laughter or snuggling under blankets and gossiping she was used to. On the occasions the conversation moved deeper—when she confided in Johanna about how helpless she felt, how frustrated she was at her inability to get pregnant—her sister's sympathy came laced with remarks about Liesbeth's poor choice in husband.

Jo waved as Liesbeth approached. She was wearing a pair of slacks, something Liesbeth would never have dared leave the house in. The editor at *Libelle* had published an editorial about how inappropriate it was for women to wear pants in public, a sign of the degradation of society and to be avoided at all costs.

Liesbeth laughed while she greeted her sister. "Trying something new, are we?"

"Oh, some days I can't be bothered. Why should men be the only comfortable ones?" She pointed at Liesbeth's goose-pimpled legs. "I mean, look at you!"

Liesbeth shrugged. "Sometimes keeping up appearances is the only way to trick yourself into carrying on."

"I thought Maurits was connected," Johanna said, as they began walking. "Surely the NSB have a whole warehouse of stockings hidden somewhere."

"Jo, I—"

"I'm kidding. Do try to lighten up." Johanna was walking at half her normal pace, and deep frown lines formed between her eyebrows.

"I'll save my favors for more pressing matters," Liesbeth said. "Now, are you planning on telling me what's going on, or do I have to coax it out of you?"

"What do you mean?"

"Your eyebrows. You're doing that thing again."

"What thing?"

"Please, spill it. Is it bad news? What is it? Should we go somewhere more private?"

Johanna didn't reply right away. Around them, birds chirped, and two children ran by, pulling a wagon with a broken wheel that squeaked and zigzagged across the path.

"It's nothing like that," Johanna said, "but you're right, I do have something to tell you. Good news." She paused. "You see, it's rather unexpected—"

Liesbeth looked back at the boy steering the wagon and understood the secret her sister was harboring. "You're pregnant, aren't you?"

"Lies, I... We weren't planning for this. We were so careful. It's the last thing I would have asked for right now."

The news hit hard, but whether with joy or pain Liesbeth couldn't tell. She stopped walking. "The last thing you would have asked for?"

"I don't mean it like that. I know I should be grateful. I am, especially since I know how much you've been trying yourself."

Ashamed that Jo had sensed her jealousy, Liesbeth looked away. "Don't worry about me. This is about you." She tried to clear her head and stepped forward, embracing her sister. "I'm happy for you. Thrilled, actually. Jo, this— You know what this means? You're going to be a mother. And I'll be an aunt."

"*Tante* Lies sounds good on you."

"*Tante* Lies, yes. It has a nice ring to it, doesn't it? Oh, this is terrific, beyond terrific. You're going to be a mother!"

"It's a wild thought, isn't it. Me, a mother? You're the one who knows everything about children."

"I suppose that's easy to say until you have a baby in your arms. I don't know the half of it. Oh, imagine, a mini you to coddle and love. What does Willem think of it all?"

Johanna smiled. "He's over the moon. He's been sharing the news with everyone in sight."

They carried on walking, but Liesbeth was so full of questions she could hardly contain herself. "How long have you known?"

"A few days. I wanted to tell you right away, but I needed some time to process it."

"Of course you did, I understand," Liesbeth said, although she didn't.

"I'm sorry I've been distant. I've been busy."

"Well, what matters is that we're here for one another now." Liesbeth had hoped for more of an explanation from Johanna but didn't want to ruin the moment, so instead she changed the subject. "Willem will be a wonderful father."

"Yes, he will, won't he?" Johanna paused and turned to face her. "Maurits will make a good father one day, too, you know."

"I hope so, I really do."

In all Liesbeth's months in Amsterdam, the sun had never quite found its way onto the rear balcony of their apartment, but she liked to sit there, perched on a white wrought iron chair with a cup of tea. Fake tea, of course, brewed with nettles she'd gathered in the park, but if she closed her eyes, she could pretend she was on a balcony in Paris, overlooking the vibrant streets of Montparnasse, dressed in a fine silk dress instead of her ratty old dressing gown and slippers.

At three in the afternoon, she was on her third cup of tea, but she'd spent more time watching the drizzling rain than she had on her work. She'd arranged some fabric scraps and a handmade pattern on the table beside her, next to a notebook and fountain pen. No matter how long she stared at these items, the words wouldn't come. Her article for *Libelle* was overdue. The editor had given her an extra day to finish it, but the notepad was still blank. She'd had a wonderful idea for a piece on converting old clothes into maternity wear, but since Jo's big news, the idea had lost its spark. Instead of writing, she flipped through the latest issue of *Libelle*. The pages featured drab, wartime colors, navy and maroon, and the models sported dirndls and embroidered cardigans that weren't available in the Netherlands.

If inspiration was a well, hers was as dry as a cove at low tide. Fabric was getting harder and harder to come by. She'd heard of women fashioning skirts out of potato sacks, of sweaters knit with fur from the family dog. Yet, with the Nazis in control of the editorial calendar, she had to pretend there was no such thing as poverty or scarcity, that Berlin was the pinnacle of fashion, rather than Paris or New York. Her editor had advised her to title a new piece "*Razzia* in Your Closet." She'd written back with a flat no, stunned by his gall. Did he think the fate of the Jews was some twisted joke?

Normally she could count on Johanna to pull her out of her uninventive slump. After all, Jo was the one who had a way with words. But her sister had been suffering from terrible morning sickness all week, so Liesbeth didn't want to bother her with her problems. Besides, Jo hadn't shown much interest in her recent articles. Liesbeth wasn't sure if she was keeping up with them.

As Liesbeth stared out at the rain, Maurits came home, his shoes clacking against the loose floorboards. He stepped out onto the balcony and gave her an appraising look. "Awfully cold to be dressed like that, isn't it?"

"You're just worried what the neighbors might think," she said listlessly.

"And rightfully so. You look the same as when I left this morning."

"I've been busy. You're not the only one who is putting bread on the table these days."

He pointed to the blank notepad with a smirk. "Working hard or hardly working? Now, are you going to ask why I'm home early?"

"Bad day at work?"

"The opposite. I thought we could have a celebratory drink."

"Oh? And how do you keep getting your hands on more alcohol when the shop shelves are bare?"

"Things are picking up," he said. "You wouldn't guess it, but there's good money to be made in my line of work."

"Is that so?" She thought of the German soldiers, lining up at the pharmacy at the day's close, the cash Maurits slipped straight into his pocket.

"It's a matter of supply and demand, my dear. And when it comes to the Germans getting their fix, I'm their man."

He opened his cigarette case and withdrew a cigarette, spinning it between his fingers. She had an urge to flick it from his hand. Why must he speak to her like she was a child, like everything needed explaining? "If you want to worry about what the neighbors are thinking," she said, "maybe you ought to look in the mirror."

He raised an eyebrow. "What are you being so sassy about?"

"I told you, I'm working. And you can leave me out of the 'finer details' of your work. I don't want to know."

"Be glad I'm clever enough to turn a profit in this war. It's the only way you can afford to mope around all day in your undergarments!"

She balled the trim of her dressing gown into her fist and reached for her pen, her irritation growing. "Please, I need to focus."

"So you won't join me for a drink? What's so important, anyway?"

"I said leave me alone, *Godverdomme!*"

Maurits stepped back. She'd never sworn at him before, but the word landed with a satisfying sizzle. Maurits swiped the notepad aside and examined the pattern she'd cut out with its label at the top: maternity dress. "So that's what's gotten you all wound up. You're still sulking about your sister's news."

Liesbeth stiffened. After a moment, she said, "I don't want to just be 'the fun aunt.'"

"Look, it's not fair. Johanna can barely cook a decent meal— Lord knows how she'll take care of a child. But being moody about it doesn't help anything. You're making me miserable."

"Maybe if we spent a little more time making a conscious effort ourselves, we'd have more success. The doctor said we should use a calendar to track my cycle."

"Well, the lack of interest you've shown lately isn't helping.

How can you expect us to conceive a child under such circumstances?" He paused. "I've given this some thought, and I think it would be advisable for you to start a treatment program."

"A treatment program?"

"To boost your mood, soften your temperament." He went into the apartment and returned with his briefcase. He opened the latch and pulled out an orange-and-blue tube. It was the same drug he'd given the soldiers: Pervitin.

Liesbeth scowled. "Don't try to play doctor."

"I've seen countless women come in complaining of a low libido and this always does the trick. We'll start you off slowly."

"I don't know if I feel comfortable—"

"And I don't feel comfortable coming home to an unhappy wife. Come on, darling, it's for the both of us. Trust me. You'll feel better in no time."

He removed the cap of the tube and held out a tablet in his open palm. She stared at it. What was the use getting mad over something she couldn't control? Perhaps it could help. And if it was as safe as a box of chocolates, what was the harm in trying? At least this way, he couldn't pin all of the blame on her. She reached out and took it, turning it over once in her hand before popping it into her mouth. The bitter taste sat on her tongue long after she swallowed.

Maurits squeezed her shoulder. "Good girl. Now, why don't you put on some clothes and finish up here? I'll be in the sitting room with a glass of wine when you're done."

He went back into the apartment, and a minute later, a cork popped. She shivered and adjusted her robe, trying not to think about Johanna, about the joy of anticipation that she also longed to feel. She traced a finger over the edge of the sewing pattern and picked up the fountain pen. If inspiration refused to appear, she would have to seek it out herself.

THIRTEEN

Johanna Vos
January 19, 1943
Amsterdam, the Netherlands

The baby elephant at Artis Zoo let out a loud trumpet and tripped over its back feet as it bolted away from the fence. I laughed and called out to it, while Willem pushed up the bridge of his glasses with his middle finger and jotted a note on his clipboard. "Strange," he said. "Something must have spooked her."

I rested a hand on the growing bump at my belly. "Maybe our little one is sending out battle cries."

"She's already as feisty as her mother."

"She?"

He winked and gave me a kiss. "See you tonight. I can't wait for dinner."

I rolled my eyes, knowing full well that he was more fed up with our meager diet of potatoes and green beans than I was. He headed off toward the petting zoo, where an overweight sow needed its medication.

Once he was out of sight, I turned to leave, thinking about what he had said, whether the baby would have my spirit, or his looks, or my build. These early months of pregnancy had toyed with my mood, creating ebbs and flows. It wasn't that I didn't want a child. I'd looked forward to the years ahead of coddling a little one, of taking my son for ice cream on sweltering days, introducing my daughter to the world of books. I knew I should count my blessings, but why did it have to happen now? People everywhere were dying, and it felt selfish to bring new life into the midst of such darkness. I was already needed elsewhere.

As I made my way toward the zoo's exit, I noticed that a peculiar restlessness had descended on the animals. The wildcats were pacing their enclosures, throwing their heads to the sky, and the penguins brayed and flapped about. By the time I reached the gate, it was obvious that something was wrong.

Then I heard the shouting.

"Schnell, schnell!" German commands, harsh on the tongue. Armed Order Police charged down the street like seething bulls. I stiffened as the metal turnstile clicked shut against the back of my thighs. It was too late to turn back.

Across the road, the front door of one of the gabled houses swung open. A family stumbled down the steps and onto the street. Yellow stars pinned to their jackets, rumpled bundles heaped in their arms, and soldiers pointing guns at their backs.

As I tried to process everything around me, the sounds and colors grew sharp and harsh and bright. My body tensed up, like a heavy weight had fallen on my chest. It was happening again—another *razzia*.

I glanced around for an escape. Looking for shadows, I inched along the gated wall, edging out of the sun. The street was barricaded. Men and women ran around me, crying out in protest, screaming as batons bashed against their shoulders, their legs. The soldiers chased the Jews from all directions, driving them onto the street. Frightened children called out for their parents as they were pushed into the middle of the intersection. And there, kneeling on the cobblestones of the tram tracks, were rows of men, their hands above their heads, their winter scarves fluttering in the wind. From where I stood, I could see their faces: the fear in their eyes, their skin drained of color.

My stomach turned. Where were the Nazis taking them? What cruel fate awaited these people? They were good Dutch men and women, our neighbors. And these vile Order Police were tearing them from their homes, trying to play God.

A truck with canvas siding pulled into the intersection, carrying more Jews. "Out!" the Order Policemen yelled.

A young man protested and doubled over as a soldier kicked him behind the knees. He curled up on the ground, recoiling as the kicks landed again and again.

I watched in horror, feeling helpless. I turned back to the walled gate of the zoo and willed Wim to appear, to open the gates and usher some of these people to safety. Nobody came.

On the opposite end of the road, a handful of onlookers gathered, gentiles, like me, all of us caught near the Jewish quarter at the wrong moment.

A woman with a yellow star emerged between the onlookers, calling frantically for her husband. She was pregnant, the bulge under her coat bigger than my own. I felt a pang of dread, of compassion, and wrapped a hand around my own belly, like that could shade my child from the hatred that had overtaken our city. The pregnant woman spotted someone on the tram tracks and lunged forward. I stepped into the street, shouting "No!" but an arm reached out to block me.

"*Ausweis*," the policeman said, holding out his hand. He had a boyish face but a set jaw, like he wanted to prove himself. Fiddling with the latch on my purse while looking over his shoulder, I searched for my identification card. Surely this woman had heard the rumors, the dark fate that might await her and her unborn child if she got deported.

The policeman snatched my identification from me and opened it. No *J* for Jew on my card. He frowned.

"Am I free to go?" I had to find the woman before she did something foolish.

He pointed to a space between some parked bicycles. "Stay here until we've cleared the area. Unless you want to wind up with this lot."

I cursed him under my breath and looked around for the pregnant woman. She had disappeared.

"Where are you taking them?" I asked.

He ignored me but pulled another gentile from the crowd and shoved him in my direction. The two of us had no choice but to stand and watch. A feeling of impotent rage washed over me when I realized there was nothing we could do as our neighbors were herded like livestock for auction.

I scanned the crowd for the woman. She wasn't with her husband, nor was she among the women huddled off to the side, with children wailing in their arms.

I could feel my anxiety building at the sight of those mothers who were struggling to soothe their children, to convince them everything would be all right. My heart was beating in my ears. A man in the back row leaped up. He was trying to make a run for it. The Order Police fired at him, one, two, three, four shots. The man screamed in agony while the force of the gunshots reverberated under my feet. For a second, there was silence. A soldier grabbed the man from where he lay and dragged him to his feet. Blood soaked his pant leg.

Then, the Germans, those filthy *moffen*, ordered everyone to march. They drove the crowd farther down the street. They were leading them to the theater, the Hollandsche Schouwburg. I'd heard stories of the countless times this painful separation had occurred before. There, men and women would be crammed into the main hall of the theater, the young ones ripped from their parents' arms and sent to the Jewish nursery across the road, where they would stay until they were deported.

A movement in the corner of my eye caught my attention.

Two women ducked out of an alley. There she was. Neither of them wore a star, but I could make out the traces of bright thread hanging from the pregnant woman's lapel. The other woman grabbed her hand and tugged her forward, down a side street. She whispered something, and from the urgency in her actions, I could imagine what it was: *Don't look back.*

As the soldiers dispersed, I, too, slipped away. Yet all I could think of was the stranger and her baby and the desperate hope that, somehow, they would survive the war.

I took one more look over my shoulder. The intersection was empty now, save for a man's cap, which having caught the breeze, swirled once, twice, before coming to rest on the cobblestones.

A few days later, we celebrated Willem's birthday. For weeks, Liesbeth had been asking about our plans for his birthday, but I'd brushed off her question, saying we didn't feel like doing much at all. What I meant was that I didn't feel like sitting across from my brother-in-law all night, trying to ignore his warped loyalties and pompous remarks about the fate of the Third Reich.

Instead, Jakob and Ida joined us for lunch, and we marked Willem's special day with streamers and candles and a cake baked with the sprinkling of sugar I'd saved for the occasion. Afterward, I turned the radio to the liveliest music I could find amid all the German propaganda, while Willem cleared off the table and set up the wooden shuffleboard his father had made us as a wedding present, and we all took turns testing our aim.

We teamed up, men versus women. Ida went first. One by one, her wooden discs shot into the slot with the highest points.

"You'd make a good sharpshooter," I told her.

Jakob grinned. "Except this sweetheart of mine refuses to do so much as set a mousetrap."

"Well," I said, "if you ever change your mind, the Resistance will find a good way to put your skills to use."

"Speaking of which," Willem said, as he bent over the shuffleboard, "I don't mean to ruin the jolly mood, but we need to discuss something."

He and I both looked at Jakob. "The *razzias*," I said. Jakob nodded, growing very serious. Three of his friends had been arrested in the latest *razzia*. They'd been marched off to the Hollandsche Schouwburg, where a mass of people huddled together inside, awaiting deportation. I thought about what I'd witnessed, the rows of people lined up, their hands in the air, terrified children clutching their mothers' coattails.

"Have you heard anything?" I asked Jakob.

"They've been sent to the Dutch transit camp at Vught. We've tried to pull some strings through our contacts on the Jewish Council, but they can't do much to stop the deportations." He pressed his thumb into the edge of the shuffleboard, his expression a mix of anger and resignation. "Too many families still haven't gone into hiding, but the damn *moffen* won't stop until they've arrested everyone they can."

"We need to help them find hiding places," I said. "Not just the performers, but everyone. I know many patrons of the house concerts have taken people in, but we haven't exhausted our network."

"It's difficult," Ida said. "Some people have the space to hide someone, but others—like us four—don't. And think about the families with infants or young children."

"I watched a pregnant woman being separated from her husband during the *razzia*," I said. "So many mothers out there must be struggling on their own."

"A friend of mine has taken in a pregnant woman whose husband was arrested and killed," Jakob said. "In a few months, she'll have to worry about the baby crying and giving the two of them away. Marijke is prepared for that, but not everyone would take on such a risk."

"What's happening to the children whose parents have been arrested?" Ida asked.

"There's a Jewish nursery by the theater. Apparently children are held there until the family is set to be deported," Jakob said.

"We need to be more creative," Willem said, "and think beyond the big villas and country houses." He stacked the shuffleboard discs at the starting line. "I've spoken to the director of Artis. He's committed to doing everything he can to arrange hiding places at the zoo."

"The zoo?" Ida said.

"We've done it before. At the beginning of the war, we housed a bunch of our own Dutch soldiers in one of the big halls. Obviously, we can't have them sleeping out in the open like that, but the point is, we have space."

"But if Jews aren't allowed to enter the zoo, how will you get them inside without detection?"

"We're still working on that, but, during the last *razzia*, someone managed to sneak some Jews in through the back entrance. If people are nearby and in danger, we'll try whatever we can."

"Please," I said to Jakob, "you know what people need. Let us know what else we can do. It's not just about the artists anymore—we need to think bigger."

"Get a pistol within short range of Hitler," he said bitterly. "Better yet, a grenade."

We stood there, the atmosphere of the night bruised while the reality of what was happening in our city sank in. I stared at the shuffleboard, that silly party game, and around the room at the streamers, our attempt at celebrating while all of Europe was falling apart.

"Come on, Jo," Jakob said. "We can't fix this overnight. You might as well take your turn."

FOURTEEN

Liesbeth de Wit
February 20, 1943
Amsterdam, the Netherlands

The grand hall was decorated from top to bottom, NSB flags and swastikas slung from the rafters. Liesbeth sat next to her husband at a round table decked with a lavish floral centerpiece and a tablecloth of fine white linen. Liesbeth admired it, imagining the shirts for Maurits and pretty sundresses she could sew if she only could get her hands on such fabric. She couldn't stop gawking. It felt like she'd stepped back in time, before the rationing, before the war had put a damper on everyday luxuries.

Maurits nudged her under the table, and she shifted her attention to the speeches. At the far end of the hall, someone had taken the podium, a tall man with hair cropped like boar bristles. Maurits said he was the local NSB branch leader. From the tone of respect in his voice, she assumed she ought to be impressed, but the man looked out of sorts in his stiff black uniform, which hadn't been tailored for his narrow shoulders.

The NSB leader saluted the crowd. *"Hou Zee!"*

"Hou Zee!" On all sides, arms shot up in forceful salutes, Liesbeth lagging behind the rest.

"Come on," Maurits whispered, "at least fake some enthusiasm."

He adjusted his tie, a flash of insecurity crossing his face. It had taken him months to convince her to join him at one of the NSB social evenings, and she knew he was counting on her to make a good impression.

The speaker raised his hands to silence the room. "Comrades," he began, "how good to see you all gathered here this evening. We're here in a show of support for Germany and our own fatherland as one united front. Our brothers have been fighting valiantly on the Eastern Front, and I have no doubt they will be quick to recover any land lost, to stifle the noxious spread of Bolshevism. Now, more than ever, it is time to join our Germanic brothers in laying the brickwork of our own legacy. We turn to the Führer to show the world our power, to guide us into a new Golden Age. We will build a country that will make our sons and daughters swell with pride!"

Liesbeth surveyed the room, baffled by the way the audience clung to his every word. Men pounded their fists on the table and women nodded in approval. Couldn't they see this man was trying to sugarcoat the truth—the fact that the swift victory Hitler had promised was disappearing under meters of bloodied Soviet snow?

The speech ended in cheers and another round of salutes. Maurits turned to Liesbeth with a proud grin. "Inspiring, isn't it? The energy tonight is contagious!"

Before she could respond, the waiters brought out the appetizer, a curry soup. She wasted no time in dipping into it, grateful for the excuse to exclude herself from the conversation. The wives at the adjacent tables looked like they perched on pincushions, their lips pursed. The exception was a younger woman who snorted with laughter in the corner, but she ignored Liesbeth's attempts to offer a friendly smile. Maurits hadn't glanced her way for several minutes. He was bent over the table in deep conversation with his friends. The only snippets she caught were phrases like "strong leadership" and "restoring our colonial empire and its wealth."

She twirled her spoon around, trying to entertain herself. One of the men Maurits had been talking to appeared to be getting frustrated with his soup. He was unknowingly using his small dessert spoon, and, with every spoonful, half of the soup dribbled back into the bowl. When the man saw her watching, she gestured shyly to the soupspoon by his right elbow.

He nodded in appreciation. "There's enough silver on this table to fund the entire Dutch army," he said. "Or whatever's left of it."

Liesbeth smiled. His shirt collar sagged from too much wear, but he struck her as the type of man who only looked in the mirror when he had to shave. He had a strong face, but one of his eyebrows arched upward, like he was permanently amused.

"You're wondering who this stranger is; I can see it on your face. That husband of yours forgot to make introductions." He stuck out his hand. "Dirk van Duin. And you're Liesbeth, the one who likes boating."

It took her a second to understand the reference. Dirk had been the one to lend Maurits his boat on that lovely summer afternoon they'd spent along the Amstel River. "That's right."

He leaned in, like he wanted to let her in on a secret. "I've lost count of how many of these ritzy bashes I've been to, and I still don't have a clue what glass is what."

She pointed out the glass for the red and the one for the white.

"Open a keg and pour me a cold one. That'll keep me happy." He winked and took a long sip of beer. "Maurits says you're a country girl, but you know a lot more than a brute like me."

Liesbeth paused. What an unusual man, so unlike Maurits. He seemed proud of his humble roots, a misfit among this room of try-hards who were so desperate to trade in their clogs and work boots for shiny Oxfords. Yet, he had a certain charm. "My uncle taught us these sorts of things," she said. "I suppose he hoped we might stumble across Queen Wilhelmina in little old Zierikzee."

"Aha, so you could dine with her while her footmen fixed the broken axle on the Golden Coach."

"Precisely. But sadly, I'm still waiting on that day."

Dirk smirked. "You'll be waiting ages if she keeps cowering in London."

Liesbeth nodded but didn't laugh. She didn't want to ruin the only half-decent conversation she'd had all evening by delving into politics, but she'd hoped that this man was more of a patriot than Maurits, that he could see that the royal family was doing all it could to protect the population.

"Who is this 'us' you mentioned a moment ago?" Dirk asked. "Your sister?"

Liesbeth smiled, grateful for the change of subject. "Yes, Johanna. However, she believes etiquette is utter nonsense, that food is food, and dining shouldn't 'sanction class struggles,' or something of that nature."

"Sounds like a communist. I bet she's not here tonight."

"No." She looked down at her lap and began pleating the folds of her skirt into her palm. Every topic felt so loaded. Out on the streets, people scorned men like Dirk, men like her husband. But here, in this hall, she felt like Alice tumbling upside down through the rabbit hole, where the opposite of everything reigned supreme.

While she searched for something to say, the scents of the main course wafted through the hall: haddock with glazed carrots and roasted potatoes. Her mouth began to water. It smelled divine. As soon as the plate was in front of her, she dug in, her appetite betraying her manners.

Maurits started speaking to Dirk, but Liesbeth was content

to savor the meal. Months had passed since she'd last tasted a good piece of meat or fish. She'd never understood how Maurits could so vocally support the NSB, not since the Nazis had marched in and parked themselves here, eating Dutch cheese, drinking Dutch *jenever*. But at least the Nazis were willing to share with their supporters. She could get used to these perks, these relics of normal life.

Between bites, Dirk caught her eye. "Let me show you a trick." He pushed away his plate and produced a deck of cards from his jacket pocket, which he began to shuffle. The ink on the cards was faded and smudged, like they had been used a lot.

"Choose a card and memorize it," he said.

"Trying to read my mind, are you? Good luck—it's one big muddled mess."

"That's life with a man like Maurits," he said and winked.

Liesbeth blushed and glanced at her husband, but he was already absorbed in a different conversation.

"Ready?" Dirk asked. "Now, I want you to select a card and sign it, so we know it's yours."

"I don't have a pen."

He gestured to her handbag, like he expected her to procure something out of thin air. After a moment's thought, she found her lip liner and drew an *L* in berry red on the two of hearts. He shuffled the two back into the deck, showing her that it was neither near the top nor the bottom of the stack.

"So where is it?" she asked.

With a snap of his fingers, he made her card appear on the top of the deck.

"How did you do that?"

"Do you want to see it again?"

She hesitated as she reached for the lip liner, not wanting to waste more of the precious lip pencil, which was so hard to come by. But curiosity got the better of her. And while she kept a close watch on his hands, he still managed to pluck her jack of diamonds from the deck without giving away a thing.

"Impressive," she said. "Have you always been a magician?"

"No, no. For years, I was a taxi driver. But I've traded in my license for something new. Bigger and better things. Working at a bank now, in fact."

"As a teller? That's wonderful. How do you find it, pushing people's savings around all day?"

"Between you and me, it's boring as hell."

"I spent most of mathematics class daydreaming up gowns and sashes, but I'm sure you're brilliant at it."

"I only had to spend four days outside their office begging them to give a poor guy like me a chance. I'm a numbers guy, though, and a lucky one."

"Which bank is it?"

Dirk held back his answer. He pointed to the waiter, who was coming by with their dessert. Vanilla *vla* with whipped cream. Liesbeth's face lit up.

"Take mine, too," he said. "I don't like the flavor."

She accepted it bashfully, conscious of her table manners, but she didn't know when she'd have another chance to taste real whipped cream again. While she polished it off, people mingled and a dance band started setting up in the front of the room. Dirk's kindness had been the one bright spot in her evening. She was curious about him, the way he behaved like an outsider, even though he seemed to know enough people. He made her feel less alone.

Maurits leaned over, resting a hand on her forearm. "I'm sorry I've been so preoccupied, darling. You realize how important it is for me to network at these functions, don't you? The business depends on it."

She nodded. He always had their best interests in mind, but surely he was less concerned about the pharmacy sales and more about promoting his shady side gig and rubbing elbows with the right suits.

"That's what I love about you. I can bring you out without having to worry about keeping you entertained—unlike those hens over there." He pointed to a couple of women who kept glancing around, looking, as far as Liesbeth could tell, not much different than she did. He kissed her forehead and excused himself.

She debated whether to approach the women who seemed equally lost. However, the band struck up and their husbands pulled them onto the dance floor. Meanwhile, Maurits had cut across the room to sidle up to some other associates. She kneaded the fabric of her skirt again, searching for a way to occupy herself. How silly she felt, standing in the middle of the room, bobbing to the music like a buoy lost at sea. Then she spotted Dirk coming back from the coatroom.

She waved to get his attention. "Do you fancy a dance?"

"Need you ask?"

He slid an arm around her waist and began to shuffle her around the room, his movements jaunty and helter-skelter. He stepped on her toe, yet somehow never missed a beat. She laughed as he spun her in circles, once, twice, until the whole room felt topsy-turvy.

Between songs, she leaned in so he could hear her above the music. "For a taxi driver, you certainly have rhythm."

He grinned. "My ma taught me. She'd go buy laundry soap and get the shopkeeper to crank the radio so she could dance with my sisters and me outside on the sidewalk. Before long, we had more soap than clothes."

She laughed, trying to picture him flapping about on the street with his mother. Her Calvinist aunt and uncle had never approved of dancing; they thought it was frivolous and ungodly.

The band started playing a new number. Dirk took her hand again for another dance, but Maurits appeared and tapped him on the shoulder. "Thank you for taking such good care of my wife. Now, let me show her how it's done."

Dirk dipped in a mock bow and made his way to the bar. Maurits pulled her close. "I love you," he said.

That familiar streak of warmth ran through her, the way a single phrase could bandage the evening's loneliness, as it had bandaged so many things he'd said and done before. She nestled her cheek against his as he guided her around the dance floor. Dirk was more of a bouncer, she thought, her husband a glider, like he moved through everything in life.

Maurits kissed her on the forehead. "Are you enjoying yourself, darling?"

Liesbeth looked over his shoulder, at the swastikas that glared at her from every corner of the room, the framed photos of Hitler and Mussert, the head of the NSB, on the wall. Then, she felt the pleasant fullness of a proper meal, the energy it brought. Her eyes fell on Dirk as he leaned against the bar, which was stacked with bottles that had long been sold out in shops across the city. She watched as he tipped his glass to the barman and drank it down in one fell swoop.

Liesbeth looked up at Maurits. "Yes," she said. "Actually, I am."

FIFTEEN

Johanna Vos
March 4, 1943
Amsterdam, the Netherlands

The instructions were to meet next to the flamingo lagoon at the zoo. Sure, Willem had intended the instructions for someone else, but I was the one waiting there, checking the time and clasping a protective hand over my belly. Part of the belly was phony: false identity cards and ration coupons padding my maternity corset, but beneath the papers, a life was forming. Our baby.

As I sat there, I tried to imagine myself one year later, pushing a baby carriage across the cobblestones, lifting up the infant to admire the pink plumage of the flamingos, the cerulean blue of the peacocks. I took a deep breath and sat up straighter as that sour taste of heartburn returned to my throat. One of the many joys of pregnancy, I was learning.

"Not exactly the courier I was expecting."

I turned to find Willem standing behind me, a stethoscope dangling from his neck. I kissed him on the cheek, and then he led me to a secluded garden, which bloomed with flowers in the warmer months but was now little more than hedges. He rested a hand on my shoulder. "You shouldn't have come. It's far too risky in your state."

"I don't see any flying bullets. I'm paying my husband a visit at work. It's hardly suspicious."

"Johanna…"

"You know I can't sit around at home for months on end."

"Why don't we have a night on the town? I heard there's dancing on the Van Baerlestraat on Thursdays."

"That NSB breeding ground? I wouldn't be caught dead there." At the sight of the worry in Willem's gaze, my voice softened. "I'll be careful, I promise. I've brought the supplies you needed, nothing more."

His face relaxed and he pinched my cheek. "I thought you'd gotten a lot rounder since this morning. Come, let's go inside."

I began to follow him. "May I meet them?"

"What?" he asked, but he knew what I meant. The Jewish people at the zoo, the ones hiding in plain sight. He gave me a warning look. "One of the macaques just gave birth," he said. "I'll show you."

He led me to the monkey rock, a big complex partitioned off by a moat, a structure with tufted peaks like meringues. It had opened shortly after the occupation began. Artis Zoo, so popular with the German soldiers, was one of the few establishments that seemed to be still expanding during the occupation. I sometimes wondered why long queues of people would still spend their precious pocket money on a day at the zoo, but they probably liked to lose themselves in the gardens and their imagination for a few hours. An oasis in a war-torn city.

"Look." Willem pointed to a macaque who carried a baby against her chest. "Just a few weeks old."

I directed my focus at what I wanted to see, yet what I hoped was impossible to see. The look in Willem's eyes told me there were people hiding somewhere in the complex. The macaques scrambled about, dipping into enclaves and out of sight. The rock must have been hollow, so the monkeys could sleep inside it. And now humans as well. I pictured them there, huddling between the cages, trying to get some peace and rest.

My mind flooded with questions: Was it overcrowded? How did they hustle the Jews inside during a *razzia*? There must have been a plank or something they used to cross over the moat. As I pondered this, I noticed that Willem's attention had strayed. He was watching a young lady who sat on a bench with a sketchbook while she chatted with some German soldiers. They cracked a joke, and she made a show of laughing at it. I frowned. Another Dutch girl fraternizing with the enemy. The soldiers got up and left, and I was tempted to go over and give her a piece of my mind.

"Don't say anything," Willem said. He could read me almost as well as Liesbeth.

"Why not? She's causing a scene."

Willem grabbed my arm, holding me in place. That concerned expression was back, but it wasn't directed toward me. I stopped and took another good look at the lady as she returned to her drawing. From where I was, I could see that detailed drawings of the monkeys filled the open pages of her sketchbook, as if she'd been sitting on that bench for hours. And her blond hair showed a hint of darkness at the roots.

"Don't meddle in things you know nothing about," Willem said. "Come on, this way."

As I followed him away from the main enclosures, I glanced back at her, at the loneliness on her face, and I understood my mistake. She wasn't trying to flirt. She was protecting herself, hiding in plain sight.

At the far end of the zoo, Willem opened a door and led me into a dimly lit storage room that smelled of damp feed. He checked around to ensure we were alone. Then he glared at me.

"I'm sorry," I said. "I didn't know."

"Get ahold of yourself, Johanna. You can't just show up here acting all righteous. You're too quick to judge. Imagine what could have happened if you started telling her off. Talk about creating a scene."

"I said I'm sorry. It was a mistake. I didn't realize they'd be milling around in the open."

"Only when it's safe. We can't ask them to stay holed up in the enclosures all the time. There's no humanity in that." He paused. "Sometimes it's easier than others. One of the men has been given a wheelbarrow of meat to distribute to some of the carnivores during the day. You wouldn't know he was Jewish if you saw him."

I wanted to ask more, wanted to hear everything, but it was not the time or the place. I reached under the waistband of my skirt and loosened the maternity corset to extract the ration cards and coupons, enough to feed a few more people for a couple of months at least. The list of demands for supplies was bound to keep growing, and I wanted to help as much as possible.

Willem stuffed the bundle into the hole behind a loose brick in the wall. He gave me another look. This unfamiliar, serious side of him surprised me.

"You need to go home," he said. "We'll talk about this later, but you need to think about the risks you're taking."

I didn't like being chastised, but he was right. We left the storage area and returned to the main path of the zoo. He accompanied me to the gate, where he kissed me goodbye. "Please," he said once more. "Think about the baby."

In an alley connecting the canals, which encircled the city like bands of pearls, was an old wooden door. The forest green paint was chipped in the corners, the latch on the door rusted and hanging lopsided. I checked the alley for prying eyes. Then, I rapped out the code Jakob had given me, and when the door opened, I slipped inside.

The space had once served as part of an old brewery: dirty glass bottles stood next to rusted machinery, and piping covered the walls. In the corner, someone was pedaling a stationary bicycle hooked up to a small generator to power the electric lights. An array of documents was spread out between huge vats. A few Resistance members I recognized sat organizing them into stacks, while two I didn't cranked out copies of an illegal newspaper on a hand press.

As I bent to pick up a handful of newspapers, I spotted Jakob sitting on a plank, which lay on overturned buckets to form a bench. A yellow star was pinned to his sweater. He waved and shuffled over to make room, leaving a wide gap to accommodate me and my enormous belly.

"Glad you could make it," he said, patting me on the wrist. "Is Wim joining us?"

I told him Willem was on his way, then held up the newspapers. The wet ink from the top sheet had smudged my skin. "Let's hand these out at the next *zwarte avond*."

"Smart thinking." Although we'd been organizing the *zwarte avonden* for almost a year, the latest *razzias* had made everything more treacherous. With so many Jews going into hiding, our concerts had to evolve, as it became riskier for them to perform. For now, Jakob was still protected, because Jews in mixed marriages had been exempted from deportation, but with every passing day, life grew more dangerous for him as well.

"Where's Ida?" I asked.

"She went to see a doctor."

"Is that so? Are congratulations in order?"

"On paper, at least. The doctor's promised to sign a statement for us, claiming she's pregnant. One more bulwark against the cattle cars."

I took his hand. "She's an inspiration, Jakob."

"Yes," he said. "She's the world as it should be." His eyes dropped to his lap. "And the reason I'm still here."

The brewery door opened again and someone ducked inside. Willem. He was carrying his veterinary bag and his hair flopped forward in that boyish, handsome way of his.

Piet, who had organized the Resistance meeting, went to the front of the room and the others stopped the printer and gathered around. Willem hopped up and sat on a keg beside us.

"Let's get started," Piet said. "The Nazis are tightening the noose across the country, showing us what they have in store. Who here knows someone who was rounded up in the last *razzia*?"

Hands went up around the room. I thought of the woman I'd seen pulling the pregnant mother off the street and I glanced at Jakob, who continued to hear of more friends and family members who had been arrested.

"We've all witnessed the risks of taking a stand: the reprisals, the executions. But still, we must ask ourselves—how did things get this bad?" A murmur passed through the group, men and women from various Resistance cells. "The time has come to strengthen our approach. And fortunately, the British SOE has sent us a gift to do just that."

He stepped aside and unfolded the blanket that lay across a long worktable to expose a bunch of weapons. Revolvers, grenades, a pinched Luger. Several people cheered. I bit my lip, and Willem looked over at me, uneasy.

"Now, I know certain Resistance cells are better equipped for these types of actions," he said, "but there are those among you who feel it's time for a more aggressive approach. The question is what to do with these weapons."

Someone spoke up in the back. "Give them to those of us who are out on active missions. No use having them gather dust in here."

I interjected. "The artists' Resistance has a whole network of people who are sheltering Jews. Many of them would feel safer with an extra layer of protection."

"She's just grumpy and uncomfortable," he said, waving his hand. He shot me a warning glance. "We should move very carefully," he said to the group. "Never open a battle we can't win."

"What do you think, Jakob?" Piet asked.

Jakob looked at me. "Johanna has a point. We have innocent citizens at the mercy of the Gestapo. Still, we need to be strategic. Where can we inflict the most damage?"

People began whispering among themselves. Willem hopped down from the keg. "As a group, we're untrained, unfit to carry out tactical missions. Let's pass on the weapons to the cells that are prepared."

With some effort, I also got up onto my feet. The others were still arguing, everyone hurling ideas to and fro. I raised my voice. "What good will it do shooting up warehouses and train depots if a whole community is wiped out in the meantime? Let's stop the traitors who keep betraying our friends and neighbors."

Everyone turned to me, and I realized what an odd sight I must have been. Keeled backward to balance my weight, my calves swollen as I tried to make my case. "I'm carrying a child into this world, a world I want to fight for, but we need to all act as one."

A smattering of cheers followed, before other voices arose, urging for caution. Willem reached out to me. "I know your intentions are good," he said gently, "but we simply cannot arm a bunch of old men and housewives. People are doing everything they can to keep those families safe. You must trust that."

At the front of the room, Piet called for a vote. I didn't have to watch to know I was outnumbered. I leaned back to steady myself, breathless from the strain of exertion. Then I wrapped a protective arm around my belly and whispered to my unborn baby, "I will be strong for you; I'll do everything in my power to bring you into a world that's safe and loving."

SIXTEEN

Liesbeth de Wit
April 12, 1943
Amsterdam, the Netherlands

Liesbeth stood outside the pharmacy, studying her reflection in the window. If she angled her body and leaned back, her coat appeared to slope downward in a healthy, motherly bump. She placed a hand on her navel, trying to imagine how her sister must feel, but the bulge of fabric flattened and her reflection shrank until it was just her again. With a wistful sigh, she went inside.

Maurits stood near the cash register, writing out instructions for a prescription. Beside him was a brown glass bottle, one of the many that lined the wooden shelves framing the counter.

"'Chloral hydrate,'" she read, examining the bottle's label with its accompanying skull and crossbones.

"Knockout drops," Maurits said, "for insomnia. Gotta be careful with this solution. If you overdo it, you won't wake up." He finished what he was doing before coming over to kiss her. She handed him a bag containing his favorite necktie.

"Thank you, darling," he said. "You managed to patch it?"

"Well, with a scrap from an old handkerchief, but as long as you're not nose to nose with your suppliers this evening, no-body will notice the difference." She paused. "What time will you be home?"

The bell at the door interrupted his reply, and he moved to help the new customer. Part of her was curious about his meeting with the pharmaceutical suppliers, but she sensed she wouldn't want to hear the details. Still, she pocketed all the extra ration coupons and the Germans' cash he came home with in quiet resignation. If his little side gig kept food on their table when so many others were struggling, she couldn't complain.

"Can you keep an eye on the door for me?" Maurits asked. "*Meneer* Van Duin is supposed to come by any minute."

As Maurits disappeared into the back room, she lifted a hand to check her hair, surprised by the little jolt she got at the mention of the man's name. She told herself it meant nothing, but she couldn't help but think back on the fuzzy feeling he'd given her at the dinner party, how he'd made her feel seen.

The bell jingled again. It was Dirk. He wore a smart knit vest with a red houndstooth necktie, but his shoes had scuff marks and his fedora sat askew. "Liesbeth," he said, "what a surprise."

"A pleasant one, I hope."

"Like cordial on a hot summer's day."

She smiled. "Quiet day at the bank?"

"Oh no," he said, after a slight pause, "but I like my long lunches at Café Ruysdael. I go there most days, helps me clear my head."

Maurits emerged from the back. "Ah, there you are, my friend, right on time. Shall we?"

Dirk opened the panel door and stepped behind the counter before following Maurits into the back room. Liesbeth strained to hear their hushed voices, wondering what business Dirk had with Maurits. He looked disheveled, and she thought she'd caught a whiff of alcohol when he'd passed—*jenever*—a strong choice for the lunch hour, but it was the same thing she reached for when she was home alone late into the night, when Maurits was caught up at one NSB event or another.

Another customer walked into the pharmacy, a young pregnant woman complaining of aching feet, for which Liesbeth advised a peppermint salve. Maurits used it for his dry hands after long days at the pharmacy, and he came home smelling of peppermint and antiseptic. She admired the customer's rosy glow with a flicker of jealousy. The woman must have only been a few weeks behind Johanna, who was growing out of her maternity clothes faster than Liesbeth could adjust them.

As the woman left the shop, the bell jingled yet again, and someone familiar came in. Liesbeth had only met Ida Cohen once or twice, but she knew Johanna was close with her husband. The two of them made a funny pair, Ida towering above Jakob.

"Why, hello, Ida. I didn't know you came here."

Ida greeted her with three kisses on the cheeks. Her dress had a high, starched collar and she wore long, mauve gloves. "Johanna mentioned your husband was a pharmacist."

Liesbeth studied Ida, searching for some hint of bitterness. She doubted her sister would intentionally solicit business for Maurits. How much had Johanna told Ida about how he'd come to own the pharmacy? "How very kind of you to think of coming here," she said.

The two men emerged from the back room, and Dirk slipped something into his pocket. She recognized the telltale orange-and-blue Pervitin packaging. *Aha*, she thought, *he has you hooked as well*.

Liesbeth gestured to Ida. "This is *mevrouw* Cohen, an acquaintance of my sister's."

Hearing the Jewish surname, Maurits hesitated, glancing at Dirk before he reached out to shake Ida's waiting hand. Dirk, in contrast, perked up at the sight of Ida, regarding her from head to toe in a way that made Liesbeth's skin prickle.

He tipped his hat to her. "*Mevrouw* Cohen—it's been too long. How are you and your husband? Dare I ask, is he still around?"

The men looked at Ida, but Liesbeth kept her eyes on Dirk. How bold of him to ask, tactless even. But was he genuinely concerned about Jakob's well-being, or was his interest selfish?

If the question upset her, Ida didn't let on. "He's well," she said, before turning to Maurits. "My back has been troubling me. Can you advise me on something to ease the pain?"

While Ida explained the source of her ailment, Maurits pulled several options from the shelves. Liesbeth seized the chance to continue chatting with Dirk, but his responses were distracted, less animated than before while he watched Ida out of the corner of his eye.

"How do you know Ida?" she asked.

"We used to live on the same street, years ago."

"And you've met her husband?" she added, emphasizing the last word.

"No," he said, "but I'd heard she was married."

"Yes, I get the sense they're very in love." She paused, gauging his reaction. "Pretty, isn't she?"

"I guess, but not my type." He turned to face her and lowered his voice. "She's got nothing on you."

Liesbeth let out a short exhale, the fluttering sensation returning. There was a richness to his gravelly voice, something enticing. She started to smile, but it disappeared as it dawned on her that she was flirting with Maurits only meters away. She took a step back and silently reprimanded herself.

"What do you think of Maurits's pharmacy?" Dirk asked Ida.

"Oh, very professional indeed," she said, dropping her change into her coin purse, "quite modern."

"You live nearby?"

"A few blocks down the Sarphatistraat, where it curves toward the zoo."

"I have an appointment that direction in half an hour. Allow me to accompany you." He didn't correct her use of the old Jewish street name, which the Nazis had recently changed.

"Oh, thank you, but you needn't bother."

"It would be my pleasure," he said. "I'm sure we have plenty to catch up on."

Ida pressed her lips together. "Well, if you insist."

Dirk turned to wave to Maurits. To Liesbeth, he said, "It was good to see you again, *mevrouw* De Wit."

Liesbeth slumped, his sudden formality souring her mood. Dirk turned and winked at her, then left, holding open the door for Ida and ensuring she didn't trip over the threshold on the way out.

SEVENTEEN

Johanna Vos
April 29, 1943
Amsterdam, the Netherlands

My bicycle slowed to a coast while I reached into my pocket for the slip of paper with the address I needed. Only the paper wasn't there. I'd forgotten I'd torn it up on the way out that morning. I couldn't afford to get caught with anything that might incriminate the kind couple who'd offered up their home for our next house concert, risking a hefty fine, or worse.

Their house was on one of the side streets that jutted off from the Apollolaan, but I couldn't remember which—pregnancy brain made sure of that. I squinted to read the name on the nearest street sign, while the baby kicked, squeezing my belly against my handlebars. Another week or two, and I'd be lucky if I could roll myself home.

I was pretty sure I needed to be on the other side of the road. I cycled farther, searching for a good place to cross the median strip without trampling the flower beds. The trees were blossoming and daffodils covered the grass. The city hadn't bothered to plant tulips: people would have dug up the bulbs to eat before the flowers had a chance to bloom.

The baby kicked again, as if it heard me dreaming about food, and I thought of the forged ration cards I had with me. My stomach grumbled and my joints ached, but I couldn't be selfish: the people in hiding needed the food far more than I did. Their savings were dwindling in the form of bribes and payment for shelter. The Resistance members did whatever they could to offer outside support. A growing network of families had opened their homes as refuge to the city's Jewish artists, and to many others in need. Friends and neighbors who could be counted on, and some who couldn't. I'd learned that you had to approach people, ask them to lend a hand or take someone in. Most people wouldn't put their lives in danger out of free will alone. But if you asked someone directly—will you help us?— you forced a decision. It was a matter of asking yourself what kind of person you were, how you were prepared to be remembered after the war. More than once, the Resistance had taken a gamble, persuading Amsterdammers with murky loyalties to take in a Jew or two. You couldn't trust people unless you knew they had something on the line themselves.

As I was about to cross the road, an automobile barreled toward me. It braked in time to careen around the corner, but I spotted the passengers crammed into the back seat, a mother with two children. The vehicle parked farther down the adjacent side street and the driver's door swung open.

"Out," a man yelled in Dutch. "Get out, all of you!"

The mother pulled her children close as they stepped out of the automobile. Word had it that a group of Dutch civil servants were being paid good money for every Jew they turned in. That made this man a bounty hunter, the dirtiest of traitors. I checked the street sign on the brick building beside me and chided myself for not taking a better look at the map. The Euterpestraat, a name synonymous with danger. The automobile was parked in front of the headquarters of the Nazi intelligence agency, the Sicherheitsdienst, or SD.

A pair of Germans in green uniforms were walking in my direction. Order Police. They stopped a student who was busy parking his bicycle and yanked the handlebars from the boy's hands. "Bicycle seizure," they snapped.

One of the soldiers pointed at me. "Hey, you there, yours, too!"

Instinctively, I took off. I heaved forward on the pedals, my belly weighing me down like a sack of potatoes, making me gasp for air. I cut down another street filled with mansions and turned two or three more times until I was sure they weren't coming after me. I braked beside a shrub to catch my breath. What had I been thinking, taking off like that? If they'd wanted to, they could have caught me. Still, I couldn't afford to lose my bicycle.

"Annie!" someone called.

It took me a second to recognize my nom de guerre. The woman called out again as she came running over. Ida. She reached out to steady me.

"What took you so long?" she asked. "Come on, it's one block over."

I wiped the sweat from the nape of my neck. "You might have told me that our hosts are next-door neighbors with the *moffen* heavyweights!"

She shushed me. Then, she projected her voice and started speaking like I was slow in the head. "Take a deep breath, Annie, nothing to worry about. We've visited these friends plenty of times, remember?"

Despite her poor acting, I was happy to go along with her charade. If the Order Police were to pop around the corner, an act like this might get me out of trouble. We approached the house of the upcoming concert. All the buildings on the street were lavish, and this one was no exception. With three stories and a manicured garden, it seemed untouched by the hardships of the war. But as I went inside and met the hostess, I couldn't shake the feeling that danger was too close for comfort.

Fortunately, our meeting with the hostess, *mevrouw* Blom, put my mind at ease. She claimed she rarely encountered anyone from the SD headquarters and promised the large hedge that encircled their yard created enough privacy to keep any illicit social gatherings under wraps. I had to take her word for that. A recent house concert in Utrecht had been broken up by the Order Police, who had stormed in to hand out hefty fines. The Jewish guests had just enough time to run and hide in the upstairs bathroom, narrowly escaping arrest. Every concert was like that—marked by both emotional highs and apprehension. Those nights, we were the custodians of our guests' well-being, and it would take only a few decibels too many or a passing policeman to put everything at risk.

The house concert was set to take place two days later, on Saturday evening. I found myself counting down the hours to the big night. An evening of music, merry conversation, plenty to distract me from my heartburn and taut skin. Although my due date was weeks away, I felt close to bursting. On Saturday morning, I ran through my usual concert preparations, ignoring my body's cries for rest and Willem's fretting about the concert's location.

"One more night," I assured him, "and then I'll wait out the rest of this pregnancy like Rapunzel in her tower."

However, as soon as I arrived at the mansion for the concert, I knew something wasn't right. The main act of the evening was a dramatist performing a one-man take on *Macbeth*, with a musical interlude by a violinist. Jakob knew the violinist from the orchestra, while the dramatist came from out of town. But when I arrived to set up, there was no sign of any of them.

I didn't mind. Despite being slower than normal, I knew our to-do list like a pianist knew his chords. I confirmed the evening's schedule with *mevrouw* Blom, checking that the seating and makeshift coatroom were in order. The mansion was only a few years old, built on the couple's newfound fortune in aircraft manufacturing. It had a large sunroom and a stained-glass window that hung over a grand staircase and glinted violet with the evening light. It was a beautiful place to pass an evening.

Because of the curfew, the guests would need to stay until dawn. This meant extra work for everyone, more food and drinks, and we had to keep up hospitable appearances regardless of how much drowsiness was creeping in. Still, these true *zwarte avonden*, the concerts that stretched into the dark hours of night, were my favorite. Friendships arose that would have been inconceivable under normal circumstances.

An hour before the concert was due to begin, Ida showed up looking very pale. "Jakob was taken in for questioning," she said.

"What?" I asked. "Where is he now?"

"I had to bring our marriage certificate and the doctor's statement to the station. They didn't believe him." She scrunched up her nose and sniffled. "They said no pretty Dutch girl would marry a filthy Christ-killer like him."

I held her close. "Oh dear, I'm so sorry. Tell me they've released him."

"They had nothing to keep him on. He's at home now, resting, but who knows what will happen now that he's on their radar."

I didn't want to admit that Ida had every reason to worry. The police were pressed under the finger of the SS. And the damn *moffen* didn't care about any flimsy marriage certificate, so I doubted it would make a difference if Ida was with child. Still, his safety net was fragile at best. If he were arrested for any transgression—not wearing a yellow star, being late for Jewish curfew, or attending an illegal gathering like our concerts—he could be sent on a train out east.

"Don't worry," I said. "He's clever enough to find a solution. Still, I'm glad he stayed home tonight."

I noticed someone standing behind Ida in the entranceway, a woman you might mistake for a bottle-blond Katharine Hepburn if you saw her in a photograph. She wore a green silk dress and carried a violin case. "Sorry for interrupting," she said, "I'm Marijke de Graaf." After comforting Ida, she added, "I'm only half the musician Jakob is, but I can help you finish setting up."

My brain had fogged up; I kept picturing Jakob arguing with the police. While I struggled to come up with some useful instructions, *mevrouw* De Graaf put down her violin and began to flit around the sitting room like she knew its every nook and cranny, straightening a crooked picture frame, laying the program cards out on the seats. "Is *meneer* Smit here already?" she asked.

"Who?" The baby was jabbing my side with its persistent kicking.

"The dramatist."

Of course, where was he? I asked Ida, who said Jakob had planned to meet the man at the train station. At the mention of her husband's name, she began sniffling again. I led her to a chair to sit down. "Do you know when his train was due to arrive?"

"I'm sorry, I don't recall."

I checked the time. The man would arrive at Amstel Station, and it would be tricky to make it there and back before the concert started. Ida was in no state to go venturing off, so it was up to me.

"Let me fetch him," *mevrouw* De Graaf said, but I politely declined and told her I'd go to the station. In the event of a delay, someone would need to entertain the guests, so I asked her to stay. After all, I certainly wasn't fit to start singing. My brain couldn't handle the names of our performers, never mind song lyrics.

By the time I made it to the station, I was panting. Luckily, *meneer* Smit was easy to spot—the lost-looking fellow by the station's entrance. A portly man with a thick beard. I greeted him and tried to usher him back to the tram.

He paused, uncertain. "Who are you?"

"There was a bit of a mix-up. Jakob ran into some trouble today."

"I had strict instructions to meet one person only."

"I believe you're hoping to find a black tulip," I said, slipping in the code marker for our concerts. "I promise, you can trust me."

This seemed to satisfy him. He followed me into the tram, and we made small talk on the way back, but I kept sweating and the baby was shifting, warning me to slow down. The man pulled out his pocket watch. The guests would all be seated now, waiting. I hoped the hostess could stretch out her opening speech.

When we reached the tram stop, we got out right when the rain started. I huffed and hurried us down the block, turning left and right and then carrying on down the Apollolaan. As we approached the mansion, a soldier stepped out of the shadows onto the other side of the road. My breath caught. It was the same Order Policeman from the other day, the one who wanted my bicycle. Did he recognize me?

He reached into his pocket for a package of cigarettes. He withdrew one and bent over it to light it, protecting the flame from the breeze. In that moment of distraction, I grabbed *meneer* Smit's wrist and led him to the right, ducking behind the hedge that lined the mansion. "Quick," I whispered. I thrust myself forward, but in the process, my heel got caught between the cobblestones. I fell to the ground, landing hard on my side. A jolt of pain shot down my spine. I winced, holding my belly, feeling for those tiny kicks.

"Are you all right?" *meneer* Smit asked, bending down to help me.

I bit my lip and felt between my legs. Everything seemed normal. "I'm fine," I said at last. "Can you please help me up?"

He pulled me to my feet and gave me a once-over. "I'm fine," I whispered again, looking around for that Order Policeman. We waited a moment, and when the coast was clear, we slipped into the house.

★ ★ ★

Inside, the atmosphere was carefree. The host was regaling the guests with jokes and everyone was laughing and nobody acted concerned that the evening's main event was late. *Meneer* Smit slipped right into character, shaking the rain from his jacket and parading up to the front of the room as if it were all part of his act. I went to the bathroom to check myself over, trying to slow my heavy panting while I glared at myself in the mirror. How stupid I'd been, rushing like that. Willem was right: I was taking too many risks. I rocked back and forth on the balls of my feet, my hands cradling my belly. When I thought I felt a kick, my breathing relaxed again. I calmed down enough to return to the sitting room, managing to settle in and enjoy the performance.

And, oh, what a show! *Meneer* Smit shone in the spotlight. His voice switched from bellowing to rasping to husky to reedy as he moved between characters. This was not the soft-spoken man from the tram. Then he broke into a musical interlude, an addition of his own design. His singing echoed through the room. I couldn't stop watching the movements of his jaw, his teeth, the spittle forming on his chin. Maybe it was a good thing that I hadn't performed myself. House concerts were too intimate a space for something as bodily as singing.

I was pulled from my thoughts when a shrill noise sliced through the room. The doorbell. There was a brief silence, then panic. People scrambled to their feet, searching for cover. Footsteps pattered in every direction, and several guests fled out the back into the garden. But I couldn't move. Sudden cramps tore at my abdomen. My back was aching. Something was wrong. Very wrong.

A hand shook my shoulder. "Annie."

I blinked through the pain, willing the face into focus. Ida and the violinist stood over me.

"Everything's fine now," Ida said. "The neighbor rang the bell; he'd found the hosts' cat wandering about."

I clutched my belly, keeling forward with the contraction. *Mevrouw* De Graaf knelt. "Are you unwell?"

"The baby," I murmured.

The two women exchanged a worried look and tried to pull me to my feet. "Come with us," Ida said. "You need to lie down."

While they helped me upstairs, I doubled over, feeling wetness between my legs. No, it couldn't be. Not here, not yet. It wasn't time.

They guided me to one of the many bedrooms and eased me onto a bed. *Mevrouw* De Graaf stayed there, rubbing my back. I moaned, calling out for Willem. I needed him there, holding my hand, promising me the baby would be fine.

Ida returned with a stranger in tow. I'd seen him in the audience, a man with a bulbous nose and long gray sideburns.

"This man is a doctor," she said, "the same one who helped me."

I tried to introduce myself, but another wave of pain overcame me. The doctor washed his hands in the washbasin and rolled up his sleeves.

"Someone get me a washcloth and some clean sheets," he ordered. He leaned over me and spoke very softly. "You're going to have to work with me here. There's no stopping this baby from coming tonight."

The hours blurred into shapes and sounds: the dark, sonorous whine of the violin, the ticking of the clock, the buzz of chatter floating up the stairs as guests mingled into the night. I clutched a pillow to muffle my screams, while Ida rubbed my back and coaxed me through the contractions. At some point, I opened my eyes to see Willem, his brow damp with sweat.

"How did you get here?" I asked, my words muffled.

He kissed my forehead. "I'm here now. Everything will be all right."

Much as I wanted to believe it, the look on everyone's faces told me this was a lie. Then, finally, after all those delirious hours of fighting and screaming and pushing, the baby left my womb in a rush of blood and tears. My tears and Willem's. But the baby was quiet. The doctor picked up the child, snipping it free, and bundled it up.

Low whispers, Willem's concerned voice. The doctor's hands fluttered around the infant's face. He dunked the infant in a bowl of water, one and then another.

"What's going on?" I asked, feeling a pang of panic. "Where's my baby?"

Willem appeared, clutching my hand. His face was white. "One minute, sweetheart. The doctor is taking care of her."

"Her?"

"It's a girl," he said, but I couldn't hear any celebration in his voice.

"Let me see her! What's happening?"

"Darling..."

"Bring her to me now!"

The pause that followed was the longest in my memory. Everything spun around me, all the activity of the night, the doctor's cool, reassuring touch, the dizzying smell of Ida's perfume as she leaned over me, the violin, the booming lines of Shakespeare. I repeated myself, demanding to see my daughter. But by the time the doctor came over, by the time I saw Willem's tearstained cheeks, I knew.

My daughter wasn't breathing.

PART THREE

The Real War
May–September 1943

EIGHTEEN

Johanna Vos
May 2, 1943
Amsterdam, the Netherlands

I had never known grief like that. In those breaking hours of dawn, I lay in a stranger's bed, inconsolable, tangled in soiled sheets. At first, the tears wouldn't come. I tossed and gasped for air and clutched the sweat-soaked pillowcase. The convulsions carried on in cruel waves, my body unwilling to accept that it was all over. Wim didn't leave my side, not once. He intertwined his fingers in mine and didn't let go.

I wanted to bury myself in the pain, succumb to the anger, the unfairness of it all. But something else lurked there. I couldn't bear it, but its weight remained there all the same. *You did this*, I thought, *you brought this on yourself.*

While Wim held my hand, I fixated on the floor, on the clump of dust that had gathered in the corner, forgotten by the maid, on the object that had fallen beneath the armchair and rolled out of sight—a crayon, a single yellow crayon, its tip dulled from use.

I couldn't face Wim, afraid he might see the truth, that I'd ignored his pleas. I'd been careless. A better woman—a fit mother—might have thought this fate was God's will, that she'd done everything in her power to shepherd this child safely into the world. But I knew better: I had failed.

Once, when I was young, Gerrit bet that I couldn't hold my breath underwater for as long as he could. I dived down to the very bottom of the pond near our house, clutching fronds of pondweed to anchor myself. With every passing second, the water clouded over, the croaking of the frogs and the green of the lily pads fading, until everything around me dimmed to shadows, the sunshine piercing the surface, far above me, impossibly out of reach.

I felt like that now, certain the world was closing in around me. There was no coming back from this. Our daughter was gone.

Once the nighttime curfew had ended and the guests trickled outside, returning to the comfort of their own beds to sleep off the drinks and merriment, Willem went to speak with the doctor. He lowered his voice so I wouldn't hear, but I could guess what he was saying. Arrangements had to be made: a burial, a certificate of birth or death or both at once.

Footsteps pattered on the stairs, and Ida's voice appeared, asking if she could interrupt. She pulled Willem away and together they went downstairs. I listened for their return, and as I lay there, the weight of our loss crept in. I tried to picture the baby, every contour of her face, the pinched shape of her tiny nose. I made an effort to sit up, to get myself out of bed. Where had they taken my child? I needed to hold her. Maybe if I cradled her close to my breast, some faint ember of life would ignite.

My hands trembled as my body forced me back down. I blinked, willing the tears to flow, frustrated by my wild desperation. The baby was gone—I had to accept that.

My feelings piled up like heavy blankets, stifling and exhausting, so much that I didn't notice Wim's return until he was kneeling beside the bed.

"What did Ida say?" I asked. Even forming the question was an effort.

"The violinist wanted to speak to me," he said, "*mevrouw* De Graaf."

That woman, what was her first name? Marijke, yes, coming to offer her condolences. "Oh?"

"It's better we talk about it later, once you've rested."

"What do you mean?"

Willem faltered. "I don't want to make this day any more difficult."

"Tell me."

"She had an idea, a proposal, but it's a big ask. A huge ask, actually, especially for you. And frankly, I don't think we should dig ourselves deeper into all of this, given what's happened."

There was something about that woman I admired, a spark of determination. The type of woman I could trust. "She's one of us, isn't she?"

Willem nodded. "There's a baby." He looked up at the ceiling, like it pained him to say this word, and my body started quivering again.

I took a deep breath. "A Jewish baby. An orphan?"

"Do you remember Jakob telling us about a pregnant woman his friend had taken in?"

I nodded.

"She got sick. She didn't make it."

A baby in need, thirsting for a mother's milk, for love. In the months following my parents' deaths, I had learned all too well what it was like to need that kind of love. And what better hiding place than amid a caring family? Like the Jews at the zoo, hiding in plain sight.

He took out a handkerchief and wiped his brow. "You need time to grieve, we both do. They can find another way."

He was right: this was no time to be rash. And to try to fill the crater that had opened in my heart—well, that felt wrong. Unthinkable, even. But a baby out there was in danger. If that child was discovered, if they were forced to give it up, it would be sent to the Jewish nursery for deportation. A potential death sentence. Even though I had pushed away from religion, I still believed that for every door that closed, a window opened. This was that window; I was sure of it.

"Is it a boy?" I asked at last.

"A girl. Not one month old."

"That simplifies things." I started making mental plans, what to arrange with the doctor, what to tell the hosts of the concert, how much to share with the rest of the Resistance. With my sister.

"Sweetheart," he said, "you've taken on so much already."

I winced, knowing what he was getting at. Had the dramatist told him I'd tripped and fallen? I wasn't ready to face that horrible truth—it was my fault the baby had come early, our darling child who hadn't lived long enough to be given a name. Willem waited for me to speak, but I sat there for a long time, considering it all, weighing the pain, the guilt, my chance for atonement. What would it feel like to rock a stranger's child to sleep, to call her your own?

"I need to see her," I said.

"The baby?"

"Ours."

He looked at me. Somewhere, a clock rang the hour. I tried to make out the time but lost count of the chimes. I waited for him to shake his head, to tell me to get some rest, not to make things harder on myself.

He stood up. "I'll get her."

"I can walk."

Reluctantly, he eased me up and helped me out of bed. I struggled to keep my balance while he guided me down the hallway to a side room, which contained a crib. I hadn't considered that the hostess might be pregnant herself, but the thought drifted off as I approached the crib. Willem squeezed my shoulder; I was shaking again. I leaned into him and bent over the crib. There she was. A crocheted doily draped over her tiny, bundled body. I reached down and lifted it from our daughter's face. The pain of seeing her overwhelmed me. Our precious child. Wim helped lift her into my arms, and together we held her close.

For several minutes, we said nothing. I kissed our daughter's pale cheek, while Willem encircled us with his embrace. At the sound of someone in the hall, we broke apart, turning to find the doctor standing there, his coat and umbrella in hand. I eased my daughter back into the crib. As I did, more pieces of my heart crumbled away.

I turned to Wim with tears in my eyes. "I don't think there's any choice in it. We can give our daughter a second chance at life."

Willem made all the arrangements, quickly and discreetly, but when our new baby was due on our doorstep the following morning, I found myself alone. His boss at the zoo had called him in for an emergency, a llama in a difficult labor. The irony was not lost on me. I sat there in the sitting room, numb, watching the minute hand tick on the clock. Whenever the minute changed, the hand shuddered and twitched before falling into place. Twenty-five, twenty-six, twenty-seven. Twitch, twitch, twitch.

I tried to picture the baby. My own. This new one. A stranger's child. An unfamiliar face. Would she resemble anyone I knew, a face I'd once passed in the park or in a shop? I cradled my head in my hands, the air drawn out from me in a long, hissing breath. What were we thinking, taking her in right then?

Over the next half hour, I worked myself into a frantic state. One minute, I felt nothing. Hollow. The next minute, the sharp pang of grief. I was depressed, then anxious, excited, then everything over again.

Footsteps approached on the sidewalk outside. I got up and smoothed the wrinkles from my dress, telling myself everything was fine, that nobody was being replaced or forgotten about. My heart had room for another child. I tried to remember the code phrase Willem had given me, in case I didn't recognize *mevrouw* De Graaf. Something about flower beds. Silly—didn't Willem know that the only flower beds belonged to our ground-floor neighbor? When I reached for the door, I glanced in the hallway mirror and saw puffy red eyes.

Outside, a couple stood in front of the house with a baby carriage. They stared at me. I stared back.

"Hello?" the woman said.

I opened my mouth to say something, but couldn't find the words. I paused, looking at the baby carriage. "Have you come to see my new flower beds?"

"Yes," the woman said, "the ones you have out back."

Yes, it was the same woman from the house concert, the violinist. *Mevrouw* De Graaf. She and her husband made a dashing couple. I blinked, told myself to sharpen up, stop gawking at the baby carriage, and invite them in.

The De Graafs carried the baby carriage up the stairs to the landing, while I tried to get a glimpse of the baby. Once we were all inside, I leaned over to take a good look. The baby lay tucked under a thick blanket, her eyelids fluttering like she was half-asleep. I admired every crease, every curve of the child's face, which was fuller than our daughter's had been. She had a big head of hair, that looked prone to curl, and while there was something angelic in the way she slept, she was still a baby, a stranger's baby. I looked at her and saw my own little one, and that ache in my chest resurfaced.

"Please, come sit down," I said, when I looked up. "I'll put on the kettle."

"We can't stay, I'm afraid." *Mevrouw* De Graaf took a few steps down the hall. I watched her peer into the sitting room, as if she were trying to assess what type of family she was leaving the baby with. Aletta, that was the baby's name—Willem had told me that much. A perfectly fine name, nothing suspicious about it. Still, it was only a name to me. Baby Aletta, this stranger's baby, who was suddenly my own to care for and love.

I waited for *mevrouw* De Graaf to say more. Part of me wanted the couple to leave, to grant me some privacy to deal with my grief. But the sooner they left, the sooner I would be all alone with Aletta. And I wasn't sure how I felt about that.

"We're so sorry about your loss, *mevrouw*," the violinist said.

The baby stirred, fidgeting as she woke. I bent down again and lifted her out of the carriage, gazing down at her. How strange it felt to hold her, knowing I'd agreed to mother her. "It's a dreadful time to bring a child into the world, isn't it?"

The couple exchanged a glance. For a moment, I wondered what they were like, if they, too, were trying to conceive. Neither of them said anything, so I spoke to fill the silence. "Well, at least I can still be of use to another young life." I started to tear up and fumbled in my pocket for my handkerchief. I didn't want these people to see me cry, to start questioning my strength and ability to care for the child. "Such light hair, for a Jew. What happened to her mother?"

"Pneumonia," *meneer* De Graaf replied. "By the time we found a doctor who would come, it was too late." He checked the clock on the wall. "I'm sorry, we need to get going. We can't thank you enough, *mevrouw*. Please hide the carriage well. Your husband knows what to do with its contents."

The carriage—yes, Willem had mentioned something about that. A false bottom, supplies for the Resistance. Weapons, most likely, or ration cards. The idea of a gun sitting right underneath an innocent baby made me uneasy.

"Of course," I said, fumbling for what to say. "You must be

very busy. Thank you for taking the time to bring her—Aletta—all the way here. You can rest assured that my husband and I will give her everything she needs."

Mevrouw De Graaf bent over the baby. She kissed Aletta's forehead and reached out to take my hand. "Please don't hesitate to ask if there's any way we can help."

They moved to leave, but *meneer* De Graaf paused at the door. "It warms my heart to see how willing you are to care for a child that's not your own."

I nodded, without taking my eyes off the baby. I was sure if I looked up, I might reach out in panic, wondering if I'd made the wrong decision, if I were the best person to care for this child. I couldn't let them see my worry. "Goodbye," I said.

The door closed with a click behind them before their footsteps receded down the stairs and onto the sidewalk outside. Then, I was left alone with her, this stranger I was to call my daughter.

The next day, I perched on the windowsill, staring out at the street. There was a queer air to the morning. A thick coat of mist hung over the cobblestones, casting the trees in gray light. Next to me, the baby cried. I glanced down at the cradle, rocked it absently, and looked outside again. A group of workers bent over the road, fixing the paving. They jiggled out the worn bricks and filled the gap with fresh ones, aligning them one by one until they formed a snug row. I watched them while they worked, observing the efficiency of it all, the smudged dirt on their hands.

The crying beside me persisted. Baby Aletta. *Our* baby now. The child's face was scrunched, prune-like. I reached out a hand, knowing I ought to soothe the baby, feed her. Do something. Aletta latched on to my index finger with a curled fist, and looked up at me. No matter what I might want to see in those eyes—love, a trace of myself, of Wim—there was nothing, just a vacant, squinting stare.

The workers were still busy outside. One man lifted a spade, striking earth. He jimmied some pebbles free, used the flat back of the spade to pat the ground flat, but all I saw in that movement was the gravedigger, the upward swing of his arm as he dug deep into the ground to bury my daughter.

Not that I had been there—everything had happened in the secrecy of night, off the record. Our poor little one lost in the dark. I couldn't push the thought away: that wooden casket, hardly bigger than a shoebox. My baby girl, meters underground, growing a little garden on her belly.

Aletta's cries pierced the silence. I rubbed my temples, fearing another headache, while her wailing grew, her mouth puckering in need. I tried to picture the baby's mother, this stranger who had died in hiding in the De Graafs' attic. She, too, had slipped into a covert grave, leaving the baby with nothing more than a worn blanket and a name.

I thought of everyone else I knew through the Resistance. The worried, frightened faces. The many names of Jews searching for hiding places, desperate for ration coupons, people they could trust, their lives teetering like acrobats on a wire. They told me what they needed, and I helped. But this baby's cries made me feel nothing aside from a dull, numbing ache.

While the workers packed up, a tall, elegant bird picked its way over the cobblestones toward them. A stork. It lifted its neck and turned its head to observe the workers with a beady eye. No, I was mistaken; it was only a gray heron.

I rubbed my temples and looked at the baby, at the wet streaks on her cheeks. The cries softened when I lifted her from the cradle. I pushed my chair back from the window and lowered the bodice of my dress. The baby shrank away from me. I tried nudging my breast toward the child, but still she wouldn't nurse. She squirmed, and I shifted my arms, struggling to find a comfortable position. How did women make this look so natural? I wished the midwife was still present, or my sister. I tried moving her around, but she kept fussing, no matter what I tried.

"For God's sake!" My harsh tone provoked more tears. I took a slow breath, trying to summon some compassion. "Come now, Aletta, you need to eat." I sucked in a breath through my teeth, trying not to lose my patience, but I felt like a failure. Here I had vowed to take care of another woman's daughter, and yet I couldn't even get her to eat.

I rubbed away my tears of frustration and told myself I could do this, that I would find a way to fill this role, to protect this child as I'd promised. I tried again, positioning her and softening my tone. "There, there, Aletta, everything is going to be fine." For a moment, the baby stopped moving. I repeated the words, repeated her name until she wriggled and latched on.

As she began to suckle, I bowed my head in relief. This was what I was supposed to feel, emotion, a need of my own, the need to protect and love little Aletta. It was time to shut out the rest of the world and focus on what was in front of me. Aletta, too, needed me, only in ways she couldn't express.

I knew I had to devote myself to this dear child. For those precious minutes, it was me and her without any other worry. And for the first time, maybe I felt something. Not love, not yet, but warmth. I held Aletta close and whispered over and over, "Everything will be all right."

However, when she finished nursing and I returned her to her cradle, that feeling began to disappear. I looked outside, hoping to see the heron or the workers, but everyone had left. There was only the mist to look at, the heavy mist that cloaked everything, sucking the color from the street.

NINETEEN

Liesbeth de Wit
May 6, 1943
Amsterdam, the Netherlands

The phone call came while Liesbeth and Maurits were away visiting Maurits's brother. When they returned, a message was waiting at the pharmacy. The baby had arrived, a little girl. The message said nothing else, no news of how the birth had gone, how mother and daughter were recovering, just the single line scribbled down by Maurits's assistant. Liesbeth read the note twice over and clutched it to her chest, disappointed she hadn't been there to help her sister through the labor; she'd always pictured herself there holding her sister's hand, helping her through the pain. She felt a niggle of resentment toward whatever midwife had taken her spot at Jo's side.

Liesbeth prepared for a visit, filling a basket with ointments and containers of soup. At the market, she bought some flowers, but the few bouquets they had were rangy and sorry looking, so on the way to Johanna's, she passed by the park to fill out the bouquet with wildflowers. And of course, some nettles for a nourishing tea.

For the first time in her life, Liesbeth felt nervous to see her sister. It had been weeks, and the last time they'd lunched together, the air between them had felt woolen, dense with unspoken thoughts. During the whole pregnancy, she'd felt more like an acquaintance than a sister. As she stood on the steps beneath Johanna and Willem's apartment, she recalled the first time she'd placed her hand on her sister's belly and felt the baby kicking, how it had also saddened her, made her feel further from Jo than ever.

Liesbeth rang the doorbell, shuffling from foot to foot while she waited. Johanna poked her head out of the window and waved before tossing down the key. Liesbeth climbed the stairs and found her sister at the landing, plump and rosy faced but with dark shadows ringing her eyes.

"Lies," Johanna said, sounding weary and relieved.

Liesbeth held back for a second before swooping in to hug her sister. Then she noticed the cradle in the sitting room behind them. Before she could open her mouth to ask, Johanna nodded. Liesbeth set down her basket and the flowers and approached the cradle. At the sight of the infant swaddled in a pale pink blanket, soft lashes brushing her cheeks, Liesbeth began to tear up. Her niece.

"She's absolutely precious," Liesbeth said. "What's her name?"

"Aletta."

"Aletta," she repeated. "My goodness, Jo, I can't believe she's really here. You're a mother!" The baby stirred. "May I?" Liesbeth asked. She lifted Aletta from the cradle, admiring her and looking for signs of Johanna's lips, her chin. Try as she might, Liesbeth couldn't spot the resemblance. "She must have more of Willem in her," she remarked.

"Wim thinks she has the same ears as his grandfather. Although that may be cause for worry. He calls her his little orangutan." Johanna smiled when Aletta nestled deeper into Liesbeth's arms. "Meet your *tante* Lies, dear one."

Liesbeth grinned. "Oh, I can hardly keep it together. She's the sweetest thing." She paused. "She's already quite big, isn't she? You wouldn't guess she's only a couple of weeks old."

Johanna shifted her gaze to something across the room. "And an early bird at that. With Wim as a father, I can only imagine what giving birth would've been like if she'd made it to full term."

Liesbeth asked to hear all about the birth, everything she'd missed. The story came out in scraps, focusing on Willem and how calm he was, how well his veterinary work had prepared him for this. A midwife was coming by to measure the baby and help with the breastfeeding. And Jo still had to get used to all the different cries that came out of Aletta, what each of them meant. Liesbeth listened, offering insight where she could, watching her sister gush one minute and retreat into her head the next.

"This greedy girl needs her lunch," Johanna said. "Lucky thing doesn't have to worry about rations and shortages. If only she'd learn to appreciate it."

She pulled down the sleeve of her dress and began nursing the baby. The intimacy of the moment struck Liesbeth, and she felt like an intruder sitting and gawking. This was what she'd always dreamed of, but instead of her, it was her sister with a child pressed to her breast. She got up and took the nettles from the basket to brew some tea, and when she turned her head, Johanna was teary eyed. Liesbeth watched, unsure when she'd last seen her sister so emotional. Sadness clouded her face.

Liesbeth sat down beside her. "It'll come, you know. Soon all of this will feel more natural. Every mother struggles in the beginning." She paused. "What can I do to help?"

"I'm exhausted. My body is begging me to rest, but being cooped up at home makes me feel so useless."

"Saving the world can wait, Jo. You've got your own little world right here now."

"You're right," Johanna said, appearing unconvinced.

There it was again, that strange detachment. This wasn't like Johanna. Liesbeth placed a cup of tea beside each of their chairs and moved to draw the drapes, adjusting them to keep the light from blinding Johanna while she burped Aletta.

"I know you won't ask for help," Liesbeth said, "but I'm here to do whatever I can. You'd be doing me a favor, letting me play auntie as much as possible."

"You're a dear."

"Let's start with you taking a nap. Judging by those heavy bags you're sporting, it's well overdue." On Liesbeth's insistence, Johanna handed her the baby and retired to the bedroom. Liesbeth sat in the armchair, rocking Aletta to sleep. While she hummed a lullaby, the baby's eyelids drooped. She had the most peculiar feeling that something was off, that her sister was keeping something from her, but she pinned it down to the distance that had emerged between them.

When Aletta drifted off, Liesbeth held her a little longer before returning her to the cradle. She tried to imagine the baby was hers, tried to picture Maurits standing over her, the three of them together as a little family. The image wouldn't form in her mind. Liesbeth reached for her purse and rummaged around until she found the little orange-and-blue tube. She opened it, and let a tablet of Pervitin slide into her open palm. One tablet would keep her awake for as long as Johanna wanted to sleep.

A month later, Liesbeth was back in her haven—gathered around the long table in the family garden in Zierikzee. It had taken some time before Johanna and the baby were strong enough to travel, plus the two sisters had to wait for a special permit to visit their family in Zeeland.

The trees in the garden had taken leaf, and the magnolia tree was shedding the last of its pink blossoms, which covered the grass like ballet slippers. Beside the vegetable patch, a group of new plants was shooting up, *oom* Cor's experiment to withstand the ongoing tobacco shortages.

Liesbeth sat next to Gerrit at the end of the table, grateful for the time with her family, away from her husband and the bustling city. Bram, the sheepdog, chased butterflies across the lawn, while Aletta napped in a wicker basket, the same basket all the siblings had slept in while they took their first breaths of fresh, country air.

Every time *oom* Cor had an excuse to get up from the table, he came by to coo over the basket. "Takes after Willem, doesn't she?"

"She's changing by the day," Johanna replied. "It's a wonder how quickly they grow." Liesbeth tried to catch her sister's attention with a smile, but Johanna seemed distracted, fixated on something in the garden.

Tante Rika brought out lunch: eel, leek soup, and bread made partly with mashed potatoes, to save on flour. Here in Zeeland they had access to the daily catch of the fishermen and home-grown vegetables. Still, *tante* Rika remained careful and pragmatic, and the portions she served shrank with every visit.

Together, they ate and laughed and tried to focus on the excitement of the new arrival to the family, but even Liesbeth could no longer ignore the war, which hovered over the table like smog. Gerrit tried to take the edge off with a joke he'd heard on the radio about the difference between a baby and a pig. Once he'd delivered the punchline, Johanna turned to their aunt and uncle. "You've turned in your radio, haven't you?" The Nazis had demanded everyone in Amsterdam give theirs up. Anything to keep people from hearing the truth about the war.

"Naturally, haven't you?" *tante* Rika said.

"Radio, what radio?" Johanna gave an innocent smile before adding, "We handed in an old broken one."

"Johanna, be careful…"

"Lies and Maurits got to keep theirs. I'm sure you can guess why."

Liesbeth bristled, trying to ignore her sister's attempts to provoke her. "A friend of Jo's makes crystal radios so tiny you can hide them in a book. Maybe they could arrange one for the two of you."

Oom Cor leaned back and lit up his pipe. "It's not worth the risk. Besides, we have bigger things to worry about."

Liesbeth looked to Gerrit. The Nazis had started calling up young men for forced labor in Germany, but she didn't know what that meant in practice. Gerrit pulled a goofy face, but there was no use trying to hide what was really in his expression.

"Gerrit?" she asked.

He shook his head. "I thought we agreed we weren't going to bring this up over lunch."

"No sense beating around the bush," *oom* Cor said.

"Please tell me this isn't what I think it is," Liesbeth said.

Gerrit pulled a rumpled letter from his trouser pocket. A call-up notice. "I've got four days to turn myself in."

Liesbeth stared at him. "What? That can't be right."

"Have you applied for an exemption?" Johanna asked.

"Give me a few years to polish my veterinary skills." He scoffed. "Or kowtow to Mussert. I hear they're getting desperate for new recruits, isn't that right, Lies?"

"Gerrit," *tante* Rika chided, "watch your tongue."

Liesbeth blushed. "He's right. There's nothing fair about this."

They all fell quiet while Gerrit read the notice aloud. *Oom* Cor and Johanna started discussing the options, the practicalities of the situation. Anyone who failed to report for duty would face punishment. Was there any way out? Liesbeth listened and tried to contribute, but she felt light-headed trying to process it all. Gerrit marching off to some factory in Germany was like dropping a fish into a shark tank. Would she get her brother back?

While their voices rose in debate, Liesbeth noticed a neighbor strolling down the lane. She raised a hand to shush her brother. "We ought to finish this conversation later, indoors."

Tante Rika nodded and waved at the neighbor with a plastered smile.

"You can never be too careful these days," Johanna said.

★ ★ ★

That evening, Liesbeth and Gerrit went for a stroll. They wandered past the grassy mound of the dike, which kept the sea at bay, along the row of bulbous pollard willows, and into the old town along the harbor, past the turreted city gate with its white drawbridge. They walked by their old primary school, where their father had been headmaster. Their parents had lived in the little white house attached to the school until their deaths, when the children were sent to live with *oom* Cor and *tante* Rika.

Gerrit pointed to the white house and told her that soldiers were billeted there. The notion of German soldiers smoking cigarettes in the very bedroom in which she'd been born, washing themselves in the same sink, struck her as absurd. She craned her neck but saw no one. They carried on walking until they reached the gnarled climbing tree from their childhood.

"Come on, slowpoke!" Gerrit said, as he swung himself up into the tree, scrambling upward with the ease of a chimpanzee.

"Oh no, you don't! I'm not sixteen anymore."

"Well, you are a bit pudgier, but I'd bet you're still as nimble." He chuckled, extending an arm to help her up. She started slipping and kicked off her shoes to get a better foothold. Gerrit climbed higher, leaving room for her on one of the strong, lower branches.

"Do you still come here as much as you used to?" she asked as she settled in.

He gestured to the pair of forgotten beer bottles in the hollow of the tree trunk. "When I need to think."

"Sometimes, when Maurits and I are fighting, I try to imagine I'm here, away from it all." She paused, swinging her dangling legs back and forth. "The croak of the frogs at dusk, the way the fields move in the wind." She didn't tell him what else she'd started imagining—that she was seated at a table with Dirk, deep in conversation, confiding in him about her loneliness.

Gerrit didn't reply right away. He stared up at the canopy,

which was still bright green with the promise of new growth. "I heard one of them crying."

"Who?"

"A soldier in the schoolhouse. On warm evenings they leave the windows open and I can hear some of them."

"Crying? Whatever for?"

Gerrit tossed a twig down into the grass. "He was homesick."

Liesbeth sat back and considered this. They were so young, most no older than Gerrit. Boys and young men, torn from their mothers and sweethearts, alone in a strange place where everyone hated them.

She looked at her brother, the innocence in his face. "With lungs like yours, do you think you could handle factory work? All that smoke and dust?"

Gerrit grunted. "I work hard around here."

"You don't have to prove yourself."

"So it's either build bombs for the *moffen* or burrow away like a mole?" he said dryly. "They'll award me a badge of courage any day now."

"Sometimes inaction is the loudest form of protest."

"Like you know from experience?"

Liesbeth frowned. "No need to get snappy."

"I'm sorry. The truth is I'm scared, scared of the prospect of living in fear, of panicking at the sound of every approaching automobile. But the factories or mines are no life, either."

"You'll be careful, won't you? No risky moves?"

He raised a hand like a pastor and crossed his heart. "I solemnly swear to stay out of sight, in the dark, until I die of boredom."

"I mean it, Ger." She looked out at the water again. "I don't want to lose you, too." Her hand closed around the tube of Pervitin in her dress pocket.

"What's that?" Gerrit asked.

She looked down, almost surprised to see the tablet in her

open palm. Taking one whenever her mood clouded had become so automatic. "Maurits gave me these to help my nerves."

"So he's drugging you now?"

She smiled. "Anything to keep the peace."

Gerrit hopped up to a higher branch. He leaned against the trunk and looked back at her. "You used to be so driven, Lies. You and Jo both, but—"

"Paris isn't going anywhere," she said, "and I hope you aren't, either."

"Remember that time you spent the whole night cutting out dress patterns for the island-wide competition?"

She nodded. "I still have them in that folder you gave me."

Gerrit sighed. He swung himself down and landed on the ground with a thump. "It's not the prints that have gone missing, sis. It's you."

TWENTY

Johanna Vos
June 7, 1943
Zierikzee, the Netherlands

I lay in the bed Liesbeth and I had shared growing up, with
Aletta tucked into the crook of my arm. The gap between the
curtains and the windowsill glowed orange with the promise
of the sunrise. In the other bed, Liesbeth was asleep, curled up
and clutching her pillow, the same way she'd slept for as long
as I could remember.

I flicked on the lamp and lowered my nightgown to nurse
Aletta. She suckled easily, and together, we settled into the
calmness of the morning. The sky outside brightened, sending
light creeping into the bedroom. I looked around. On the shelf
in the corner was the abacus that Pa had used to teach me my
sums, before the accident. On the bed, the quilt that *tante* Rika
had made, with crocuses—Ma's favorite flowers—trimming the
border. The books Gerrit and Lies had given me for my seven-
teenth birthday: *The Three Musketeers*, *Jane Eyre*, and *Frankenstein*.
For years, the three of us had shared this bedroom, so curious

about the world beyond Zierikzee. And now that world felt too real, impossible to escape.

Aletta wriggled, slipping off my breast and letting out a garbled noise. I soothed her, tilting her until she latched on. Lies hadn't stirred. She lay there, in a peaceful sleep, her face angled toward me. As a child, she had slept facing me, our foreheads so close they almost touched.

Now it was Aletta nestled up to me, her skin against mine. I bent over her, watching the subtle twitches in her cheeks as she fed, the way her fingers folded and clenched into a fist. There was such innocence to her movements, to everything about her, and I felt an urgent need to protect her, to shelter her from our grim reality.

After some time, Aletta pulled away, letting me know she was done. I rested her on my shoulder. After several weeks, I had fallen into the rhythm of this routine, gotten used to the feel of her, attuned to her needs. When I finished burping her, I laid her on the mattress. She peered up at me with those blue eyes of hers, eyes that would probably darken and change into a color that wasn't mine or Wim's. I held her close, amazed by the changes I already saw in her.

Then, she smiled. A soft upturn of the lips, but it grew into something more, a proper smile. A jolt of warmth went through me. I smiled back, trying to capture the moment in my mind, registering everything about that precious smile. I looked up at the window, wondering what my daughter's smile would look like, the baby I'd lost. What changes would I have seen in her? The green of Willem's eyes? Hands growing long, slender fingers like my own?

These questions would follow me around for the rest of my life. But I tried to push them aside while I bent over to admire Aletta. I began to imagine her first words, her first steps—so many changes that her birth parents never got the chance to witness. She was here in front of me, ours to love. I knew I had to relish every little smile.

TWENTY-ONE

Liesbeth de Wit
June 9, 1943
Zierikzee, the Netherlands

The wind blew hard, tugging strands of hair from Liesbeth's barrette as she and Johanna walked along the beach early in the morning. Bram trotted along behind them, kicking up sand with his paws. Liesbeth faced the wind and inhaled the salty sea air while gulls cawed overhead. The Germans had blocked off most of the coastline while bunkers and dragon's teeth—concrete, pyramid-shaped obstacles—began to replace the cottages and fishing shacks she'd known since childhood. If you knew where to go, you could still find short, secluded strips to walk along.

Liesbeth spread a checkered picnic blanket out across the grassy bank of a sand dune, and they sat and ate the sandwiches she'd packed for breakfast. It was the first time in months that she had a chance to talk to her sister alone, without the distraction of family or a crying baby. Yet so many topics felt off limits, and she found herself turning to rub Bram's belly when the conversation ran dry.

Johanna stood up and scanned the coastline. "I'm going to

take a quick dip while no one is around." She stripped down to her undergarments and ran toward the waves. "Come join me!" she yelled.

Liesbeth stayed put. Not only would she be horrified to be caught in public half-naked, but also she didn't have the confidence to swim in such a current. The wind was kicking up sea foam across the waves, and she'd heard stories of fishermen overwhelmed by huge waves in their rowboats. After a minute or two, she called out, "It's getting rough. Come in closer, won't you?"

Of course, Johanna ignored her. She swam farther out, past the protection of the rocky outcrop. Liesbeth watched, concerned, as Jo dived under the surface, reappearing seconds later when a wave pushed her back toward the shore.

When Johanna returned, Liesbeth decided to speak her mind. "You're a mother now, you know."

"I can watch out for myself," her sister replied, while she dried herself off with the hem of the picnic blanket.

"You had me nervous."

Johanna let out an exasperated noise. "You don't have an adventurous bone in your body, do you?"

Liesbeth recalled what Gerrit had told her, that she'd lost herself. Coming from him, the words had stung.

Johanna continued getting dressed. "You're like Wim, worrying nonstop. You wouldn't get it. I need a moment to myself. It wears on you, being on call every waking minute, a child sapping every ounce of your energy."

Bram tried to snuggle up between Liesbeth's legs, but she brushed him off and stood to face her sister. "I can't believe you. Look at you—you have everything I've ever dreamed of. Don't you know what I'd give to be in your shoes?"

"Don't try to say I'm not grateful—I am. I just don't feel like myself lately."

"Understandably. Having a baby is a huge step, but it's not going to completely change who you are."

Johanna gave her an acid look. "If a baby doesn't change you, a marriage might."

"What are you trying to say?"

"Carefully consider the type of advice you give out."

"All I'm saying is you don't have to shoulder everything on your own. Please let me in."

Johanna spread out the picnic blanket again and lay down on the dry half. Liesbeth watched her, torn between her frustration and her reluctance to get into another fight. Things had been tense for so long.

"I need a minute," Liesbeth said. She walked off down the beach, Bram running along ahead of her. They followed the curve of the coastline, where it dipped into a shallow cove. Clouds had started to roll in, bringing the threat of rain on the horizon. She stewed in her anger. Johanna was in a slump, but Liesbeth couldn't ignore the feeling that something else was wrong. Aletta was growing so quickly, already a roly-poly baby and responding to her mother's voice. Yet Johanna acted so detached.

Bram bounded over with a long stick. She threw it for him, and then circled back to Gerrit's remark. He had a point; she was starting to feel like a shadow of her former self. In her attempts to appease her husband, to fit into his world, the two of them had grown so close she could barely peel apart her thoughts from his, his plans from hers. They had become fused. Maybe that was what kept bringing her mind back to Dirk. He represented something different, so fresh and free, someone who took an interest in her without trying to hold her down.

She called for Bram to bring over his stick. He was approaching the edge of a tide pool, where the sand had a mirrorlike gloss. "Bram, *kom eens!*" He ignored her command as he ran up to sniff something: a grayish lump, with something white that kept catching the breeze. Probably flotsam from a fishing boat. No, she thought as she approached, something larger than that. A beached seal, perhaps.

"Bram, leave it!"

After a few more steps, she stopped. She had been wrong. The gray-blue color was not from the hide of a seal, but from a uniform.

TWENTY-TWO

Johanna Vos
June 9, 1943
Zierikzee, the Netherlands

"Johanna!"

I glanced up from my book. Liesbeth was nowhere in sight, but I swore I'd heard my name over the gust of wind. The pages of the novel drew me back, but there it was again, an urgency to her shouting. With a sigh, I rose, packed up the picnic basket, and headed in the direction she'd sulked off to.

When I rounded the bend, Liesbeth waved her arms and Bram came running toward me, with that same look he got whenever he'd been out tormenting the sheep down the road from our aunt and uncle's house. Then I saw it—the bulk visible on a protected strip of shoreline. All the serenity from the morning swim drained away as my skin began to prickle. "Is he alive?" I called out.

"Doesn't look it!"

The body was facedown in the muddy shallows of the tide pool. My first instinct was to turn and run before the Germans caught us. But I couldn't see anyone up or down the coast.

Bram scampered around, prodding the man with his nose. The man wasn't conscious; that much was evident. I recognized the uniform: RAF, the British Royal Air Force. He wore a leather bomber jacket and wool-lined flight boots. The webbing of his parachute harness had gotten tangled in his life vest, and a section of parachute billowed out, soaking wet and trailing seaweed.

Liesbeth stood several meters away, her face twisted in fear. "Bram," she said in an insistent whisper. "Come now!" The dog sniffed the pilot's arm.

I scanned the beach. Someone must have heard the crash, but where was the plane and where were the Germans? After a moment's doubt, I set down the picnic basket and approached the pilot, moving in to kneel beside him. Maybe he still had a pulse.

"Careful," Liesbeth said.

When I saw the pilot's face, I jerked back. His goggles were askew, one lens shattered. Blood had coagulated at his temple—from shrapnel, perhaps?—and his skin was bruised and swollen. He was dead all right, and must have been before he hit the water. For his sake, I hoped so.

"I'm surprised a patrol hasn't found him," I said.

"He must've drifted in with the tide. Let's get out of here. The Germans will be searching for the wreckage."

The last two nights, bomber planes had broken into my dreams with their drone, a noise so cold that it was easy to forget the young men buckled into those planes. Bram was still sniffing around. I shooed him away and gave the body a push to roll the pilot onto his side. "We need to take his tags."

"Are you mad?"

"Who knows what will happen to his body once the Germans find him, but I bet they won't be sitting down to write their condolences to his family. If we take the tags, we can get word to the RAF of his death."

I stared at the body, anticipating the German patrol that would throw the pilot into the back of a truck and dump him in some unmarked grave. This reminded me once more of my daughter, the baby from my womb, and the stranger who had dug a grave for her some short weeks ago. I felt suddenly very cold and weary.

"Let's check his pockets," I said. "Maybe there's a letter or something, family we can contact." I swallowed, taking another look at the man's swollen limbs. Then, I grabbed the knife from the picnic basket and cut the straps of the harness to access his breast pocket underneath his jumpsuit. I withdrew a metal cigarette case and passed it to Lies while I fiddled to remove the man's dog tags. The sight of the cigarette case made me think of Maurits, and I felt a flush of resentment toward Liesbeth and my brother-in-law. This poor pilot had died fighting for our freedom, while Maurits was all too happy to fraternize with the enemy.

Liesbeth leaned down beside the pilot's torso and fingered the folds of the parachute, the edge of white silk torn and grainy with sand. The rest was still tucked inside, the package that had failed to save his life. "Such beautiful silk." She opened her mouth to say more but somewhere in the distance, a truck engine rumbled.

"We should go," I said.

"Wait." She tore off the soiled, exposed bit of the parachute and cut the bundle that hadn't deployed free of the harness. I didn't have time to ask questions, but when she wasn't looking, I slipped the pilot's revolver into the picnic basket, just in case. The sound of the vehicle disappeared and then reappeared, but it seemed to be going the other way.

"Come on," she said, casting one final glance at the pilot over her shoulder while we hurried back toward our bicycles. She dumped the waterlogged parachute bundle into the saddlebags of her bicycle. Then we cycled off into the cover of the trees.

"Why the parachute?" I asked, surprised she would want to

take it, to do anything that might get her into trouble. At least the revolver could save our lives.

"The fabric. I want to give the silk a new life."

"What?"

"I'll make a christening gown for Aletta."

I stifled a laugh. Of course she expected little Aletta to be baptized. For a split second, I considered letting her in on the secret. Then I thought back to the pilot's cigarette case, to Maurits, to the gap that had grown between us sisters. No, some things were better left unsaid.

The discovery of the British pilot had disturbed me more than I was willing to admit. Something about the sight of him, the mottled blue of his skin beneath the goggles, that briny smell of seawater that was giving way to rot. I'd looked at him and seen what I myself had lost, that missing shard of my heart.

The image of him lingered. I kept opening the cigarette case, which bore a monogram, the initials G.J. It contained a photograph, presumably of a woman, but this was too water stained to make it out. When I wrote a letter for Piet in the Resistance to pass on to his contacts in the RAF, I imagined the pilot preparing to fly out, getting into his jumpsuit, joking with his friends about the navigator's proclivity for awful hangovers. I imagined him pulling out the cigarette case to admire the photograph of his sweetheart and thinking of their baby at home whom he'd yet to meet.

For days, I worried the doorbell would ring, that the Nazis would show up and demand to know what we'd been doing at the beach, whether we had information to share. But when the bell did ring, the visitor was a welcome one. My Wim.

He had journeyed down from Amsterdam for Aletta's christening, which would take place that Sunday. I had hemmed and hawed about the baptism, but Willem claimed it would be safer for her to be seen as a Christian from the start. I couldn't argue with that. Besides, nothing would make my aunt and uncle happier than seeing us all gathered as a family at the baptismal altar, with Aletta wearing the angelic christening gown Liesbeth had sewn with the parachute silk.

After the baptism, Gerrit was to go into hiding on a nearby farm. We all knew he dreaded this and wanted to make the most of his last few days with the family. The morning after Willem arrived, *tante* Rika shooed us out of the house so she could prepare the food for Sunday. She handed us two buckets and a hammer and sent us down to the cove. Mussel season had begun.

The day was promising, a clear sky with wispy clouds high above the horizon. The moon's pull had pared back the sea, exposing a beach dotted with sea life: barnacles and rock pools and half-crushed clamshells. Willem parked the baby carriage next to a bench and lifted Aletta to his chest, arranging the blanket to shade her face while we started down the beach.

"Over here," Liesbeth called. She approached a clump of rocks where mussels clung to the sides like butterflies at rest.

Gerrit pushed past her. "Make room for the expert." With a flat-edged knife, he jimmied the mussels loose. They broke off the rock with a satisfying crack, and he scooped them into the bucket.

Liesbeth made the same prying maneuver, but the mussel shattered under her clumsy attempt. I took the tool. "Allow me." I pulled at the biggest ones, and the mussels gave way, printing a salty film on my fingers when I transferred them to the bucket.

"Atta girl," Willem said. He gave me a teasing kiss. "Exactly what I signed up for."

"Enough, enough," Gerrit said, with mock revulsion. "Let's try up ahead."

He started walking, but Aletta chose that moment to kick up a fuss. She wriggled in Willem's grasp. "What's wrong, little orangutan?" he asked. He tried to soothe her, but she began to wail. "Is she hungry?" he asked, holding her out to me like I could magically fix things.

I stared at Aletta, her sour pucker. That familiar wave of exhaustion washed over me. "I fed her before we left."

Liesbeth took one look at us and stepped in to take Aletta. "I'll watch her. I don't much like mussels anyway."

Willem asked Liesbeth twice if she was sure, but Aletta settled in against her shoulder. I looked away, unsure whether to feel relieved or guilty. Liesbeth smiled and told us to go on while she sat with Aletta on a bench.

Gerrit was far ahead, but Willem and I took our time catching up to him, sensing the effects of each other's absence, how good it felt to be together. He pulled me close. "I've missed you."

I realized then how much I'd also missed him those weeks, his lighthearted quips and levelheadedness the antidote to my exhaustion and restlessness. At times, when Aletta had cooed or reached out a sleepy fist, I had wished he were there to see it. As I looked at him, the shadow of stubble on his chin, his knowing smile, something inside me stirred. How I loved him. He had always been there for me and was now there for Aletta. More than I ever could be myself.

"Are you ready for tomorrow?" I asked.

"You mean presenting our daughter to the one true Lord?"

"We can still change our minds—storm out of the church, spilling the holy water as we flee."

Willem laughed. "It's the right thing to do, but don't think we won't teach her about her own heritage."

I tried to picture us bringing her to a synagogue in the future, trying to explain it all, to honor her birth family and the life she'd lost. Already, the thought filled me with an uneasy dread. Was I prepared for all of this? I bent down to pry loose some mussels. My boots squelched in the mud while I hunted for more.

Willem didn't join in. He grew quiet and looked back down

the beach toward the bench where Lies sat with Aletta. What-ever he was planning to tell me, I didn't want to hear.

"Have you told her the truth?" he asked.

I shook my head.

"She's so good with her, isn't she? Such a pity. What a mother she'd make."

"A real natural." I couldn't hide my bitterness. The last thing I needed was another reminder of the kind of mother Liesbeth would be. The kind of mother I wasn't.

"Maybe you should tell her. If something were to happen to us—"

"What? And let Maurits find out that his new niece is a fu-gitive?"

"Johanna. Don't you see you're being a little unfair? They're both still family."

"What's unfair is that she doesn't recognize her husband for the dog that he is. There's a clear line, and she's crossed it."

"This is war—everything is blurry. To call things black-and-white is as dishonest as a Nazi blessing the seder."

"We can't trust her. I'd love to, believe me, but we all know Maurits is God to her. As long as she worships him, we don't tell her."

He kicked at a rock buried in the sand. Up ahead, Gerrit beckoned us to join him, pointing to the treasure trove of blue-silver mussels he'd found. Willem waved back but didn't move.

He looked me in the eyes. "I need to tell you something. Marijke de Graaf and her husband are dead. Or as good as dead. Missing, hauled away at night."

I set the bucket down, my stomach turning. The woman who had brought us Aletta arrested—whatever for? What had hap-pened? How much did they know? I sat down on a rock, ignor-ing the mud that splattered on my dress, ignoring the sharp edge of the barnacles digging into my thighs. "When?"

"Nobody's seen them since the first weekend in May."

"When we took in Aletta."

"Indeed, the timing is troubling."

"How much do you think the Gestapo know?"

"No idea. Theo was making foxhole radios for two different Resistance cells, so he had a big network."

I could see it before me: the Gestapo swooping into the De Graaf house in the cover of darkness, bright lights blinding the couple as they filed into the back of a truck. Had we saved Aletta just in time? Or was it her the Gestapo had been searching for?

Gerrit called our names again.

"One minute!" Willem shouted before turning back to place a hand on my shoulder. "There's no use trying to decipher what happened, but the message is clear." *Lie low*, he meant. Keep your head down, for the baby's sake. Anger coursed through me, anger at the thought that two good people had been arrested, anger at the idea that Aletta's mother, her real mother, would never again wrap her arms around her child, anger at our hundreds of neighbors whose lives were in danger, all thanks to the deluded ideas of some German tyrant with a stuffy mustache.

"Yes," I said. "I'll take it to heart."

"Thank you. I don't mean to frighten you, but we must think of Aletta now."

"Of course," I said. But if I knew one thing, it was that Aletta would grow up wanting to know that we'd done everything in our power to stand up for her people, her true family—a family I knew almost nothing about, aside from the names Marijke had scrawled on a notecard she'd tucked in Aletta's baby carriage. Why hadn't I asked the De Graafs more about Aletta's parents while I'd had the chance?

"You two are no fun," Gerrit said, as he walked back toward us, waving a full bucket above his head like a trophy.

"Sorry." I leaned down, fished some seaweed from the shallows and draped it over the bucket to keep the mussels fresh. "I guess we city slickers can't keep up."

"Speak for yourself," Willem said. He held out the empty bucket suggestively. "How much are you willing to wager on that?"

Gerrit grinned. "Tonight's dessert?"

"You're on."

I rolled my eyes and left the two of them to their game. I knew I ought to go keep Lies company. But as I turned to head back, Willem caught my gaze, and I knew what he meant to say. *We're safe for now. Let's keep it that way.*

TWENTY-THREE

Liesbeth de Wit
July 14, 1943
Amsterdam, the Netherlands

The tide of the war was turning and, with it, Maurits's mood. Liesbeth had begun to follow the news more closely, if only to be able to predict when he would come home brooding. First the developments in North Africa and then the Allied landings in Sicily. Whatever brightened her spirits darkened his. She was beginning to wonder if her husband still loved his country at all.

One evening in July, Maurits came home after work and hung his hat on its hook without saying a word. Liesbeth rose to greet him, giving him a peck on the cheek when he didn't meet her kiss. His face was hard and lined.

"Rough day?" She eased him down into his armchair and began to massage his shoulders.

He shrugged her away. "Put on the radio, won't you?"

Liesbeth turned it on and adjusted the volume, but the German broadcaster spoke too quickly for her to follow. "What is he saying?" she asked.

Maurits shushed her. "I can't understand if you're going to talk through it all."

Liesbeth bit her lip. When was the last time he'd behaved warmly toward her, showered her with compliments? Her heart ached trying to keep up this act all the time, playing the patient, understanding housewife.

Across the table, Maurits's briefcase sat open, a telltale blue-and-orange tube poking out from the side pocket. Liesbeth went over and opened the tube, popping a tablet into her mouth. She relaxed a bit, anticipating the relief that would come, that giddy weightlessness that washed everything else away: the fatigue, the resentment, the coldness.

Maurits watched her swallow the pill. "Are those helping? Maybe we should increase your dosage."

Liesbeth considered this. How tempting it was to suppress it all, to remain suspended on that bed of clouds. Tempting, but also a little frightening. She thought of the headaches the pills brought forth, those palpitations that had her believing her heart was jackhammering out of her chest. "They're working just fine," she said.

He turned his attention back to the radio, so she began to prepare dinner. Rations had been decreased again, and she had to get more creative with whatever lousy vegetables she could get her hands on. Maurits was never pleased at the sight of his plate, but she couldn't blame him. Tasteless pap and dense, flourless bread: a diet for baby Aletta, not a grown man.

From the kitchen, she heard Maurits swear. *"Godverdomme!"* She stayed put. No need to enter the lion's den uninvited. However, his cursing continued and then came a loud smack. She hoped it wasn't their radio—or the sewing machine, for that matter.

Maurits entered the kitchen, shaking his head and muttering. "How long until dinner?"

Liesbeth took the bottle of *jenever* down from the cupboard and poured her husband a drink. Maurits had received the bottle from Dirk, who had his own steady supply in the same way her husband never seemed to run out of cigarettes. At the thought of Dirk, she felt a spark of excitement. She passed Maurits the glass, hoping his expression would soften. It didn't. "Twenty minutes until dinner," she said. "Why don't you sit and read until then?"

Maurits slugged back the *jenever* in two sips.

"Another?" she asked.

He shook his head. She reached for the bottle, topping up his glass anyway, hoping it would soften his temperament. "An aperitif to stimulate your appetite."

He pushed the glass away with a little snort. "Says the one who pops Pervitin right before dinner."

"The Pervitin you're feeding me!"

"A lot of good it seems to be doing."

The effects of the drug were beginning to surface, the first tinglings, enough to make her bold, but not enough to dissolve her growing irritation. "What's that supposed to mean?"

"Well, for one, I never asked for a wife that questioned everything I do."

Liesbeth's cheeks flared hot. "All I ever do is bite my tongue around you. There's plenty I'd love to say, but you wouldn't accept a word of advice from me."

"With good reason. You have your book of sketches and your silly dreams, but a girl like you doesn't know the ways of the world." He pulled his cigarette case out of his breast pocket and strode out of the kitchen.

Liesbeth stood there smoothing the wrinkles from her apron and trying to calm herself down, until smoke started billowing from the stove. She snatched the pot off the burner and used a wooden spoon to scrape the mashed potatoes from the bottom. Who was he to try to crush her spirit like that, after everything she'd done to support him? She'd stood by his side without complaint, even though it had driven a wedge between her and Jo, even though she'd had to weather cold, suspicious looks from half the neighborhood.

She dropped a wallop of half-burnt potatoes onto a plate. She brought this out to the dining table and placed it at Maurits's spot before fetching her coat.

He glanced up from the newspaper. "Going somewhere?"

She didn't grace him with an answer. With a solid clap of the door, she left the apartment and descended the stairs two by two, not looking back until she was well down the block. No sign of Maurits in the window. She turned a corner and carried on, walking until her shoes started to pinch. At a bridge, she paused to wiggle her sore toes and peer out over the canal. A few boats passed by. An old man leaned out of the last one, a shabby construction of old boards and riffraff. "Smoked eel!" he called. "Get your smoked eel!" No one else paid him any mind.

She picked up a stone and tossed it at the ripples formed by the boat's wake. *Damn Maurits*, she thought. This was not the man she'd married, not the man who had fought for her attention, who had teased her and kissed her wrists and whispered sweet promises in her hair, promises of love and laughing children, of happiness that couldn't be broken. Was this his idea of happiness, speaking to her like she was incapable of doing anything for herself? He never considered her input, brushing off her ideas and dreams the same way Jo did. That familiar loneliness returned to her, the feeling that she didn't belong, that she was someone easy to brush off or ignore. How she longed for a little comfort. She picked up another stone and turned it over in her palm, thinking of Dirk, that little jolt she got whenever he was around. Dirk, with his card tricks and his disheveled charm—an outsider, like her.

Liesbeth glanced down the street. If she continued across the bridge, she would reach De Pijp neighborhood. Dirk lived somewhere nearby, though she wasn't sure where. She had a sudden desire to see him, to find distraction in his card tricks and easy conversation. This was the Pervitin talking, but, oh, he was so much simpler than her husband! An easy man to please, who wouldn't take what he had for granted.

She tossed the stone aside and wandered around as if he might step out of a side street into her path. Her feet started complaining again, coaxing her toward home. However, she wasn't ready to face Maurits, not yet. A name came to her, the bar Dirk frequented, Café Ruysdael. It was on the way back. Liesbeth walked in a couple of circles until she found it, where the Albert Cuypstraat met the Ruysdaelkade. A small brown café, with dark wooden paneling on the walls and a smoky interior. Two art deco lamps hung over the bar. She peered through the windows but didn't recognize anyone.

On an impulse, she went inside and approached the bartender. "Good evening," she said. "I'm looking for a friend, *meneer* Van Duin."

The bartender wiped a tea towel across the inside of a glass. "Old Dirk, you say? He left five or ten minutes ago."

She brightened up. "Which way did he go?"

The bartender gestured farther down the canal. She thanked him and hurried outside. It didn't take her long to find him, standing on a corner, puffing on his pipe in a pin-striped suit while he leaned against a streetlamp. She slowed to a casual pace, hoping he wouldn't realize she'd been searching for him. "Hello."

Dirk glanced up, angling his head to get a good look at her under the brim of his fedora. He removed the pipe from his mouth. "*Mevrouw* De Wit?"

"Liesbeth."

"What are the odds?"

They walked back to Café Ruysdael and sat at a table tucked in the corner, with Dirk facing the window. The bartender winked at her, and she looked down at her lap. Though she preferred *jenever*, the bars rarely served anything hard anymore, so she joined Dirk in ordering a beer. She sipped hers self-consciously, feeling out of place at this late hour and too forward for chasing him down.

Dirk set his drink on the beer mat and gave her a curious smile.

"I suppose you're wondering what I'm doing here," she said.

"Your eyes already tell half the story."

Liesbeth blushed. She was beginning to regret her rash decision. Still, there was that effervescent glow of the Pervitin, egging her on. Its heat settled over her like a halo.

"Does Maurits know where you are?"

"He was worried about something on the news."

"Ah, Kursk."

"Kursk?"

"Hitler has called off the offensive, a blow for Germany."

Liesbeth let a small smile escape. No wonder Maurits was on edge. She wanted to ask Dirk what he thought of it all, if he, too, was bothered by the changing fortunes, but before she could reply, he cocked his head to the side and studied her. "Tell me something, Liesbeth, if you could be anywhere right now, where would it be?"

"If there was no war, you mean?"

He nodded.

"I'd want to be in Zeeland, with my brother and everyone at home, safe and sound." She hesitated when she said this, afraid she was letting on too much. The last thing she wanted was to create problems for Gerrit.

Dirk leaned forward. "Is that right? I think you're playing it safe with that answer. Tell me, where would you be?"

The look in his eyes made her feel at once naked, as if he could peel back her skin and peer into her thoughts. It was a startling feeling, alarming, but oddly comforting.

"I suppose," she began, "what I'd love is to be in Paris, studying fashion. Wandering down the Champs-élysées, sketching passersby in the Jardin du Luxembourg." She locked eyes with him while she traced her index finger along the rim of her glass. "But that's a castle in the sky."

"With or without Maurits?"

"Pardon?"

"You didn't mention him. Would he be there with you?"

Liesbeth blushed. "Oh, of course he would."

Dirk smirked. He gestured to the barman for another round. When the beers came, he took a big swig of his. "I've been to Paris. An old man with too much money to burn paid me a week's earnings to drive him there and shuttle him around all day. Wide, busy boulevards, nothing like here. Dames dolled up in pearls, painted eyebrows. Giant signs with flashing neon lights. People chasing highs over absinthe and Gitanes."

He stopped, and she understood he was waiting for her reaction. "That sounds wonderful."

Dirk laughed. "It stank there that summer, foul and brackish from the river."

She ignored this remark and tried to picture herself there, amid a sea of fabric: lace, taffeta, silk. Being given swaths of mink fur to trim dresses, designing daring cuts and cinched waistlines. No more drab, wartime shades, but vivid colors: an artist's palette at her fingertips. The thought of all the glittering lights and glamour was intoxicating.

She looked down to find a fresh beer in front of her and realized it was probably the alcohol that was making her head spin. Now would be a good time to stop. But Dirk raised his glass in a toast—"to making it all come true"—and she drank more, her mood bolstered with every sip until she stopped worrying about the time, about Maurits, about everything else.

Dirk reached into his jacket pocket and pulled out something narrow. A tube of Pervitin. He opened it and shook a tablet onto the table. "A little nightcap."

Liesbeth was buzzing all over. "May I?"

"I didn't realize Maurits had you on the stuff." He tipped the tube into her hand, his fingers lingering against her skin.

Liesbeth swallowed the pill with the last of her beer. "Enough about Maurits," she said. "Let's go out and enjoy the night air."

While Dirk settled up, Liesbeth shimmied into her coat, trying to steady her balance. The clock on the wall chimed. One hour until curfew, one hour to make the most of Dirk's company. He slid his arm around her waist as they left the bar.

"You okay?" he asked, as she teetered on her heels.

Liesbeth looked up at him, at the long, shadowed curve of his jawline. She admired his lips, wondering what it would be like to kiss him, and she knew she wouldn't be going home until she found out. "Never better." She gave him a smile. "Now, show me the side of Amsterdam I've been missing out on."

She clutched his shoulder while they carried on down the street, breathing in the smell of his jacket, of him, ripe and enticing, the way the leather of brand-new gloves invited you to try them on, to dress your best and pretend you were someone else for a night, someone wild and daring. He led her down a few blocks, making small talk, telling her that he'd just moved house, that he was still trying to find a sense of home amid the piled boxes. She asked polite questions and looked at the rising moon, increasingly aware of the buzz of the Pervitin, the way her legs seemed to wobble beneath her.

"It's getting late," she said.

"I'll walk you home."

"That's probably not a good idea."

"Well then, can you find your way back from here?"

She nodded, but her body was tingling, unwilling to let him go. She locked eyes with him for a second too long, taking in the wrinkles that already creased his face, his stocky build, the cleft in his chin. This was not someone trying to play a part; he was himself, through and through.

He lifted a finger like he meant to stroke her cheek. A set of headlights veered onto the street, turning toward him. He reached for her wrist, tugging her off into the shadows while they ducked into a side street. She listened, trying to judge if it was a German patrol, but before she could tell, he had pushed her up against the brick wall. He held her face and kissed her hard, his tongue parting her lips.

"Dirk," she said, but his name got lost in the moment. She wrapped her arms around his neck, drawing him closer, trying to savor the heat of his breath on her mouth, the desire in his touch. Every part of her felt every bit alive.

Then, the vehicle sputtered past them, pulling her out of the kiss and back to the shadows of the street. "Dirk," she said.

He stepped back and looked at her. "You need to get home."

"Yes."

"I'll see you soon."

"Maybe," she said, but she smiled as she said this and kissed him goodbye, knowing she was already treading in deep water.

TWENTY-FOUR

Johanna Vos
July 15, 1943
Amsterdam, the Netherlands

Two weeks after our return from Zierikzee, Willem opened the newspaper to find another requisition notice. The Germans wanted bicycles. Bicycles to ride, bicycles with rubber tires they could recycle. Simply put, they wanted to make life harder for us and easier for them. First, they had confiscated all the Jews' bicycles, and then the men's bicycles, and now they were broadening their reach.

"Looks like we're stuck this time," Willem said. He and Maurits had both gotten an exemption on account of their medical jobs, but I had no such wall to hide behind.

I dropped my knitting in a heap on my lap, frustrated by both the news and my pathetic attempt at a baby sweater. "The nerve they have. Can't they let us be? Must they pluck every bit of joy from our lives?"

Willem tore the notice from the paper. "Here's the address for the collection point. Tomorrow at noon." The sparkle in his eyes suggested a challenge.

"I refuse to deliver anything into their hands. We can hide it for a few days." It wasn't a foolproof plan, but some of our neighbors had done this before. The soldiers tended to forget about the collection once they'd hit their quota. I tried to bury the memory of the last time I'd tried to dodge the Germans with my bicycle, how that had kick-started the worst experience of my life. I'd never told Willem about my fall. Some things were too shameful to repeat aloud.

Willem laughed. "I pity the soldier who crosses your path, but I think I know a good place."

Three days later, we found ourselves standing beside the drainage ditch that ran behind Jakob and Ida's street. It was dusk, dark enough to obscure our faces, but approaching curfew. When I told Liesbeth that I'd hidden my bicycle, she'd offered to watch Aletta whenever Willem and I went to retrieve it. The offer had surprised me, but I'd accepted immediately. How good it felt to have a couple of hours back amid the buzz and the lights and sounds of the adult world.

I stood guard next to the drainage ditch, but the road was quiet, aside from a mouse that scampered across the cobblestones in search of crumbs. Behind me, Willem and Jakob hunched over the water, fishing with a makeshift rod for two women's bicycles. Ida had stayed home. After months of relying on a forged document to protect Jakob, she was actually in the early weeks of pregnancy.

The water was probably shallow enough to stand in, but the bicycles had settled into the sludge. "Take a look at how murky this is," Willem said, his pole stirring up sediment.

"Land me a pike and I'll give you a kiss to remember," I said.

"No fish that big in these canals," Jakob said.

"You bet there are," Willem replied. "Although by now they've probably all ended up on people's dinner plates." He wriggled the rod until it caught something. "I've hooked a handlebar."

The men made a show of wrestling my bicycle out of the water, which was slick with grime. As Jakob wiped it down, he lowered his voice. "Speaking of all things fishy," he said. "I know you're trying to take a step back from all of this, but I thought you would want an update."

I moved in closer. "Yes, please tell us what you've heard."

"Piet has had three recent reports of families in hiding being rounded up, including the surgeon and his wife from our first concert. All of them in some way involved with the *zwarte avonden*."

"Oh no." I thought of the De Graafs and caught Willem's eye. "But that's a coincidence, right?"

"You've heard the gossip, right?" Jakob said. "Men who are paid a bounty for every Jew they arrest. Apparently some department at the LiRo bank has been set up to 'eliminate the Jewish problem.'"

Willem shook his head in disgust.

"Despicable," I said, "a new low. How can these people call themselves patriots?"

"The weird thing," Jakob went on, "is that everyone at those concerts is trusted. Everybody knows someone. But each time, the house of one of the guests is raided a couple of days after a concert." He stood to help Willem lift Ida's bicycle from the canal.

My mind spun like a pinwheel. It could be an inside job, but who would be passing on information?

A sudden sputtering noise shut us up. A motorcycle, a block away. A patrol. Jakob froze. If they checked everyone's papers, they would see he was half-Jewish, and he could be arrested for being out past curfew. Any black mark on his record could mean deportation. I grabbed him by the wrist and led him across the street and up the set of stairs to the alcove of a darkened entranceway. Willem dropped the remaining bicycle back into the water, but he had no time to move. As the motorcycle veered around the corner, I thought fast, pulling Jakob toward me until our noses touched.

"Pretend," I said, throwing my arms around him in what I hoped looked like a passionate embrace.

He caught on and tilted his hat to cover our faces and we acted like lovers lost in the heat of the moment. Hopefully the patrol would ignore us. I held my breath while the engine slowed to a stop, but I didn't dare look. Jakob's fingers dug deep into the neck of my sweater while the Order Policeman got off the motorcycle and approached Willem.

"What are you doing with that bicycle?" the man asked in German.

"Fishing. Not much of a bite today."

"You have a permit for that bicycle?"

"Yes, sir." A long pause followed. Was Willem presenting his papers, or had the officer noticed us in the shadows? I pulled Jakob closer, my lips grazing his cheeks, trying to look convincing. His pulse beat wildly beneath my fingertips.

"This is a woman's bicycle," the policeman said.

"Someone stole mine, so I've been using my wife's."

"Get another."

"But you saw my permit."

"Men don't ride women's bicycles. Find another one."

A long, excruciating pause followed. Jakob and I stood so still, we almost forgot our act. First came the sound of the bicycle pushed across the path, and then the motorcycle sputtered back to life. I waited, fearing the policeman would choose that moment to look up at us in the stairwell. Jakob sensed this and shoved me back against the wall. He kissed me hard. The absurdity of it all hit me, but all I could focus on was Jakob's papers, that threatening yellow star.

The moment passed and the sound of the engine faded to a

distant putter. Jakob and I pulled apart, unable to meet one another's eyes.

"Quick thinking," he mumbled.

Willem met us at the bottom of the stairs. Seeing our embarrassment, he patted Jakob on the back. "Not much of a kisser, are you? Don't worry, I'm not looking to pick a fight. We both know who's taking her home tonight. And I promise I won't tell Ida, either."

We laughed a little, all of us shaken. What Wim meant was that Ida wouldn't let Jakob outside ever again if she knew he was cutting corners and taking risks. Funny that he was concerned about safeguarding Jakob's freedom to fight back, but not my own.

"Did he see us?" I asked.

"He looked up at you," Willem said. "Maybe that's why he insisted on taking the bicycle—the closest thing he could get to a real woman."

"Sorry about your bicycle," Jakob said to me.

We all knew things could have ended much worse. "At least he didn't get Ida's as well. Now, let's hurry up and get this over with."

The two of them had no trouble reaching the bicycle this time, since the bell protruded from the water like a silver pebble. At the count of three, they heaved it out of the drainage ditch, jumping back to avoid the dirty splash on their clothes. Jakob picked Ida's bicycle up off the grass, wiped it off, and made a move to leave. "You'll be all right?" he asked.

"Go on, get home to your wife," Willem said.

"Wait," I said, "what are you going to do about that bounty hunter?"

Jakob shook his head. "We'll take extra precautions. But you're right, it's probably nothing more than a coincidence."

After he left, Wim took my hand and pressed it to his lips.

"I love you," I said.

"I love you, too, even when you are a philanderer." We chuckled and started on the long walk home. Along the way, I peered at all the darkened houses, wondering what they concealed—frightened families hiding in attics, or traitors opening their purse strings? As we turned onto the final stretch of canal before our house, Willem slung his arm around my shoulder. "Stop worrying, sweetheart, you've done enough."

I didn't reply but stared up at the darkening sky, that first crust of the waxing moon. This helpless feeling was going to eat at me. I had to figure out who was behind the arrests before it was too late.

TWENTY-FIVE

Liesbeth de Wit
July 25, 1943
Amsterdam, the Netherlands

Liesbeth opened the windows of her sister's sitting room to welcome in some fresh air. It was the last Sunday in July, and the afternoon heat had settled into the house's bricks and mortar, making the apartment stuffy and warm. Aletta lay in the cradle beside Liesbeth, oblivious to everything outside: the bells ringing and cyclists weaving past one another, the girls playing hoop games and teasing boys in shorts and knee-high socks. Aletta dozed through it all.

Liesbeth had to admit she was also trying to slip into a dream, to distract herself. When Jo had asked her to watch Aletta for the afternoon, she'd been all too happy to accept. Since the incident with Dirk, she'd jumped at any reason to get out of the house, away from her wifely duties, away from Maurits.

She sat in the armchair and rummaged in her purse for the tube of Pervitin. The truth of what she'd done was gnawing at her. That was what bothered her most, she thought while slipping another tablet into her mouth; it wasn't a feeling of guilt she was left with, but exhilaration.

"What do you make of it," she asked sleepy Aletta. "What's wrong with me that after doing something horrid, all I want is to do it again?"

Liesbeth opened her sketchbook, trying to come up with some ideas for her next article. Women had to make do with whatever fabric scraps they could find, which meant hemlines were shrinking, and skirts couldn't be gathered or pleated as they had been before. But she currently had no interest in designing something from her husband's castoffs, so instead drew beaded evening dresses with long trains.

Aletta stirred and woke, crying for attention. Liesbeth picked her up, tucking her against her chest while she rocked her. "Hush, darling, everything is fine. Your ma will be home soon to feed you."

Aletta grabbed at a loose tendril of her hair. "Ouch!" Liesbeth said playfully. "Oh, Aletta, what am I going to do? I've gotten myself into a real bind."

Aletta gurgled and Liesbeth laughed, but something inside her ached. Everything she wanted was in front of her, that bundle of joy and love. She couldn't help but feel it wasn't fair: Why should Johanna have a child if she was too preoccupied to give Aletta the love she deserved?

The Pervitin was starting to kick in. It bloomed warmth across her chest, tingling as it spread to her fingers. She looked at Aletta. No, she was certain she could still be a mother under the right circumstances. She tried to picture Dirk, bouncing a toddler on his knee. The image appeared so much sharper than it ever had with Maurits.

A few minutes later, Johanna arrived home. "There you are, my little orangutan," she said. She put down her bag and lifted Aletta up with great enthusiasm, but Aletta wasn't ready to be disturbed and began to cry.

"You're a godsend for watching her," Jo said, while she tried to soothe the baby.

Liesbeth smiled halfheartedly. Her sister only doled out this type of praise in thanks. "How was your visit with Jakob?" she asked. "Does he have any good news about his cousins? It breaks my heart to think of those poor little children torn away from their parents."

"No, nothing."

She should have known better than to expect a proper response. Lately, Jo clammed up the moment Liesbeth tried broaching the subject of the war or politics, as if she couldn't be trusted any more than the walking uniforms that patrolled the city. For once, she wanted her sister to see her as she used to, as a friend, a confidante. An equal.

Liesbeth held out Aletta's rattle. "She often quiets down when I sing to her," she said. "You know the lullaby Ma used to sing? She likes that one."

She watched Johanna's expression tighten, knowing very well her sister wouldn't take to the idea that Liesbeth knew how to care for her daughter better than she did.

"She needs to eat, that's all," Johanna said. She sat down and undid the upper half of her dress, one of her best dresses, which Liesbeth had only ever seen her wear on special occasions. At the sight of Jo's swollen breasts, Liesbeth felt a flash of envy. Regardless of whether Jo acted on her responsibilities, she still looked every bit the epitome of motherhood.

"Mama is here," Johanna said, as Aletta stopped fussing and latched on to her breast. "Mama missed you, so, so much." She gazed adoringly at Aletta, but Liesbeth wished her sister had stayed away a little longer, given her a few more minutes to linger in the illusion of motherhood, before she became the aunt again, the babysitter, nothing more.

"What time is it?" Johanna asked. "Could you jot it down for me in the notebook? It's in my bag."

Liesbeth retrieved the notebook and flipped through it, look-ing for the section her sister used to track Aletta's feedings. The most recent page had some scribbled notes, a numbered list of songs. "What is this? A set list?" She eyed Johanna's outfit. "Are you singing again?"

Johanna blushed, which she never did. "Singing? No, this little one eats up all my spare energy—I couldn't imagine try-ing to prepare something."

"But you do have the energy to dress up on a Sunday, and you are awfully dressed up for coffee with Jakob. He and his band have found somewhere to perform, haven't they?"

"Where? One of Jakob's bandmates has already been deported, and you'll have to search hard to find the others."

Liesbeth shook her head. "You're keeping something from me, I can feel it." She flipped back a few more pages. In between the list of feedings were more notes: Chopin, pianist; *Swan Lake*, ballet duo. "What is all this about?"

Johanna adjusted Aletta. "Daydreams, that's all. A list of music that stirs my heart."

"And your outfit? What were you and Jakob doing all after-noon?"

"Having coffee, keeping his pregnant wife company, pretend-ing we were elsewhere."

"I mean it. I won't take care of Aletta anymore if you're dis-honest with me. What have you been up to?"

"It's better you don't know."

Liesbeth studied her sister. Those words could only mean one thing: Johanna was involved in the Resistance. With Jakob, most likely, and probably Willem, though he at least had a good dose of caution. "Does it involve music?" she asked. "A performance? Am I right about that?"

"I'm doing some private concerts, that's all." Johanna gave her a tight smile but said nothing more. Liesbeth sat back. Be-tween the NSB parties, Dirk, and now this, they had never harbored so many secrets. She missed the days back in Zierikzee, when they raced home from school and flopped on the bed and swapped stories about everything that had happened that day. Who would have guessed that politics would have built such defenses between them? And now there was so much more on the line: treachery, broken hearts, her sister's safety.

Liesbeth stood up and prepared to leave. She squeezed Aletta's hand and leaned down to kiss Jo on the cheek. "If you are ever in any trouble," she said, "you let me know, all right? Be safe. Aletta needs you, we all do."

As the summer progressed, the Allies bombed Hamburg, the Italians tried to engage in peace talks, and Maurits lay awake at night, restless. Liesbeth curled up next to him, listening to the rustle of the Pervitin tube at midnight and again two hours later. The tablets boosted his mood, soothed his worries, but they also stole his sleep. A part of her wondered if he knew what she'd done, but he gave no indication, so she assumed he lay there wired, his heart thrumming, while he contemplated his next move.

Still, it surprised her when he asked if she would deliver a package on his behalf. One morning, the package was waiting for her on the kitchen table, wrapped in brown paper and tied in a neat bow with a piece of string.

"My birthday's not until February, you know," she said cheekily.

Maurits pushed it toward her. "Can you be sure Willem gets this? There's a note inside explaining everything."

"What is it?" She picked up the package, taken aback by its weight. Something clinked inside. "I need to know. What if I get stopped by a patrol?"

"They won't stop you. That's why I'm sending you. It's medication. I thought it might be useful."

"For the animals?" she asked, bewildered by his sudden interest in his in-laws. Maurits hadn't reached out to Willem since the early days of the war, and he rarely asked about either of them.

Maurits looked at her like she was daft, but there was also an awkwardness to his expression, embarrassment. "It's for the Resistance."

He had never even acknowledged the Resistance without some spiteful remark about "useless rabble-rousers" or "their foolhardy stunts," but he must have assumed his in-laws were somehow involved. She tucked the package into her bag. "Willem will never accept your help."

"You don't have to tell him it was from me. But I'm certain they need everything they can get ahold of."

She moved to leave, knowing he was right. In the doorway, she paused. "Why are you doing this? Why now?"

"Perhaps I've seen the error of my ways," he said weakly.

Liesbeth gave him a tight-lipped nod before heading down the stairs. She wanted to believe him, oh how she did. She wanted to believe some part of her other half was still loving and good.

TWENTY-SIX

Johanna Vos
August 5, 1943
Amsterdam, the Netherlands

With every passing week, Aletta grew—cooing, gurgling, teething, peek-a-booing, grabbing, rolling over—and I watched, astounded by her emerging personality. But whenever I started dwelling on my real, blood daughter, on Aletta's real parents, it only led me to think about all the arrests. People betraying their neighbors, slipping information to the Gestapo, to the bounty hunters. By my latest count, almost two dozen Jews connected to the *zwarte avonden* had been betrayed. Discouraged and restless, I kept pacing the apartment and contacting Jakob to ask when the next house concert would be, what the Jewish artists needed. Any way I could help.

I was skeptical, to say the least, when Liesbeth showed up with a delivery of medical supplies from Maurits: muslin bandages, iodine, sulpha pills and insulin. I wanted nothing to do with his ploys, his attempts to win favor with both sides while the fate of the war tilted back and forth, like a wayward lever. But medicine was medicine. So, on a warm August day, I jumped at the excuse to be helpful for a change. I packed the insulin into the false bottom of the baby carriage and laid a blanket on top. Then, I bundled up Aletta, placed her in the carriage, and set off.

Jakob and I had been growing concerned about three children in hiding at a house near the Vondelpark. The woman sheltering them, a *mevrouw* Dijkstra, had complained about the eldest boy's medical needs and the extra burden this created, since his food had to be weighed and portioned, and it was getting harder to find foods he could eat. Delivering some insulin for the boy offered the perfect opportunity to check in on the woman.

On my way to the Dijkstra house, I met Ida for a morning stroll. Lush trees shaded our route as we circled around the park. Ida's belly had popped, and her pale skin glowed, but she wasn't her calm, graceful self, seeming instead like a bird on a windowsill, apt to take flight at any moment.

"How is the pregnancy going?" I asked.

"Pregnancy suits me. It's everything else that ails me. The uniforms in the streets, the constant worrying."

"I understand. Wim would have loved it if I never left the house during those nine months, but I couldn't sit back and relax."

"You seek out the action, but trouble seems to find its way to me. All I want is to stay home and shut everything else out." She glanced at Aletta in the baby carriage. "You're up to something today, aren't you?"

When I told her about my plans for the insulin, she stopped and looked at me. "You're going there this afternoon, to the Dijkstras'?"

"Yes, after this."

She shook her head, looking flustered. "You shouldn't go."

"Why not?"

"Taking Aletta with you on such an errand?"

"Nobody would suspect a doting mother out for a stroll."

"It's a bad idea," she said, frowning.

"It's fine."

"What about the medical supplies? Isn't it odd that Maurits gave them to you?"

"He's trying to hedge his bets, playing both sides, that's all." We had rounded the park to the exit I needed to take. "I'm dropping in for tea, as anybody would."

Her concerned look didn't fade. "I wish you wouldn't. Wim is right. You should leave these kinds of errands to the men."

I gave her a kiss on the cheek. "Don't worry about me."

"Go then," she said, "but be quick about it."

I continued with Aletta toward a house that lay beyond the park gates, arriving to find a placard on the door: *Achtung— Scharlach*, a warning that the occupants were battling scarlet fever, a trick to ward off unwanted visitors.

Mevrouw Dijkstra opened up before I knocked. She'd seen me enough at the house concerts to know my face. "Come in, come in," she said. "Sweet of you to drop by."

I peeked around while *mevrouw* Dijkstra cooed over Aletta. Large portrait photographs hung in a gallery on the wall and a cello rested on the stand in the corner. The woman's husband was in the Concertgebouw Orchestra, which was why they'd agreed to take in the three Jewish children, while the children's father took refuge elsewhere. The father was one of the best pianists Amsterdam had ever seen.

Mevrouw Dijkstra beckoned me over to the table, which was laden with a Persian table rug and a silver tea service. We made polite conversation for a few minutes over nettle tea, until she asked to see the insulin. "It's a real nuisance, I tell you. Where are you supposed to find a steady supply of insulin with no questions asked? His father could have been more up front about the boy's condition."

I bit the inside of my cheek to keep myself in check. As far as I knew, the children's father paid the Dijkstras a fat allowance to cover their expenses. The woman probably didn't so much as blink when she pocketed the bills that bought her trust or when she pawned off the diamonds that had been sewn into the seams of the children's clothes. I'd heard far too many stories of fates flipping overnight, trust broken over a few valuable gems.

"If it's become too much for you," I said, "we know of farmers up north who have offered to take in children."

"And take the risk of moving them out to the countryside with total strangers? Out of the question." She sipped her tea. "You know, it was their father who got my Herman a contract with the orchestra. He marched into the conductor's office and said he wouldn't leave until they hired the man who could make music like stardust."

The woman tipped her head back, lost in nostalgia. "It breaks my heart," she said. "These children should be learning to play the cello, running outside with friends. Instead, they can only leave the crawl space when the neighbors aren't home."

I sat back. Everyone had something to complain about when circumstances got tough, but this woman appeared to feel genuinely responsible for the children's well-being. Much as I wanted to meet the children, we couldn't risk any unnecessary noise, so I finished my tea and left with Aletta, feeling content, my faith in the woman restored.

However, that evening, Jakob showed up at our house with troubling news. Only three hours after my visit, *mevrouw* Dijkstra and the children had been arrested. "The lady across the street believes it was bounty hunters," he said, "two men in plainclothes, but she didn't see their faces."

On hearing this I sank into a chair at the kitchen table. I sat there, feeling defeated, while Willem poured us nettle tea. I was lost in thought, and the tea grew cold. Whatever Jakob said, whatever words of comfort he offered, I didn't hear them. *Mevrouw* Dijkstra might come back with only a fine, a slap on the wrist, a warning. Her husband was well respected. But the children would suffer a different fate. By now, they would be on their way to the Jewish nursery by the Hollandsche Schouwburg, awaiting deportation. And once they got on that train headed eastward, they would be all alone. They might never see their father again.

I kissed Aletta on the forehead, holding her tightly, understanding the danger I'd put her in by bringing her with me that day. How I wanted to find those bounty hunters. I wanted to make them hurt.

TWENTY-SEVEN

Liesbeth de Wit
August 7, 1943
Amsterdam, the Netherlands

Dirk had moored his boat to the side of the quay, not far from his house. Liesbeth reclined in the bow, resting her legs on the thwart while Dirk tinkered with the engine and cleaned off a smear of motor oil. The still surface of the water mirrored the vivid sky and the buildings across the canal—the towers of the Rijksmuseum and the indoor pool where Johanna liked to swim.

Liesbeth rubbed her bare calves, adjusting her skirt to find a balance between demure and daring. Her house was fifteen minutes away, but all it would take was one nosy neighbor walking back from the market to ruin things. She tried to think of a good excuse in case Maurits happened by. He was supposed to be at an NSB meeting.

"How come you didn't go today?" she asked Dirk.

"And get stuck passing out flyers in Dam Square? I told them I had a personal emergency." He moved to massage her thigh. She glanced around before leaning over to kiss him. Dirk grinned. He folded some loose washers and a screwdriver into an old rag and tucked them into the compartment next to the engine while he whistled a cheerful little tune.

He poured her a glass of cordial, placing it on the thwart in front of her. "Staring at a pretty girl all morning will make a man thirsty."

Liesbeth recalled the wine she and Maurits had drunk when they'd borrowed Dirk's boat. How they'd left it on the thwart when they'd shimmied out of their clothes and jumped in, laughing and splashing one another. That version of Maurits felt lost. Feeling a sudden stitch of guilt, she opened her handbag for her Pervitin. She popped a tablet into her mouth and moved closer to Dirk. The boat rocked beneath her, throwing her off balance. Dirk reached out to steady her.

"Not much of a sailor for someone from Zeeland," he said.

"No, I sure haven't earned my sea legs. I've never understood the appeal of venturing far from land." Again, she thought of that day with Maurits, how his eyelashes had glistened with water droplets while he held her in the shallows, laughing and kissing her neck.

"Come on," she said, "your repairs can wait. Let's go inside."

Dirk's apartment was not at all what she'd expected. Her husband was a man of regimen; he kept books shelved by subject and author name, his hats hung from casual to formal. She had assumed a bachelor would fall into bad habits, but this was something else.

Disarray. Newspapers three days old strewed across the floor, a glass candy dish filled with enough pipe ash to suggest a volcanic eruption. The kitchen, oddly, was tidy, but knickknacks and paraphernalia cluttered the other rooms. On a windowsill, a schooner in a bottle. On a side table, a pair of brass binoculars. And on the bookshelf, a small menorah. Liesbeth touched its branches, the dark spot where a candle once sat. "Why do you have this?"

"I'm a collector," he said, as if that explained everything. He paused before adding, "It belonged to my family's old landlord."

She caught the bitterness in his words. "And he gave this to you?"

"A parting gift."

Liesbeth nodded, wondering who would think to give such a gift to someone who couldn't value it. Strange that he'd kept it all these years.

"I'm still in the process of settling in," Dirk said, gesturing to the pile of empty crates in the corner. "You'll have to come to my housewarming party in a few weeks." He pulled her away from the shelf and kissed her, inhaling the scent of her hair. She felt the comforting sensation of the Pervitin kicking in, making her want him more.

"I promise you," he said, "the bedroom is much more interesting."

Liesbeth laughed, and let herself be led toward the attic room. The walls sloped inward around the unmade bed. But she didn't care about that as she focused on his touch, the tingle as his fingers raked through her hair.

They made love, twice, and by the time they fell back with their rosy faces against the pillows, Liesbeth felt giddy. Her body hummed with the Pervitin. With Dirk, intimacy was a completely new experience. No need for flattery or false promises. No worries about cycles or the best positions to conceive a child. There was simply the two of them and the thick passion between them.

Dirk traced a finger around the curve of her ear. "You're different than when I first saw you."

"How so?"

"You seemed so removed from everything, maybe a bit uptight."

She flinched. That was how she came across to him? It was a miracle he was interested in her.

He sensed her reaction and smirked. "There's nothing wrong with steering clear of all those marionette housewives with their wooden small talk. But this Lies is different—more present, more free."

It was true; he had knocked down some barricades. There were no rules, no marital expectations to fulfill. She considered everything she'd told him: how she'd secretly never wanted to stop working at the tailor shop, how she longed to put her sewing talent to good use, rather than spend her days dusting the lampshades and preparing for dinner parties with people she barely knew, women who only opened their mouths to ask for a serviette or comment on the rain. She feared she'd become that same woman, hardened into that mold.

"I suppose," she said, "I don't have to pretend with you. Everyone else seems to have something they're fighting for. Sometimes I feel like a reed caught in the wind."

"Well, you need to understand what makes you tick, what gets you excited." He reached over to the nightstand drawer and withdrew his own tube of Pervitin, which he opened and offered to Liesbeth. She popped it into her mouth, but her jaw felt stiff from the earlier dose, so the bitter, floury flavor stuck to her tongue as she tried to swallow it.

"So what gets your heartbeat up?" she asked.

He untangled himself from her and got up from the bed. "Good question." She waited, hoping he would say something else, but instead he went to the bathroom. The question stayed with her. What made her own heart beat faster? The shock of what she was doing, the possibility of Maurits finding out, the risk of getting pregnant—or was that what she secretly wanted? She shook the thought away, knowing she had to be careful. Besides, Dirk had pulled out in time.

She sat up and opened the drawer of the nightstand to put the tube of Pervitin back. Something inside the drawer caught her eye. The gold chain of a necklace glinted in the lamplight. A garnet set in a pendant with geometric details. Art deco, if she wasn't mistaken. She held it up, angling it so the stone caught the light. Did he intend to give it to her? It was gorgeous, one of a kind. Then another possibility crossed her mind. She recalled his attention for Ida, the way he'd looked her up and down in the pharmacy. Did Dirk have another lover?

Downstairs, the toilet flushed. She tucked the necklace away, shutting the drawer right as Dirk reappeared in the attic. He slid back into the bed. When he reached over to the nightstand, she perked up, but instead he grabbed his glass of water. They lay there together until she couldn't stand the curiosity any longer.

"What is that necklace?" she asked, trying to sound casual.

"What necklace?"

"In the nightstand."

He paused and then chuckled. "You little snoop! How will I ever be able to surprise you?" He opened the drawer. The necklace rotated as it dangled from his fingers, its stone sparkling, making her think of Paris and couture and limitless dreams. He gestured for her to turn around, and when he slipped the chain around her neck, her whole body softened, the tension she didn't know she'd been holding melting away.

"Thank you," she said. "It's exquisite."

"A family treasure." He leaned in, his lips grazing her temple. "You deserve it, and so much more."

The following weekend, Liesbeth journeyed down to Zeeland to visit her aunt and uncle. The Nazis had imposed more and more travel restrictions while they prepared the coast for battle, building it up like a fortified castle. People speculated about forced evacuations, precautionary flooding, but she struggled to picture the countryside she knew so well turned upside down. She had the chilling awareness that this visit home could be her last for some time.

By the time she made it to the island, the day had slipped away and the vendors at the market had packed up and gone home, the cobblestones slick with runoff from the fish stalls and the gulls squawking while they fought over the carcasses that littered the gutters. The salty tang of the air mixed with the smells of horse dung and tobacco and fresh bread. The soldiers had stolen *oom* Cor's bicycle, so she walked with her uncle from the wharf back through the winding streets, toward the welcoming candlelight in her aunt and uncle's front window.

Tante Rika had dinner waiting: potato soup and bread topped with grated carrots. Liesbeth scraped the bowl clean, trying to keep her eyes on her food and off the empty chair next to her. She couldn't remember a single night in the house without Gerrit. *Tante* Rika did her best to lighten the mood, spouting off gossip about the neighbors: the senile Belgian who was convinced she was Joan of Arc reincarnated, the cabinetmaker who'd been executed for brawling with a German soldier.

"You remember the minister's daughter, the ginger girl? She's given birth to twins, two healthy boys."

Liesbeth picked a piece of lint from her skirt. Any news but baby news, she thought. *Tante* Rika must have sensed this, because she cleared her throat and changed the subject. Liesbeth raised a hand to her neck, feeling the imprint of the necklace she wore tucked under her sweater. The thought of it, of Dirk, made her smile, their own little secret.

When everyone's plate was empty, Liesbeth cleared the table. She was placing the dishes in the sink, when a soft rap came at the back door. Liesbeth and *tante* Rika started at the sound— nobody came knocking so late.

Oom Cor moved to answer it, grumbling something about "foolish risks." Then Gerrit's big grin appeared as he wheeled his bicycle in through the back entrance.

"Ger!"

He set a wicker basket filled with vegetables on the table and he moved to greet them.

Tante Rika wagged a finger at him. "Give your old aunt a heart attack, why don't you? How many times do I have to beg you to stay put at night?"

"What, and miss out on a rare chance to pester Lies?"

"Don't pretend this is about me," Liesbeth said. "You're itching for *tante* Rika's cooking!"

Gerrit grabbed a tea towel and chased her around in an attempt to flick it at her.

"You win, you win!" Liesbeth said, laughing. They finished washing up together, falling into easy conversation. Gerrit had found work on a nearby farm, a half hour cycle from Zierikzee. The Germans rarely bothered to check the farmhands' work permits, so as long as he stayed on the property, it was a good hiding place. Liesbeth scolded him, but she was glad to see him.

Once they had dried the dishes and stacked them away, they retired to the warmth of the heated back room. Liesbeth tossed a block of peat into the stove and lit a few more candles. The electricity had been out more often than not that week, *oom* Cor told them. They sat together while Gerrit regaled them with stories of farm life, of the one-eyed goat that kept bursting in on the farmer's wife in the bathroom, of the runt piglet that he'd nursed back to health. "Won't last long, poor little fella. Even at his size he's got enough pork chop in him to be the biggest prize in town."

He talked about how busy they'd been, preparing for the sugar beet harvest. The work was draining, leaving him with sore feet and a persistent heat rash, but the farmers reasoned that the beets would be the lifeline to pull the Dutch through the harsh winters. Liesbeth reckoned she'd already eaten enough sugar beets to last two lifetimes.

When the conversation began to die, *oom* Cor pulled out the evening newspaper and cleared his throat.

"That's my signal," Gerrit said. He grabbed his bicycle from the back entrance and carted it into the room, setting it up on the stationary bicycle stand. He hopped on and started pedaling like a maniac, until the mechanical bicycle lamp kicked in and cast a yellowish glow across the floor. *Oom* Cor sat down on the rug next to the bicycle and started poring over the latest dispatches from Sicily. Liesbeth laughed at the sight: two grown men ogling the paper, debating the likelihood of the Italian surrender.

Tante Rika snipped out ration coupons for the pair of brown leather shoes she was saving up for, while Liesbeth opened her mother's old sewing box. There wasn't a shred of decent fabric left in the house, but she'd resolved to fashion a dress from *tante* Rika's old flour sacks. She didn't get far, the dim light making it hard to see her stitches.

When the candles had burned to stubs, everyone tidied up and went to sleep. Liesbeth lay in bed and listened as, across the room, Gerrit's breathing turned into snores. When they were little, the siblings used to all pile into one bed and stay up giggling until *tante* Rika told them to go to sleep. Looking back, she wondered if this had been their way of coping with the long, empty nights after the loss of their parents. But that evening, Liesbeth lay by herself and stared at the ceiling, thinking of the two men in her life and feeling very alone.

In the middle of the night, she woke up. Someone was pounding at the front door. She rubbed the sleep from her eyes, trying to make sense of it. A barked order followed. *"Aufmachen, schnell!"*
Order Police.

Liesbeth hissed her brother's name. As her eyes adjusted to the shadows, she heard a shuffling, the sound of something clicking into place. Gerrit had vanished.

Downstairs, more yelling. *"Aufmachen!"* The sound of the door creaking open, her aunt's and uncle's muffled voices. The Order Police were asking about the bicycle in the middle of the room. Liesbeth glanced at the two messy beds. She yanked the quilt back over her own bed, straightening it as best she could, placing her childhood dolls on the pillow. Boots clumped on the staircase. Adrenaline rushed through her as she tiptoed across the room and clambered into Gerrit's bed, which was still warm with the imprint of his body. She curled up, burying her head into the pillow to feign sleep.

A second later, two Order Policemen burst into the bedroom. "You, get up!" Their faces looked angry and mottled with drink. Her hands trembled as she pulled back the covers. *Tante* Rika appeared behind the men to pass her a robe. Liesbeth made a noisy show of putting it on over her nightgown, drawing her arms through the sleeves in big, disruptive movements while the Germans scoured the room. They held up a framed photograph of Gerrit, a snapshot of him showing off the medal he'd won for the regional swim meet. They shoved it toward her. "Where's your brother?"

"We haven't seen him in months." She tried her best to match their stare but inside she was terrified. She weighed every pause, afraid the sound of Gerrit's nervous breaths would drift up through the floorboards. The rug beneath the bed lay askew. Would they notice? While her aunt and uncle waited anxiously in the corner, the men rifled through the cupboards, discarding the contents on the floor. They looked so certain of what they'd find, like they'd had a good reason to come looking for Gerrit in the middle of the night. Had he done something? After all, by being in hiding, he had already broken the law. She took a step back, trying to push the thought away, appalled she could think such a thing. Of course the Germans weren't justified in their search, not at all.

One of the men yanked open the bottom drawer of the wardrobe, turning it on its side. She saw her chance to distract them. "Oh, please be careful with those papers. Those are some of my drawings, fashion sketches. I've had them for years." She babbled on, coating her words with cheerfulness. One of the men flicked through the papers, turning them over to glance at the sketches before tossing them aside.

The Order Police moved on to her aunt and uncle's bedroom.

Liesbeth stood there in the hall, clutching *tante* Rika's arm, silently begging them to leave. Once they had pulled the clothes from the shelves, knocked over the vase on the bedside table, and ground the yellow blossoms into the fibers of the rug, they retreated downstairs. Liesbeth watched from the bedroom window while the men left the house frustrated and empty-handed. One of them swore and kicked the bucket next to the chicken coop, sending feed scattering across the yard. The chickens awoke in a flurry of squawking and flapping wings.

In the next breath, the men were gone. When fifteen minutes had passed and they hadn't returned, Gerrit climbed out of the crawl space beneath the floorboards. His face was as white and stiff as starched linen. He hugged *tante* Rika, rubbing her back and promising everything was over.

He turned to Liesbeth with a plastered smile. "Look at you, talking their ears off like that. Forget the sewing; you'd make an ace actress!"

That rush of shame returned, how, for a second, she'd questioned her own brother, believing the Nazis correct for enforcing the rules. How could she possibly think that?

"Don't you dare laugh this one off," she said. "For goodness' sake, don't set one foot off that farm, you hear me?"

He clicked his heels and shot up his arm in a salute. *"Jawohl, liebe Schwester!"*

The two of them stayed up for a long time, huddling together in the darkness, each of them replaying the events of the night. Liesbeth took a Pervitin to soothe her nerves, but all it did was keep her awake. She flinched at every sound outside, the branches scraping the windowpane, certain the Germans would return. When Gerrit fell asleep, his chest rising and falling in a soft, gentle rhythm, Liesbeth stayed there beside him, her hand on his shoulder. For the first time, she understood the real stakes of the war, how much she stood to lose.

TWENTY-EIGHT

Johanna Vos
September 3, 1943
Amsterdam, the Netherlands

Aletta looked up at me when I turned onto the wide street that led into Jakob and Ida's house. Since the arrests at *mevrouw* Dijkstra's, I hadn't dared to venture out with Aletta. Whenever I thought of those poor children alone in some camp—or worse—I shriveled up inside. Plus I'd put Aletta in harm's way. Who knows what might have happened if we hadn't left when we did.

I couldn't stand by and watch the bounty hunters pick off more Dutch children. Someone close to us was involved in the arrests, someone with intimate access to our network. How else could you explain the way the artists and the good people who hid them kept disappearing after our *zwarte avonden*, plucked like chestnuts from low-hanging branches? I'd scanned the concert guest lists, searching for names I didn't recognize. What about the dour-faced lawyer who'd sat in the back two concerts in a row, or the spice merchant who'd grumbled about his business losses? Would one of them make some phone calls in exchange for a handful of guilders per head? However, the concert hosts vetted the lists before Jakob and I saw them, ensuring that everyone who entered their homes were familiar faces. And so, I circled back to that same question: Whom could we truly trust?

I hoped Jakob would help me go through the lists, since he knew the Jewish network much better than I did. He and Ida lived on the fringes of the Jewish quarter, not far from the zoo. I was struck by the emptiness of the neighborhood. One of those telltale moving trucks glided down the road like an omen of death, stopping in front of a gabled canal house. The movers would strip the home of its possessions—the cuckoo clock the family had bought on a trip to the Alps, the rolltop desk where the husband had written love letters to his wife—whitewashing the memories of the occupants on the pretense of "relocation" and "temporary resettlement."

I crossed at the intersection to avoid the moving truck and checked on Aletta, savoring the little gurgles she made as she stared up at me. I adjusted the fabric of the carrier to shield her from the breeze. The wind had blown all night, carrying gusts of desert sand up from the Sahara that coated the parked automobiles and the shop windows in a grainy film. While passing the bookstore, I glanced inside. A woman in the back of the shop caught my attention, her pregnant profile visible beneath a beautiful blue coat. Her head was turned, but I could have sworn it was Ida. She plucked a book from the shelf, a leather-bound volume with a red spine. She opened it and slipped something into the spine of the book, but, before I saw her face, she disappeared farther into the back of the bookshop.

A few minutes later, Aletta and I arrived at Jakob's doorstep. We stood there a long time before he answered the bell.

"Were you spying from upstairs?" I asked.

"Well, I was grumbling about having to entertain another visit with you, but I changed my mind at the sight of this little monkey." He invited us in. Once I had unwrapped Aletta from the sling, he lifted her up above his head and she let out a giggle.

"We need to talk about these disappearances," I said. He led me into the sitting room, and I settled in a chair between the piano and Jakob's contrabass. We were interrupted by the sound of Ida returning home. She appeared a minute later wearing a long-sleeved dress that seemed fit for a funeral, an outfit Liesbeth could have spent hours picking apart.

Ida's face brightened at the sight of Aletta on my lap. "Why, hello, little princess."

Jakob smirked. "Don't let Jo hear you say that."

"No princesses here," I said. "Explorer, medical pioneer, philanthropist, all-around good person—any of those alternatives would do."

"I shouldn't expect anything less from your daughter," Ida said.

I smiled. Aside from the doctor at the house concert, Jakob and Ida were the only ones—alive, anyway—who knew Aletta's real identity, yet Ida spoke of the girl like she was my blood. It was almost as if she had forgotten how Aletta had come to join our family. Or perhaps now that she was expecting, she understood the need to feel like a proper mother.

"I saw you just now," I said. "Did you pick up anything of interest?"

"What do you mean?" she asked.

"At the bookshop."

"You must be mistaken. That wasn't me."

"Well then, I suppose you have a doppelgänger." I paused to unhook the sleeve of my blouse from Aletta's grasp, before glancing back at Ida. The skin at her temples pulsed, stretched taught from her chignon while she busied herself with something in her handbag. I motioned for her to join us. "I was telling Jakob that I want to get to the bottom of these disappearances. We have a traitor in our midst."

Ida hesitated before taking a seat next to her husband. "You two are the brains here."

With my free hand, I retrieved the lists I'd drawn up. "The timing between each concert and the disappearances is uncanny. They must be gleaning information from the concerts about everyone's whereabouts."

I passed the documents to Jakob, who unfolded them across the coffee table. Ida leaned over his shoulder to scan the lists. "So you think we've had a bounty hunter at our music salons?"

"Or an informant," Jakob said.

"Who knew that the Dijkstras were hiding those children," I asked, "aside from the three of us?"

Jakob rubbed his chin. "Marijke de Graaf, for one, but that doesn't help us. Probably a few other members of the orchestra." We spent a few minutes compiling names, trying to figure out who had the best motives, whom we trusted.

"All this speculating," Ida said, "we could be here all day and not get any closer. What would you even do if you solved this riddle?"

I looked at Jakob. "I have a revolver."

"Johanna!" Ida wrapped her arm around her belly. "You wouldn't want Aletta to lose another mother, would you? Would you risk everything for revenge?"

"Now," Jakob said, "there's no need for talk like that."

Ida ignored him. "Maybe this is exactly what she needs to hear. These are powerful men, men who don't blink an eye about betraying their countrymen. If she goes looking for them, she's putting everything we've worked to safeguard at risk."

"At least I understand kind words aren't enough to save lives," I said.

Jakob waved his hand as if to clear the air. "Enough, ladies. What's the point in arguing?" He walked over to the piano. "We have the information in front of us. Now it's a case of seeing how things fit together." He sat down at the piano bench and ran his fingers across the ivory, stopping to play a few notes, a piece from Rachmaninoff in C Minor. He turned to me. "What about your brother-in-law?"

"What about him? Maurits doesn't know about the concerts."

"He gave you the insulin. Maybe he was trying to set you up."

Ida touched the high collar of her dress. "I told you I had an uneasy feeling about that."

"You might have a point," I said. For months, I'd suspected that Maurits was in deeper than Liesbeth had let on. "Think of all the addresses and information he can access, knowing all the ins and outs of people's medical needs."

Aletta began to cry on my lap. She was getting hungry. I told Jakob and Ida I had to go but that I would investigate our suspicions. Maurits was exactly the sort of person who might let a few names slip if it meant securing his own fortunes.

As I got up to leave, Ida took my hands. "Promise me you won't make any hasty decisions, dear. Men will say anything when they're feeling cornered."

I nodded and assured them I wouldn't, but I could already feel my pulse quickening. I tucked Aletta back into the baby carriage and said my goodbyes. As I closed the door behind me, I glimpsed Ida's coat hanging in the hall closet. A bright, beautiful blue.

On my way home, I passed by the bookshop. The shopkeeper was about to close for lunch. "Be quick," he told me. I hesitated, trying to recall where she'd stood, and I leaned forward, Aletta gurgling at my chest, while I scanned the shelves. Tucked beside *The Three Musketeers* and *The Count of Monte Cristo* was a thin, leather-bound volume with a red spine. *The Black Tulip*. I paused, thinking of the black silk tulip that we used to mark the house concerts. I opened the book and cracked the spine until I could see straight through it to the floor. Nothing fell out. I left the store no further ahead, mulling over the coincidence, questioning Ida's strange behavior. But soon my thoughts returned to Maurits, my need to confront him. I had bigger things on my mind.

TWENTY-NINE

Liesbeth de Wit
September 4, 1943
Amsterdam, the Netherlands

"You know," Liesbeth said, while Dirk caressed her hair, "they say this is the same sound silkworms make."

"What do you mean?"

She pointed to the window of his attic bedroom, and they listened to the raindrops pattering against the glass. They lay naked, their limbs twisted in the sheets, her head resting on his chest. The gas had gone out, so she curled into him until his breath warmed her neck.

"It's the same sound?" he asked, and although she couldn't see his face, she heard the amusement in his question. "Tell me more."

"For years, the Chinese fiercely guarded the secret of how to make silk. But legend has it that it leaked out when a princess was married off. She couldn't bear to be without her precious silks, so she smuggled cocoons of silk moths and seeds from the mulberry tree out of China."

"How did she do that?"

"By hiding them in her hairpiece, naturally."

Dirk sat up. "Sounds like something you would do."

Liesbeth laughed, but she didn't tell him how wrong he was. She couldn't imagine risking her life over something so trivial. Seeing Dirk, being in bed with him, was the most daring thing she'd ever done. She balked at her boldness, the shame she felt, pooling in the backdrop. Maurits had left town for two days. An uncle of his had passed away, and he'd offered to go to Rotterdam to sort out the man's affairs. Maurits had invited Liesbeth along, trying to appeal to her desire for fun and distraction. "We'll treat it like a holiday," he said. "I'll book a hotel. We can see the sights, wander along the harbor, maybe visit a dress shop." But Liesbeth knew how it would go: she would end up spending the days packing up musty old items, possessions of an in-law she'd never met. Besides, the Nazis had practically flattened Rotterdam at the start of the occupation—what was there left to enjoy? No, she'd told him, it was better she stay home and rest.

Two whole glorious days, and this was how she was spending it. Dirk had ample time for her. His work was slowing down, so he often could leave early in the afternoons. He said the job might end soon. She found it odd that a position at a bank could wrap up like that, but she didn't dwell on this. Bigger things were afoot, and while they lay there together, the afterglow from their lovemaking fading to a languid daze, she found herself in troubled thought, worrying about her family.

Dirk reached for his tobacco tin. He took a pinch of real tobacco and mixed it in with the surrogate and began filling his pipe. He fumbled for a match, glancing sidelong at her. "Something's bothering you; it's all over your face."

She reached for her Pervitin, unsure how to reply. She avoided talk of the war with Dirk; it was all she ever heard at home anymore. What they had—their affair, she supposed she ought to call it—existed on neutral territory, and any reminder of his allegiances only clouded her mood and reminded her of her guilty conscience.

"It's my aunt and uncle," Liesbeth said. "They may have to leave Zierikzee in the next few months."

"Ah, so the Germans are making preparations."

She nodded, knowing that if she spoke he would hear the tremor in her voice. Rumors had started circulating that the Allies were planning to attack somewhere along the Atlantic coast. She couldn't imagine they would zero in on Zeeland— she hoped with all her heart that wasn't the case—but there was a chance the Nazis would flood the islands to thwart any Allied invasion. If so, her aunt and uncle would have to pack their life into a couple of suitcases, unsure of when they would be able to return home, if there would be a home left for them.

"You must be very worried," he said. "I wouldn't wish that on anyone. Will they live with you and Maurits for the time being?"

Dirk never had any qualms about mentioning her husband. He accepted the strange reality of their affair without reservations, which both soothed and unsettled her.

"No, they'd like to stay nearby. We have relatives in Brabant." She didn't tell him the real reason—they wanted to stay near Gerrit. He couldn't travel all the way to Amsterdam, nor could she expect Maurits to welcome her fugitive brother with open arms. By staying on farms in the vicinity, Gerrit could still be protected.

Dirk reached for her hand. "I'm sorry. This war has torn apart so many lives. If only we'd known in the beginning what a long slog lay ahead."

"I should be there to help them. Every week I hear something in the news or receive a letter that puts me on edge, wondering what's yet to come."

"Are they still letting visitors into Zeeland?"

"It's almost impossible, but I need to find a way to help."

"Selfless to the core," he said, "that's admirable of you."

"No, that's Jo," she said, more to herself than to him. "She's the one out saving the world, every week a different cause."

"How are her house concerts going? Have you attended any?"

"How do you know about those?"

"You mentioned them at some point."

She was almost certain she hadn't, given that she barely knew the truth herself. His comment gave her an uneasy feeling, something she couldn't pin down. He cocked his head like he wanted her to go on. When she didn't, he tapped the ash from his pipe and ran his hand up her thigh. "You're so worried about everyone all the time—Maurits, your sister, your aunt and uncle—why don't we focus on you for now?" His lips moved to her neck, trailed down her collarbone. She tried to relax and let him please her but the images remained in her head: the Nazis blowing up the dikes, water lapping at the door of the family home, flooding the yard with its orchard and the chicken coop, flooding the cemetery down the lane.

She thought of her parents' graves, no one there to tend them, to pluck the weeds and trim the grass and lay the fresh flowers every week. The water would rise up, obscuring the headstones, eroding the soil, disturbing their peace.

Dirk touched her elbow. "Liesbeth, what's wrong?"

She looked at him blankly.

"You're pulling away from me."

She gathered the sheets around herself, pressing them to her naked chest, and avoided his stare.

"Look at me," he said, more of a question than an order.

When she raised her gaze, she saw genuine concern.

"You can talk to me, whatever it is."

If only it were that simple. Gerrit was the only one in the family who ever spoke of the accident. Whenever her aunt and uncle mentioned her parents, they stuck to fond memories, speaking of them with the casual air of someone who had gone off on some errands, who might return at any moment.

Liesbeth chewed her lip and looked down at the sheets. "I don't want them to be left there all alone."

"Who?"

"My parents."

He waited for her to continue.

"It was my fault they died. For weeks, I'd been whining, begging them to bring me to visit a cousin who had moved across the islands. They had just dropped me off when their boat crashed, right into the ferry. If I hadn't been so insistent, they never would have been out on the water."

Dirk brushed a tear from her cheek. "An accident like that could happen at any time."

"But I insisted. They wanted me to wait until the weather was calmer, but I wouldn't let it go."

"How old were you?"

"Seven."

"Exactly."

"I robbed them of so much." She paused, noticing in the silence that the rain had stopped. The only sound was the hum of the bedside lamp. "They never got to see their children grow up, never got to see their first granddaughter."

"You can't cling to what-ifs. Who knows what else might have happened, what the war would have made of them."

Liesbeth nodded and thought of Gerrit, stuck in hiding. Dirk had a point. These past few years, everyone's fate seemed as uncertain as a coin midtoss. "I suppose you're right. Still, I can't help but wonder what kind of life our family would have built together if it hadn't been for me."

Dirk got up out of bed and put on some trousers. He passed Liesbeth one of his long button-down shirts before leading her downstairs, where they opened a bottle of *jenever*. He motioned for her to join him on the divan and held out a glass. "My last bottle. This seems like a good time."

Liesbeth snuggled up to him, tucking her feet up beneath

her. As he poured the drink, she felt a sense of relief. He hadn't judged her for her shame about her parents' deaths; she felt like she could tell him anything. He kissed her on the forehead and clinked his glass to hers. "You're a sweetheart. Maybe too sweet. Don't let anyone take advantage of that."

Music blared from the gramophone, competing with the laughter and murmur of voices that filled Dirk's house. The day before, Liesbeth and Dirk had had the place to themselves, but now she leaned against the sitting-room windowsill, observing the guests at his housewarming party. By now, she was beginning to know the corners of Dirk's house intimately: how dappled afternoon sunlight streaked through the curtains, the trick to flushing the toilet, the way the floorboards shifted as you approached the piano. It felt strange to her now, pretending it was her first visit to his new home, admiring the artwork on the walls with the curiosity of a newcomer.

Still, it forced her to take a step back and marvel at the place. In preparation for the party, Dirk had hired a cleaner, so the house was tidier than she'd ever seen, which allowed her to appreciate the furnishings. He had welcomed her into his house without much explanation—to be blunt, she'd hardly noticed the decor when he'd first led her by the hand up the stairs to his bedroom. But the house was huge. Two floors, with ornate rugs and polished wooden cabinets and moody landscape paintings of Dutch fields and windmills. Now that she could look past the disarray and clutter, it struck her how unlike Dirk this house was, as if he'd inherited the furniture from a wealthy aunt. Since when did he play the piano?

She wished he would come over and talk to her. Surely, he could think up an excuse for some innocent conversation. However, he'd been chatting with a trio of women in the hall for over twenty minutes. He had caught her briefly as she went to powder her nose, his hand brushing her wrist when he'd turned to wink at her. "Always so stuffy, these parties," he'd said, "aren't they?"

A group of women had edged toward the windowsill, their drinks sloshing on the floor as they swapped gossip. Liesbeth searched around for a familiar face. She was relieved to see Maurits approaching with two glasses of beer in his hands.

"Quite the place, isn't it?" he said, lifting his glass to cheers her.

"It doesn't suit him," she said. "I would have expected something a little more modest."

Maurits chuckled and leaned in, the stubble on his chin tickling her ear. "Oh, darling," he said, "you're adorable. You do know how he got this house, don't you?"

"He said he acquired it through his position at the bank. Isn't that true?" But as she said this, she heard her own naivete. She watched Dirk across the room, debating whether she was prepared to hear the truth. Just then, he clapped his hands to get everyone's attention, and the chatter died down.

"Ladies, gentlemen," he said, "you're in for a treat." He stepped aside to reveal a bulky device perched atop a table, the sort of thing you'd see in a cinema.

"It's a projector," Maurits told her.

Dirk motioned for some of the guests to move aside, clearing a space in front of a wall, where a large white sheet hung. He passed around a box of cigars, and she knew from Maurits's nod of appraisal that they were expensive and hard to come by.

"Everyone, gather round," Dirk said, fiddling with the projector.

Liesbeth hooked her arm through her husband's. "His own private cinema. Can you imagine?" She was surprised Dirk hadn't shown it to her on her visits, hadn't mentioned anything about the house or its former owners. But she was beginning to realize the truth and it was a bitter tincture, hard to swallow.

Maurits lit his cigar. "You wait, darling, one day we'll be on the inside looking out."

Dirk called for someone to dim the lights. The guests dragged the chairs and the divan to face the hanging sheet, but Liesbeth and Maurits stood in the back, next to a large potted plant that was wilting and crisp at the edges.

The film projector crackled on, shooting a thick beam of light across the room. The guests cheered and clinked glasses when the sheet came to life with moving images. Liesbeth tilted her head, trying to make sense of the scene that was playing out. A long, panning shot of a coastline: a sailboat, a sandy beach, lounge chairs. Five people lounging under a striped parasol—a family. A mother in a sun hat, flirting with the camera as she bounced a baby on her lap. Next to her, two young children sat in the sand, filling buckets and tipping them over into castle turrets. The little girl grinned and sucked on a licorice stick.

Liesbeth watched, dumbfounded, while the children raced into the crashing waves. "They're Jews," she whispered.

"Mmm-hmm," Maurits said, "looks like the French Riviera."

Liesbeth looked around, appalled. The other guests were either refilling their drinks or watching enraptured, oohing and ahing at the novelty of the film. She glanced back at the movie, at the Jewish family who had privately filmed their summer getaway. Had those children played with toy locomotives on the very floorboards on which she stood? Had their mother done her embroidery in the same alcove where two bawdy women now perched? Had their father watched in horror as the Order Police marched the family out of this very house, handing it over to the bank? And what about the bed where she and Dirk made love?

The children on the screen doubled over, splashing each other silly. Liesbeth wriggled free of Maurits's arm. She had to get out of there.

"Where are you going?" he asked, without taking his eyes off the film.

She didn't answer. She rushed out, past the bawdy women, past the cloud of cigar smoke, past Dirk. She opened the door to the balcony and stumbled outside. The night air was crisp, and bright stars twinkled in the darkness. She stared out at the rooftops and closed her eyes. Dirk was living in a stolen house, and she had lain intertwined with him in another couple's bed. Everything she believed about him had changed. But how was this any different, she wondered, from taking over another man's pharmacy?

THIRTY

Johanna Vos
September 4, 1943
Amsterdam, the Netherlands

Willem and I sprawled out on a blanket in the middle of the Vondelpark, taking in the last remnants of summer. Between us, Aletta let out a happy babble while she rolled onto her tummy and tried to grab at the picnic basket we'd brought along. I watched her, feeling that my whole universe could be contained within those four corners of the blanket—so why did I feel the constant need to focus outward, to busy myself with problems that played out away from my loving family?

Willem reached over and lazily rubbed my knee. "What's on your mind, dear?"

"Nothing," I said, "and everything."

Aletta tried to push herself up. Wim picked her up. "Baby orangutan, is it jungle time?" He swung her through the air, like she was swinging from vine to vine, and my heart wanted to burst with love. I began to sing to her, a silly ditty Wim and I had made up, about the many other types of animals she would meet on life's adventures. All the other animals, that is, if the Nazis didn't try to poach them all.

Wim set her back on the blanket, propping her into a sitting position so she could look around. I let her wrap her fist around my pointer finger and turned to Wim. "Do you ever wonder about her real parents?"

"Constantly," he said. "I try to imagine what type of people they were, if they'd approve of the way we're raising her."

We watched Aletta spread out her hands, transfixed by the discovery of her fingers.

"Jakob and Ida and I have a suspicion about who could be behind the arrests," I said. "We think Maurits could be involved."

"What gives you that impression?"

"Think about it. He has access to plenty of information: names, addresses, people's medical history. He would notice patterns when things change. And isn't it a bit too coincidental that he made a show of sending us medical supplies?"

"What does that have to do with the house concerts?"

"Lies knows about them. I tried to keep it from her, but she figured out something is going on. Who knows what she told Maurits."

Willem looked unconvinced. "Liesbeth wouldn't do anything to hurt us."

"Not intentionally, but Maurits would."

"He was my friend. I'll be the first to say he's made some terrible decisions, but I doubt he would take it so far as to have innocent people arrested."

"Never question how far a man will go in pursuit of power and status," I said. "I'm going to ask Lies about it."

Willem chuckled. "And you think she'll be willing to tell you the truth?"

"We are sisters."

"You haven't been acting like it."

His remark hurt, although it rang true. The only times I

spoke to her was when I needed help with Aletta, and surely she sensed my reasons for getting in touch were selfish. I felt I barely knew her anymore.

"I've been meaning to tell you something," Wim said. "Things are getting trickier at work. The director has tried his best to spare us from the labor call-ups, but the Germans are rejecting more and more exemption requests. I'm not sure how much longer he can protect us."

"What does that mean?"

"There's a chance that I would need to go into hiding."

I bit my lip. It was hard enough managing with Aletta in these circumstances already, and to be without Wim—I couldn't imagine not seeing him every day.

"Where would you go?"

"Hiding in plain sight," he said, referring to the young Jewish lady drawing at the zoo. I tried to imagine him scrunched up between the monkey enclosures, but I found it too hard to picture him anywhere but at my side.

"Let's hope it never comes to that." That prickly sense of injustice came back stronger than ever. I wanted to put a stop to it all before anyone else got hurt. "I'm going to speak to Liesbeth. If I'm correct about Maurits, we need to know. That's one thing that's still somehow in our control."

"If you insist. But please, be careful. Reckless accusations leave behind septic wounds."

I nodded and looked once more at Aletta, her content smile. Once we got up to go home, the universe would expand beyond our little trio. But for a few more hours, we could stay there together on that blanket, pretending we were safe, that everything would turn out all right.

I set off for Liesbeth's midmorning on a Monday, after Maurits had left for work. The more I thought about it, the clearer the connection seemed to be. If the occupation had taught me one thing, it was that most people were preoccupied with saving their own skins. People stole, bartered, lied, and cheated. For so long I'd believed morals would persist in these dark hours, but that was a lie.

Liesbeth answered the door with the pin curls still setting in her hair. Seeing Aletta in my arms, she lit up but her glee faded when she registered my mood. "Is something wrong?" she asked.

"You'll have to tell me." I carried Aletta into the sitting room while Liesbeth prepared the coffee. A collection of baby toys and crocheted blankets lay piled in a basket on the floor, awaiting Aletta's visits. I rummaged through the basket for a rattle, trying to suppress that uneasy feeling, the reminder that Lies had never been anything but loving and pure toward my daughter.

Liesbeth brought in a pot of imitation coffee and two biscuits. "I made the flour from tulip bulbs," she said, gesturing to the biscuits, "not my best experiment."

She sat down and I waited until she'd poured the coffee before speaking. "Lies," I began, "we haven't been very open with one another about our activities during the war, but what I want to ask you is of critical importance."

"Of course. There are no secrets between us." She fidgeted in her seat and I could practically see the NSB uniforms marching through her mind, all the glitzy dinner parties she'd failed to mention.

"People we are trying to help keep disappearing. Jakob's entire family has been taken. His parents, his brothers, even their toddlers."

"Those poor children. How can the Nazis push things so far?"

"Not just the Nazis. Someone is betraying these families, someone close to us."

"Surely you don't believe that?"

"No? What about an ambitious man, someone who wants to gain favor with the Germans?"

Liesbeth glowered at me. "Well, come out and say it then.

Ask me what I know, and I can tell you with full honesty that my husband may have his flaws, but he's no executioner."

"He wouldn't need to be. All it takes is a few phone calls and then he can go home to his darling wife without ever getting his hands dirty. And all the while he can play it off like he's had a change of heart and is helping the Resistance. I'm describing him to a T, aren't I?"

She frowned, considering what I'd said. She started fiddling with a necklace at her collarbone, one I'd never seen her wear before. Her fingers passed over the hexagonal pendant, rubbing the red stone set in the center. Something about it looked familiar.

"Maurits would never do anything that could hurt a child," she said.

As I was about to reply, it came to me. I'd seen the necklace at one of the early house concerts, the stone glinting in the candlelight, the hostess telling me its story. I reached out to examine it. "When did he give this to you?"

Liesbeth pulled back, but, sure enough, it was the same pendant with its art deco shapes and lattice backing. "What?" she asked, her hand closing around it.

"Did he tell you it was a family heirloom, that his grandfather made it?" I couldn't hide the cutting edge to my words. "It belonged to a Jewish woman. A kind, upstanding lady who helped the Resistance before she was captured."

At this, she blanched. The necklace slipped from her hand, dropping back against her chest.

"I knew it."

"You don't understand. Maurits didn't give me the necklace."

"Who, then?"

She averted her eyes. For a moment I sat stock-still, watching the color rise in her cheeks. An awful realization dawned on me. "No," I whispered. It all made sense: my sister's buoyant mood, the way she seldom mentioned Maurits anymore, for better or worse. How had I missed the signals?

"You're having an affair."

She cringed, as if the word was a heavier blow than the act itself.

"Who is he? Is he an artist? What does he know?"

After much hesitation, she spoke. "He's not a bad person. I'm sure there's been some misunderstanding." But I could see her thoughts churning while she pieced things together.

"Tell me everything. Don't leave anything out."

Liesbeth pressed her lips into a thin line. After all the years we'd spent swapping secrets, giggling about sisterly things while constructing forts from bedsheets, now she couldn't bear to let me in. I placed my hand over hers. "Please, think of all of those innocent families."

"His name is Dirk van Duin. He's an acquaintance of Maurits's, but he has a respectable job, and he's never been anything but good to me."

"Go on."

She burst into tears. "I can't." She looked up at me, the way she did when we were much smaller and much more innocent. "You don't understand how hard it has been. I've been so lonely."

She sniffled and brushed away a tear. Once she had composed herself, she began to tell me about the affair. It felt like she was relaying someone else's story because I struggled to picture quiet, pensive Lies locked in a passionate embrace with some man in the shadowy streets. But everything she told me about this man—his house, his job at "the bank," his character, the niggling doubts that grew in her mind as she spoke—convinced me it was him. Our bounty hunter.

"Did you tell him about the house concerts?" I asked.

"The house concerts?" Lies looked confused, and I tried to remember how much I'd let on about our work with the artists' Resistance.

"My performances."

"I don't know." She paused. "Somehow he knew about them, but I don't remember telling him. I'm almost certain I didn't."

I withdrew my hand, flushed with a sudden anger. "Tell me his address. Where can I find him?"

She shook her head.

"Think, Lies, who do you think owned this necklace?" I held it up to her eyes.

"There must be some mistake," she whispered.

"I'm not trying to hurt Dirk. I only want to confront him, to hear the truth."

"I can't. I—"

"You must." I got up and tucked Aletta into the cradle Liesbeth kept for her in the corner. I sat back down with a tightness in my chest, and, looking at her once more, saw how different we were, how different we'd become.

"Who are we, Liesbeth," I asked quietly, "if we are not honest?"

"I can't tell Maurits." She unfastened the necklace and held it in her palm. "It would destroy him."

"Then maybe someone else will."

"No, no, you can't."

"Tell me where I will find Dirk tomorrow evening before curfew."

"You cannot do this, Johanna. You can't just bend me to your will!"

"Tell me, for God's sake!"

"The dry dockyards in the harbor," Liesbeth said flatly. "On Wednesday. He's going to fix up his boat on Wednesday evening." She dropped the necklace to the floor, as if it burned. When she looked up at me there was fire in her eyes. "Don't confront him. Don't you dare send anyone after him, Jo."

THIRTY-ONE

Liesbeth de Wit
September 6, 1943
Amsterdam, the Netherlands

Dirk wasn't at home when Liesbeth went searching for him. He wasn't at home and he wasn't by his boat, and when she asked Maurits if Dirk would be joining him at the evening's NSB meeting, all she got was a queer look and a shrug.

She had to find him. The second Johanna had left that morning, Liesbeth had collapsed on the bed in a bout of tears. What had she done? She didn't know which she feared most—the possibility that her sister might tell Maurits about her disloyalty, or the idea that Johanna might try to do more than simply ask Dirk for the truth. The conversation with Johanna had made it clear that her sister had a lot to hide; whatever she was doing with the Resistance, she was in deep. Helping her was the right thing to do, but Liesbeth's feelings for Dirk felt like wild horses faced with the open countryside. She had to somehow lead him away from this trap.

She found him at Café Ruysdael, surrounded by a throng of men. Friends, coworkers, or perhaps fellow bounty hunters?

No—she refused to believe it, refused to believe the truth of the necklace, not until she had real evidence.

He was standing at the bar, tapping his deck of cards against the counter and leaning in to joke with the barman while waiting for his beer. Liesbeth helped herself to another Pervitin tablet. The buzz from the last one was still going strong, propelling her forward. She worked her way toward him, until he turned and saw her. "Lies!" His voice sounded a pitch higher than normal, and he threw an arm around me, the beer heavy on his breath. "What are you doing here?"

"I need to talk to you."

Dirk turned to the barman. "Tom, get this lady a drink."

"Please, somewhere private."

He hesitated, and she wondered what sort of celebration she had crashed. But he passed his beer to one of his companions and led her outside and around the corner, to the very alley where they'd first kissed, where she'd first dipped a toe into these tainted waters.

"Now," he said, "as much as it's a treat to see you, I can't help but ask myself what is so urgent."

She looked up at him, at that impish arch of his eyebrow, the laugh lines that softened his stare. Even half-drunk, he was charming. He pulled her closer, and she kissed him—a deep, longing kiss.

"Are you still going to fix your boat on Wednesday evening?" she asked. Perhaps he'd changed his mind; perhaps all of this could be avoided.

"I was planning on it."

"Take me out instead. Please? Maurits will be at his brother's. We can do whatever we'd like."

"Tempting," he said, giving her waist a squeeze, "but I need to get this caulking done. They need to make room for other boats in the warehouse. I'll make it up to you on Saturday."

"No, that won't do. Can't you go to the dockyards in the afternoon instead?"

"Some of us have to work, my dear."

The mention of work caught Liesbeth off guard, and those thoughts bobbed back again, his profuse lies. The job at the bank, the necklace. She thought of his party, the film projecting on the bedsheet: the children frolicking in the sand. Jewish children.

Dirk cupped her chin and tilted her face toward his. "Since when do you want to be seen in public with a scoundrel like me? What's going on?"

She clasped his arm. "Don't go there on Wednesday night. Promise me you won't."

"Why? What aren't you telling me?"

"I have a bad feeling about it, that's all."

"Tell me the truth. What do you know?"

"I'm afraid some people are out to hurt you."

"Who? The Resistance?"

"I don't know."

He stepped toward her, pinning her against the wall. The beer on his breath was overpowering now, and she smelled something stronger beneath it. It brought a wave of nausea, and she wanted to duck away, away from the hardness of his stare.

"Your sister? The one with the baby?" He moved his hand to her collarbone, his fingers splayed, pressing deep into her flesh. She coughed, sputtered, her lips salty with tears. "Tell me," he demanded.

"Yes." She couldn't remember ever mentioning Aletta to him—but how else would he have known? Unless Maurits had told him.

She pleaded for him to stop. "Please, you're hurting me!"

His grip tightened and he raised his other arm, as if he was winding up to hit her. "You'll tell me everything she said. Unless you want me to ask your husband."

She began to sob. "She just wants to talk to you." She choked, trying to get the words out. "She believes you've done something dreadful, that you're betraying the Jews."

The hand around her neck loosened, and he took a step back. She looked at him through a blur of tears. "Promise me you won't go."

THIRTY-TWO

Johanna Vos
September 8, 1943
Amsterdam, the Netherlands

I stood in the shadows of the dockyards, the barrel of the revolver tucked in the lapel of my jacket. Sailboats crowded the dock, their bare masts like sentinels in the darkness. A sloop navigated through the narrow canal, and its muted light cast a greenish sheen across the water. I waited for it to pass, until I was alone again, the dockyards quiet. Ahead of me was the warehouse Liesbeth had mentioned. The sliding door stood ajar. He was inside, everything as we'd planned. I tried not to think of my sister, what she'd done with that awful man, the feelings she had for him. How blind she'd been, how desperate.

The revolver felt cold against my chest, my breasts swollen and tender with milk. I would be home before Aletta woke, and the city would be a safer place for her. I would be home in time—I would.

I planted my feet wide, my pulse hammering in my ears, my muscles taut and strained with rage. I considered the weight of the gun, the weight of what I was about to do. It wasn't too late to turn around, to slip back through the darkened streets and return to the warmth of my kitchen. But then this barbarian would be free to destroy more innocent lives. The surgeon and his wife's. Marijke de Graaf and her husband's. My sister's. And so many more. People who had cared for me, invited me into their homes—gone, hurt, thanks to this monster. All I needed was the name of his informant. As long as he gave me that, I wouldn't have to pull the trigger.

I approached the warehouse, careful not to make a sound. A lamp was lit, and from inside came the gentle taps of someone working with a screwdriver or a wrench. I slipped off my shoes, stepped across the threshold, and peered in. A long, shallow boat rested on wooden stocks, its motor exposed like the tail of an overturned duck. Even in the faint light, the boat looked slick with grime.

There he was, crouched on the floor at the stern of the boat, bent over a can of paint or pitch. A boxy man with a solid build. His back was to me. I raised the revolver, but it was too far for a reliable shot. I took another tentative step forward and then another. I took aim, the revolver pointed right between his shoulder blades. He was humming to himself, a strange tune that reminded me of another, happier time, of vendors at the Zierikzee market singing as they sold their wares. I paused. What if I had the wrong man? What if I'd made some mistake? My hand wavered. I shifted my weight ever so slightly, and in that instant, he turned around.

"This ain't no place for a lady—" he started to say. Then he saw the gun.

"You lied to her, didn't you?" I said. "You lied to Liesbeth the whole time."

He raised his arms and started getting to his feet.

"Don't move!"

"I'm just going to stand up."

I trained the revolver on him, pointed it at his heart. He stood still and met my eyes. His expression was calm, almost amused, and I immediately understood how he'd charmed my sister. He had the face of a rascal, the type of child who got to take off the dunce cap and leave his spot in the corner because the teacher had melted at his sorry pout.

"Tell me your name," I said.

"Dirk van Duin."

"Occupation?"

"I'm a banker."

"Bullshit. Tell me what you really do."

"You can look me up. Registered banker at the LiRo."

I scoffed. "You're a bunch of swindlers, stripping good people of their livelihood. You're a bounty hunter, admit it."

"And you?" Dirk laughed. "A housewife playing hero?"

I took another step closer. I was only a couple of meters away now. "Who's been helping you? Who's your informant?"

His reply was slow and measured. "Maybe you don't know your inner circle as well as you think you do."

"My sister—"

"I'm not talking about her."

"Who, then?"

"You think the Resistance acts in the name of what's just, but even your own friends are selfish."

My finger wrapped around the trigger. "Tell me."

He looked from my face to the gun. "Ida Cohen."

I stiffened and let out a terse laugh. "You're lying." It couldn't be, not Ida. But the name hit me with a coldness in my core. She was a woman who had a lot to protect. I shook my head, repeating myself. "You're lying." But I remembered her coat, her bright blue coat in the bookshop.

Dirk's eyes narrowed, his focus shifting to something behind me. I turned to look, and he lunged forward, throwing me to the floor. What happened next was a blur. Lights, shining in my eyes. Gestapo, yelling harsh orders, holding me down. The clatter of the revolver as it fell. Dirt and gravel grinding into my cheek. A flash of pain as my arms were twisted behind my back. Then the handcuffs, encircling my wrists. Dirk was standing there, looking down on me with a smug smile.

"It seems your sister has also made her loyalties clear," he said, while they led me out of the warehouse. He had been one step ahead of me, all along.

I sat on a wooden chair in the middle of a basement room, my hands cuffed behind my back. The room was empty, save for a cupboard in the corner and the bare bulb that dangled overhead. They'd brought me to the SD headquarters on the Euterpestraat. Two blocks from here, I'd given birth. Two blocks from here, I'd lost part of my heart. And here I was again, glaring up at my interrogator.

The officer drummed his fingers against his leg and bent down to stare at me. "Let's make this quick, shall we?" he said. He stank of cigar smoke and garlic, and his wide-set eyes were bloodshot, like he'd been living off Maurits's drug stash.

I looked away. I tried to replay the events of the arrest, but all I could see was Dirk, that arrogant expression when the Gestapo slipped the cuffs over my wrists and took me away. Liesbeth was behind this, my own sister. How dare she endanger Aletta and Willem?

Something tapped the underside of my chin, drawing my head upward. The officer's baton. He held it there, forcing me to look at him. "That requires you to cooperate. Now." He smiled like he'd made a wisecrack and waited a moment. "I want to know your accomplices. Names, addresses."

"I acted alone. I was protecting my sister, that's all this was."

"Don't expect me to believe that." He lowered the baton and circled me in slow, controlled steps. "In ordinary times we might see this as a simple familial spat—jealous sisters pulling each other's hair over a man—but you look like the type who's trying to prove something of herself, trying to show you disapprove of *Herr* Van Duin's patriotic activities."

"Sending innocent children to their deaths for a few extra guilders," I said, my voice rancid with hate, "how is that patriotic?"

"Haven't you noticed how much sweeter the city smells without those droves of swine?" he laughed. "Maybe you don't appreciate it now, but you will once the air clears. Once every last one is gone."

I thought of Aletta's twinkling smile. But the officer noticed the flash of vulnerability on my face and stepped closer. "They'll be caught, that's inevitable. But you can make it easier on yourself and your family if you play along." He paused. "You have a young daughter."

The anger inside me was bubbling up with such ferocity, I was sure he could feel its heat.

"This was about my sister and her poor decisions and nothing else."

"You wouldn't want to leave your little girl without a mother, would you?"

I gritted my teeth and stared at the high curve of the officer's widow's peak. He didn't know, did he? He couldn't. Nobody knew, except—Ida. Would she have told him? I thought back to that day I was certain I'd seen her in the bookstore, her shady reaction when I'd mentioned it to her. Something wasn't right. A panic rose inside me, but still I didn't speak.

The officer opened the cupboard and pulled out a bottle of spirits and two glasses. He poured them both and offered me one. As he untied my hands, I shook my head.

"Drink."

The shot burned my throat. He was trying to loosen my tongue. I thought of Aletta, of Willem, my strong, calm Wim. No sign of weakness would escape me, nothing that might betray our secret. The officer poured another shot. And another. With each shot, the fire in my throat grew, but still I didn't speak.

"I'm waiting." He grabbed me by the wrist. "Such pretty fingers," he said, holding my hand down. "So little time, so much to lose."

I shuddered and recoiled at his touch. He poured shot after shot, fired question after question, but I refused to cooperate. The alcohol pooled in my stomach, making me woozy. I felt myself slipping, slumping sideways in the chair. His questions slurred together in a blur of words.

Then, he hit me. Smacked me upside the head. I pitched forward and cried out. My cheek stung, hot, burning pain.

He poured another shot. "Drink."

Still, I did not speak.

PART FOUR

Hunger
September 1943–May 1945

THIRTY-THREE

The water in the bathtub was cold, but Liesbeth didn't care. She'd lost track of how long she'd been lying there, counting the floor tiles, examining her cuticles, trying to distract herself from what she'd done. Shame stuck to her skin, and try as she might, there was no scrubbing it off. Thanks to her, Johanna was shivering in a jail cell somewhere, away from her husband, away from her daughter.

How could she have robbed Aletta of a mother? How could she have chosen some other man over her own kin? And a bounty hunter, no less! She recalled Dirk's reaction when she'd warned him about Jo, the disdain he'd made no attempt to hide. He saw her sister no differently than the Jews he rounded up—a nuisance, a pest needing extermination. And this, this coming from the man she'd thought she was falling for.

Liesbeth drew her goose-pimpled legs to her chest and buried her face in her knees, recalling the rushed words in the note Willem had scrawled and left in their mail slot, informing them of Jo's arrest. He didn't know the man responsible, only that Jo had walked into a trap. Liesbeth was afraid to face Willem, afraid of the many questions he might ask, so she hadn't left the house since hearing the news.

Still, she wished she were somewhere else, protesting outside the jail, pulling strings to change the mind of the Gestapo. Instead, she had locked herself in the bathroom, avoiding everyone, even her own reflection in the mirror.

What bothered her most was the feeling that seemed to surface the longer she lay there. The anger, the frustration, the guilt, all seemed to diffuse with the steam of the bathwater. The emotion that was left horrified her, this flicker of relief. More than anything, she wanted her sister back. At the same time, some dark part of her felt at ease again, unconfined by her sister's silent appraisal, her words of admonishment. When was the last time she had been herself around Jo?

In some ways, it felt like sewing. Sometimes, the stitches Liesbeth made on the sewing machine came out jagged, the fabric puckered, while the thread of the bobbin was pulled through the seams. The harmony was off: too much tugging in a one-sided tug-of-war. However, if she rotated the tension dial too far back the other way, the thread would spill onto the back, bunching up in a jumble. That was how she felt now, like a spool of thread that had been released, allowed to unravel and escape, with no clear sense of direction.

Her head pounded, a tight band of pain arching across her brow. She reached over the side of the tub, fumbling on the floor until her fingers closed around the Pervitin tube. Although the drug brought on the headaches, it also numbed them, staved off the hurt, and all she wanted was to feel nothing.

While she lay there in the water, picturing her sister, alone in that prison cell, picturing Aletta, crying out from her crib for her mother, Maurits came home. All he knew was that Jo had been arrested for her Resistance work, but she wasn't sure how long it would take for Dirk to fill him in on the rest.

She heard him dig into the potatoes she'd left on the counter. Then he came into the bathroom. "Hello, darling." He came over and placed a hand on her arm while he leaned down to kiss her. "You're freezing." He dipped a finger into the bathwater and gave her a perplexed look. "And no wonder. How long have you been sitting here?"

He picked the towel off the floor beside her and handed it to her. She sighed and climbed out of the bath.

"I'm sorry about your sister," he said, "truly, I am. Rotten luck. But that's what happens when you try to outsmart the Germans. Nothing gets past them."

She tried to read him, but there didn't seem to be any deeper meaning buried in what he said aside from a sincere attempt at sympathy. "Can't you help her somehow, maybe ask your friends for a favor?"

"The SD has her. You know that's out of our reach." He patted her head the way one might pat a dog before returning to the kitchen for his dinner leftovers. She toweled off, boggled by the strange nature of her marriage, how she could resent him and depend on him in the same breath.

She got dressed and went into the sitting room. Maurits had the radio on, some program that was nothing but propaganda, proclaiming all things glorious about the Third Reich. He patted the armrest of his chair. "Come here. You look like you could use some cheering up."

Liesbeth searched for an excuse. It was far too early to retire to bed, but she had no desire to join him, listening to his hollow promises about her sister's well-being. He could call the Nazis sophisticated, call them civil, but she was certain Jo would have to fight to stay afloat.

"I'm quite tired." She turned down the volume on the radio and moved to close the drapes.

"Look, forgive me for what I said earlier. Regardless of what she was doing with the Resistance, I would never wish something like this on your sister. I hope you know that."

Liesbeth yanked the drape with more force than she'd intended. But as she drew it toward the center of the window, a movement on the street below caught her attention. A man was approaching the door to their building, and when he saw the drapes shift, he looked up. Dirk. She cursed under her breath. But was he coming to see her or her husband? She whipped around. Maurits took a cigarette from his cigarette case. Was he expecting company? Was he setting her up for this?

"What are your plans for the rest of the evening?" she asked, praying the doorbell wouldn't ring.

He smiled. "Are you suggesting something?"

So that was a no to Dirk's visit. She thought quickly. "I'm feeling a little light-headed. I'm going to take a stroll around the block."

Before he could ask more questions she put on her shoes and left. She raced downstairs and went outside. On seeing her, Dirk perked up and tried to say something, but she motioned for him to be quiet and follow her down the street. The sound of his footsteps beside her grated at her, every step reminding her of what she'd done.

When they rounded the corner, she stopped to face him. His tie was loose and mustard stained, and she saw how sloppy he looked, how little care he took, even of himself. She thought of the disarray in his house, the assortment of trinkets, the menorah, the necklace. He'd called himself a collector, but whose stolen property had he crammed into that house—whose heirlooms and precious memories?

"I needed to see you," he said. "I owe you an apology. And the truth." His eyebrow was raised in its permanent arch, so this looked more like a question, like he didn't mean this.

"You owe me a lot more than that."

"I'm sorry. I had to protect myself."

"From whom? Toddlers? The elderly? A singer?" She took a step back and glared at him. "I thought you were like me, that we understood each other, but I've never been so ashamed of myself as I am now."

"Let me explain." He reached out to touch her but she jerked away.

"No, this is it. You stay away, leave me and my family alone! If you don't, someone will come after you. I'll make sure of that."

Liesbeth left him there, alone in the middle of the sidewalk. She turned and walked home, her head held high. But inside, she was crumbling. She couldn't hold on much longer.

The following evening, she sat staring at the brown glass bottle on her dressing table. Maurits had yet to notice that it was missing from the pharmacy, or if he had, he hadn't thought to look for it at home. She circled both hands around the glass of liquor she was holding and took a swig, sputtering at the taste. She'd poured it from a bottle hidden in Maurits's desk drawer, but it tasted horrible, more moonshine than *jenever*.

Picking up the brown bottle, she tilted it sideways so that a few drops of the solution spilled into her drink. Knockout drops, Maurits had called them. Potentially lethal when diluted in alcohol. She poured some more. Her sister appeared like an apparition in front of her: Jo in handcuffs, a look of contempt. Jo, alone in a dark, dingy cell. Then Liesbeth saw her brother and *tante* Rika and *oom* Cor, the hatred they would feel if they found out she had provoked Jo's arrest. She reached for another capsule and then another. It would take a lot to bring her down from the Pervitin, which had long since stopped boosting her mood, to bring her down where she belonged. What kind of cruel, warped person would betray her own sister?

The doorbell rang. A full minute passed before she reacted. She sat there, staring at the brown bottle, wondering how quickly the solution would work, if death would hurt. The doorbell rang again and then again. Someone was shouting from the road. She got up and answered the door.

Willem stood outside, holding his hat to his head against the wind. "Finally," he said, hurrying up the stairs. "Is Maurits home?"

"What's wrong?" Immediately, she feared for Jo's safety. But Willem refused to say anything until they made it upstairs into her apartment. Inside, he set his hat down on the kitchen table. His hair was plastered flat with sweat and his movements were twitchy, anxious.

Liesbeth grabbed his arm, forcing him to look at her. "What's happened?"

"They came for Aletta," he said, his voice choked.

"What are you talking about?" They already had Johanna; what did they want with her child? She stared at him in disbelief. But when she saw the desperation and fear in his eyes, she understood; the answers had been there all along.

"She's not our child, not really," he said. "She's Jewish. We took her in after Jo had a miscarriage."

Liesbeth was surprised by her calmness, how acknowledging this felt more like a relief, like Jo had let her in somehow. But then the direness of the situation hit her, and she had to grip the kitchen chair to keep herself steady. "Where did they take her?"

Willem paced back and forth, shaking his head. "I don't know; I came here from the police station. They wouldn't tell me anything." He paused. "They've been taking Jews to the Hollandsche Schouwburg to await deportation, but surely they wouldn't deport a baby, not all alone."

Liesbeth shuddered, unable to bear the idea of her beloved niece alone at the hands of those horrible men. Men like Dirk. "We need to find out more. Don't your contacts in the Resistance know anything?"

"A lot of them have been arrested. I've asked one of the cell leaders, Piet, to ask around, but who knows how long it will take before we can locate her."

"We can't afford to wait around for an answer."

"No, we can't. If the rumors are correct, the Nazis are preparing for one more big purge, before they declare the city *Judenrein*."

Hearing it now, that word hit her in a way it hadn't when she'd first seen it in Maurits's NSB newsletters. *Judenrein*—cleansed of Jews. For the first time in days, her head felt clear, free of fog. But that bottle of chloral hydrate still sat waiting on the other side of the kitchen wall. She pictured Aletta, her dimpled laugh. Blood or not, her niece was the closest thing she had to a daughter.

She gestured for Willem to join her at the table. "Tell me everything you can about the deportations, about how you've been trying to stop them." He hesitated and she saw herself from his perspective: his sister-in-law, married to a traitor. His sister-in-law, who attended NSB dinner parties. Maybe he knew more; maybe Johanna had told him about the affair and he sensed her role in Jo's arrest.

What right did she have to help; why had he come to her? The draw of the concoction in the bedroom returned; she had a way out, a way to free herself from the guilt. She fiddled with the sleeve of her blouse before placing her hand over his. "You can trust me."

"I know." He looked like he wanted to say something else, and she braced herself for an accusation. Instead, he began to tell her about the *zwarte avonden*, about Jo and Jakob's work to organize the concerts and help coordinate hiding places for the Jewish artists and their families. "I'm not sure how she wound up in trouble with this man who had her arrested. Whatever happened, she acted completely on her own." He paused. "Last I heard, she wanted to talk to you about Maurits."

Liesbeth swallowed. "She did. And I told her that Maurits is busy with his Pervitin and nothing else. I'm certain about that."

She knew she should share the full truth, but she worried that if she did, he would no longer trust her to help find Aletta. And that was most important of all. The truth would have to wait.

"I hope you're right," Willem said. He asked her for a notepad and a pen. "I remember something else that may be relevant. There's a nursery near the theater."

"A nursery. So they're keeping children separate from their parents?"

"Possibly. I cycle past it on my way to the zoo."

"We need a way to find out for sure," she said, "and a credible cover story to get inside."

Willem fidgeted, unable to sit still. "We can't be too hasty. One mistake and our efforts will be in vain."

"Just as we can't afford to wait," Liesbeth said. She tried to comprehend the danger of what she was suggesting, but her desperation to get Aletta back outweighed everything else. They sat together for over an hour, puzzling out the possibilities, and by the time Willem stood up to go, Liesbeth found herself sketching a map, giving instructions, taking charge.

After he left, she retired to her bedroom, her head filled with questions and ideas. As Liesbeth got ready for bed, her eyes fell on the dressing table, at the bottle of chloral hydrate. She poured her drink down the sink and tucked the brown bottle deep into the drawer with her undergarments. Should she ever need it, the knockout drops would be there, waiting.

They had the poor luck that the next day was a Sunday, when most of Amsterdam lurched to a standstill. Aside from the people congregating at the entrances of the churches, the streets were almost deserted, as were the tram stops, the cafés, anywhere that might offer Liesbeth the opportunity to blend in while she staked out the Jewish nursery.

She stood at the address Willem had given her, the tram stop on the Plantage Middenlaan, up the street from Artis Zoo. On her left was the Hollandsche Schouwburg, the theater with its grand, neoclassical facade. The Nazis called it the "Joodsche" Schouwburg, to remind everyone that it was a theater for Jews, and only Jews, but now the building served a grimmer purpose.

Liesbeth peered up at the theater's elegant columns and nude sculptures and then down at the SS man guarding the entrance. Inside, dozens of people camped out in days-old clothing, fearing for their children and contemplating their fate. On the opposite side of the street stood the nursery. It, too, was an imposing building, framed by stained-glass arched windows and topped with a Star of David. She'd passed these buildings countless times, without ever stopping to consider their purpose.

She tried to make herself inconspicuous—a task that shouldn't have been difficult, given that she'd spent her whole life taking up little space—but she didn't know how to loiter without making it obvious.

Twenty minutes passed without any sign of activity at the nursery. Liesbeth walked farther down the road, trying to appear engrossed in her book. Now and then, she sneaked glances at the guard outside the theater, but he didn't pay her any mind.

When a door eventually opened, it wasn't the grand double doors of the nursery's main entrance, but a side entrance that had slipped Liesbeth's notice. Two young Jewish nurses came outside. Willem had told her the nursery staff was Jewish, that the job spared a handful of young women from deportation, at least for now. They both wore a white pinafore and blue dress with white short-sleeved cuffs, a neat white cap over their hair. While they walked down the road, Liesbeth studied their uniforms, trying to memorize every detail. If she could replicate the uniform, maybe she could sneak into the nursery undetected. However, where would she find all the fabric?

After leaving the nursery, Liesbeth met with Willem, who'd done some sleuthing of his own. He had good reason to believe Aletta was being kept in the nursery. The transports left the theater for transit camps three nights per week, so Aletta could be shipped off with the detainees at any time. Worse, the Nazis had recently deported the director of the nursery, as well as some of the Jewish nursery staff, so there was no telling whom they could still trust.

"We have to do this on our own," he said. "And we must act fast."

Back at home, Liesbeth emptied out her sewing cabinet: tissue paper for sizing out the pattern, her measuring tapes, and all the fabric she'd saved for an emergency. She set to work with her pencil and ruler, and before long, she had sketched out a rough pattern for the various pieces of the uniform.

Unfortunately, the scraps of white fabric she had wouldn't fit a pinafore, and she didn't have anything blue. If only it were as easy as dropping by the nearest fabric shop and buying a bolt. She thought back to the christening gown she'd made for Aletta, the soft parachute silk slipping through her fingers while she sewed, how angelic her niece had looked on the changing table, folds of white fabric flowing around her in a long train.

Looking back, Liesbeth found it funny that Jo had arranged a baptism—all part of the big ruse. After the service was over, everyone had returned to the family house for lunch and *tante* Rika had pulled out her finest linens and they'd sat around the table laughing and talking as if the war was raging on Jupiter instead of the battlefields and airspace around them.

Table linens, that would do the trick. Liesbeth opened her hope chest, retrieving a white tablecloth they used at Christmas and Easter. Perfect. She still had to come up with something for the dress, however, that particular shade of blue. And where on earth would she find that?

THIRTY-FOUR

Johanna Vos
September 12, 1943
Amsterdam, the Netherlands

The prison cell was cold and bare. I sat on the stool next to the bucket I was supposed to use to relieve myself and curled into a ball. I'd never felt so small, so useless. For days, I'd replayed the events leading to my arrest, examining every detail, trying to figure out where I'd gone wrong. Each pathway inevitably led to my sister, my personal Judas.

Now, I was too weary to think back on it all. All I could see was Aletta. Would she be confused when her mother wasn't there to feed her, to rock her to sleep? Would she notice?

From what I'd gathered, they were holding me at the Weteringschans detention center in the middle of Amsterdam. It was strange to think that Willem might pass by the building on his way to work. Sometimes I swore I felt his presence on the other side of the thick concrete walls.

I tried to imagine all of us together, the whole family in Zierikzee, celebrating the end of the war. Aletta bouncing on *oom* Cor's lap, Gerrit climbing onto a chair to make a wisecrack, Liesbeth sketching the scene from the shade of the magnolia tree. No matter how much I wanted it to be real, there would never be a celebration like that again, so happy, so careless. There couldn't be. Unless there was some other explanation for why Dirk had known to expect me, my own sister had betrayed me, had chosen that vile leech of a man over her own kin. Just thinking about it left a bitter tang in my mouth.

Someone approached in the corridor: loud, booted footsteps, like all the guards. You could tell when they had a prisoner with them because some footsteps were softer, resigned to whatever fate awaited them: a concentration camp, a firing squad. Sometimes, the prisoners were dragged back to their cells kicking and wailing. More often, they were dragged because they could no longer stand.

I watched the entrance to my cell, wondering if it would open, but the footsteps passed. Names and dates were scratched into the heavy iron door, other Resistance fighters who had suffered before me.

Harmina Janssen, March '43.
Greetje van Lier, weeks 卌 卌 |
June '43. Truus Cox—I will get you, traitor, if it takes the rest of my life.

Who had betrayed Truus? And where was she now: in another, grimmer cell, or rotting in a shallow grave in the sand dunes? Was it noble to be here, one of many who had risked their lives for a cause? Or was it all in vain?

I recalled that afternoon at the zoo, when Willem had taken my hands and begged me to step back from the Resistance. Now I saw that it had been reckless to ignore him, to put everything else before family.

Lies had told Dirk to expect me—I could assume that much—but what about Ida? I couldn't bear the idea that what Dirk had implied was true—that Ida was playing informant. Maybe the De Graafs had revealed Aletta's hiding place when they were interrogated, but then the Gestapo would have come after her months ago. Still, it was easier than accepting the alternative, that what Dirk had said was true, that Ida had given up countless people in hiding, including Aletta. What would possess her to do that?

That night, I woke to a commotion in the corridor. The cell next to mine clanged open and the guard roused the prisoner inside. "Tomorrow is judgment day for the rest of your crew. You have five minutes—say your goodbyes."

There was a shuffling in the hall and a yelp, like a hound who'd been kicked, followed by muffled, teary goodbyes. *"Ik hou van je, sterkte!"* I love you, stay strong.

When the door clanged shut, I lay back on my cot and stared into the abyss, that phrase circling my thoughts. I stayed like that for the rest of the night.

THIRTY-FIVE

Liesbeth de Wit
September 14, 1943
Amsterdam, the Netherlands

Liesbeth and Willem stood by the tram stop on the Plantage Middenlaan, watching the early-morning traffic. "Here comes another one," Willem said, gesturing to the oncoming tram and then to his pocket watch. "It's a small window, but that grants us more chances if something goes wrong."

They pretended to be absorbed in conversation and watched from a distance while the tram lurched to a stop. As they'd hoped, it blocked the view of the Jewish nursery. Passengers filed out and then on, and a bell clanged when the tram switched back into gear and carried on down the track.

"Remember," Willem said, "I'll be there for a diversion should you need one."

The theater guard stared straight ahead, like a gargoyle that might spring to life at any minute. Only his finger moved, while he rubbed the trigger of his gun, back and forth, back and forth.

"Thank you," Willem said. "Thank you for doing this." In

the past few days, his face had sunk inward. She wondered if he had faith in her ability to find Aletta and get her out safely.

"You're doing everything you can," she said, as calmly as she could. If only she'd decided to take a Pervitin that morning, something to give her that boost she was trying so hard to fake. They walked farther out of sight, and she removed her coat to reveal the uniform she'd hastily sewn, with the yellow star pinned at her breast. She'd managed to get some light blue fabric through the editorial staff at *Libelle*. The shade was slightly off and it wasn't cotton, but she had to make do. Still, the matter of the blue fabric had cost them a day, a delay that could mean everything for Aletta's safety. Willem had monitored the comings and goings at the theater, and as far as he knew, no transports had left, but neither of them could be sure.

She kissed Willem on the cheek, raised her chin to bolster her confidence, and set off across the road with her big, quilted carpetbag. Before the war, the strip of sidewalk in front of the nursery must have been crowded with mothers filing in and out to drop off their children on the way to work. Now the nursery felt like a prison looming in front of her.

She opened the main set of doors and entered a small vestibule, remembering only then that the nurses had used the side entrance. A noise came from inside the nursery. It sounded like someone rustling through papers, tossing open drawers, sounds that brought her back to that night in Zierikzee, when the Gestapo had turned the bedroom upside down in pursuit of her brother. Her nerves picked up, thrumming inside her, urging her to turn back while she had a chance. But when the noise subsided, she forced herself to push through the second set of doors. She hurried forward, past the office to her right, giving the person inside no time to register her face.

Farther down the corridor, she tried opening a couple of doors, but they led to a kitchen and a laundry room with washing vats that reeked of soiled diapers. The sound of laughter brought her up the stairs to a large, sunny room where children sat drawing at several tables. These children looked four and older. One of them waved a hand to ask her a question. "How long until lunchtime?"

"Well," Liesbeth said, "not much longer. Once you've finished your drawings."

"Who are you?"

Liesbeth spun around. A nurse stood in the corner of the room, holding a little girl by the hand.

"Well? What are you doing here?"

Liesbeth chose her words carefully. Hopefully this Jewish nurse would understand, unless she feared for her job, her own safety. "I'm looking for my niece."

"Your niece?"

"My sister's been arrested. She was doing everything she could to help."

The nurse studied her, frowning. Then, she let go of the girl's hand and beckoned for Liesbeth to follow her to the corner, where they were out of earshot of the children. "Your niece is Jewish?"

Liesbeth held up a photograph to show the nurse, one of her and Aletta playing in the park, and told her, in as few words as possible, what had happened. The nurse glanced at it and grabbed Liesbeth by the elbow, leading her back down the stairs.

"What are you doing?" Liesbeth asked. "Please, I need to know if she's here."

"Keep your eyes low," the nurse whispered. She didn't say anything else until they entered some sort of waiting room on the main floor with the door shut behind them. "I don't know what you expected, breezing in here with this outfit. But everyone here knows everyone else. You're lucky I'm the one you ran into."

"Can you help me? Have you seen Aletta?"

"I'm not sure. If she's here, she'll be in the front room, beside the main entrance. But it's too risky to go there right now. You saw the SS officer?"

"He was searching for something, turning the room on its head."

"That's the director's office," the nurse said. "Well, was. Who knows what he hopes to find, but we're not dumb enough to keep the records of our efforts in there."

"You mean?"

"You can't look for your niece now. I have my suspicions about the girl who is supervising the nursery. Come back at three o'clock. I'll see what I can do."

"And if they come for Aletta?"

The sound of boots echoed down the corridor. The nurse put a finger to her lips and pushed Liesbeth toward another door. "Go!"

Liesbeth did as she was told, emerging in a narrow passageway that opened to the street—the side entrance. When she stepped back outside, she could hardly face Willem. He stood at the tram stop in the middle of the road, pacing back and forth. He turned to her, fixating on the carpetbag. She shook her head, and his shoulders sagged. She was apologizing before she reached him, the words spilling out with choked emotion. She had let him down and failed Johanna once again.

"I'm sorry," she said, "bad timing."

"Not here," he said, hushing her. She winced. Everything she did felt like a misstep, a lapse in judgment.

Willem passed over her coat and took her hand as if they were a couple, leading her away from the theater toward the zoo. He raised a hand in greeting to the ticket booth attendant, who let the two of them pass through the gates. "This way," he said. They followed the lane lined with lime trees toward a small garden and found a bench between the manicured hedges where nobody could hear them. "What happened?" he asked.

She told him everything, trawling her memory for every detail. As she spoke, the gravity of her situation hit her, and she began to question their chances. The notion of going back in there felt daunting.

"No," he said, "this is promising. If only we had a guarantee that she was in there."

"Nothing is certain. Maybe it's too dangerous to return—for all we know, it could be a trap."

Willem winced, and she felt the blow of her words, how he took it as an admission of defeat, of giving up on Aletta. And after all, hadn't she let her own sister walk straight into a trap?

"I didn't mean it like that," she said.

"Did anyone else see your face?" he asked.

He looked at her impatiently. Much as she wanted to give him the assurance he needed, the promise that they could fix this, she felt her strength dissolving. She had let Jo down once, and now a second time. What was to say it wouldn't happen again? If she closed her eyes, she saw Dirk showing off his film projector, the clip of the Jewish family at the beach looping over and over.

Liesbeth stared at the hem of her skirt. "I told him," she said.

"What?"

"I didn't think it through. I had to warn him. I was afraid, nervous of what would happen. I know that's no excuse, but I feel horrible."

"Who? What are talking about?"

"Dirk. A man I was having an affair with."

Willem flinched and leaned back to study her. "What are you saying?"

Everything tumbled out, the lies she'd been living with, the guilt she'd been trying to stuff down out of sight. She told him about the arguments with Maurits and her affair. She told him about Jo's determination to uncover the truth, about her own selfish feelings for Dirk, her dread that Maurits would find out what she'd done.

"I'm sorry," Liesbeth said, her voice crumpling. "I wish I could take it all back."

Willem sat still, focused on some spot in the dirt. The noise of squawking birds and the shrieks of the monkeys and lemurs filled the unbearable silence between them. He let out a heavy sigh. "Johanna's heart is in the right place," he said, "but she often acts before she thinks. We all do sometimes, don't we?"

Liesbeth nodded, but his dejected tone filled her with shame.

"This time, we think before we act." He paused. "Are you still prepared to help me?"

She thought of Aletta, crying in a crib somewhere in that imposing building. She thought of her sister, locked in a cell where she couldn't see the sky. It was up to her to feign some confidence and pull herself together, for Willem's sake.

"I am."

"Good. Then we will try at three o'clock. And we'll just have to hope for the best."

A few hours later, they returned to the same spot between the theater and the nursery, waiting for a tram to show up. "You'll find her," Willem said. "I have faith in you."

Liesbeth nodded, but the rush of nerves came back to her. "I'll find her," she repeated. When the tram arrived, she adjusted the cap of her uniform and crossed the street, veering off toward the side entrance. *You can do this*, she told herself, locking Aletta's cherub face in her thoughts. This was no different than the times she'd gone to pick up Aletta from her sister's; Aletta would be there waiting, giggling and kicking her tiny feet.

She headed through the covered passageway and opened the interior door a crack, only to spot a nurse standing at the far end of the waiting room. Liesbeth faltered, but the sound of playing children came echoing toward her. She clenched a fistful of her skirt, her nails digging into her skin. When the nurse had disappeared, she pushed open the door and entered the building, with what she hoped was a confident stride.

She worked her way through the maze of rooms, trying to reorientate herself. The laughter and teasing shouts to the right suggested the older children, the ones she'd seen upstairs earlier. The nurse had told her to go left, hadn't she? Or was it right? She paused, listening until she picked up another sound: the faint wail of a baby.

She followed the sound down the corridor to the left, toward the main entrance. She stopped and listened before carrying on, entering the room opposite the office. Inside were rows of wicker bassinets and several cribs with babies and toddlers—some sleeping soundly, others grabbing at the bars of the cribs. In the center of the room was a baby girl with tousled brown curls: Aletta. The nurse from earlier approached from the far end of the room, gesturing toward the middle crib. "This is her, isn't it?"

"Aletta," Liesbeth said, unable to contain her relief. Aletta grew animated, squealing and flapping her legs. Then the heavy footsteps returned. Liesbeth stiffened, afraid to make a sound.

"Quick," the nurse said, motioning toward a side door, "in here."

Liesbeth slipped into the broom closet, closing the door behind her. She stood still, trying to quell the panicked breaths rising in her chest. The footsteps entered the room. Two people.

"As you can see," a female voice said, "we're down to half the babies we had last Wednesday."

A man: "Good, we'll ship the last of them out in the next week. By Rosh Hashanah, the whole city will be *Judenrein*."

Liesbeth bit her tongue, furious. Hearing Maurits and his friends regurgitate Nazi propaganda was one thing, but it felt far worse to imagine those innocent babies loaded up onto a train headed to Poland. She clutched the carpetbag to her chest and struggled to stay still, desperate to burst out and scoop Aletta into the safety of her arms.

The voices faded as the tour carried on down the corridor, but Liesbeth didn't budge until the closet door swung open in front of her.

"Take her," the nurse said, "now. We try to smuggle out as many as we can, but some parents cling to the hope that their children would be better off staying with their mothers as they make their way to the camps."

Liesbeth rushed toward Aletta. "I'm here, sweetheart, I'm here," she murmured, pressing her lips to her niece's forehead.

"Hurry out the way you came," the nurse said. Together, they opened the clasp of the carpetbag and tucked Aletta inside. The nurse grabbed a bottle of milk and wiggled it into position, until Aletta took to it. "Be quiet, little one."

Liesbeth thanked her. She hurried out of the room, almost bumping straight into the SS man as he headed into the director's office.

"*Guten Tag,*" he said, looking her up and down.

Liesbeth returned his German greeting. She tried to hold the bag straight, conscious that any shift in her weight might startle Aletta. A foot kicked the corner of the bag. She prayed Aletta would be quiet.

"You work here? I didn't see you on my tour."

"I was taking stock of our supplies. I need to go out to pick up some extra—nappies." She raised her voice to distract from any noise coming from the bag.

"To pick up what?"

She must have used the wrong German word. She listened, trying to judge if the tram was near. Every second wasted with this man was treacherous.

"You know," she said, forcing a smile, "the things babies soil."

"Ah," he said, slapping his leg, "you mean *Windeln.*"

"Yes, that's it, *Windeln!*" She stopped, midlaugh, at the sound of the approaching tram—her window, her chance to get out.

She smiled again, as sweetly as she could manage. "I'm sorry, but I have to run. The head nurse hates when I dally."

He wished her luck, and she stepped outside as the tram screeched to a stop, blocking the view of the guard at the theater. She darted into the street and saw Willem heading toward her. He grabbed her by the elbow and guided her forward into the gaping mouth of the tram. The doors shut behind them as they crammed in between all the people. When Willem handed her her coat, a cry came from the carpetbag, a loud, single sob. Frightened, she looked up at him.

He placed a protective arm around her as they clung to the pole. The tram lurched forward, and Aletta fussed again. If any passengers understood what was going on, they gave no sign of it.

As soon as the tram stopped, the two of them got off. "Beautiful day, isn't it?" Willem said, his voice loud and clear. "A beautiful day to be alive."

Liesbeth arrived home late in the afternoon, flushed and beaming. She collapsed on the bed, her arms spread wide above her head, and let her breath rush out, all the nerves, the worries that had been ballooned up over the past few days.

Willem and Aletta were safe. For now, at least. Tucked in the rafters of the predator gallery at the zoo, sleeping above the lions and leopards. From there, Willem would still be able to conduct some of his work, and the others in hiding could lend a hand with the baby. Liesbeth recalled the feeling that had overcome her when she saw the hiding place. The shock of seeing the curious, pale faces looking back at her. People who had spent all summer hidden from the sun, trying to make do on insubstantial rations. Members of the Resistance, young men like her brother, and Jews. Women her age, young children, bundled together on wooden partitions. These people could have been her neighbors. They could have been her friends.

When it was time to leave, she'd held Aletta to her chest and whispered over and over, "I'm sorry." Sorry for what had happened to Jo, sorry for her role in it. Sorry for the hate in the world, sorry for everything.

"Don't be so hard on yourself," he'd said. "You rescued her."

Now, lying on her bed, Liesbeth felt almost giddy. "We saved her," she said to herself.

She pulled out the bottle of chloral hydrate from the back of the wardrobe and turned the bottle over, considering all the problems she'd thought it would answer. In the bathroom, she poured its contents into the toilet. When she stared at the empty bottle, she had a rush of resolve, so she scrambled around her room, checking her handbags and jacket pockets until she had collected her tubes of Pervitin. One by one, she emptied them into the toilet, watching the tablets swirl around and around until they disappeared.

"Liesbeth, darling?" Maurits stood at the edge of the bathroom, glancing from the empty containers in her hand to her outfit. "Why are you dressed like that?"

Potverdorie, she'd forgotten all about the uniform. She scrambled for an excuse, but there was no point. Besides, something inside her dared her to speak up, to tell him the truth. "Willem needed help," she said.

He frowned. "You mean you did something for the Resistance."

"Aletta was in danger."

She let the remark dangle, unwilling to fill in the details, but he didn't act surprised. Had Dirk told him about Jo's secret? Or worse, their own?

"So you put your life in danger, and mine, for what? To help Willem? For a sister who looks down on you?" Maurits pulled the tie from around his neck in one slick motion and coiled it around his hand. "Think, Liesbeth. Did you stop to think about how foolish that is? What it could do to our reputations, to everything we've been trying to build here? Or worse, our lives?"

"You pandered to the Resistance when it suited you."

"I was being strategic, not prancing around in costumed theatrics."

"Maybe I'm done toeing the centerline."

He turned and left the room. "I'm going out. Don't bother waiting up for me."

THIRTY-SIX

Johanna Vos
October 18, 1943
Camp Vught, the Netherlands

Halfway through October, I was transferred with a group of other political prisoners to a concentration camp in the south of the Netherlands. We arrived at Vught train station late in the evening and were forced to walk the long road to the camp. Blackout paper covered the windowpanes of all the houses in town, but slivers of light appeared as people lifted the corners of the paper to peek at us passing by.

We trudged onward, out of town and into the woods. My legs felt as if they'd forgotten how to walk. Others around me struggled with heavy suitcases, but I only had a single change of clothes in my possession. Trees towered on either side of us, their tangled branches stretching to reach the moon like a grandmother's age-curled hand. Stars shone in the midnight sky. I listened for the sounds of nature above our dragging steps— bats swooping through the canopy, the distant hoot of an owl. Months had passed since I'd breathed in country air. I took it all in, the coolness tingling my lungs.

The name Vught stirred up memories from childhood. My parents had brought us there for a weekend at the beach the summer before the accident. I remembered the thrill of swimming in the calm lake, so different from the sea, the water fights Pa and Lies and I had while Ma entertained Gerrit on the shore. I remembered the tall legs of the lifeguard stand, hovering over us.

This time, it was not a stretch of beach or a lifeguard stand that greeted us. The forest opened onto a wide pitch enclosed with barbed wire, and I stared up at the tall legs of the watchtower, at the rifles trained on the moat that surrounded the fence. I closed my eyes and willed back that summer's day, the picnic basket Ma had carried and the songs we'd sung while we skipped through the woods.

A guard appeared in front of us, a Dutch woman, like us. She hollered and sneered and pushed us along without any sign of shame. *"Loop door!"*

We filed into the open square and fell into rows. SS men gathered around us, ordering us to line up straighter and shut up while they took stock of us like sailors at a whorehouse. I tilted my head back to the sky. There was Andromeda, the chained lady, shining back at me. Unlike her, I would have to save myself. I thought of Willem and Aletta, and I hoped they could see her, too.

Every morning when we were marched out from the barracks to work, I looked to the sky. It kept me going while I swept the camp premises, my back bent over a broom for hours on end. A glance at the sky, at the birds overhead, at the promise of sun or rain. When I blocked out the fence and the watchtower and the sight of our blue jumpsuits, I felt free.

If there were no buildings left to clean, the guards sent us into the woods to sweep the forest floor. Anything to keep us busy. On the weekends, they pointed to a heap of sand and forced us to shovel it back and forth across the pitch, from one pile to another, from dawn until nightfall. Hours trudging back and forth in the drizzling rain, until we collapsed from exhaustion. Anything to drain our energy.

When the SS men grew bored, they announced a delousing. A little game to keep them entertained. All of us were to be inspected for lice, despite the frosty mornings and the cold that kept us awake at night. The guards placed a narrow plank across two stumps and forced us to strip one by one. I lay there on the plank, shivering and naked, as one of the SS men told me to lift up my arm. He prodded my armpit with a pencil while he searched for lice. When he moved down lower, I tried not to shudder and focused on the sharp blue of the sky above me.

Anything to break our dignity.

The trouble started with braids and a pair of scissors. If there was one thing we women at Vught hated, it was a traitor. Many of us had fought tirelessly against the Nazis and anyone who befriended them, but betrayal persisted in the camp. When the lights went out in Barrack 23B, a hand might creep out to snatch a crust of bread, a coveted fork or spoon.

In the middle of January, a German woman with a loose tongue began crossing us. She'd been imprisoned for insulting a soldier, and she made no show of hiding her view that she didn't belong in the camp, that she would succeed in getting her sentence shortened. She tried to earn our friendship, eager to make conversation. Yet, whenever one of us smuggled a potato from the peeling stations in the camp kitchen or flirted with a lover across the barbed wire of the men's camp, this woman was there, blabbing this in the guards' ears. This time, she'd snitched on some women who were due to be released, leaking their plans to link back up with the Resistance. She had violated the sanctity of trust within the barracks and did so in the light of day, with no remorse.

We had to teach this traitor a lesson. We yanked the straw

mattress from her bed, and someone threw a bucket of icy water over her. Still, she tried to deny everything, so we devised another approach. She wore her hair in two long braids that hung down her back. In the evenings, she perched on her bunk, combing out the knots and tangles, boasting that men in her village had compared her hair to spun gold. So when my bunkmate Nelly snipped that braid clean off during a factory shift, we knew this woman would feel the insult. She returned to the barrack that evening with her kerchief knotted tightly over her shorn locks, lashing out and cursing "that wretched Delilah."

I laughed despite myself, feeling only a hint of pity. Something told me she still hadn't learned her lesson. Sure enough, she reported this to the head guard, and Nelly was imprisoned in a detention cell in the bunker building.

When the rest of us heard the news, we held a heated meeting in our barrack. Nelly didn't deserve to take the fall; after all, so many of us had made teasing remarks or shunned the traitor for her brownnosing. We penned a letter to the camp commandant declaring our solidarity with Nelly. That traitor kept her distance, slinking off into the shadows outside, while around ninety of us signed the letter.

On Saturday afternoon, the fifteenth of January, we were called to roll call in the square—everyone who had signed the letter. One of the guards, a Dutch woman we called the Hyena, grumbled at us. "*Godverdomme*, hurry up and get in line." She was missing her day off because of us, her visit with her son.

It was barely above freezing, and we shivered in our rows while we waited to find out what was happening. She ordered us to march toward the bunker. Most of us were giggling, taking it in like schoolgirls awaiting detention.

The Hyena turned to snap at us. "You won't be laughing soon enough."

I looked at the woman next to me, pleased by the way we'd ruined the guard's day off. Here we thought we were standing our ground. We thought we'd gotten our message across. It wasn't like they could lock all of us up forever; they simply didn't have the space.

When we arrived at the "bunker," the new prison block they were constructing, we were told to go to the bathroom. We milled about, trying to guess what the guards had planned. The commandant showed up with more guards. They opened the door to Cell 115. One of the guards grabbed my wrist, pushing me and five others into the cell. It was a small room with a tiled floor and a stripe of grayish paint encircling the walls. High up near the ceiling was a narrow window that had been boarded up so no light came in.

"Get in," the Hyena said, driving another five women toward us. We crowded together. Then, Nelly was there, shoved in beside us. She stumbled and fell into my arms. We hugged. "We couldn't let you take all the credit for snatching her braid," I joked, but I cut myself short as more prisoners came tumbling toward us.

The cell was no more than three meters across on each side. Twenty women crowded inside. "There's no more room," I called, but the Hyena looked at me and laughed.

Twenty women, then forty. Then fifty. We packed together like tinned herring. Nelly also called out in protest, but the commandant gestured for more. More, more. We tried to claim our space, pushing toward the doorway, but one of the guards climbed up onto a bench, peered into the back of the cell, and ordered us to squish farther back. I couldn't see the guards anymore.

"That's enough," the commandant said, and the guards heaved their weight against the door to force it shut.

Seventy-four of us in nine square meters.

The moment the cell shut, voices picked up all around me, shouting. "Come back!"

"Help us!"

"We can't stay like this!"

The cell next to us clanged shut as they locked up the remaining women. "Settle down, you mutinous whores," the commandant yelled, "or I'll get out the fire hose!"

The footsteps receded and we were alone in the dark, left there to panic. I was boxed in. Skin on skin on skin. The hair of the women next to me pressed up against my nose. Already, the heat was rising. We were stuck. We couldn't move; we couldn't even sit down.

"What are we going to do?" someone asked.

"We could die in here!"

The noise grew dizzying as everyone shouted, clamoring for help. At first, some of the women tried to reason with the others, to soothe them. "They'll come back in an hour. They're trying to break our resolve."

But no one came. The hours passed. I grew light-headed. My limbs shook. I was thirsty, so thirsty. Around me, women wept, they prayed, they wailed. The noise of fear rose up like some Satanic symphony, reaching crescendos before crashing into silence. The cell became muggy, the heat stifling. Around me, limbs wriggled free of uniforms until we all stood naked, sweat against sweat.

The woman to my left began to waver. Her head rocked forward and she began to pass out, her body lodged between ours. "Sleep," she mumbled, but Nelly and I grabbed her by the shoulder.

"You can lean on me," I said, "but you need to stay alert."

The thirst became unbearable. The women next to the walls began to lick the condensation that was beading on the cement. Anything to quench the thirst, to still those demons in our heads. The chaos carried on into the night, swelling up whenever one woman's panic set off another's. The air felt thinner by the hour.

"Stop it!" I called into the noise. "We must preserve oxygen. Stop shouting. Be quiet."

For a few seconds, people listened, but then the noise picked up again. "'Even though I walk through the valley of the shadow of death, I will fear no evil.'" Someone led the room in prayer, but I refused to join in. I counted low, shallow breaths, trying to let my energy sap out slowly, drop by drop. I thought of Willem and Aletta and tried to grasp hold of a memory. A stroll through the zoo, Aletta beaming with curiosity at the seals' splashing tails, the breeze ruffling Wim's hair as he threw back his head in laughter.

Breathe. Slowly. In: one, two, three, four. And out.

None of us slept a wink. The noise subsided in the middle of the night, but the cries never ceased. The air grew foul as urine trickled down our legs and some people began to vomit. A woman near me started raving, muttering like she was in a trance. Someone else cried out, claiming the woman had bitten her. In the late hours, my knees gave out. I imagined the coolness of the floor tiles against my cheeks, the relief of sitting. More and more women fainted, leaving no room to stand on both feet, so I leaned on one leg and then the other.

Nelly held me fast. "There's no oxygen left down there." She was right. If I fell asleep, I wouldn't wake up. I reached for that memory once more and held on to it with all my might.

Early the next morning, the door to Cell 115 opened. The light was blinding. Everything had blurry edges. The female guards swore and recoiled at the stench. "Fuck," they said, and then they slammed the door, locking us back in.

Soon, the door reopened. The guard slapped one of the women near the entrance, yelling at us to stay put, but we tumbled out of the cell in a surge of prisoners, crouching, leaning on the walls for support, many blue in the face. When the fresh air hit me, I collapsed on my knees, unable to take another step. Behind me, I saw what had silenced the guards. In the middle of the cell, which was steamy with the heat of us, a heap of women lay motionless on the floor. Twenty, thirty women. A fly began to buzz around one of their toes. The doctors came over to carry out the bodies. Some of them, they managed to revive. Many of them, they didn't.

We tumbled out of one cell, barely clinging to life, and straight into another. A few minutes' respite, long enough to fetch water from the taps, to feel cold relief pouring down our throats, sputtering from our mouths as we struggled to take it all in. Our wooden clogs clunked against the tiled floor, but otherwise we were still.

This time, we were thrown into cells in small groups as we awaited questioning. I huddled in the corner next to four other women, trying to breathe, trying to forget.

Only there was no forgetting those bodies, lifeless on the floor. Women I'd worked and slept beside. Women who had laughed and talked dreamily of the soft scratch of their husbands' beards, the mischievous twinkle in their children's eyes as they made off with the last slice of cake. I could easily have become one of those corpses.

A hairline crack ran up along the cement wall. I imagined its path like the Maas River, snaking its way back across the map, bringing me home to Zierikzee, where Aletta and Willem and my aunt and uncle would be waiting. The sound of a dripping pipe pulled me from this fantasy. A rust-tinged puddle was collecting in the corner of the cell. I hugged my shoulders and watched the droplets gather.

Some moments, rage flowed through me. Anger at Maurits, at Liesbeth, for letting their own ambitions and indiscretions trump what was good and right. At Ida, for whatever role she'd played in helping Dirk. Other moments, that anger turned inward. I had been the one who ignored Willem, who kept taking risks, unable to step aside. My thirst for justice—or was it vengeance?—had landed me here. I'd never been there for Aletta, not in the way I should have been.

I imagined my daughters—both of them—frightened and alone. All that work: all that money we'd raised, the people it protected, and what good had it done? Families had still been arrested, sent off to camps, likely to their deaths. Despite everything I believed in, despite everything I had worked toward, I had failed the two people who meant the most to me. Even Ida, despite her treachery, had strived to protect her family.

Only one option remained. For Aletta's sake, I had to survive. The war could end any day, and my daughter needed a good, loving mother for whenever freedom came. I sat up straighter and promised myself I wouldn't stop fighting, not until I was reunited with my family. How else would I ever find a way back home?

THIRTY-SEVEN

Liesbeth de Wit
March 20, 1944
Amsterdam, the Netherlands

Liesbeth climbed into the rafters above the predator gallery at the zoo. "Hello, little butterfly," she said, spotting Aletta's beaming face between the hay-covered pallets, where several people sat reading and playing cards. Liesbeth greeted Willem and crouched down beside her niece. "What are you doing?" she asked, pointing to the bundle of unsharpened pencils at her side. "Are you having fun?"

Aletta shoved the pencils at Liesbeth, who clutched them to her chest. "For me? Why, thank you."

Aletta sneezed, once and then again.

"All this dust up here can't be good for her," Liesbeth said to Willem. She took a handkerchief from her pocket and wiped Aletta's nose.

"You'd think that, with this many idle hands, we'd manage to keep the attic clean, but all the hay makes that impossible."

The young Jewish couple lying on the nearest stacks of hay overheard this and grinned. Who would have thought they would have to trade in their canal-side house for a bed of animal feed?

Liesbeth perched on the edge of the makeshift mattress and unpacked the food she'd brought along. She'd tried to make it look appetizing, but most of the vegetables she could find were withered, the biscuits gritty and bland.

"Thank you," Willem said, "your visits have made all the difference."

Aletta tried to crawl across the mattress. She fell back onto her bottom and stretched out her arms. "Pa-pa," she said.

Liesbeth looked up in astonishment. "She's speaking!"

"For a couple of days now." He picked Aletta up and she latched on to his arm. He sighed. "Her first word should have been *mama*."

Liesbeth leaned over to squeeze Willem's shoulder. "You've done everything you can in Jo's absence. She will be forever grateful for that, both of them will."

"That may be so, but I'd give anything to take her place in that camp. It's been weeks since I've heard from her."

"She's strong. She'll push through this; I know she will."

He shoved his hands in his pockets and nodded. A few weeks earlier, Jakob's wife, Ida, had given birth to a baby boy, but the birth had left Ida weak and malnourished. Their experiences weighed on Willem, a stark reminder of everything he and Jo had endured.

"How are you managing?" she asked.

"Better now that the gray winter months are behind us," he said. "Now we can bring Aletta outside more often. You should see how big her eyes get when she spots the giraffes."

Fortunately, Willem could still work when there was no risk of encountering soldiers. Often, he tended to the animals after hours. Liesbeth dropped by to help whenever she could, but one could only visit the zoo so many times without arousing suspicion. The others hiding in the attic had been a blessing, caring for Aletta.

Liesbeth smiled, proud of Aletta's inquisitive nature. She often worried about the impact these long months in hiding would have on her niece. What she wouldn't give to be able to take Aletta out to the seaside together with Jo, to hear the squawking seagulls, to feel the salty wind against their cheeks, to watch the evening light dance across the shore while the sun dipped beneath the waves.

The Jewish couple on the next mattress put down the newspaper they had been reading. "Willem," the woman said, "didn't you say your wife was at Camp Vught? You'd better look at this."

Willem gestured for Liesbeth to sit next to him so they could read the newspaper together. She moved over and looked over his shoulder. It was a recent edition of *Trouw*, one of the most reliable Resistance publications. She scanned the headlines.

"Second page," the woman told them.

Liesbeth pointed to the article and began reading aloud. "'While we are generally opposed to the dissemination of horror stories, we must make an exception for the account of events that occurred in Camp Vught on the fifteenth of January...'"

She looked at Willem, who had fear in his eyes. They read on, the horrible night in the Vught bunker unfolding on the page before them. Ten women were dead. Others, those who had licked the condensation off the cell walls in thirst, had chemical burns on their tongues and bodies from the fresh lime coating. Countless women were still weak and struggling to recover.

"My God," Liesbeth said. A numb, tingling feeling spread across her chest as she envisioned those bodies, piled in the middle of the cell. She prayed her sister hadn't been a part of this, but something in that spark of sisterhood that bound them told her that Jo had been there, cramped and frightened in the cell with all the others.

Willem said nothing. He slumped forward, his elbows on his

knees and his head in his hands. The two of them sat there, at a loss for words. Between them, Aletta cooed and called out for Papa. Liesbeth reached for her and then put a comforting arm around Willem. "She's alive," she said, "I know she is."

Willem leaned into her embrace, shuddering with tears. She repeated this, promising him Jo was safe, and she held him and Aletta close while she summoned Jo's strength, trying to be strong and supportive, like they needed her to be.

The fifth of September should have been a Tuesday like any other: Maurits had a busy day at the pharmacy, and Liesbeth had a doctor's appointment, after which she planned to sneak in a visit to the zoo. But when they woke up that morning, she could tell something was wrong. A strange buzz filled the city streets, the hum of rumors passed balcony to balcony, from butcher to baker.

Maurits turned on the radio, but the German stations were broadcasting mundane stories about the weather, vague updates about the Wehrmacht strongholds on both fronts. When the family on the fourth floor across the street opened their window to fasten orange streamers—the color of the Dutch royals—to the balcony railings, Liesbeth told Maurits to change the station. "Put on Radio Oranje. They'll set the record straight."

He looked like she'd asked him to play football across the rooftops. "Why take a gamble? The Germans are jamming the receivers anyway."

Liesbeth got up and played with the dial, adjusting it to the frequency of the BBC, ignoring Maurits's protests. It picked up static, no matter how much she tried to play with the antenna. Another noise came from outside, the sound of cheering. Maurits let out an exasperated huff. He went into the bedroom, returning with a *moffen* sieve to filter out the German interference.

"Oh?" she said. "This is a surprise, coming from you."

Maurits fiddled with the wooden contraption until Radio Oranje came through. "Listen," he said. "It's Gerbrandy."

She leaned forward in her chair to hear the Dutch prime minister's announcement.

"Now that the Allied armies have penetrated the Dutch borders, I am convinced you will give them a warm and dignified reception, which they deserve as liberators of our country and for destroying the tyrants. The hour of liberation has struck."

"It can't be," Maurits said. He combed his fingers through his hair and got up to look outside, like he expected to see the liberators marching toward them, Union Jacks awaving.

The broadcast continued. Gerbrandy reported that the Allied troops had pushed through Antwerp and had crossed the Dutch border, arriving in Breda in the south.

"It may only be a matter of days, hours even," Liesbeth said. She joined him at the window. Somewhere, people were banging pots and pans, making a jolly ruckus.

"Look." She pointed farther down the street. Soldiers on bicycles were speeding past, heading out toward the edge of Amsterdam. A family spilled from their house, arms piled high with luggage. Liesbeth recognized the woman, the chair of the National Socialist Women's Organization. The couple loaded the suitcases into the carrier of a cargo bicycle, and with the children perched on top, they cycled off.

Maurits went very pale. "We need to evacuate," he said.

"Are you mad?"

He walked from the window to the armchair and back, playing with the clasp on his cigarette case. "Germany will be safer. We'll adapt. It's what we're best at, isn't it?"

Surely, he had to be joking. Those NSBers on the street were traitors on the run. Fleeing meant admitting guilt and no chance to return, not ever.

"Why run, Maurits? What do you have to hide?"

He hesitated but then his face grew steely. "Don't use that

tone with me. If I say we're leaving, we're leaving." He went to the bedroom and began throwing clothes into an empty suitcase. "I need to collect some things from the pharmacy, but we can stop there on the way to the station. Come, get packed."

Liesbeth thought of Amsterdam, the sight of Dutch flags hoisted back onto the flagpoles. She thought of Zierikzee, the beach stripped clean of bunkers and concrete dragon's teeth. Of her sister and Willem and Aletta, all of them free. She tightened the sash on her dressing gown and went to pour herself another cup of coffee.

"I'm not coming," she said.

"What do you mean? We don't have time to play games, Liesbeth."

"I'm not. If you want to run, that's your choice but my home is here." The confidence in her words came as a surprise; it felt good to say this, powerful.

He reddened but before he could make his retort, a plane roared overhead. They went to the window and angled their heads to look up at the sky. British planes were swooping low over the city. The fleeing German soldiers on the ground below didn't bother to glance up.

Maurits went back to packing with renewed haste. Now and then he called out to her. "I'm packing a bag for you. Come on, be reasonable!" She ignored him.

Left alone, Liesbeth was faced with the gravity of what was unfolding. Liberation, the chance for a fresh start. A day she'd waited on for four long years. A day, she now realized, her husband had dreaded. She considered what an Allied win would mean for her marriage, for her future. And what was the cost of this victory? How many innocent young men had shed blood to make it this far; how many had stumbled on the road to Breda, only to never get up? She thought of the RAF pilot dead on the beach, the sodden photo of his sweetheart in his breast pocket. How much love had been lost for her freedom?

The noise outside grew louder. Liesbeth opened her sewing box and lifted the tray of thread to retrieve something from the compartment in the bottom: a strand of orange ribbon. She tied this into her hair and got up to leave.

"Where are you going?" Maurits asked. He stuffed his watch and a wad of bills into his briefcase. She didn't have to ask where the cash had come from.

"I'm not going to hide inside all day," she said. "Goodbye, darling." She gave him a kiss, which felt cold and lifeless, a reminder of everything the two of them had thrown away.

He called after her. "As soon as the madness settles down, I'll send for you. I'll find us a beautiful home, you'll see."

Outside, Liesbeth found her way to a small square where she could blend in and no one would recognize her as the wife of "that NSB pharmacist." The square had taken on new life: women and children gathered in the center, wearing bright colors, singing and dancing to folk songs. Liesbeth joined in the circle, letting strangers spin her around and around until she became dizzy with laughter.

Several schoolboys paraded around with the German traffic signs they'd dislodged, waving them above their heads like lassos.

A constant stream of traffic blew past: soldiers with horses and wagons piled high with cabinets and boxes; NSBers with baby carriages filled with odds and ends—a mass exodus to the train stations. Liesbeth watched the wives who were following their husbands out of the city—their panicked movements, the cowardice in their eyes—and knew she'd made the right choice. She didn't want a life on the run, hiding from her family for a cause she didn't support. It wasn't clear what awaited her, but in that moment, it didn't matter.

At eight that evening, the remaining soldiers passed through the streets, ordering everyone to return home. At nine, Liesbeth was eating a slice of bread when the key scratched in the lock. She opened the door to find her husband standing in the hall with his suitcases, his wrist bandaged in a sling.

"What happened?" she asked. He looked like he'd aged five years over the course of the afternoon.

He collapsed onto a kitchen chair. "They fired at the train. Allied Spitfires. I saw women and children among the dead." His voice was thick, and his free arm hung heavily at his side. "A passenger train, they shot at a fucking passenger train!"

"Good heavens." She took Maurits's hand and pressed it to her lips. "I'm grateful you're safe," she said, which she mostly meant.

"The Resistance is laying nails on the roads out of the city. I don't see any way out, at least not tonight." He cradled his head in his hands. "I'm sorry for what I said earlier, but everything is spiraling out of control. I can't tell you how many officers have come by the pharmacy recently asking for cyanide capsules." He looked at her wearily. "If the Tommies come marching in, our world won't ever be the way it was before. You understand that, don't you?"

After she heated up some leftover soup, they sat there at the table for a very long time. Maurits stroked her wrist and told her he was sorry, that he would never leave her. His apologies went right through her. She thought of Dirk and wondered if he'd been one of the many who had taken off. She thought of the children she'd seen earlier, perched high on a stack of luggage while their parents tried to flee, and prayed they had made it out unscathed. She thought of herself and the children she hoped would one day grace her future—and she was determined to build a life they would never need to escape.

THIRTY-EIGHT

Johanna Vos
September 6, 1944
Western Germany

The air in the cattle car grew hotter by the hour, until we felt like roasts left to burn in the oven. I huddled on the floor, sandwiched between so many women that I could no longer tell whose limbs were whose. We stank of each other's sweat and filth, but I took the hands of the women next to me in the dark and tried to pretend we were somewhere else, anywhere other than on our way to Germany, running away from our Allied liberators.

"We're going on holiday," I said, "the picnic basket is packed and I've put on my favorite sundress, the one my sister sewed for my birthday, with bright blue polka dots." I squeezed Nelly's hand. "Tell me what you've packed, my dear."

A long pause followed. Around us, groans and whimpering in the sweltering, sauna-like heat. Stomachs rumbling, so loud they were like a choir. It was all too familiar. We hadn't been fed a scrap of food since they'd loaded us up—all the remaining women at Vught—and crammed us into these cattle cars. Countless hours ago, maybe days now.

"Come on, Nel," I said, "what's in your suitcase?"

"Sunglasses. A white pair with green lenses, like the Hollywood starlets wear."

A voice spoke up to my right. "Nobody wears those anymore."

Another woman started to cough, cutting her off. "Oh, don't be a spoilsport."

"Spoilsport? While I'm stuck here, my nose next to this damn bucket of shit? Trade me places and then try saying that."

"Ladies, ladies." I clapped my hands together. "Where were we? On a train, on plush seats with a lovely view of the countryside. Headed to the sun. Where?"

"Italy."

"Biarritz."

"Monaco."

"You couldn't find that on a map."

"Oh, shut your trap."

"Enough!" I said. "We've made it through so much already. Don't let them destroy us now."

The women went silent, but I knew what they were picturing. Their homes, their families, their loved ones. Everyone and everything they'd fought for, fought through to get to this. I closed my eyes and tried to see my Wim, Aletta. But then the cattle car rattled and jolted over a bend, pitching me sideways. For a second, I was back there in that tiny cell. Smothered. Gasping, my lungs tingling. Fumbling in the blackness.

Breathe, I told myself. *In and out, in and out. Deep, into the diaphragm, like you would in your vocal warm-ups. In: one, two, three, four—and out.*

I tried to anchor myself there, with Jakob and his bandmates, rehearsing for one of their shows. I hummed my scales, but the sound got lost under the rumbling of the tracks.

Nelly nudged me. "Sing something for us," she said, "something happy."

Normally, my head was full of music, but I felt empty, punctured. The notes took a long time to come to me. I started to sing, and the women around me began to laugh as they recognized the tune, a song about making the most of the hard things in life. One by one, they joined in. By the time we reached the chorus, the song had caught on on all sides, booming through the cattle car. Louder and louder, until we were belting it out at the top of our lungs.

Ravensbrück. A name that had meant nothing before the war, nothing until I'd arrived at Vught, where the rumors began to spread. Every week, new names reached our ears. Ravensbrück. Majdanek. Bergen-Belsen. Auschwitz. German names that tasted like poison on the tongue. Names synonymous with fear.

I arrived at Ravensbrück weary and brittle from the six-day journey, covered in my own filth. I knew whatever waited for me inside the women's camp would be cruel and spiteful, designed to break. When I settled in on my wooden bunk, squished between strangers—Dutch women, Polish, French, and German— my tired limbs trembled in the cold. But I forced myself to stop and take stock. After all, I had survived so far. And the trickle of strength left in my body told me I still had Wim and Aletta, too. I had to count on that to be true.

Within a few days, I was put to work in the sewing department. It sounded simple—after all, Liesbeth made it look so easy—but I soon learned how wrong I was.

At sunrise, we marched over to the workshop at the back of the camp. The noise inside was deafening: the whirr of rows and rows of sewing machines like a barrage of artillery fire. That first day, one of the guards showed me to a vacant machine and gave me cotton slippers to wear while using the pedal. Thick dust filled the hall. It creeped into my lungs and sent me into a coughing fit. I stared at the bobbin, trying to recall how to thread it. For years, I'd passed all my mending on to Liesbeth, and now I felt as useless as a tax collector in front of the machine.

One of the Dutch women next to me leaned over and showed me what to do. "Your job is to sew this trim on the collar. Be fast. They time us to the second and you don't want him to see you slipping."

"Who?"

She indicated the man who had emerged from the office. A stout man with an oblong face that seemed stretched out of shape. He pulled out his stopwatch and patrolled the aisles with a fixed scowl.

I set to work with the pieces that were handed to me down the line. We were sewing shirts for the soldiers in the Wehrmacht, preparing them for the months ahead on the battlefields, as if the Germans still hoped they could turn the war around. The first collar I botched within seconds, pressing the pedal too hard so that the needle jumped forward in a zigzag line. The woman beside me pointed to a crevice between the tables. "Quick, toss it there." She checked for the supervisor before bending over to speak in my ear. "You can't afford any more mistakes—trust me."

By the third shirt, I'd started to get the knack of it. My hands coaxed the fabric through the machine with ease, and I trimmed the stray threads only a few seconds after the next set was passed to me. I fell into a steady rhythm. I realized how little I'd valued my sister's talents. What could Lies accomplish if she had total freedom to work?

I was so preoccupied that I didn't notice the supervisor coming to stand over my shoulder. *"Du bist zu langsam,"* he said. "Hurry up!" He picked up the collar I'd finished and tugged at the seam. "Too loose," he said, holding it up for everyone to see. "Unacceptable quality."

I didn't see what happened next. It came back to me later in bits and pieces. A loud smack against my head. My nose hitting the sewing machine. Pain like forks of lightning. Drops of blood trailing crimson across the stainless steel side plate.

When the room came back into focus, he had moved on, and two half-finished shirts sat beside me, demanding my attention.

With time, my nose healed and my sewing improved. I learned to sing while I hunched over the shirts, but the drone of the machines was so overpowering that only the woman next to me could hear. Now and then she requested a song: Judy Garland, Billie Holiday, Vera Lynn. But the songs that made us smile were the ones we knew from childhood, ditties our mothers had sung while they bounced us on their hips and stirred the pots of soup on the stove, the lullabies that had rocked us to sleep.

Between songs, I kept watch for the supervisor, who seemed to grow fouler by the day. When, after our eleven-hour shifts, we failed to meet our daily quota, he would come out from his office and throw a stool or revoke our bathroom privileges or hit whichever poor woman sat within reach.

Maybe he knew the end was coming, that fate had something terrible in store for him. For every morning I told myself, *The war might end today. The war might end, and I'll go home to my family, and everything will be well.* You had to have something to believe in.

In November, I took over the sewing station of a woman who had died. We'd all seen the SS man who had yanked her out of line one evening and led her to an abandoned shed. She came back to the barracks late at night, weeping, torn and bleeding between her thighs. I'd tended her wounds as best I could, but the water was dirty. Something in her had already broken. A week later, her sewing station was empty, and I was the one left to sew on the buttons.

There was a bright spot to all of this. The supervisor was a creature of habit. When he walked down the aisles, he stopped two or three times to check the quality of the stitching. He never checked the buttons. And so, I began to reposition them, millimeters at a time, until they no longer lined up with the holes. I imagined the last line of soldiers on the Eastern Front, cursing while they fought to get dressed in the morning. Maybe they would be late for roll call. Maybe they would shiver in the cold and misfire.

Wishful thinking, maybe, but it brought a shred of cheer to those dismal days.

THIRTY-NINE

Liesbeth de Wit
September 6, 1944
Amsterdam, the Netherlands

The day after the celebrations in the streets, the truth hit like one of Göring's bombs, sending a shock wave over the country. It was all a mistake. The Allies hadn't liberated Breda; they hadn't even crossed the border. The prime minister had misspoken. And while many people still clung to the possibility that it would be a matter of days, Liesbeth understood in her gut that the occupation was far from over. She woke up the next morning with Maurits by her side, pressed into the curve of her back like nothing had happened.

Despite everything, the world around them shifted in the weeks that followed that chaotic Tuesday—Mad Tuesday, as the newspapers began to call it. Hopes grew and withered away, and all the while, Liesbeth tried to find her place amid everything. The German government moved eastward, away from The Hague and the encroaching front line, and in Amsterdam, barricades and barbed wire took over the square by their house.

Maurits tried to further pad his earnings by increasing his

dealings with the Germans. The extra money would get the two of them through the coming winter, which promised to be bitter cold. Liesbeth spent her days visiting Willem and Aletta, canning food, and mending the never-ending holes and tears in their clothing. *Libelle* magazine had stopped publishing, which she found out the day before an article was due. Everyone was bracing for some unknown horror ahead.

Meanwhile, the NSB was splintering under the weight of its uncertain future. Many of Maurits's friends had taken refuge in Germany, afraid or unwilling to show themselves back home, whatever semblance of authority they'd once had reduced to mere feathers and sequins. A letter arrived for Maurits, informing him that all members of the NSB had to assume an official function.

"Mussert is scrambling to maintain appearances," Maurits told her. He suspected he would be posted to the Landwacht, forced to guard the railway yards against the ongoing strike. It was hardly a position to be proud of, a step down the ladder. One evening, Liesbeth came home from the zoo to find her husband surrounded by sheets of paper while he wrote a letter of resignation.

"I'm renouncing my membership," he said. "The NSB is a disjointed mess, and frankly, I don't want to be part of an organization that lacks strong leadership."

"Good," she said. "You've come to your senses."

But of all the changes, one worried her to no end. In early October, the Battle of the Scheldt began along the southern coast, near Zierikzee. Earlier in the year, their aunt and uncle had moved eastward, with Gerrit concealed in the bottom of their borrowed car. He was hiding on another farm while her aunt and uncle stayed with relatives in a nearby town. But now this felt too dangerous, too close to the front line.

Liesbeth lay awake at night wondering what was happening to her childhood home, whatever was still left of it. The Germans had flooded the region to slow the Allied advance, and Liesbeth couldn't help but picture the flowers in their garden afloat, the seesaw from their childhood submerged under a meter of water.

Let this end, she thought, *let the sea come and wash this evil away.*

"Darling?"

It was late one evening in late October, and Liesbeth lay in bed, bundled beneath the covers. When she didn't reply to Maurits, he knocked again and entered the bedroom. His face was set in a grim expression. What was it: resentment, suspicion? Had Dirk admitted to their affair?

Liesbeth folded her arms across her body. "Please, I'd like to be alone."

Maurits waved a folded piece of paper at her. A telegram. "This is important."

"Who is it from?"

He sat next to her on the bed and passed it to her. She unfolded it nervously, knowing it could only be bad news. And there it was, the words cold and clear:

ATTN: Liesbeth de Wit
G in hospital. May not survive the night. Call tomorrow, 08:00.

Liesbeth let out a low, warbled cry. She read the telegram once more, willing the message to change. Maurits wrapped his arm around her, and she clung to his shoulder in heavy sobs. Her aunt and uncle wouldn't risk blowing Gerrit's cover unless the situation was dire.

"We have to go there," Liesbeth said.

"I'm sorry, but that's out of the question. It's far too dangerous. The trains aren't even running that far."

For once, she knew he was not trying to be difficult. The whole region, including her relatives' place beyond the main conflict zone, was cut off from the rest of the country. Maurits stroked her hair. "I'm sorry, I truly am. Try to get some sleep. We'll speak to them first thing. He's strong, you know he is."

Liesbeth nodded, trying to hold on to hope. Gerrit would be all right; he had to be.

By morning, Gerrit was dead. When the phone rang at the pharmacy at eight o'clock sharp, Liesbeth already felt it in her heart. She picked up the phone and heard it in the trill of her aunt's voice. He was gone, the light flickering from his eyes at dawn. Diphtheria, *tante* Rika said. For days, his condition had been worsening, but Gerrit had begged the farmer not to go for help, since the only doctor nearby was an NSBer.

When she heard this, Liesbeth slumped against the wall. How could it be true? Her sister and her brother—the only siblings she had left—both stolen from her in a single year? Was it foolish of Gerrit to refuse the doctor, or brave? She wondered what might have happened if the doctor had turned him in, and for the first time, she understood the deep hatred Johanna felt for the NSB.

"I was there, holding his hand," *tante* Rika said, between sobs. "Your uncle's company sent a car to pick us up when they heard. We got to the hospital just in time."

In time to say goodbye, something she would never be able to do. She listened to her aunt go on about funeral arrangements without absorbing any of it. She wouldn't be there, couldn't walk across the room to see her brother in the casket, to kiss him on the forehead one last time. Her aunt kept talking and talking, crying about how she was losing her loved ones one by one, worrying about Jo's well-being, lamenting the fact that they couldn't tell her the news. When it became too much to hear, Liesbeth motioned for Maurits. He took over the phone, and she ran out of the pharmacy, and all the way home.

The funeral took place that Thursday. Liesbeth didn't get dressed all day. Instead, she sat on the sitting-room floor, reading the Bible, adding Gerrit's name to her regular prayers about Johanna. She tried to convince herself he was in a better place. However, the more she read, the more the psalms and verses blurred, until they became hollow, meaningless phrases.

The day dragged by, her sadness like a vulture, circling overhead. Afterward, she relived the funeral through her *tante* Rika's many letters. They held a small wake at their relatives' house, and *tante* Rika had mentioned three times how nice it had been. She described the funeral in every detail, down to the trim on the tablecloths.

All the guests had to disinfect themselves after the funeral. *Tante* Rika had stripped the house from top to bottom, cleaning everything with vinegar to ward off any diphtheria.

And Gerrit. His body lay on display in the sitting room. *Tante* Rika wrote nothing of how he looked but Liesbeth could fill in the rest: his face gray, his neck swollen. Nothing left of his laughing, fiery spirit.

They buried him quickly, to prevent the diphtheria from lingering. There was one matter left to decide, *tante* Rika wrote. The wording on the headstone.

Oom Cor suggested, "If God so will, I know that will is love."

Liesbeth wrote back, her penmanship surer than it had been in days. "I think he'd rather something else, something more him." She paused and thought for a minute before picking up the pen again.

He is gone, but his memory lingers
In the hearts that knew his smile.

FORTY

Johanna Vos
January 3, 1945
Western Germany

No sooner had I begun to adjust to the routine at Ravensbrück was I loaded onto another cattle car and transported back across the country, this time to a prison in the west of Germany. All alone again. Perhaps the constant movement was designed to keep us from settling in and forming friendships, but it also reminded me that the Nazis were on the run, their grasp on power breaking up like canal ice under the blazing sun.

Being back in a prison felt like a small gift after the crowded bunks and terrible hygiene of the camps. But the gloom of solitude set in when I returned to my cell at night, alone and unhappy.

For weeks, one of the German guards had been watching me. She hovered around while we devoured our potatoes and then lingered near my workstation. *Frau* Kraus was a short woman, with a thick coiled bun and brows that had either been overplucked or were falling out.

One day at the beginning of January, I stood with the other

women in the exercise yard, making our daily laps. Beyond the yard was a small military airfield, with the constant noise of planes coming and going, and nearby, the men's prison. It was freezing cold. We were allowed to walk, nothing more, and so I circled the yard the way I often did my cell, thinking of the mistakes I'd made, thinking of everything I would give up to see Aletta and Wim again. We all straggled forward, forbidden to speak, although when the chance was ripe we swapped a few words: *Where are you from, do you know so-and-so?* Some women had grown weak and had to be prodded forward so they would keep moving, but others took long, assured strides, their faces raised to meet the light kiss of the January sun.

That morning, when filing out of the exercise yard, I over-heard the guards talking about us. "Striking, isn't it," *Frau* Kraus said, "how normal these ones seem. Nothing like the last batch."

The other guards mumbled in agreement. As I reported for work duty, I mulled over her remark. We Resistance women weren't their regular crowd of prisoners, women arrested for distributing a pamphlet that reported the truth about the war, or for sheltering Jews. Maybe they couldn't decide what kind of treatment we deserved. Unlike the Hyena at Vught and the sewing supervisor at Ravensbrück, these guards didn't seem like the type to sleep with *Mein Kampf* tucked under their pillows.

I spent my afternoon work duty bent over a hot iron, pressing the wrinkles from the guards' uniforms. Some of the guards had brought in their personal laundry, so I worked between heaps of long underwear and pleated skirts and dirndls with little bows, which felt far too delicate for women with bludgeons at their waists. The ironing left me exhausted and sweaty, with burn blisters on my thumbs from careless movements.

When I came across two matching wool sweaters, I paused. Someone had placed them in my ironing basket by mistake. Both were plain and gray, like they'd been issued to the guards. I ran my hands over the wool, which felt far warmer than the coarse skirt and bodice I had to wear. If I ever hoped to escape, I would need civilian clothing. I checked around. The guards were busy topping up on imitation coffee. I made sure the other women were distracted before opening an empty drawer and slipping one of the sweaters inside. My heart rate quickened. I reached for the iron and continued working, hiding my guilty face behind a cloud of steam.

After several hours, my arm ached from the repetitive movement, and I couldn't wait to get off my feet. The bell rang, summoning us for dinner. I glanced at the drawer. As I calculated my move, I heard *Frau* Kraus's heavy footsteps behind me.

"Forgetting something?" She pulled me aside as the others filed out of the room.

Prickles ran down the back of my neck. I composed myself and turned to her with a straight face. "I'm sorry?"

"The sweater."

I fumbled for a good excuse, but she continued. "It's not a sin to be cold, especially not if you're in the cell with the cracked windowpane." She opened the drawer and handed me the sweater.

I paused, unsure what to make of the gesture, and searched for some sign it was a trick. *Frau* Kraus didn't smile, but her eyes told another story through a flicker of understanding.

"Thank you."

"Go on, now. You'll be late for dinner."

I hurried to catch up with the others, wondering all the way if I hadn't been too quick to judge. Perhaps things weren't as black-and-white as I wanted them to be.

Frau Kraus's small acts of kindness did not end there. One evening, I returned to my cell to find a pair of thick tights. Another time, I entered the laundry room and discovered an old newspaper folded at the top of the trash bin with headlines about the Allied advance in the Netherlands. Together with the other prisoners, I pored over the articles, trying to see through the propaganda. At the news of the terrible famine that was sweeping the frostbitten fields, we wept. At the news that Canadian troops had arrived in numerous Dutch villages, we squealed like schoolgirls. It would be a matter of weeks before the whole country was free.

Meanwhile, more and more alarm bells disrupted our nights. Air raids, Allied planes flying overhead. At the whine of the alarm, the guards unlocked our cells, and we all filed down into the basement cellar, where we crouched in rows, equipped with buckets of sand to douse any sudden flames.

Each time that siren went off, I was transported back to that night in Amsterdam, clinging to Wim as we waited in fear. How long ago that felt. I missed the reassuring weight of his arm around me and wished I was there to comfort Aletta in the dark nights.

For several weeks, I watched *Frau* Kraus with the same scrutiny she watched me. I wasn't sure if I could trust her—a total stranger, an enemy—but I couldn't see any other way. I refused to sit by waiting for the Allies to pry open the prison gates. There would be trials, an assessment of all the prison records. It could be another year before I saw my family. I had to take the chance.

One day, after our walking circuit of the courtyard, I held back, hoping to snatch a moment with *Frau* Kraus. She saw me shuffle to the back of the line and came over.

"You're going to be late for work duty," she said.

"May I ask you something?"

She nodded and motioned for me to step off to the side.

"Will you stay on here once the war ends?" I asked.

She looked across the yard, toward the fence. "I don't know. It pays well. It depends what I have to go home to."

"Is your husband off fighting somewhere?"

"He died. Stalingrad."

"I'm sorry." I tried to think of something else to say, some deeper offering of sympathy, but I was caught by the image of this woman in mourning. How easy it is to forget that grief seldom takes sides.

"I've made peace with it. It's the camps I'm more worried about." She squinted into the afternoon sun. "You've heard what they say?"

"The gassings?"

"I have someone I hope will come back to me." She gave me a sad, tender look, and I asked myself what she saw whenever she was watching me, if she saw something of that person—perhaps a woman—she was missing.

"Home has a way of calling us back." I wanted to know more, but every second was valuable. Now or never. "I was wondering if you could help me."

"With what?"

"I could use some warmer shoes. Please, a proper pair of shoes."

"You know I can't give you that," she said. She looked down the hall, where another guard had appeared. "Go on, *schnell*."

I nodded. Disappointed, I started down the hall.

Frau Kraus called after me. "No more requests!"

Even with her back turned, I caught the stifled smile in those words.

FORTY-ONE

Liesbeth de Wit
January 22, 1945
Amsterdam, the Netherlands

What a cold, a terrible, unforgiving cold. Icy winds and frosty nights and snow that wouldn't let up. It was the harshest January in Liesbeth's memory. The newspapers called it a famine, a "hunger winter."

For four winters, she had gotten by on the coattails of Maurits's inner circle. But in 1945, everything had changed. Maurits had revoked his NSB membership and, with it, his privileges. So in the early mornings, Liesbeth joined the long, winding lines outside the shops, waiting hours for meager scraps from the greengrocer, tulip bulbs, and pulpy sugar beets and potatoes that let out a steady drip of water when squeezed. On the days the milkman had anything left to offer, she came home with half a bottle of milk so thin it looked blue.

At night, they huddled next to the stove for warmth. They spoke little to save their energy and went to bed early, to avoid the hunger pangs that came late in the evenings. They spent the holidays bundled up in bed, trying to stay warm as they made do on red cabbage instead of a Christmas roast. Maurits took Pervitin to keep the hunger at bay. At times, Liesbeth stood in the bathroom, running her finger over the edge of the tube, considering the relief it could bring, but she let it be.

Across their neighborhood, the trees and the wood from the tramlines started to disappear, pried away or chopped down in the cover of night by those who dared to steal it for fuel. Maurits began tearing apart furniture—the kitchen cupboards and the sitting-room table—anything for a little firewood.

For weeks, Maurits tried to play the optimist. They were still better off than most, he said. The elderly man two doors down had died of starvation, his five-year-old grandson, too. Willem had told her stories of the people who broke into the zoo at night to snatch a pig or goat from the petting zoo. Everyone knew someone who was barely managing. Maurits would rather starve than join the crowds outside the soup kitchen, but luckily, Liesbeth always found a morsel of something or other for the table, even if it meant paying a week's salary on the black market for a loaf of bread or a handful of eggs. Willem and Aletta depended on her for food as well, but there wasn't enough for all of them. Amsterdam had been stripped bare. Aletta was growing thinner instead of bigger, and Liesbeth couldn't remember the last time she'd gone to bed with a full stomach. One day, she found herself standing in front of the stove, dropping her fashion sketches into the fire and watching the ink sizzle and spark before curling up into cinders. One sketch at a time, to keep the stove going longer. Nothing was for certain anymore. Whether Maurits would admit it or not, they needed more food.

On a cold January morning, Liesbeth got up early and packed up her best linens to barter for food. She wrapped strips of cloth around her hands to cover the holes in her gloves and put on two sweaters, each knit from scraps, old scarves she'd unraveled to combine into one colorful mess. In a note, she told Maurits what she was going to do. Better to ask forgiveness than permission.

She set off on her bicycle in the rose-gray light of dawn. It didn't take long for the icy air to seep through her layers. The rising sun drew more people into the streets. Without a way to warm the classrooms, the schools had closed, and parents sent their children out to scavenge what scraps they could. A group of scrawny boys rifled through the overflowing garbage bins. One of them scooped something yellow from the heap of mold and rot, licking the palm of his hand clean. When she cycled past, he looked up at her with big, glassy eyes. Liesbeth cringed, but her stomach still rumbled at the thought of what he might have found.

She turned onto the street that led out of the city and fell into a long line of other cyclists, all loaded with bags and baskets they hoped to turn into loaves and fishes. Hundreds of people. She chided herself for not leaving earlier. They cycled without speaking, wheels whooshing through the fresh snow. Her bike wobbled over the ice. The Germans had commandeered all the rubber, so she had to make do with wooden tires, which made a terrible racket. It was a miracle she still had the bicycle at all. At one point, a tabby cat darted across the road. Liesbeth braked, shuddering when she recalled the rumor of the people who caught pets to cook for dinner. She kept an eye on the cat until it was safely out of sight.

The ride out of Amsterdam dragged on. The icy roads glistened as the sun peeked over the horizon. Liesbeth turned her face toward those first rays, trying to eke out their warmth. Friends had warned her that it was useless to beg for food at the farms on the outskirts of the city. Tired of the endless pleas for help, the residents had long since locked their gates. She followed the long, winding train of people north.

The road grew very crowded as she caught up to everyone on foot who had set out in the middle of the night: a pair of sisters pulling a wagon, boys whose toes gaped through their shoes, mothers with babies in their arms. Everyone weary, try-

ing to brace themselves against the wind. Once or twice, someone collapsed. In shock, Liesbeth stopped but she didn't move,
watching with shame as someone else rushed over to help the
stranger to her feet.

Hours passed. Liesbeth worried about her aunt and uncle
down south. They were staying with relatives in a small town
with access to food, but she didn't know for sure how they were
faring. To keep herself distracted from worrying and from the
cold, she tried to dream up their lives after the war. The gift
of freedom, the image of her family all together, complete. A
Christmas spent, not shivering in bed, but dining together in
a house warmed with laughter. Only Gerrit wouldn't be there.
The reality came rushing back to her: her family would never
be complete.

She tried to summon happy thoughts, imagining the beautiful clothes she would make once the war was over, once there
was fabric again. Dresses for picnics, dresses for evening soirees.
She thought of opening her own seamstress shop, how wonderful that would be. She thought back to the conversation she'd
once had with Dirk. He had made her believe it was possible.
But Maurits would never approve of the idea. She was, after all,
a married woman. And what did that mean in terms of freedom?

Her legs felt leaden, her fingers numb from the cold. The sky
began to rumble as the Tommies flew overhead, the broad wings
of their planes casting shadows across the white fields. The children pointed in excitement, but when the planes ducked low,
everyone scattered, jumping into ditches. Who knew what the
Allies thought they saw from above: hungry civilians or a long
convoy of German soldiers?

After the third such scare, Liesbeth paused to survey the horizon. Up ahead in the distance was a quiet-looking farmhouse.
She cycled up the access road and rapped on the farmhouse door
until a woman answered, a woman with a deep, healthy complexion.

Liesbeth hesitated. "Please, *mevrouw*," she said at last, "can you spare any food? I've brought towels and good bedsheets to trade."

"I'm sorry, we've given everything we can."

"Please? A carrot or two?"

The woman opened the door farther, so Liesbeth could see inside. A group of ragged children crowded around the table, drinking warm milk. "You're too late. These little ones got the last of it. You can try next week."

Liesbeth nodded. By the looks of it, the children had traveled a very long way on their own. Who was she to ask for this woman's generosity?

"There's several farms down the road," the woman added, "but skip the next house. That grouch is more liable to set a trip wire for any trespassers than dole out his crops."

Liesbeth thanked her before turning back down the road. She tried farm after farm, but everyone told her she was too late. Too healthy, she assumed, based on the judgment in their eyes. Her gnawing hunger was nothing compared to what so many of these strangers had fared. Her thoughts returned to Aletta, who was almost two. If only Liesbeth could return home with enough food to soothe her cries for a little while.

The sun was high above her now. She had to hurry if she was going to make it back before curfew. Many people would find refuge in barns overnight, sleeping together in one room amid the stacks of hay. Yet word had spread of the odd farmer who demanded sexual favours in return for the hot soup and a place to sleep. No, staying the night wasn't an option. She pressed onward. One, two more houses, with long, snaking lines to the door. She left both empty-handed. And then a third. Several people were leaving the farm with bulking bags, their wagons piled high. She slipped into the lineup.

At the front gate, she sighed in dismay. Someone had scribbled a message on a sign that was fixed to the latch. "No more linens."

"No linens?" Liesbeth asked, turning to the women behind her.

The older of the two held up a pair of candlesticks. "They'll take silver."

Liesbeth lowered her head. After all this, would she return home empty-handed? She thought of Aletta, her protruding ribs, her tiny arms that should have been chubby with baby fat. The way Aletta played peek-a-boo and tried to spit out *tante* Liesbeth" in a slobbery mess of consonants. Had she ever learned to say "Ma"?

"Mevrouw?"

The farmer's wife was at the door, several crates of potatoes and carrots stacked beside her. Liesbeth shuffled forward, sheepishly pulling out her towels and bedding. "It's good cotton. I'm sorry, it's all I have."

The woman's wrinkled face folded into a frown. "I have enough sheets to sleep Moses and the Israelites, and their donkeys. So unless you have something of value, you'll have to step aside."

Liesbeth patted her pockets, trying to wish something into existence. A few guilders were all she had on her. She owned a coral necklace that would have been worth something, but that was at home. Why hadn't she thought to bring more?

She stuttered. "Perhaps I could give you some money and come back tomorrow with something else."

The woman scowled. "We don't work on charity." She looked over Liesbeth's shoulder. "Next!"

"Wait." Liesbeth tugged off her glove. "You can take my wedding ring."

The woman reached out to examine it. The second Liesbeth passed it over, she second-guessed herself. Maurits would be appalled.

"This will do." The woman pocketed the ring without so little as a smile. She began to weigh out the potatoes and carrots. Liesbeth considered asking for the ring back, getting back on her bicycle and returning with an excuse instead of food.

But the sight of those potatoes, the bright orange of the carrots, made her stomach growl, and she thought of Aletta crying in her crib. Her niece's well-being was worth a lot more than whatever was left of her marriage. The vegetables tumbled into her open bags, and she left the farm with a renewed energy, happy and light-headed with relief.

FORTY-TWO

Johanna Vos
March 24, 1945
Western Germany

Once I had a better pair of shoes, I didn't have to wait much longer. In late March, we were filing out to start our workday when a loud wail broke through the morning.

"Downstairs, ladies," *Frau* Kraus called. Before she could repeat the order, a plane engine tore low overhead. What followed was a terrible roar, a sound like the earth was splitting open. The bricks in the walls seemed to quake.

Frau Kraus glanced at the other guards, searching for direction. The noise became deafening.

"Look!" a guard shouted. The men's compound across the way had caught fire. Flames ruddied the sky.

Another explosion followed and then another, these ones closer. We threw ourselves to the floor in panic. One of the guards screamed and took off down the corridor.

I could barely feel my legs. My heart was hammering. I ran back to my cell to snatch my sweater from its spot on the mattress. Then I found *Frau* Kraus, who stood rigidly in the middle of everything. I tugged on her sleeve. "Please, do something. We can't stay here!"

She looked from me to the ring of keys at her waist and then headed toward the exit that opened up onto the main prison grounds. "Everyone," she said, "find cover!" She struggled, the key sticking in the lock, until I threw my weight against the door. It opened into thick smoke. *Frau* Kraus coughed, and I waved a hand to clear the air in front of me. The heat of the flames engulfed us. *Frau* Kraus motioned to the women.

"Come on," I yelled. "It's safer out here."

I followed *Frau* Kraus's line of sight to the manned watchtowers at the edge of the grounds. But I saw no weapons, no pointed guns. Only panic. *Frau* Kraus tore into the center of the field, waving her arms at the planes, trying to alert them to our presence.

I took off running. I listened for someone behind me, but everything blended into the noise of the planes, turning back for another pass. I ran to the edge of the complex, making a break for the fence. Nobody came. Nobody shot at me.

The fence towered high overhead. I looked back at the watchtowers. With all my strength, I hoisted myself up, scaling the posts, faltering at the top, my arms shaking. Someone fired a shot, but I threw myself over to the other side. My feet hit the dirt hard. Shouting. Another shot fired. I didn't look back. I ran and ran, until the tree line rose to meet me, and I slipped into the protection of the woods.

I kept going until the prison complex behind me disappeared in a tangle of branches. I collapsed against a tree trunk, tugging at the collar of my sweater, gasping.

The sound of the planes faded into the distance. I stopped and listened. Then I let out a laugh. Finally, freedom!

My elation abated when shouts began to fill the void left by the plane engines. It was only a matter of time before the guards recovered and came searching for me. And while *Frau* Kraus had chosen to unlock that door, I had no idea whether she would stall the manhunt or if she'd feel mad and betrayed. I took a deep breath and started running into the unknown.

The coiled tendrils of Aletta's hair, which grew darker by the day, the tinkle of her laughter, like bottled joy—my memories seemed so clear now, all the details that had slipped away during my imprisonment. I ran on, across the railway lines, dodging patrols and farmers on wagons, toward home, toward my little girl.

I headed what I hoped was westward. Twice, I reached a village but stayed far out of sight, too far to catch any place markers that would set me on course. My legs began to ache, my knee threatening to give out. I was very thirsty. I slowed to a pace that wouldn't cast suspicion. Then, I began my hunt for water.

At the edge of a farm, I found an old well. A dirty bucket dangled from a chain on the side. It was probably meant for livestock, but I hoisted up some water and drank until my throat tingled from the cold. Then, something came charging across the field. A German shepherd, barking loudly. I took off, pain shooting across my kneecap, slowing me down. The dog growled and snapped its teeth. It was closing in. I reached a small stream. An easy jump for a dog. I leaped over it, waiting for the dog's paws to hit my back. Suddenly, it halted behind me. In the distance, the keen piercing of a whistle. The dog hesitated, and I ran on until it gave up its pursuit and bounded back toward the farmhouse.

As sundown approached, the path westward grew clearer. I kept going as far as I dared, but I needed to find shelter. I cut off toward a side road, hoping it would lead to a farm. Dusk set in, and I saw a barn silhouetted against the purple-gray sky. I stood behind a tree at the edge of the property, waiting, watching. When I was sure I was alone, I crept through the shadows toward the barn.

The iron latch clanged as I tugged open the barn door. It took a minute to adjust to the dark, but the sounds of heavy breathing and rustling straw warned me I wasn't alone. It smelled like manure. Cattle.

I paused, wary of disturbing the animals. Once the shadows had taken form, I edged forward and placed a hand on one of the cows' snouts. "Here," I whispered, "you can trust me."

The cow jerked back. I whispered again, until it stepped forward to nuzzle my fingers, its nose hot and wet. I turned to survey the barn. Several bales of hay were piled up in a sort of loft. A storage cupboard stood beside the ladder that led to the loft. I opened it to find several jars of sauerkraut and a crate of onions. My stomach complained noisily. I bundled the food into the fabric of my skirt and climbed up the ladder.

In the corner of the loft, I curled up on the hay, exhausted. I'd done it. I was no longer a prisoner. I raised an imaginary glass in a toast, congratulating myself for making it so far. But a long, difficult journey lay ahead. I still had to cross the border and traverse a battle zone. One challenge at a time.

Sleep was a fickle friend, slamming doors in the passages of my mind and leaving me more fatigued than before. Dawn came too soon. When the cows began to stir, I got up and slipped outside, certain the farmer would not be far behind.

It was a beautiful spring morning, but the roads were quiet. I passed a road sign that told me I was going the right way. Once, I saw two girls, twelve or thirteen, walking down the road and asked them for directions to the border. It was several days' walk, they replied. One of them said their father was headed west toward the towns. The children were unlikely to give me away, but who knew about their father. Still, I had little choice. I followed them home and met the man, who was busy loading vats of milk onto a wagon.

As his daughters had, the milkman looked me up and down. "You're not German," he said. "I hear it in your Gs."

I stumbled on my reply, aware that lying was bound to build defenses. "That's right," I admitted. "I'm trying to return home."

The man seemed satisfied with this answer. He tugged on his beard and then offered me a crust of bread from his jacket pocket. "Here," he said, "for the ride."

The journey was bumpy, and the cold air nipped at my face more than it had while traveling by foot, but I was grateful to this stranger and his willingness to help someone he should have called an enemy. He kept to himself, but I got off at every stop and helped pour the milk into people's tins and glass bottles. He accepted my help in begrudging silence.

When we reached the center of town, I tensed up, wary of the soldiers in the streets. The milkman turned onto a quiet side road and slowed the wagon to a stop. "Best get out here." He gestured in the other direction. "That's the road you'll want."

I thanked him and carried on, keeping my head down. At the edge of town, I skirted away from a group of soldiers who were stepping out of a house of ill repute, chortling like they were still half-drunk. Morning turned to afternoon. I walked through the ache in my feet, the persistent thirst. I caught another ride, this time with a peat farmer, who brought me a few kilometers farther. Asking for a ride was one thing, but it took hours of walking to work past the shame of begging for food. When my stomach couldn't take it anymore, I approached a farmer who was dumping a pail of potato scraps into his pig pen and asked if I might have some of the peels. He looked like he was going to refuse before he turned back to the farmhouse and called to his wife, who brought out some bread with a thick slice of cheese.

By the time evening fell, I was more tired than I could ever remember. My joints ached. My jaw felt stiff from the constant teeth chattering. I couldn't feel my toes. The damp air had permeated my clothes, settling into my skin. Lost in worry, I failed to notice the automobile parked up the road until it was too late. A man in an SS uniform knelt on the road as he jacked up the rear wheel of the vehicle. He glanced up at me. "It's a cold evening to be out without a jacket."

I flailed for an excuse. "I forgot it at my cousin's. The weather was much milder when I left this morning." I articulated every word, trying to shed any traces of my accent.

He wriggled the flat tire off the wheel. "Where are you headed?"

I named a German town near the border, hoping he wouldn't push for details.

"That's quite a walk. Not something for a woman on her own, especially not at night." His words were clipped, but he kept his focus on the spare tire he was wriggling into place. "I'll tell you what. I need ten minutes to finish up and then you can come home with me." He saw me stiffen and smirked. "The widow I'm billeted with has a spare room."

I knew I had no choice in the matter. I cleared my throat and gave what I hoped came across as a grateful nod. "Thank you, Officer."

The officer kept working, humming as he switched the tire. I considered whether to offer my help, but that would mean more talking, more risk of being discovered. He picked up a wrench and said there was a blanket in the back seat if I wanted to warm up. I opened the door to retrieve it. A briefcase lay on the floor of the automobile, the glint of something metal poking out of the side. A spare Luger. I eyed it, wondering how quickly I could get it out. I saw a flash of Dirk, standing over me while the police pinned me down. Right as I extended my arm to reach for the Luger, the officer stood up.

"Find it?" He gave me a strange look, as though he'd remembered the weapon.

"Yes, thank you." I wrapped the blanket around my shoulders, leaning into its warmth.

"All done here. Come on, get in."

We drove in silence, down a picturesque, winding road. Several horses were being led from the pasture, their manes tousled in the breeze. I watched their clopping hooves, wishing I could leap from the car and ride away into the night. Instead, I was stuck with this brute, who was one step away from asking for my identity papers, from realizing I was on the run. I tried to conceive a way out, something heavy to hit him with over the head. But when I looked over, he seemed oblivious, pleasantly tired from a day's work.

He turned right, onto a long driveway toward a farmhouse with white gables.

"You like sausage?" he asked.

I looked straight ahead and bit my tongue.

"Currywurst," he added. *"Frau* Fischer makes it better than anyone I know, although she'll be cross that I didn't warn her of the extra mouth."

My stomach grumbled at the prospect of a proper meal, which I hadn't had for over a year. The officer went on about the accommodation, how the widow's husband and son had died in France, how she devoted all her spare time to baking for the German soldiers in town, how her apple strudel created lineups around the block. "The Führer couldn't ask for a more loyal citizen," he said with pride.

A light appeared as we pulled up to the farmhouse. I braced for more questions; things could take a turn at any moment. The woman who greeted us was a petite brunette, who only spoke when spoken to, but the officer talked enough for the both of them.

Frau Fischer showed me to the spare room, and I had to hide my excitement. A real bed, with clean sheets, already made up for me.

"I'll heat some water for you to wash with," *Frau* Fischer said.

"That's very kind."

The woman cocked her head. "You're not from here."

"I'm not."

The two of us stared, sizing up one another. I spoke first. "Thank you for your hospitality. And my condolences for your losses."

Frau Fischer pursed her lips. She left the room and didn't say anything more when she returned with a hand towel and a jug of steaming water. I rinsed the grime from my neck and face and removed my boots to examine my damp, bluish toes. I wrapped them in the bedsheets to warm them. While waiting to be summoned for dinner, I tried to put myself in the woman's shoes: having an SS officer billeted at your house, having to share your precious food with him and an unwashed stranger with a Dutch accent. Had it been me, would I have kept my mouth shut or would I have revealed the truth? One less mouth to feed.

Frau Fischer didn't say anything that evening, but it felt like an understanding had settled between us over the serving of potatoes and sausage when she split her own portion into two. Two women on opposite sides, both trying to survive, whatever that may take. For much of the meal we sat listening to the scrape of utensils on the porcelain, the smacking of lips. The officer remarked on the high water levels in the rivers and asked about my home, if I was married. My answers were terse but polite. "Yes, married, to a veterinarian" and "one daughter, of almost two years." I regretted sharing this, worried it might come back to hurt me. But he reached into the breast pocket of his uniform and pulled out a paper sachet. He shook the contents onto the table. Out fell a photograph and a flower, a pressed violet.

He held up the photograph, a shot of a young girl on a swing set. Her eyes twinkled, her mouth opened midlaugh. "This is Anna."

I admired the photo, recalling back to the British pilot on the beach, the snapshot he carried. I wondered if his family had received word of his death. "She's beautiful," I said. He smiled and tucked the photo away without any mention of the girl's mother.

After dinner, I helped *Frau* Fischer clear the plates. We washed up in uncomfortable silence. Afterward, she bid me good-night and retired to her own quarters. I intended to do the same, but when I passed the sitting room, I heard a velvety voice coming from a gramophone. I paused outside the doorway to listen. It had been so long since I'd heard music.

"You know her?" the officer called out.

I stepped out into the room, berating myself for not slipping off to bed while I'd had the chance. "Lale Andersen," I said.

He nodded, gesturing for me to join him. I took a seat at the opposite end of the room and declined his offer for a nightcap. His Luger rested on the table, and the insignia on his uniform glinted in the lamplight. Maybe he expected me to sidle over to him, to kiss him or please him. Was that the price to guarantee my safety, to deliver me home to my family? The possibility made me flinch. I thought about all the times I'd passed Dutch girls flirting with German soldiers and had scorned them. Perhaps they, too, had secrets to protect.

The song came to an end, and the officer lifted the needle on the gramophone. I looked from the gun to the strong slope of his jaw. But in that second of indecision, the needle landed back on the record with a scratch. He had skipped tracks. I recognized the new song, "Lili Marleen."

The officer stared absently out the window. Here I was, listening to a song about love and a homesick soldier with a man who had every possibility of killing me, but instead he was caught in his own daydreams. Did he know Goebbels had called the song "unpatriotic," that the singer, Lale Andersen, was rumored to be enamored with a Jew? If he did, he didn't appear to care. The song held him, transporting him somewhere I could only speculate.

I hummed along and then, softly, began to sing. He turned to me. "It's all over, isn't it?"

"Maybe this chapter. But who knows what comes next."

"The journey home," he said. "Facing what you left behind."

He took a drink of his schnapps and tilted his glass to examine it, like he was searching for answers in the crystal. Then, he looked at me, the light revealing the rings of sleepless nights under his eyes. "Where was it you said you lived?"

"Meppen."

"Right. We'll go down to the train station in the morning and get you a ticket."

"Thank you," I said, although I knew this was impossible. A ticket might require identification papers, something I couldn't provide. No, my journey would have to continue on foot. "I hope I'm not being rude," I added, "but I'd like to turn in for the night."

"Yes, get some rest." He bid me good-night. As I got up and left, the gramophone crackled as he returned the needle once more to the beginning of the song.

I returned to my bedroom, shaken. If the officer had picked up on my accent, he hadn't let on. He seemed done with the war, done with the orders and cold-blooded killings. But I wouldn't be around in the morning to find out for sure.

A nightgown was waiting out on the bed for me, but I didn't change into it. I splashed some water on my face to keep the sleep at bay, and I sat up in bed, fully dressed. In the other room, the music played on and on. The record ended and then started again from the beginning, followed by the soft clink of glass. My breath fluttered while I strained to listen, eager for a chance to slip away. I tried to think of what I would say if he were to have a change of heart, barge into my room, try to force me to repay the favor of his hospitality. I pictured his heavy hands pinning me down and shuddered. I looked at the clock. Two hours had passed, and I hadn't heard a sign of movement for over fifteen minutes.

I peered out of the doorway. The only way to get to the back door was to pass by the sitting room. As I inched my way down the hallway, a floorboard creaked under my weight. I froze, bit-ing my lip as I listened for some reaction, but heard only Lale Andersen's deep, soothing voice from the gramophone. I carried on down the hall, peeking around the corner into the sitting room. The officer lay passed out on the sofa, his hand sprawled to the side like he was reaching for his drink. When I was certain he was asleep, I tiptoed by, the music muffling my steps. Slowly, I turned the handle of the back door and slipped outside, into the cover of night.

FORTY-THREE

Liesbeth de Wit
March 26, 1945
Amsterdam, the Netherlands

As soon as Liesbeth climbed up into the rafters of the predator gallery, she knew Willem was preoccupied. He sat cross-legged at the edge of one of the stacks of hay, with Aletta on his lap, but he ignored her attempts to play with the collar of his shirt, to bury her face into his knit vest.

"Lies." He pushed up the brim of his glasses with his middle finger. "It's so good to see you."

She waved to the others in the rafters and seated herself across from him. Aletta slid off his lap and came over for a warm, sticky-kissed hello. The Hunger Winter had taken its toll on her. She moved slowly and her thin limbs stuck out at rigid angles. Liesbeth squeezed her, wishing she could transfer some of her own strength into Aletta's frail body. She unpacked a tin of cabbage soup and handed it to Willem.

"Great timing," he said, "I wasn't sure I could stomach another meal of the bread they're baking with the zoo's remain-

ing grain stores. Yesterday it was dotted with rat droppings."
He smirked, but the worry lines on his forehead didn't soften.

"What's on your mind?"

"I have some news, but I'm not sure how you're going to
take it."

"Jo?" she asked, feeling like a bag of marbles had dropped
into the bottom of her stomach. But no, Willem was too calm
for that. His mouth twitched as he looked at her, perhaps trying to think of how to word it.

"Dirk is dead."

"Oh." She looked down at Aletta, at the worn straps on her
niece's leather shoes. The straps had little white flowers on them,
but the shoes didn't belong to Willem. They were hand-me-
downs, passed on from someone else in hiding, a Jew whose
daughter had been sent away to a farm, where she would be
safer, where her life might be spared because of the light color
of her hair, the fact that she could pass as someone she was not.
She looked at those white flowers and it all returned to her, everything she'd believed about Dirk, about the way he'd made
her feel. She felt sick to her stomach.

"Lies?"

She set Aletta aside and scrambled to get up, looking for something, anywhere, a spot of privacy. A bucket stood at the opposite end of the attic, meant for washing. Liesbeth bent down
and splashed her face with water, trying to clear her head, trying to wash away those thoughts of his card tricks, his charming smile. How she'd fallen for it all.

Willem called after her. "Can I get you something?"

She shook her head and waited until the nausea settled down.
She'd tried so hard not to think about him those past months,
but he had never fully left her thoughts. And now he was gone.

She walked back to Willem and Aletta, trying to ignore the
others' curious expressions. "Tell me how it happened," she said.

"There's no delicate way to put it. We got him. Piet did, one of our Resistance leaders."

"How?"

"You sure you want to know?"

She nodded.

"Piet shot him. He was sitting on his boat, moored to the side of the canal. He was shot in the back, wouldn't have seen it coming."

For a second, she pictured a dartboard, a dart flying and marking a bull's-eye. But then that image disappeared and she saw him again, slumped over the engine of his boat, blood seeping through the fabric of his tweed jacket.

"I see." She blinked, surprised at how calm she now felt. The anxiety and prickling feelings had settled down, leaving her with nothing but the facts. "Well," she said, turning to Willem, "I suppose he got exactly what he deserved."

FORTY-FOUR

Johanna Vos
March 27, 1945
Western Germany

The encounter with the SS officer stayed with me like the sharpness of ginger, imprinting itself on my senses. I couldn't forget his forlorn stare, the way I'd prepared myself to hate him but ultimately failed. While I continued on my way, I recounted every minute of our encounter, trying to hit upon some hint of his depravity. But maybe he was another homesick person. The thought crossed my mind that not everyone was free to make the conscious choice of fighting for his or her beliefs, of what side he or she was on. Sometimes, you had to act simply to survive.

Two nights later, I came back to this thought while hiding in a thicket by the Dutch-German border. The moon shone overhead but clouds gathered on the horizon. For three hours, I crouched there, pinching myself to stay awake until the clouds obscured the moonlight. I hadn't eaten all day. Somewhere along the way I'd shed the last of my dignity and knocked on farmers' doors, begging for bread and a place to sleep in exchange for help with chores. Mostly, they'd obliged without too many questions, but that afternoon, I'd been turned away.

The wind picked up from the west, and the gust of cold wind made me shiver, but it was Dutch wind, a sign that home was near. I hunched my shoulders and rocked back and forth to stay warm. For two days, I'd moved up and down this strip of border, trying to gauge my chances. From what I'd gathered, the Allies had reached Coevorden and Emmen, two towns across the border, but the Wehrmacht troops were still putting up a fight in places. I refused to fall back into their hands. Farther along the road was an armed border stop, and I'd passed some rowdy soldiers who were camped out for the night, but here, between the farmers' fields, there was only the occasional passing patrol.

Soon, the moon disappeared behind a mask of clouds. I watched the houses for lights. The last thing I needed was a frightened farmhand sounding the alarm. I pictured Aletta and Willem. Then I counted down from ten.

On one, I ran.

I ran as fast as I could, the wind whipping my cheeks, hammering in my ears. Home. Faster I ran, crouching low, keeping my eye on the ground. I hopped over roots, tore across a field, leaped over a ditch. Somewhere, a dog started barking, but I didn't look back. I kept running as the parceled fields shifted direction, like the world was rotated beneath my feet. I kept running until I passed the farmhouses and hit another narrow thicket. I stopped to listen. The barking had ceased. The night was still. Once I'd caught my breath, I crept out of the thicket and rounded a bend. I straightened up, emerging onto the road only to come face-to-face with a bright beam of light.

Soldiers. Four of them, standing there with the flashlight trained on me. One held a cigarette pinched between two fingers; another had his hand on his gun.

"What are you doing?" the one with the flashlight asked.

Allies. Canadians, judging by the armbands of their uniforms. I sighed in relief.

"I'm trying to make my way home," I said in English, "to Amsterdam."

"From Germany?"

"I was taken prisoner. I was in the Resistance."

The men exchanged a glance and leaned in. The one with the cigarette tossed the butt on the ground and crushed it with the heel of his boot. Then, he stepped forward to take a good look at me. He had a thick mustache and a strong nose, the type of man who could be kind or intimidating, depending on his mood.

"What a convenient story."

"It's true, I swear. I've been traveling for weeks."

"You expect me to believe the Krauts let you just waltz back across the border?"

"I had a lot of luck."

The soldier laughed. "You can come up with a better story than that." He turned back to the others. "Whatd'ya think boys, is she telling the truth? Or did the Krauts send us one last Trojan Horse?"

My mouth went dry. Had I made it into safe territory, only to be recaptured as a spy? Couldn't they see the Germans were on the retreat? What good would it do to send a spy all on her own to liberated towns?

The men spoke among themselves: "Too pretty to be a spy."

"That's exactly what they'd want us to think."

"Give the lass a break, George, send her home."

The soldier with the mustache held up a hand to silence them. "Search her."

Before I could protest, hands shoved into my pockets, patting me down. They ordered me to turn around and remove my shoes. My sore feet glimmered white under the flashlight, and I began to shiver.

"I'm innocent. Please, you must believe me!"

"She's clean."

The mustachioed soldier looked me up and down, but I couldn't read his mood. No malice, but no pity, either. "You two," he said, pointing to the two who had searched me, "bring her to the captain. He'll decide." He gestured for the other soldier to follow him and they continued down the road. At the junction, he turned and hollered back, "Give her something to keep warm. She's liable to catch pneumonia."

The men threw a jacket over my shoulders and nudged me forward. If I was taken prisoner by the Allies, who knew how long it would take me to get back home. I had to find a way to change their minds.

The Canadians brought me to a countryside estate where they'd made camp. The sunroom on the side of the villa had been destroyed, its remnants a pile of glass and plaster. I thought back to the mansion where I'd given birth, the way the guests had congregated near the sunroom, the atmosphere of joy and relief, that temporary suspension of fear. It, too, felt like a lifetime ago.

The captain had set himself up in the former study. A burly redhead, he sat at a mahogany desk, with various maps and charts arranged in front of him. When the soldiers led me into the room, he frowned. "What now? Who is this?"

"Johanna Vos, sir," I said. "The Nazis arrested me for my work in the Dutch Resistance. I crossed the border by foot."

The captain stood up, his kilt swishing as he walked up to me. He said something, but his accent was so thick I couldn't make it out.

"I beg your pardon?" A bout of dizziness hit me. How many hours had it been since my last meal?

"Get this woman a chair," he ordered the soldiers, "and tell me someone has thought to give her something to eat. She looks like hell."

A minute later, I had a biscuit in my hand and a cup of steaming tea. The captain waited until I'd taken a couple of bites before launching into his interrogation. I told him my story, from start to finish, removing my shoes to show him my blistered feet, evidence of many days on the run.

The captain called for a translator, someone who could probe deeper, possibly pick up the trace of an accent or some inconsistency in my story. While we waited, I looked the captain in the eyes. "I promise," I said, "every word I'm telling you is true. Please, all I want is to go home."

A flicker of compassion passed over his face. He nodded, like he was inclined to believe me but was trying to uphold his duties. I needed to give him no reason to doubt me. I leaned over and indicated one of the maps on his desk. "I passed a few German soldiers who were camped out close to the border. They were loud, drinking, an easy target. If your men can point out where they picked me up, I can show you where they were."

The captain waved over one of the soldiers who had accompanied me. The soldier placed his finger on a spot, and from there I worked my way backward, offering my best guess as to where the rowdy lot had been. As the translator came in, the captain ordered the soldier to send out some men to investigate. Then the captain turned to me. "Tell this man what you told me and answer his questions. If he has any reason to suspect you're lying, I'll hear about it. Otherwise, he'll find you a place to sleep and ensure you have a hot meal."

"Thank you, sir."

I followed the translator out of the study, but the captain called after me. "Have some patience and you'll find your way home. We've almost beaten them, almost."

FORTY-FIVE

Liesbeth de Wit
May 8, 1945
Amsterdam, the Netherlands

At last—freedom! Free on paper at least, the capitulation signed and dated. But while much of the country was soaking in the first days of freedom, Liesbeth had yet to see any sign of their liberators. Rumors trickled through the street: the Canadians were in nearby Utrecht, their arms laden with delicacies nobody had seen in months; the Canadians were greeting the farmers on the outskirts of Amsterdam; the Canadians were grinning and handsome, leaving a path of blushing young women in their wake. The anticipation was intoxicating. Liesbeth wanted to be in the thick of it all, sucking everything in, catching the stories, spinning her own fantasies of what it would be like to walk worry free through the city, to sink her teeth into a cream-filled pastry made with real flour. To find her sister.

That hint of doubt creeped in when she thought back to Mad Tuesday, how the disappointment had settled over the city for months. "I'll believe in this liberation once I see it," she said to

Maurits, to keep her hope in check, and in part because she was afraid of tarnishing his mood.

In those final days, Maurits spent hours at his desk, poring over newspapers and pharmaceutical journals, snapping at Liesbeth if the imitation coffee wasn't how he liked it. Other times, he would slip into a frenzy, sweeping her up into his arms, spinning her around as he announced his grand plans for after the war: the places they would see—Paris, Milan, Budapest—the shows he would take her to in the ritziest theaters and catwalks of Europe.

The newspapers declared the eighth of May V–E Day, marking victory across Europe. And this time, the rumors could be verified. The Canadians had been sighted, driving in from the southeast. Liesbeth was up early. She and Willem planned to watch the procession of soldiers filing into the city. It was his and Aletta's first full day out of hiding, back in their own home, and she didn't want them to celebrate alone. From the looks of it, the entire city was spilling out onto the streets. Everyone except Maurits. Liesbeth tried to rouse his spirits, but he would have none of it.

"After what happened yesterday," he said, "the last thing I want to do is get tangled up in a massive crowd."

He had a point: the day before, a handful of German marines had opened fire on a celebratory crowd in Dam Square. Some people speculated that the Resistance had tried to strip the marines of their weapons, sparking the chaos. Others believed one of the marines had spotted a Resistance fighter flirting with his girlfriend and fired a shot in a jealous rage. Whatever the truth of the matter, it had been a bloodbath. Dozens dead and even more wounded.

Although the news had frightened Liesbeth, she assured Maurits she would be fine, that the Germans would no longer be a threat once the Canadians arrived. But he insisted on spending the afternoon at home with the latest pharmaceutical periodical. "We can celebrate in our own way tonight," he said. "Go have fun. But be careful."

Liesbeth was fully set on doing both. She pulled out her orange ribbon and a crepe paper flower for her dress. When she left the house, she got swept up in the joyful shouts of the children running by, the flags hanging from balconies, the long-hidden red, white, and blue.

Willem and Aletta were waiting for her at the end of the block, and together they made their way toward the Amstellaan. Willem carried Aletta on his shoulders, and, after months cooped up in the zoo, Aletta acted like she'd stepped into a new world, enraptured by the sights and smells around her.

"How does it feel to be out on the streets, in the thick of everything?" Liesbeth asked.

"It won't be easy to move past these nightmares. But one day at a time, life will return to normal."

Liesbeth knew what he was thinking, the same thought that had been lingering in her mind for weeks: that the letters from Johanna had stopped, that she should be freed. Yet, they'd heard nothing. Where was she?

"She'll find her way home," Liesbeth said quietly, "or we'll find her."

At the head of the Amstellaan, the throng grew so thick that trying to push through it became next to impossible. They squeezed into a space near the curb, managing to get a good view of the bridge ahead and the road leading out of Amsterdam. Liesbeth took Aletta in her arms and pointed out all the people, how nice everyone looked. Women with their hair in ribbons and braids, bobby socks, and skirts they'd saved from tired wear with the hope that this day would come. The men had shaved and polished their shoes. If it weren't for how skinny and gaunt everyone looked after that cruel winter, you might have thought it was a regular day, a festival like the ones they'd had before the war. Before it all.

Up ahead, someone cried out in excitement. One by one, jeeps and armored vehicles crested the bridge. And for the first time in five years, it wasn't the cold field gray of the Germans' uniforms coming toward them, but a brigade of khaki. Canadians. Liesbeth waved, dumbfounded, as the streets erupted into cheers. Everyone began to clap and sing and dance.

"They're here," she said, "they're really here." She and Willem fell into an embrace, holding Aletta between them, raising her little arms into the air. Aletta giggled and gaped at it all.

They stood there for over an hour. Within the first few minutes, people began to flock over the road, swarming the incoming troops. Men tossed their caps in the air. Children in paper crowns waved flags. And the girls tossed handkerchiefs and bouquets of flowers, blowing kisses to the soldiers, who invited them to scramble up into their jeeps and ride along with them, arm in arm. People lifted the Canadians up onto their shoulders and decked the tanks in streamers. Lipstick dotted the cheeks of the soldiers, who grinned ear to ear beneath their berets and mustaches, overwhelmed by their reception. Liesbeth felt giddy, exhilarated. This was it—freedom.

She wished Gerrit and Jo were here to see this. "It feels like some crazy dream," she said.

Willem smiled, his eyes alight. "No, we're waking up from one."

She embraced him again, turned to greet strangers and joined in renditions of "Het Wilhelmus" until her voice grew hoarse. The power of the words surprised her, how moving it felt to be able to sing the national anthem without fear of retribution.

Soldiers in berets began handing out chocolate and tins of preserves. Children ran up to them, begging in their best English, "Have you some food for us?" They followed behind the jeeps, dancing and bending down to collect the cigarette butts that fell on the ground, for their parents to smoke later.

While the procession paused, slowed by congestion, Aletta

caught the attention of a Canadian officer on a motorbike by waving a floppy hand at him. He chuckled and slowed to a halt beside them.

"Why, hello, little miss." He pulled a banana out of his bag, which he peeled and held out to Aletta. She stared back at him.

"She's never seen a banana before," Liesbeth said. She took the fruit and offered a small piece to Aletta, who chewed once, twice, before spitting it out. The banana slid down her chin, making the officer laugh again.

"Ba-na-na," he said, sounding it out for her. "Plenty of time to get your little monkey hooked on these." He glanced back at the procession, which had started rolling, and passed Liesbeth two tins of braised beef. "You take good care of her, won't you?"

Liesbeth thanked him and promised she would. She handed the tins to Willem, and they looked at one another, Johanna's absence heavy between them.

Aletta's babbling broke through their thoughts. "He go bye-bye?"

Willem nodded and took her, pressing her close to his chest and stroking her curls. They moved to a quieter spot farther back, where they could sit on the grass and rest their feet. Willem tried to feed Aletta the rest of the banana, singing as he clapped her hands. She puckered her mouth and pushed it away.

"Well," Willem said, "if she prefers to grow up on a diet of tulip bulbs and turnips, my wallet will be happy."

Liesbeth laughed. "She's tired. And after all this excitement, she's not the only one who could use a nap."

"It's a lot to take in, for all of us." Willem started getting Aletta to her feet. "And I'm sure you'll want to check on Maurits." He raised his voice at the end in question, but Liesbeth didn't know how to answer. It had been blissful, these few hours in which she'd managed to forget about all the problems at home. Her husband, the man she was meant to love. Her affair. The lies and betrayal that masked it all.

"Yes," she said, "I suppose he'll be wanting some lunch."

She gathered her things, adjusted the orange corsage that had come loose from her dress, and followed Willem while he wove a pathway back through the crowd. There would be more celebrations in the days to come, so she knew it was time to leave, but the idea of returning to the storm cloud at home dulled her energy.

Suddenly, someone bellowed her name. "Liesbeth, Liesbeth!" A male voice, a Canadian. She turned, confused, searching for the source of it.

"Liesbeth!" A handsome young soldier was waving at her from a jeep. He grinned and pointed to the woman beside him. A woman with hair cropped short and a sallow complexion. It took Liesbeth a second to register the face, the woman calling and waving and hopping off the moving truck, rushing toward her. But there she was, her sister.

PART FIVE

Rebuilding
May 1945–May 1946

PART FIVE

FORTY-SIX

Johanna Vos
May 8, 1945
Amsterdam, the Netherlands

"Jo!"

The moment I locked eyes with Lies, everything changed. All those months I'd spent wondering, anticipating what it would be like to find my sister, and there she was. I jumped down from the jeep that had brought me into the city. We found each other in the middle of the crowd, Liesbeth wrapping me in the tightest of hugs. She pulled back to look at me. She looked thin and tired but still full of color. "Jo," she said, "it's really you!" She kissed me on the cheek and hugged me again, but then she stopped and scanned the sea of people around us, reaching out an arm for someone. "She's here!"

I felt my breath cinch and turned my head, searching. I saw Willem first. My darling, strong, capable Wim. But then there was a child, pudgy cheeked with wild, dark curls. For a moment, I was confused. Although I'd known it would happen, Aletta had changed, transformed from a baby to a little girl. A sharp pain wedged itself into my chest as I tried to grasp everything I'd missed, all those milestones I should have been there for, holding my daughter's hand.

"Sweetheart!" Willem's arms encircled me now, holding me, comforting me. I reached out for Aletta, lifted her up, surprised by the weight of her. Those round little cheeks, that cascade of curls, smelling like imitation soap. Big, searching eyes. Sticky, fruit-stained hands.

"Aletta," Wim said. "This is Mama."

I became aware of the stares of onlookers. Curious celebrators awaiting their own reunions. They watched Aletta turn her head away from me and scrunch up her nose, reaching out in the other direction, reaching out for Liesbeth. My daughter was here, in front of me. Ready to be loved, to be cared for. But she no longer needed me.

"Give her some time," Wim said.

Didn't he understand that this moment was all I'd been counting on for all those months in prison? The one thought that had kept me going.

Aletta wriggled, calling out for "Papa." I kissed Aletta on the forehead before handing her back to Willem. She settled in against his shoulder, while I tried to conceal my disappointment.

"We're so relieved to see you," Liesbeth said. "With every wave of soldiers that came over the bridge, I had my hopes, but we thought it could take weeks, months even. We want to hear everything."

I smiled weakly. "I'm quite tired."

It was Liesbeth's turn for disappointment. "Of course, you must need your rest."

"We'll get this Resistance hero straight home to bed," Willem said with a laugh.

I shook my head. "Please don't call me that."

As we retreated through the crowds, I caught the glance that passed between my sister and husband. No doubt, they were wondering what kind of dark clouds I was bringing back and whether they'd been better off without me.

★ ★ ★

Arriving home felt like slipping into a dress I'd worn before my pregnancy—although I knew it intimately, it felt strange, suited for some version of me that had long disappeared. In the hallway, one of my hats hung in the same place I'd left it. I picked it up and ran my fingers around the brim, which Liesbeth had dressed up with fur from an old stole. I wanted to give it to Aletta, to play dress-up with her in funny voices, but I worried that she would only cry if I tried to place it on her head.

Willem poked his head around the corner. "What do you feel like, sweetheart? Are you hungry? I'm still trying to get the house in order, but whatever you need, you tell me and I'm your man."

"I'm going to need some time myself," I said, "to rebuild." I wasn't sure what I meant by that. Rebuild our family? My life? My relationship with Liesbeth? Even though the country was free, the barbed wire still cordoned me off from my former life.

"Come," Willem said, placing a protective hand on my shoulder, "let's get you something to eat."

For the rest of the afternoon, we sat at the kitchen table, talking and laughing and crying, catching up on everything. Willem had a bottle of wine he had saved for the liberation, but I asked for water. My stomach couldn't handle much more than that, and I was afraid the drink would make my worries and insecurities bubble over.

I told him of the bunker and the rats and the sewing workshop and the German guard and my fortuitous escape. Willem, in turn, told me how he and Aletta had lived between the animals, like so many others. He told me that Aletta had been taken, and how helpful Liesbeth had been through it all, how she'd orchestrated a plan to sneak into the Jewish nursery, all the risks she'd taken to get my daughter back. He told me Jakob had survived, having made it through several months of forced labor in a German munitions factory, but that Ida hadn't, her body unable to recover from birth and the starvation of the Hunger

333

Winter. I took all of this in, struggling to picture the sister I knew acting bravely and selflessly. I wasn't yet ready to process what I felt about my sister, what I believed about Ida.

Then, he told me about my brother's death. Although I had sensed Gerrit's absence for some time, I hadn't expected the news to hit so hard. I slid to the floor and sat in a heap, fixating on the geometric fans of the wallpaper. I recalled all the times he'd snuck up on me in the neighbor's field while I belted out cabaret numbers and leaped from hay bale to hay bale, how I'd chased after him, cornering him and tackling him to the ground. I thought of his warmth toward Aletta, how much he'd wanted to settle down and start a family of his own.

Aletta toddled over from across the room. She stared, unsure what to make of my tears.

"Go see Ma," Willem said, but she didn't budge. I closed my eyes. The distance between us seemed unfathomable.

"You can pick her up," Willem said, "she'll be fine."

I couldn't force my daughter to love me, not after everything I'd put her through. But a sneaking fear crept into my mind: What if my sister had taken my place in Aletta's heart? And wasn't it deserved? For Liesbeth was the one who had been there to care for her while I was in prison, had helped Willem in every way she could. Maybe that was already fixed in Aletta's memory.

Willem watched the standoff between us. His face was lined with a mix of happiness and concern. It must have been so hard on him, trying to navigate the war and parenthood, not know-ing if I would ever return. I recalled all those cold nights in the camp, when I'd huddled on my lumpy mattress between strang-ers and tried to imagine him at home, croaking out off-key lul-labies as he tucked Aletta into bed.

"I don't know how you did it," I said, "keeping her so strong in spirit."

"I couldn't have managed without your sister," Willem said. He lifted Aletta onto his lap. "She helped every step along the way."

"I don't want to hear it. Not now."

I stood up and walked over to the window. Outside, the guardrail by the canal was covered in orange paper streamers. I thought of the heron that I'd watched all those times while I breastfed. There was no sign of him now. Perhaps someone had hunted him, eaten him in the Hunger Winter. So much of the city had been stripped bare. And much as I ought to be indebted to Liesbeth, for how she'd lent Willem a hand in my absence, I wasn't ready to forgive her.

Across the room, Aletta fidgeted on Willem's lap. "She needs sleep," I said, "and so do I."

"You go lie down. I'll put her to bed."

"No, I'll do it. I need to start somewhere."

FORTY-SEVEN

Liesbeth de Wit
May 26, 1945
Amsterdam, the Netherlands

For Liesbeth, the days after the liberation passed in a daze. She felt the elation of her sister's safe return, the guilt that bobbed back to the surface, that feeling of trepidation as she tried to explore this new freedom, avoiding the main squares, flinching at every loud noise.

Maurits only left the house for work, and he returned home early, before the afternoon rush. They ate their meals in an uneasy silence. Now and then, he commented on the weather or asked for the salt, but that was it. After two weeks, Liesbeth convinced him to join her on some errands. His stack of paperwork had been filed away and it was a fine day, perfect for a picnic. He had no excuse.

They strolled down the long avenue that ran parallel to the Vondelpark. The birds were chirping, and the sun was shining but Maurits kept his hands in his pockets and his head to the ground. Liesbeth didn't mind. It would have almost felt strange to intertwine her fingers with his, to lean into him as she once had. They lived in two adjacent worlds, and she wasn't sure if any love still smoldered in the cinders of their marriage. After everything she'd felt for Dirk, the passion he'd brought out in her, it felt so hard to trust her own feelings. She knew she owed Maurits some loyalty, to repair what was lost, make up for her mistakes. But all she could think of were her own dreams, the hope that maybe, now that the war was over, she had a chance for a fresh start.

They turned a corner by a tailor's shop and milliner that had closed during the Hunger Winter, lacking fuel and customers. Maybe one day, she could return to her sketches and make something of them. "Soon these places will reopen, don't you think?" she said.

Maurits grunted. "Wouldn't count on it."

Liesbeth wondered if she wouldn't have been better off having the picnic by herself. When was the last time they'd managed to have a lovely day together? She recalled the afternoon they'd spent boating at the beginning of the war. How much fun they'd had, swimming and sunbathing, until he'd ruined the day with his news about taking over the pharmacy. Back then, she'd seen him as someone pure, someone with principles. Yet if she'd been so opposed to his morals, why had she never stood up to him about this?

They kept walking in silence until they reached the bakery. A line wound out the door.

"Maybe we should come back," Maurits said.

"We won't have much of a picnic at all without bread." She joined the line and started going through her ration coupons. The people in front of them lived two buildings over. They turned up their noses at Maurits, but Liesbeth pretended not to notice. When the baker called out for the next in line, the two of them entered the shop.

The baker looked Maurits up and down. "Out," he said.

Liesbeth took a step back. "I beg your pardon?"

"I won't have the likes of him in my shop."

"But we've been coming here for years."

"You're welcome to stay, *mevrouw*. But he needs to leave."

Liesbeth played with her purse strap, unsure how to react. She waited for Maurits's temper to flare up, but he simply grimaced and strode out with his head held high. Liesbeth stuffed her ration coupons back into her purse. He was already at the opposite end of the small square before she caught up to him. She didn't look back at all the prying eyes behind them.

"There's another bakery two blocks down," she said.

"Let's go home." As he lowered his hat over his brow, she saw his weariness and frustration. They walked home as they'd come, without speaking. Liesbeth thought of all the newspaper headlines she'd seen, the government's promise to bring justice to Dutch society. There was no room in society for traitors; that point had been made clear. But was her husband guilty of treason, or just of taking the advantages that had been handed to him? And where did this leave her?

That afternoon, Maurits stayed indoors, bent over a journal he'd read several times over. A classical program was playing on the radio, but when the news came on, Maurits switched it off.

Feeling stifled in their small apartment, Liesbeth set off for a stroll in the next neighborhood, where she could wander in blissful anonymity. How different it felt from the days she'd wandered there with Dirk, trapped in her own romantic fancies. She mulled everything over, trying to decide the best course of action, for her marriage, for her own future. There didn't seem to be any clear answers.

On her way home, she encountered a commotion down the road from their house. Several people were dragging a man from a taxi. The man kicked and yelled, writhing in protest. "Leave me be," he said, "let me call my lawyer!"

Liesbeth stopped, nervous. A group of bystanders had gathered. More men joined in, some of their neighbors. They knocked the poor fellow to the ground and beat him with whatever they had: brooms, sticks, dustpans.

A woman spit at him. "Traitor!"

Liesbeth made a move to cross the street, but the man on the ground looked her way, panicked, like he was seeking an ally. She recognized him; he had been in the Landwacht, the branch of the NSB Maurits would have been assigned to, had he kept his membership. Liesbeth averted her gaze and hurried on home.

When she got to their building, she looked up at their window and saw Maurits staring outside, watching the lynching. His face had hardened. While she ran up the stairs, she heard a loud crash, followed by cursing. She gripped the railing, her heart drumming in her chest. Traitor—that was her husband, all right. He knew it as well as she.

She waited five minutes before continuing up the stairs. She nudged open the door to their apartment and found Maurits sitting on the floor, a table lamp shattered beside him. He held his head in his hands.

"Maurits?"

When he looked up at her, he was crying. "Lies," he said, "I need you here. I need you here beside me."

One month after Johanna's return, Liesbeth received an invitation for dinner. It arrived by mail, written in careful handwriting, which felt uncharacteristic for Johanna. The notecard was addressed to Liesbeth, with no mention of Maurits. "A dinner to thank you," it read, "for everything you've done for my daughter."

In the end, Liesbeth didn't need to devise an excuse to tell Maurits, because he had left town for several days to visit his brother. Took refuge was more like it, away from critical eyes. She showed up at Jo's with a tin of biscuits she'd managed to claim from one of the Allied food drops, the boxes and sacks that had floated down from the sky like trinkets from heaven.

Liesbeth arrived to find Aletta in bed, earlier than normal, and she couldn't help but wonder if that was intentional. She couldn't blame her sister, nor did she want to compete for her niece's affection, but the apartment felt too still without Aletta's babbling and monkey hugs. At the sight of Aletta's toys tucked away in the corner, Liesbeth felt that pining ache return to her womb.

Johanna had managed to get her hands on a small piece of fish, which came out of the oven dry and charred at the edges. Liesbeth washed down each bite with plenty of water and a polite smile, while the dinner unfolded over awkward remarks and toasts. Johanna preached about freedom, about what it would mean for Europe, the long process of rebuilding and taking stock of their losses in people and property. When her tone grew vindictive, Willem cut her off, but this only made Liesbeth feel worse. After all, didn't Jo have every right to be resentful? Liesbeth didn't know if she could ever expect things to go back to how they were before the war or whether she deserved that. But it was up to her to lay the first stone in that bridge.

"Jo, I've been meaning to say something—" Liesbeth began.

"Yes?"

Liesbeth glanced at Willem, who fixated on his plate as he edged his knife around the blackened bits of fish.

"You were right," Liesbeth said, "about Maurits. I should have trusted your judgment." She let out a breath of relief. While it was not the full confession she owed her sister, it was still something she'd never admitted. With every passing day, she felt it growing in her heart—the knowledge that she couldn't live out the rest of her days with any hope of happiness with a man like her husband.

"Yes," Johanna said, "well, we all misjudge people, don't we?" A brief hint of something—vulnerability, guilt?—flashed across her face, before she tensed up again. "Are you going to leave him?"

"I don't know."

"There's no place in society for traitors," Johanna said. "He'll get what's coming to him."

Liesbeth fiddled with a stray thread on the tablecloth. She knew this was true; it was only a matter of time. She'd seen the girl-friends of the German soldiers marched naked through the squares, their heads shaven and their bodies tarred. She'd heard the stories of spontaneous arrests, NSBers rounded up and sent to camps, where they awaited prosecution.

Johanna went on. "If he's convicted, they'll strip him of his citizenship, and you, too, if you're unlucky. Everyone will know what side you were on."

They already did, Liesbeth thought. The past few weeks, she'd felt like she and Maurits had been walking around with sizzling brands on their foreheads. She shifted in her seat. "I'm frightened," she said, in almost a whisper.

"You should be." There was heat in Johanna's words, like she wanted to see Liesbeth suffer. And maybe Liesbeth deserved it for what she'd done. If it hadn't been for her ridiculous concern for Dirk, Jo would have never been sent away.

Willem cleared his throat and shot Johanna a warning look. "It's a lot more complicated than that. We may have won, but we can't run around like a bloodthirsty lynch mob with no re-gard for due process. It's not easy to decide who was truly bad and good. And who has the authority to make that decision?"

"The government," Johanna said.

"The government that was stuck on the other side of the English Channel for the past five years? What do they know of the many shades of gray that shaped our actions?" Willem said.

"And what do you think?" Johanna asked Liesbeth. "Was Maurits too blind to see the masses of Jews herded into the back of trucks? Too deaf to hear the cries of starving children across the city? Were you?"

Willem interrupted her. "We owe a great deal to Lies."

"That's true," Johanna said. "And I'll be forever grateful for your help. Wim says Aletta wouldn't be here with us today if it weren't for you."

Liesbeth looked up, hoping this marked a turn in the evening, that Johanna was willing to forgive her. However, whatever hint of compassion her sister had shown vanished as quickly as it had appeared.

Johanna took a sip of water. "As grateful as I am, this doesn't change the fact that you made some very poor decisions along the way."

"Johanna," Willem said.

Liesbeth dabbed her lips with her serviette. "It's all right," she said, although she was trembling, "she's right." She got up. "I understood Maurits was wrong. Maybe not in the early days, but I did soon enough. But I was too much of a coward to do anything about it."

"Please, Lies," Willem said, "sit down and have another drink. We'll talk about something else. I have a funny story about the sea lions at the zoo."

It took all her will to keep her emotions from spilling over. She brought her plate to the kitchen. "I should get going. It's getting late."

Willem tried once more to change her mind while Johanna sat there without saying a word. When Liesbeth tried to kiss her goodbye, Jo turned her cheek.

"Good night, sister," Liesbeth said. "I hope we will be able to mend our relationship in time."

"Good night."

Liesbeth walked out into the warm evening. A clear divide had settled between them, and it was time for her to accept the consequences of her loyalties. In all those years of occupation, everyone had faced the same choice. Maurits had collaborated. Johanna had resisted. She herself had hoped to adapt. And at the end of the day, they were left trying to make sense of it all, and everything seemed so much more black-and-white in retrospect.

She knew she wouldn't be part of Johanna's life, or Aletta's, if she continued on the same course.

She stared up at the gabled rooftops that lined the block. The sun was dipping out of sight, casting a reddish glow over the roof tiles. The blackout paper had long been taken down and shredded, but still, many houses had their curtains closed. Something told her the city would stay that way for many years to come.

FORTY-EIGHT

Johanna Vos
July 2, 1945
Amsterdam, the Netherlands

The tense dinner with Liesbeth had set something off in me, a series of tiny explosions like the firecrackers the neighborhood boys would light on New Year's Eve. I knew the war's end would bring its own set of problems, but I hadn't anticipated the frustration it would unleash. Something was eating at me. I felt like I was still on the run, being hunted, unable to sleep in peace. I rarely left the house and found myself avoiding the friends I'd missed so dearly.

In need of an escape, I took Aletta down south to visit my aunt and uncle, who were still staying with relatives while they waited for the damage in Zierikzee to be repaired, for the sea-drenched fields to be drained and the sodden houses made livable. I spent two heartwarming weeks with them, sharing what we'd endured over the past year and swapping memories of Gerrit that made us cry and laugh and then cry again. Every day, stories poured out of me, the ones I could speak aloud and those I chose to keep to myself and put down on paper. The weight

I'd been carrying lessened, yet, still, whenever *tante* Rika or *oom* Cor mentioned Lies's name, I grew tense and tried to change the subject. When two weeks were up, I knew I wouldn't sleep peacefully until I put the truth to rest. I needed to hear Jakob's side of the story, about what happened with Dirk and Ida.

I returned to Amsterdam and dropped in on Jakob one afternoon in early July unannounced. Maybe I was afraid to face the great loss that had become his reality or maybe I wasn't sure I could replay the events of the betrayal yet again, but I circled the block three times before convincing myself to approach the apartment, and when the door swung open, I paused, for once at a loss for words.

Jakob let out a whoop and pulled me into a hug. "You're back! Willem said so, but I refused to believe it until I saw you in the flesh. Those *moffen* just couldn't sink their teeth into you, could they?" He chuckled, a laugh laced with pain. I thought of Ida and wondered what other bad news had started trickling back to him from the death camps out east.

I pulled back to look at him. No words could capture what I needed to say, express the hurt I felt for him. He hadn't just lost a wife but a whole community. "I'm so sorry about Ida," I said.

He pressed a fist to his lips, like the words wanted to spill out, the list of names of everyone else he'd lost as well. Instead, a tiny voice interrupted, calling "Papa."

Jakob stepped aside to reveal the little one teetering toward him, a boy with a fine head of hair and Jakob's wild eyebrows. Jakob bent down to pick up his son. "Rudi, this here is Johanna. Your *tante* Jo."

The word *tante* gave me pause, reminding me how excited Liesbeth had been to call herself auntie for the first time. But I pushed this thought away and leaned in to admire the boy. "Rudi, what a handsome young man you are," I said, as he waved a floppy hand at me. I smiled at Jakob. "And the mirror image of his father."

"Sometimes I wish I saw more of Ida in him," Jakob said. He kissed Rudi's forehead and tousled his hair before leading me into the sitting room. "Come here, there's someone you'll want to see."

At first, I thought it was Ida sitting in the reading chair in the corner. The woman looked vaguely familiar, as if I'd seen her once in a dream. A second passed before the connection came to me. It was Marijke de Graaf, the violinist who had been there during my labor, the very woman who had brought Aletta into my life.

"*Mevrouw* De Graaf," I said.

She stood up to say hello. "Please, no need for formalities. After all we've been through, we're hardly strangers."

"What a relief to see you. Nobody knew what had happened." The phrase hung in the air, its true meaning unspoken: *if you would make it out alive.*

"They had me at Ravensbrück," she said, "and then Buchenwald."

"Ravensbrück—I was there, briefly, near the end."

My heart went out to her. Buchenwald was a men's camp, but something told me I shouldn't ask what had brought her there. Marijke looked so frail, her skin that luminous milky blue of a pearl, veins crawling up her thin arms, and her eyes held a deep, stirring sadness, so haunting I wanted to look away. Whatever this woman had been through in the camps, it was far worse than what I had seen. She nodded and something passed between us, a kinship, built on an understanding of things too painful to share.

Jakob placed Rudi in the crib and gestured for me to sit down beside Marijke. "Coffee?" he asked, on his way to the kitchen.

Marijke turned to me. "I often thought about you and the baby. Is she well?"

"Aletta grows stronger every day." I opened my purse to show her a piece of paper, a portrait that a young Jewish woman hiding in the zoo had sketched of Aletta. It captured her months earlier, at an age I'd missed, and I found myself reaching for it whenever I was away from my daughter for more than a few minutes.

"She's beautiful," Marijke said.

"Can you tell me something about her parents?"

"Aletta's mother was a kind soul, the type of woman who would never say a bad word about anyone. And her father was a mathematician, apparently brilliant, although I never had the chance to meet him."

I nodded, trying to add these pieces to the puzzle of Aletta's life. "And your husband, is he—"

"He's fine." She laughed, her voice tinkling like a china teacup against its saucer. "Well, fine, fine—what does that mean anymore? He's alive. Weak, but alive. He was one of the lucky ones."

We sat there, mulling this over, both of us mourning our own losses. I thought of Gerrit, of Ida, of Aletta's birth mother. When Jakob returned with the coffee, I asked him about his family.

"So far, nobody has returned," he said, "not a single person." There was talk of a second cousin someone had seen alive, but that was four months earlier, before the Nazis marched prisoners for days on end across frostbitten terrain. Jakob feared the worst. As I tried to grasp the extent of it all, I blinked away tears. So much death, so much sorrow.

"We did what we could, Jo," he said. "It could never have been enough, but every bit helped. And with each loss comes fresh beginnings." At this, Marijke rubbed a hand absently against her belly. Jakob didn't seem to notice, but I wondered if she was carrying a child. A blessing after all she'd been through.

"Theo is waiting for me at home," she said. "It was so good to see you, Johanna. I'm glad Aletta is safe and well."

"Let's make music together someday soon," Jakob said. "It would be good for you, for all of us."

"I'd love to hear you play," I said.

Marijke turned to me with a melancholy smile. "Yes, perhaps one day."

★ ★ ★

When she left, the atmosphere in the apartment shifted. Jakob topped up my coffee and took a seat across from me, sitting straight and tall. Somehow a wall had formed between us, a wall that needed to be dismantled brick by brick.

"That poor woman," I said. "I can only begin to imagine how much she's suffered."

"All for trying to help people in need," he said.

"And to think that it was probably one of her friends or neighbors that turned her in. Who else would have been close enough to monitor her every move?"

Jakob must have sensed that I needed to unload, because he sat back and let me talk.

"Haven't you noticed," I said, "how many people are coming out of the woodwork, with gutsy tales of everything they did for the Resistance?" I'd heard such claims from people I'd never seen lend a hand. The neighbor who had stood by and done nothing, the butcher who had closed his store to Jews. Everyone wanted to make it clear that they had secretly been good; they had been loyal beneath it all.

"A nation full of heroes," Jakob said dryly.

"Exactly. But where were these people when we went to them for help? Full of excuses on why they couldn't take someone in, why they weren't the right person to ask. And now we're supposed to believe they were fighting evil all along?"

"We all did what we could, within our limits."

"Did we? Did we really act out of the goodness of our hearts or did we act on our own agendas?"

He raised an eyebrow. "Come out and ask it, Jo. Ask and I will tell you everything I know."

I paused. For so many months, I'd sat in that cell, trying to construct answers—full of rage, full of hatred, judging my sister and Ida for everything they might have done. What good would it do now to draw my own conclusions? That hadn't gotten me anywhere in the past. It was time to truly listen.

"Why did she do it?"

Jakob folded and unfolded his hands on his lap, his eyes clouding over. "If only I'd known," he said. "If I'd known in time, I would have turned myself in and put a stop to all of it."

"I thought your marriage protected you. That and her pregnancy."

"From what? From a capricious beast with talons that reached across the continent? Nothing was certain, Johanna. Nothing." He let this sink in before continuing. "My friend Rifka, who was married to the Catholic headmaster? They arrested her for walking her dog after curfew. They sent her to Bergen-Belsen. She hasn't come back. My cousin Abraham, the one who fell in love with a good Calvinist girl? Sobibor—for running across to the neighbor's without a star on his jacket."

"I am so sorry."

"I could go on. You see, the fact that I'm still here while so many others are gone is nothing but a fluke. Maybe the Almighty was watching out for me, or you might say I had enough strings to pull, enough agility to dodge a few near misses. Or you could say it was Ida who saved me."

"Yes, but at a terrible cost."

Jakob cleared his throat. "She told me everything before she died. Of course, she never meant to hurt anyone, but Dirk's threats got worse by the week. The guilt of what she'd done consumed her, most of all with Aletta. You have to believe me when I say that Dirk forced that out of her. He came asking for dirt on you, anything she had. He had her trapped."

Like he had my sister trapped.

"She shouldn't have given in," he added, "shouldn't have given him any names. I wish it had been me in those camps, instead of everyone else, instead of you. I'll never forgive myself for it."

He wiped at his eyes, while I sat numbly, trying to take it all

in. He told me how Dirk had found out about the house concerts—the ideal opportunity to gather names and addresses of
Jewish artists in hiding and their protectors. He told me how
Dirk had instructed Ida to leave this information tucked in the
spine of a book at a used bookshop.

"*The Black Tulip*?" I asked, recalling the day I was sure I'd
seen her in the bookshop near Utrechtsestraat.

"Yes, by Alexandre Dumas. How did you know?"

"Like the black tulip that had marked the house concerts."
I grimaced. "A man with a sense of humor to match his soul."

"He was relentless. Once, when Ida said she wanted out, he
showed up here at the apartment while I was away. He had a
copy of a form all filled in for my arrest, awaiting a date and
signature."

"No wonder she was so frightened."

"She should have let him arrest me. What's one death compared to dozens?"

I got up and picked up a framed photograph of Ida and Jakob
from the side table. Ida looked down at him adoringly, clutching
his hand like she couldn't let go. I remembered taking the shot
during Willem's birthday celebration. Had she already known
then the threats that lay ahead? When I looked at the image,
at the love in her gaze, I didn't feel the rage I had before. All I
saw was a wife who would do anything to save her husband. If
Willem's head had been on the chopping block, wouldn't I have
done anything to try to save him? What about Aletta's?

"Dirk is dead," Jakob said. "You know that, right?"

"I know."

"Piet did it, but I wish I'd done it myself."

The anger seemed to ooze from his pores. I didn't want to
tell him I couldn't imagine him ever pulling a trigger. Even
now, his hands were trembling. "You don't need to say anything more," I said. "It's over now. And it was her choice, what
she did, not yours."

A soft suckling noise came from the crib, Rudi sucking his thumb as he dozed. I walked over to the crib and looked down at him. Here was another little boy, waiting for love, just like Aletta.

"Besides," I said, gesturing to Rudi, "it wasn't only you she saved."

"Yes," he said. He nodded several times, like he was trying to convince himself of that. "There's no telling what might have happened to him otherwise."

"Just like there's no telling what any of us would have done. I admit, I was very angry at her for a long time. But now I realize all we can do now is try to heal and move forward." I bent down to adjust the blue baby blanket, tucking it over Rudi's shoulders. In that moment, it was my sister I was thinking of, my sister and Maurits, my sister and Dirk. If I could forgive Ida, could I learn to forgive Lies, too?

FORTY-NINE

Liesbeth de Wit
October 19, 1945
Amsterdam, the Netherlands

The notice arrived in their mailbox on a Friday, just before noon. Liesbeth saw it on the hall landing on her way out for a walk, lying there inconspicuously, as if it were any regular piece of mail: a bill to be paid, a flyer advertising the reopening of a department store. She picked it up and studied it. Maurits's full name was stamped on the front.

She slipped it into her jacket pocket and continued out the door toward the park, where she found a lone bench that over-looked the pond. Before the Hunger Winter, lush trees had framed the pond and played home to chattering birds. However, like so many teddy bears, books, and rags, the branches of the park's trees had disappeared into the bellies of the city's stoves and now the park looked bare.

Liesbeth sat and looked out over the water. In two days, it would be the anniversary of the darkest day in her memory. One whole year since Gerrit had passed. On Saturday morn-ing, she and Johanna would take the train down south to meet their aunt and uncle. While Liesbeth couldn't wait to spend some time with *tante* Rika and *oom* Cor, she couldn't say the same of the trip down with Johanna, which she was certain would pass in silence, if her sister didn't find a way to end up on a different train all together.

Something beside the bench caught Liesbeth's attention. A scrap of tartan fabric, part of a doll's dress, by the looks of it, maybe a gift from a relative who had traveled to Scotland before the war. A lifetime ago. She closed her eyes and thought of the outfit her mother had sewn for her own childhood doll. It was dressed in the traditional costume of the island, with a little floral dickey and a jacket over a long skirt and apron. Gerrit had fashioned the lace cap himself, and he'd been so proud to present it to her. Never once had he refused to play with her; never once had he pushed her away.

She clung to those memories of him: his flippant smile, like a joke was constantly on the tip of his tongue, how he'd pulled her aside and pointed out her sketches, telling her that they were good, really good. Now he would never get to play uncle to Aletta or to her own children, if she were ever so lucky to be blessed with them.

But the notion of having children with Maurits no longer left her with the elated feeling it once had. Instead, she felt cold and empty. She resented him for everything he'd done, not just to her, but to her family. Everything he stood for. She saw it now, as clear as the North Star on a cloudless night. The only thing Maurits cared about was himself.

Her fingers met the envelope in her pocket. She pulled it out and turned it over. It was neatly typeset, aside from the letter *s*, which was worn out in the lower curve, but what caught her attention was the return address, a department of the Ministry of Justice. She pressed it to her chest. Whatever the letter contained, it would certainly shape their fate.

No, she assured herself: *his* fate. This was her final chance.

If she wanted a future of her own, real prospects for a family, for following her dreams, she had to seize it. And that was only possible if she first pulled out some shears and cut the threads that bound them. It was time for her to create a life that was worth living.

She got up from the bench and left the park in a hurry. Any delay would only create room for doubt, and for once, she felt certain about her decision. On her way to the pharmacy, she practiced everything she intended to say.

However, she arrived at the pharmacy to find a delivery driver unloading a shipment of medicines, and his crates and clipboards cluttered the tiles of the waiting area. She stood in the corner, egging herself on, as Maurits finished up with the supplier.

"Hello, darling," he said to her, when the shop was empty. "Aren't you the perfect way to brighten my day." He kissed her on the lips, looking delighted to see her.

She paused, that wave of doubt crashing in. There were periods when he was so sweet and caring, when his love seemed so genuine. *No*, she told herself, *this is your chance to be free. It's now or never.*

"You may want to hold that sentiment." She passed him the envelope. His expression hardened as he saw the return address. When he opened it, he seemed to shrink, his chest caving inward.

"What does it say?"

He handed it to her.

This is to inform you that you are under investigation for reputed activities during the occupation that were disloyal to the crown. You must report to the authorities by October 30 or face impending arrest.

This meant prison time; that much was almost guaranteed. Liesbeth thought of those men she'd seen rounded up in the neighborhood, the rumors of the internment camps for the "traitors." She tried to picture Maurits sleeping in a bare cot, washing himself in a dirty latrine, as Johanna had been forced to do.

"Maurits."

He backed away, his eyes darting around the shop. Then he turned and swiped his arm across the counter, sending medicine jars shattering to the floor.

"Maurits!" She reached out to steady him but he shook her off.

"Pull yourself together," she said, her voice shaking. She became aware of the passersby gawking through the window, wondering what the fuss was about. She considered closing the blinds, bolting the door, but this was his mess to clean up. "I'm going home," she said. "I'm leaving in the morning to visit family. I'm done with us, I really am."

FIFTY

Johanna Vos
December 5, 1945
Amsterdam, the Netherlands

As 1945 drew to a close, life returned to its normal pace, and the signs of war disappeared one by one. Ships left Rotterdam's harbor: some carrying soldiers bursting to return to the wheat fields and mountains and family they'd left behind, others bringing young brides to their new homes in Canada. City squares were cleared of armored vehicles, signs with Jewish surnames hauled out of storage and returned to the proper street corners. Men like Maurits were rounded up and thrown in camps where they belonged, the very camps that had held so many innocent people.

However, the biggest change, the one that kept us holding our breath and checking the post, was the people. Stragglers returning from the east—members of the Resistance, Jews, homosexuals, and more. And with everyone who returned, came the reports of those who hadn't. For every joyful reunion, like the one we had with Marijke, came telegrams and letters and tears of grief. We mourned the dramatist, *meneer* Smit, who had died on a death march. We mourned the surgeon and his wife, who had been gassed as soon as they'd left the cattle cars. We mourned Jakob's cousins, his brothers, his parents and so many more. And for those who had yet to resurface, we launched formal inquiries and waited for news.

The evening of December 5 was Pakjesavond. Dutch children had been counting down to it for weeks, eager for Sinterklaas's visit with his sack full of presents. The older children clung to the hope that, this year, the holiday would be as they remembered: full of laughter and treats aplenty. On the nights leading up to the fifth, they filled their wooden shoes with hay and left them out in hopes of marzipan and chocolate letters. Instead, they woke up disappointed by mealy cookies or empty shoes, unable to understand why this was happening if Sinterklaas didn't have to deal with ration cards and food stamps.

Lucky for Willem and me, Aletta was too young to know the difference. She fed off the energy of the children around her, toddling around the house like the little orangutan we saw her for.

As the sun set on December 5, Jakob brought Rudi over to our place for the celebrations. Willem and I had decorated as best we could with candles and paper cut-outs of Sinterklaas and his white horse, which Aletta had scribbled over in bright colors. As Jakob set Rudi down on the floor, he handed me an envelope.

"This was on your doormat," he said.

The postmark was British, with a stamp bearing the likeness of King George VI. I opened the envelope and started reading the letter aloud.

"Dear Mrs. Vos,
I apologize for the delay in writing you, but your letter with my son's dog tags took a very long time in finding me..."

I scanned the rest and pulled out the photograph the woman had tucked into the envelope. There he was, the RAF pilot who had washed up on the shore. A name was scrawled on the back of the image: Gilbert Johnson, 1941. I reread the letter, noticing the love in his mother's careful handwriting for the son who had never come home.

Willem rested his hands on my shoulders as he leaned over to read the letter. "She'll rest better now knowing she has some answers."

"Yes, I'm sure she will."

Jakob checked the time. "Let's get the children seated. Sinterklaas is due any minute." He led Aletta and Rudi over to the chairs in the sitting room. "Is your sister joining us?"

I shook my head, all too aware of the glance Jakob and Willem shared behind my back. I hadn't spoken to her for weeks, but I assumed she'd made her way down to *tante* Rika and *oom* Cor for the holiday. She wouldn't spend Pakjesavond on her own.

Three loud knocks on the door interrupted my thoughts. "Children," Willem said, "who could that be? Shall we sing to invite him in?"

Jakob and I sat down with the children to sing the Sinterklaas songs while Willem went to answer the door. Aletta bounced on my lap, waving her arms in her attempt to sing along. As we finished the last line, Willem turned the handle and threw open the door to reveal the good saint.

Dressed from head to toe in red-and-white robes, his face covered by a long, snow-colored beard, Piet was almost unrecognizable as Sinterklaas. He winked at me and stepped into the room with a grand sweep of the arm. "Did I understand correctly that there are some very well behaved children in this house? Should I open my sack of presents?"

Aletta squealed, and Rudi mimicked her, pleased to be part of the excitement. Piet made a big show of distributing the modest gifts we'd managed to get for the children: a wooden train for Rudi, a handmade doll for Aletta. If my pride hadn't gotten in the way, I would have asked Liesbeth to design a set of costumes for the doll, but for now it wore a plain blue shift, the pinnacle of my own sewing abilities.

Jakob and Willem got fully into the mood, oohing and ahhing at everything that came out of the burlap sack, much to the delight of Aletta and Rudi. I held back, watching it all from a distance, the happiness on the children's faces, as though they'd already forgotten what the war had put them through. I thought of Lies, how much she missed Aletta, and I hoped I was right in believing that she wasn't at home that night, all on her own.

Piet stroked the long white beard and bowed toward the children as he took his leave. Willem burst into song again, and Aletta clapped her hands as Sinterklaas made his way out. I followed Piet into the hall.

"Thank you," I said, "you made it an evening to remember."

"Something tells me those two won't remember a bit of this once they've slept off their sugar rush."

"If only we could all say that of the last five years."

He smirked but then he grew serious as he pulled the cotton batting of the beard from his chin. "You'll get through this, you know, all of us will."

"What about Aletta?" I asked. "How can I be sure she'll make it through this without too many scars?"

"Surround Aletta with good people, and she will be fine, good people who love her."

He said goodbye and headed home, leaving me there in the hallway, staring at the plaster fixtures on the ceiling. *People who love her*, I thought. My mind returned to what Willem had said to me the night before, the same thing he'd said on many nights since my return. *Your sister did everything she could to help Aletta, you know, and she kept Aletta's identity a secret, even though that secret put her own life in danger. You're lucky to have her. Isn't it time to forgive her?*

FIFTY-ONE

Liesbeth de Wit
December 5, 1945
Amsterdam, the Netherlands

The letters from Maurits poured in one by one, but Liesbeth refused to read them. However, she gave in once, only once, on Pakjesavond, while everyone else was celebrating and she sat at home, darning her stockings. Much as she tried to tell herself it didn't matter, she couldn't help but wonder what she was missing out on: teasing jokes as poems and gifts changed hands, Aletta's gleeful smile. If only she'd gone to visit *tante* Rika and *oom* Cor for the holiday, but the relatives who were hosting them while they waited to return to Zierikzee had little space. Besides, she felt she'd overstayed her welcome with her many trips down south in the weeks since she'd left Maurits.

When she finished darning her stockings, she got up to pour herself a glass of *jenever* and found herself opening the top drawer of Maurits's desk. The letters he'd sent sat in a neat stack, fastened together with a black ribbon. She took the top one from the pile and pierced the seam of the envelope with his ivory letter opener, the paper ripping with a satisfying tear. Once the envelope was open, it had a magnetic pull, but she was afraid she would regret reading the letter. It felt like inching up to the edge of a cliff, hoping to catch the view, but one step too far would send her tumbling.

She sat there with the letter folded on her lap, until the glass beside her was empty, the *jenever* leaving her throat warm and burning. On lonely nights like these, she longed for the familiar boost of the Pervitin, that confidence in a tube. However, the drug's spell had been temporary, wearing off to leave her emptier than ever. She reminded herself that she was her own person, independent of her husband, and that she could choose the power his words would have over her.

Still, when she began to read, Maurits's voice came through with such force that she had to put the letter down to catch her breath.

Liesbeth, darling,
I miss you terribly. You wouldn't believe how bad it is here at Camp Vught, how they do everything they can to humiliate us. Thoughts of you are the only thing that keep me sane. Come back to me. I need to know you're waiting for me, that you'll be there when my time is done. Promise me that.

Liesbeth didn't read the rest. She couldn't face him or the hold he'd had on her. Although she'd known he had been sent to Camp Vught, it felt jarring seeing the name in writing, the understanding that her husband was lying in the same barracks, eating from the same vats of soup, as Jo had, not so long ago. Liesbeth's heart ached as she considered this. No doubt, Johanna was satisfied with this turn of events, if not pleased, but for Liesbeth it was just another reminder of how she'd failed her family, how everything had changed for good.

A week earlier, a newspaper had shared reports on the treatment of the NSBers in the camp, of the games the guards played to torment the traitors: chasing men around with a rubber bat, making them hop around like frogs, blasting their genitals with a hose. The journalists spoke of the need for "reeducation and reintegration," but Liesbeth knew Maurits didn't have the strength to weather such humiliation.

She folded the letter in half, and then in half again, folding it until it shrank to a size that she could conceal in the palm of her hand. For a long time she'd sat there, the sharp corners of the folds pressing into her skin. Then went to the kitchen, and lit the stove, letting the flames consume the letter, the paper curling and crumbling into ash. She recalled the long, cold evenings during the Hunger Winter, how it had been her sketches that she'd dropped into the stove, her designs and hopes for a different future.

She returned to the other room feeling lighter and promised herself she would not read another letter, not a single one, no matter how many more showed up at her door. Instead, she rummaged through the other desk drawers until she found some scraps of paper and a stub of charcoal pencil. She sat by the window, watching the heavy snowflakes twirl between the rooftops, and she began to draw—hesitant strokes at first, the curved figure of a woman's silhouette. Then, she closed her eyes and envisioned it all before her: a shop with her name stenciled in the window, dresses hung in a splash of colors, a sewing machine in the center where the designs came to life. With every stroke, her hand became surer, until it felt like it was all in front of her, waiting for her to grab it.

Two weeks later, Liesbeth had a meeting with a lawyer to discuss her plans. Given Maurits's record, nothing would be easy, but some light offered hope. She took the long route home through the Vondelpark to mull it all over, wishing she could discuss the options with her sister, who would know how to take a step back and gauge the best course of action. She wished she could simply drop by and cozy up under a blanket with her as they weighed the situation, like they had for so many troubles throughout the years.

Liesbeth was still thinking about this as she rounded the corner to her apartment. A stranger stood in front of the entrance, scanning the nameplates.

"Can I help you?" Liesbeth asked.

He turned, tipping his fedora to reveal his gray, U-shaped hairline. "*Mevrouw* De Wit?"

"Yes, that's me."

He presented her with a card stamped with a government insignia. A hot flush spread down her neck.

"What can I do for you, sir?" she asked, but in her heart she already knew why he'd come.

"We've been trying to contact you. Perhaps you wish to step indoors for a little more privacy."

She reached out a hand to steady herself against the brick wall. "He's dead, isn't he?"

The man nodded. "I'm sorry for your loss."

She felt a sudden tightness in her chest, like someone had reached in to squeeze out her heart like a dirty sponge.

She took a deep breath and tried to picture her husband's face, tried to summon the warmth and comfort of his touch, the blissful memories they'd made together. Nothing came to her.

"How?" she asked.

"I beg your pardon?"

"How did he die?" In her gut, she knew this was something her husband had wanted, had chosen for himself.

The government man looked from her to the salesman that was making his rounds a few houses farther down. "Please, *mevrouw*, let's continue this conversation indoors." The concern on his face suggested that one too many housewives had broken down in front of him, but Liesbeth felt oddly detached, like she'd stepped outside her body to watch this play out.

She unlocked the door to the building and beckoned him into the front hall, but no farther. "How did he do it?" she repeated.

"Poison, a cocktail of drugs he managed to steal from the doctor's stores. They found him in his bunk. It was too late to save him."

So, Maurits had found his way out, the cowardly choice when facing a lifetime of loneliness. The government man kept talking but Liesbeth had stopped listening. She was wondering what she would say to the salesman when he arrived at their door. Or might he have noticed the tense encounter and have the civility to pass them by? What would she tell her aunt and uncle about Maurits? And Jo, if speaking to her sister was an option? She tried to imagine herself dressing in black, hiding behind a crepe mourning veil. The image didn't fit.

"*Mevrouw*? Did you hear what I said? We'll also need you to sign some papers."

"Yes, whatever is necessary."

The bell rang, but she made no move to answer it. She stared at the government man, at the clipboard with the forms he'd removed from his briefcase, the forms that would mark the end of her marriage, and mark her as a widow. There was no getting her husband back, no changing him, no more hoping he would revert back to the person she'd fallen for. She kept waiting for the pain to take over, the reality that he was gone forever, but instead she felt as if she'd shimmied out of a tight corset and, for the first time in years, she could breathe freely.

So much uncertainty seemed to spiral around her. Packing up Maurits's belongings, selling what she could, finding a place she could truly call home. She had so much to arrange. A lot would have to change. But she could build her own life, one decision at a time. And she would start that now, by taking the forms, saying good-day, and showing this gentleman out.

FIFTY-TWO

Johanna Vos
May 11, 1946
Zierikzee, the Netherlands

The long table that had once spanned the back garden of the house in Zierikzee was gone, rotted away from the waterlogged soil, but rows of chairs had taken its place, ready for the guests who were due any minute. *Tante* Rika and *oom* Cor had spent the past several months making the house inhabitable: scrubbing the brine stains from the doorframes, tearing out the flooring, rebuilding the chicken coop. Willem and I had helped whenever we could, but this was the first time we were all gathered there together, the first time since the autumn that I'd had to face my sister.

While Willem finished tying the ribbons to the chairs outside, I lingered in my old bedroom upstairs, Aletta clinging to my knees as I fixed the buttons on my dress.

"Mama," she said, reaching up for me. I would never tire of hearing that word. I picked her up and danced with her, pointing out her reflection in the mirror, but I found myself remembering when I'd stood in that same spot with Liesbeth, the joyful bride on her wedding day. How excited we'd been, ready to start a new chapter of our lives together, both of us settling down in the big city. A day full of promise. I shook away the thought and carried Aletta downstairs, where everyone was filing in. Willem found me by the side door and gestured to Jakob and Marijke and her husband, who had made the trip down from Amsterdam for this special day. I greeted them and gushed over Marijke's newborn daughter, whom she cradled in her arms. "Every bit as beautiful as her handsome parents," I said.

Marijke gave me a wooden smile. Maybe she found it difficult to accept a compliment. Almost a year after the liberation, her face still bore so much sadness. "Thank you for organizing today," she said. "I can't think of a better way to honor everyone we lost."

I showed her husband to his seat and brought her, Jakob and the other three musicians who filled out the string quintet to the sitting room, where they could tune their instruments and warm up. Across the room, Liesbeth lifted a framed photograph from the mantelpiece, a snapshot of Gerrit grinning proudly with a swimming medal dangling from his neck. She carried it outside and laid it down on the table with all the other photographs, of the sisters and aunts and cousins and lovers whose lives the war had claimed, evidence of all the death and heartbreak. I debated following her outside, telling her everything I meant to say, the words that felt so difficult. I'd promised Willem and promised myself that I would make things right. However, while I hesitated, she found her way to a seat next to a man I'd never seen before.

"That's the doctor," Willem said, coming up beside me.

"*The* doctor? You mean the one who sold her the building for her new shop."

"We both know it's turned into more than that. I'm certain we'll be seeing lots more of him." He nudged me. "Have you said hello to her yet?"

I shook my head. So much had changed for Lies since Maurits's death. The news hadn't come as a surprise. On so many occasions, I'd pictured him standing behind the fence at Camp Vught, staring up at the barbed wire and feeling very much alone. Secretly, I was proud of Lies for picking herself up and starting over, trying to turn her talents into something she'd always dreamed of. In so many ways, Maurits's cowardice had freed her. And maybe, it had opened another door for her and me, a chance to reconcile and find our way back to one another as sisters.

Before Willem could push me further, *tante* Rika came over to say that everyone was here. It was time to begin.

Outside, the rows of chairs were filled all the way back to the magnolia tree, which was in full bloom. Willem sat in the front row, by *tante* Rika and *oom* Cor, with Liesbeth and the doctor on the other side, next to Marijke's husband. Rudi and Aletta had flopped down in the grass with their toy blocks, and our friends and other members of the artists' Resistance sat in the remaining seats, faces that had been part of our secret circle during the war, and family members of those we'd lost. Some artists had traveled from all over the country to join us on this beautiful spring afternoon. I looked around at all the people, at the line of photographs, and up at the cloud-dotted sky. The sun was shining, and the scent of freshly cut grass filled the air. It was hard to believe that, not so long ago, tanks had rolled down the back street, while bomber planes dived overhead.

Jakob and I took our places to open the concert. I read out the list of names we'd gathered, the people we'd lost—musicians, actors, dancers, poets, patrons of the arts, family, and others who were dear to us. At Ida's name, I squeezed Jakob's hand. At Gerrit's, my gaze fell on the far end of the garden, his old spot along the long table. In the front row, Liesbeth reached for a handkerchief.

It took several minutes to get through the names. When I finished, the audience seemed to let out a collective sigh, and we paused for a moment of silence. Then the music began. First, Jakob and Marijke set up with the other members of a string quintet. I sat down beside Willem as they began to play, Schubert's String Quintet, the last work Schubert completed before his death. Jakob had adapted it to include his contrabass, and the deep tones of his instrument brought out a quality in the music that was as haunting as it was beautiful. The music was lush, bursting with emotion, joyous one second and dark and somber the next. Like life, I thought, always changing, like rain rolling in with the clouds, only to clear to a bright, promising sky. I peeked at Lies, who sat with her head cocked to the side, a trace of a smile on her lips. The doctor reached, almost imperceptibly, for her hand, and her smile grew. She turned toward me, but I quickly looked away.

Maybe it was all about accepting the change in the weather, the moments and decisions of others that lay beyond your control.

The quintet played on, and we all slipped into the serenity of the music, the comfort of the notes. Even Aletta and Rudi stopped playing and sat still, transfixed by the movement of Marijke's bow. When the last movement came to a close, we were still, all of us caught in our own memories, until someone remembered to clap.

Then it was my turn. Schubert's composition had held me in such a close grip that I hadn't had the time to get nervous, but that feeling returned as I got up and faced the audience, as I faced my sister. She looked up at me with such earnestness, such love, and such sadness, that I almost forgot what I wanted to say. Willem nodded, encouraging me. I thought about the clouds rolling in, the storm that faded into spring sun. We had weathered the storm. Barely, but we had made it. And I wouldn't have my daughter there beside me if it hadn't been for Lies. I had rehearsed the songs I'd intended to perform the day I'd found out I was pregnant. But suddenly, I knew what I needed to sing instead.

"I hope I won't disappoint any Billie Holiday fans out there," I said, "but I'm going to sing something a little different than what you see in the program." I turned to Lies. "A song about dreams, about second chances."

Her expression shifted as my words registered. I began to sing "Somewhere over the Rainbow." Wim smiled and Aletta waved at the sound of my voice and tried to make her way toward me, but he scooped her up and held her close, whispering in her ear. Lies didn't take her eyes off me. Right then, I knew we would find our way back to one another, one step at a time.

I looked up and closed my eyes and pictured the world I wanted for her and for my daughter. A world without hate, a world in which we tried to find one another, through a little hope and understanding. Maybe that world wasn't so far away.

When I opened my eyes, something atop one of the nearby buildings caught my attention. It couldn't be, or was it? I gestured to Lies, and she followed my gaze. A nest, high in the chimney top, the highest spot on the horizon. A stork's nest. I looked at her and she looked at me and a silent word passed between us: maybe, just maybe.

★ ★ ★ ★ ★

HISTORICAL NOTE

When we think of the damage inflicted during the Second World War, we tend to think of the ravaged battlefields in Northern France and Russia, of bombed-out buildings in London, of the gas chambers at Auschwitz. But, in May 1940, when Nazi Germany invaded the Netherlands to little resistance, the Dutch people had their hopes for neutrality erased and faced a new reality: occupation.

In the early months of the occupation, the impact on daily life for the average citizen, while notable, was still moderate. Many things carried on as usual. The Nazis were inclined to give preferential treatment to their "Germanic brothers." In some circles, cooperation with the Nazis evolved into staunch support, as the Dutch National Socialist Party (NSB) gained prominence. But the notion of everyday life faded when the Nazis began restricting more and more personal freedoms, starting with those of the Jewish community.

The Dutch then faced a choice: Do you collaborate, keep your head down, or actively resist? This gray area is what I wanted to explore in *The Dutch Orphan*. Would you offer shelter to a stranger, even if it meant risking your life? Would you refuse to register your vocation in a show of support for others? What if this meant you could no longer afford to feed your children? Would you do business with the Germans if that led to some well-needed nourishment in return?

According to Yad Vashem, the World Holocaust Remembrance Center, more than three-quarters of Dutch Jews were murdered during the Holocaust, higher than in any other Western European country. This was in part due to the efficient bureaucracy set up by the Germans in the Netherlands and the relative independence of the German police there. Another important factor was the swift reprisals for the general strike that was held in protest of the first major *razzia*. Fear of more reprisals contributed to the delayed setup of organized resistance.

Another thing that struck me when researching the persecution of Jews in the Netherlands was the introduction of bounty hunters. These Dutch men were paid a bonus for every Jew they managed to arrest. Incentives like these in desperate times were one of the countless reasons that certain citizens struggled with their expressions of loyalty and trust. Does the wrong choice become the right choice if you're fighting to support your family?

Many of the events that happen in this book are inspired by true occurrences. As in other countries, the zoo in Amsterdam offered refuge to people in need throughout much of the war. The house concerts in the novel were actually held throughout the Netherlands and featured some of the country's best artists. Johanna's initial performance at Café Alcazar was inspired by the performance of Jewish trumpetist Clara de Vries, who was later arrested and murdered at Auschwitz. Similarly, the stories surrounding the children at the Jewish nursery are a nod to the many children who were rescued by nursery staff and other members of the Resistance. Finally, the traumatic incident in the bunker building at Camp Vught is also based on real events, a reminder that the horrific torture in concentration camps extended beyond the gas chambers and crematoria of our common narrative.

Writing this novel while living in Amsterdam has reminded me of the many small signs of the occupation that remain to this day, like the brass stumbling stones that mark the former homes of Holocaust victims; the test blast of the city air sirens; and the 1940s newspapers and hiding place that were discovered in the renovation of my old apartment. I'm grateful to the many friends and loved ones who've shared stories of their families' experiences during the war, and to the countless people who have taken the time to preserve their stories and diaries in the Dutch archives.

In some cases, I've played with the timeline of events to better fit the narrative. For example, I condensed the February Strike to play out over one day instead of two and changed the dates of a subsequent *razzia*. Similarly, I show word of the German invasion reaching Johanna and Liesbeth during the afternoon of their wedding party, whereas they likely would have woken up to the news.

To list all the books and archival resources that helped me give life to this story would require a great many pages. A few titles that proved indispensable include: *Hitler's Bounty Hunters: the Betrayal of the Jews* by Ad van Liempt; *Hier Woont een NSB'er* by Josje Damsma and Erik Schumacher; *Blitzed: Drugs in Nazi Germany* by Norman Ohler; and *Muziek in de Schaduw van het Derde Rijk* by Pauline Micheels.

ACKNOWLEDGMENTS

I wrote this novel during those dreary days of lockdown, a process that brought new meaning to the idea of the solitary writer and came with its own set of challenges. This process reminded me that writing a novel takes a village, and I am so grateful for all the advice and support I received along the way.

I'm deeply grateful to my first editor, Patrick Crean, for believing in me like no other and helping me find my voice. An enormous thank-you as well to Janice Zawerbny, for later picking up this project with enthusiasm and keen perception, and to Erika Imranyi for such thoughtful feedback and ongoing support. To the rest of the teams at HarperCollins Canada and Park Row Books—including Iris Tupholme, Nicole Luongo, Greg Stephenson, and many more—thank you for your hard work in bringing this book to life.

Thank you to Rachel Letofsky and everyone at CookeMcDermid Agency for always being there with ideas and a listening ear.

When it comes to the research, I spent many a comforting hour between the archival stacks at the NIOD Institute for War, Holocaust and Genocide Studies in Amsterdam.

I also appreciate all the writers of the London Writers' Salon, who bring sunshine to my writing days. To the International

Writers' Collective, thank you for giving me a space to continue learning about this craft. And to the faculty at the University of British Columbia's MFA program, who have taught me so much along the way.

Thank you to Julie Hartley, Laura Nicol, Jill Goldberg, and Sarah Richards for always helping and cheering for me from afar. To Jen Gryzenhout and Melanie Veenstra, for the friendship that started with a cheese platter and a blank page and has turned into something much deeper.

Thank you also to the many friends who offered encouragement and ideas along the way, especially to Dyon Vocking, Wilco van Bokhorst, Andrea Spithoff, Lauren Titus, Lisa Süss, and Lauren Tan.

To Nita Pronovost and Matthew Lawson—despite being continents apart, a special friendship has taken root. Matt, your feedback and words of motivation were integral to helping this story take shape.

Finally, to family: thank you to my grandmother, Harmien Deys, whose own experiences in the war inspired many moments in this novel. To Hannie de Vries and Han Kooistra, for always being there. And to my brother, Peter, and my parents, Rod and Evelyn Keith, for the constant love and support.

In many ways, writing this novel while so much of daily life was on pause reminded me how small the world really is, and how stories continue to bind us together.

Read on for a sneak peek at The Dutch Wife, *Ellen Keith's sweeping story of love and survival during World War II.*

It is, in fact, far easier to act
under conditions of tyranny than to think.

HANNAH ARENDT

CHAPTER ONE

Marijke de Graaf
May 3, 1943
Amsterdam, the Netherlands

The infant in the baby carriage opened her eyes and saw that I was not her mother. Her face grew red, wrinkling up like a walnut. I forced myself to swallow and glanced ahead, where three German soldiers patrolled the gated entrance to the Vondelpark. Beside me, Theo's voice dropped to a hush. "You go on alone. It's less suspicious. Just act calm." He pressed his lips to my hair before ducking off into the nearest shop.

I leaned down to coo at the child. "Shh, quiet now. Everything is all right." But my pulse betrayed me. My knuckles blanched around the handle of the carriage, and I adjusted the blanket to conceal the telltale seam beneath her, the hidden compartment that would give us away. Forged ration coupons and foxhole radios Theo and I had built, secreted away in cigar boxes. Not to mention a pistol.

Through the fog, swastikas flying from a nearby building

caught the morning sun, and the soldiers smoked as they checked the identification of passersby. A few meters back, Theo pretended to be absorbed in a rack of newspapers. He nodded in encouragement. The little one stared up at me as I carried on, but when the wheel of the carriage stuttered over a loose cobblestone, she started to cry. Loud, grating wails. I debated turning around, but the damn *moffen* had already noticed. The soldier who looked my age, or no more than twenty-four, stepped forward. "And where are you rushing off to?" He hitched the rifle strap up over his shoulder. "You're the first pretty pair of legs to come by all morning."

The nape of my neck tingled. The baby's cries escalated while the soldier held out a hand for my ID papers, and his gaze dropped to my chest as I drew them from the pocket of my peacoat. I tried not to cringe, hoping Theo was too far away to notice.

The other soldier approached, his brow like a pan greased for baking. He peered into the carriage. "What a racket. Does it need to be rocked?"

I checked the padding, the blanket, but nothing had shifted. "She's just hungry." My words were too sharp, and as I tried to calm her, I wondered if he recognized the inexperience in my actions. Sweat dampened the folds of my blouse while I waited for them to demand I pick her up. The men looked me up and down unabashedly.

The one studying my identification squinted at me. "Marijke de Graaf. Just how old is this photograph?" He held it up for his companion to examine. My curly hair was longer in the photo, my face a little fuller.

"Four months."

The child, finally quiet, sucked her thumb, her cheeks scarlet with tears. After an unbearable pause, the soldier handed back my papers. "Well, it sure doesn't do you justice." He winked and waved me on my way.

My mouth was dry, my arms tense as I continued on into the park, humming a nervous, shapeless tune. I found a bench near the teahouse, where more uniforms were scattered between the suits and dresses at the tables: soldiers eating pastries, looking out over the water at the ducks and squirrels as though our city had always been theirs.

Within a few minutes, Theo found me. He bent down to check on the child before giving me a kiss. "They took their time with your papers, didn't they?"

I shook my head. "They're just searching for entertainment."

He lifted the baby from the carriage.

"Darling, not here. Let's get her to safety."

"But look at this tiny frown." He pulled faces at her until she gurgled a laugh and stretched out as if trying to tug on his big ears, and I watched with yearning as I imagined us with a daughter of our own to comfort and love.

"If only we could keep her." He placed her back with a wistful sheen in his eyes that made me want to take him in my arms.

"But you know we can't. Plus, she needs to be breast-fed. Our time will come, I promise."

He sighed. "I know."

From there, we cut across the park and exited through another set of gates, these ones thankfully unguarded. Women bustled down the streets, and collectively they formed a walking fashion catalog from three years earlier, colors fading and hems showing their wear. Since the invasion, everyone had learned to keep their heads lower, their movements more purposeful, and the few men in sight were prepubescent or already wrinkled, so many others afraid of venturing out, only to be rounded up in the impending call-ups for forced labor.

As we approached the address the resistance had given us, the front door of the house opened a crack, and a woman peeked out, observing the baby carriage. She recited our code in a stiff voice that wouldn't have fooled anyone. "Have you come to see my new flower beds?" On hearing our response, she checked for onlookers and beckoned us into her front hall. Inside, she bent over the baby carriage with a look of heartbreak, her eyes ringed red, her skin showing the toll of sleepless nights. "Please, come sit down," she said at last. "I'll put on the kettle."

"We can't stay, I'm afraid." I glimpsed an empty bassinet in the sitting room, a baby blanket crocheted with initials draped over the side. The sight of it made my throat tighten. "We're so sorry about your loss, *mevrouw*."

She picked up the baby and gazed down at her. "It's a dreadful time to bring a child into the world, isn't it?"

Theo and I exchanged a glance.

"Well," she said, "at least I can still be of use to another young life." Her chin started to tremble, and she retrieved a handkerchief from her pocket. "Such light hair, for a Jew. What happened to her mother?"

"Pneumonia," Theo replied. "We were hiding them in our attic, and by the time we found a doctor who would come, it was too late." He glanced at the clock on the wall. "I'm sorry, we need to get going. We can't thank you enough, *mevrouw*. Please hide the carriage well. Your husband knows what to do with its contents."

I leaned to kiss the baby on the forehead and squeezed the woman's hand in farewell. Theo paused in the front entrance. "It warms my heart to see how willing you are to care for a child that's not your own." She nodded, but kept her focus on the baby, and once the street was clear, we left the house without looking back.

SHORTLY after eight the next evening, the blackout curtains went up across Amsterdam, erasing the city from the sky. The Nazis had cut the electricity again, so I lit a candelabrum and sat beside the darkened window to play the violin. Nobody went to the symphony anymore, yet I still practiced every day. My bow glided across the strings while the grandfather clock ticked like a metronome, counting the passing minutes. I put down the instrument and drummed my fingers against it, wondering what was taking Theo so long, raking my thoughts for the forgotten mention of some appointment, but all that came to me were the signs in the squares, threatening forced labor in Germany, men picked up from the streets at random and carted off in trucks. I thought of Theo's favorite student, who had disappeared the week before.

I'd set a potato-and-nettle soup to cook in the hay box, and when the aroma wafted over, I rose to go stir it. In the hope of a distraction, I surveyed the kitchen, our good Delftware, the tablecloths from my trousseau, making a mental inventory of what we'd next barter when we ran out of eggs and butter.

A key jiggled in the front door lock. With it came that balm of relief, soothing my ever-fried nerves. Feeling silly for letting my imagination get the better of me, I resisted the urge to rush over to Theo, to run my fingers through the lone wave in his hair, to chide him for keeping me on edge. Instead, I bent over the pot, humming to myself, until he came up behind me, encircled his arms around my waist and lifted me into the air, the wooden spoon in my fist dripping soup across the tiles. He whispered into my neck, "I missed you."

"You know," I said, "it's impossible to think straight until you make it home."

When he put me down, his thick eyebrows hung lower than normal, like a shelf over his eyes. "Sorry, dear. I had a few stops to make. Piet is coming by in an hour to drop off some newspapers."

"One of the resistance publications?" I took his cold hands in mine, pressed them to his chest. "Where does he want you to deliver them?"

"I'll pass this batch on to my students."

"Good idea. You can tell me more about it over dinner."

"Later. It's almost nine." He led me upstairs to our bedroom, where he reached into the back of our wardrobe, pulled out the old atlas and opened it to reveal the small radio hidden within its pages. I lay beside him on the rug as he hooked up the *moffen* sieve and fiddled with its modulator dials to filter out the interference from German jamming stations. The Westerkerk chimed the hour, one of the few churches that hadn't yet lost its bells to the Nazi armament factories. As silence spread across Amsterdam with each passing week, it felt as if the city were holding her breath alongside us. But then came the sound we waited all day to hear. The first four notes of Beethoven's Fifth, the Morse code *V,* for *victory. Radio Oranje* on the BBC, the broadcast from our exiled royal house.

Theo passed me a headset and held my hand while we listened by candlelight. The government spoke of the recent factory strikes, the growing Nazi retaliations, but urged us to stay calm. "Resist the pressure to answer the labor call-ups. Stand strong or go into hiding—we must persevere."

I leaned over until my cheek brushed his and tried to picture the house empty at night, Theo deported for work in Germany. I couldn't bear the thought. He turned to kiss my hair. "Don't worry, love. We'll find a way."

After the broadcast, we stayed there on the rug, with my head resting on his shoulder. I wanted nothing more than for us to lie in bed all night and all day in an armor of blankets, sheathing ourselves from the troubles of the world.

"That child will have a good life with those people, won't she?" I asked.

"They're devout Christians. They'll treat her like their own, I'm sure of it."

I looked up at him. "And do you still think we're making the right choice by waiting?"

He hesitated. "It'll be hard enough for even the two of us to get through the war with all these food shortages and wage cuts. The last thing I would want is—"

A knock came at the front door. I moved to spy under the blackout paper, but Theo was already halfway to the stairs. "No use looking. It's dark as a cave out there. That'll be Piet, right on time."

I got up and followed him, but right before he reached the entrance, there was a loud noise, the splintering crack of wood. The door flew open. I saw the guns first and then the uniforms. The Gestapo burst into the house, yelling at us in German not to move. While they searched the rooms, we stood there in terrified silence, our hands above our heads. A lamp crashed to the floor. Drawers were flung open, papers sent fluttering, my violin tossed aside with a clunk. The smell of warm soup grew nauseating. Shaking, I rubbed my thumb against my ring finger, my wedding band cool against my knuckles. I lowered my gaze along the tiled floor until this granted me a glimpse of the corner of Theo's shoe, the anxious tap of his foot. One of the Gestapo shouted from upstairs. He'd discovered the radio supplies, the secret alcove in our attic. I thanked God we had nobody left in hiding.

The *moffen* circled us with taunting expressions, the barrels of their Lugers staring like deadened pupils. "Hand over your identification," the head agent said. "You have two minutes to pack. No talking."

One of them escorted us to our bedroom, where my undergarments lay strewn across the rug. As Theo reached for our luggage, his face met mine. His hair was disheveled, and behind his glasses, his eyes looked wild, all whites. We packed our warmest clothes, and I took our wedding photo off the wall, placing it in Theo's suitcase. I refused the *moffen* the satisfaction of seeing me cry. On our way downstairs, Theo laced his fingers through mine, sending a silent plea. *Don't tell them anything, don't let them win—I love you.* The Gestapo agent smacked him against the temple, knocking him sideways and ripping him from my grasp. When I reached out for him, they held me back, rough hands choking my wrists. I whispered his name, but it got lost in the noise. In front of me, Theo cradled his head. Then they shoved us forward and marched us out into the night.

★ ★ ★

WE Dutch girls climbed out of the frigid darkness, that nest of sickness and death. Outside the cattle car, dogs snapped at our ankles. The train whistled as it set off again and German guards shouted, pushed us into waiting trucks. When we arrived at the Ravensbrück camp compound, we were led around like parts on an assembly line. Examined. Assessed. Tagged. Sorted. We filed into a warehouse, where female guards ordered us to undress and turn in our clothes, and while I bent to remove my stockings, an SS man leaned in and whistled at the sight of my dangling breasts. Two gaunt prisoners handed out stained uniforms, and I put on the striped tunic and long, gray knickers, the fabric coarse against my thighs. The leather shoes had frayed laces and pinched at my toes, but many of the women around me were forced to squeeze their feet into bulky wooden clogs.

The Jews with their yellow stars emerged from the hall, heads shorn, nicked and bleeding from a careless barber. Skin spotted from lice. The women sobbed as they tried to cover their scalps with kerchiefs, any shred of fabric they could find. I understood the weight of their loss, and with a wince, I fingered the red triangle that marked me a political prisoner and raised a hand to my curls, grateful I still had a fraction of my own identity.

We slept two or three to a bunk, the sneezes and coughs of strangers on my skin. The sick urinated on the straw pallets where they lay, too weak to climb down from the top bed and drag themselves to the toilets. I learned to sleep with my cup and bowl tied to my clothes. In the beginning, Dutch mothers told folktales to their frightened daughters while a trio of cabaret stars swapped bawdy riddles across the beds, but these soon turned to quarrels over stolen bread. One woman drove herself mad, writhing on her mattress, yanking out clumps of hair and muttering to herself. Sometimes she whined like a puppy, going blue in the face with distress, while the others yelled at her to keep quiet. My pity for her became fringed with fear. Madness lurked there at Ravensbrück, tugging at us all. Survival depended on a stable mind, so I had to stay strong.

The latrines often clogged, spilling brown puddles onto the floor of the barracks block. Water became tainted from the fluids of the dead that had seeped into the camp sediment, taking on a tang and leaving many with swollen bellies. I made a constant trudge back and forth to the toilets as my body tried to purge itself of the contaminated liquid, the molding potatoes from the soup.

I soon came to understand that camp life played out in a different key for certain groups. German gentiles had the best chance at survival, in part because they easily understood the orders thrown at us throughout the day. Some of us—the Germans, the Dutch, whichever races the *moffen* deemed "human"—were permitted to keep our hair, but we had to wear it combed back, tucked under caps and kerchiefs. I forged hairpins from strips of wire from the factory. One night, I sat on my bed, teasing my bunk mate's thick waves into rolls and decorating them with ribbons torn from the edge of her kerchief. She became Ginger Rogers and I Betty Grable, and we fell asleep imagining a lavish banquet, with satin gowns and pearls and Champagne and *confit de canard*. The next morning, I woke to her body cold and lifeless against mine.

As days passed, the growls from my stomach grew louder, the sores on my hands redder. We poured the mucky ersatz coffee into our bowls to warm our cold feet and, each night, I picked the crusted mud off my shoes and polished them with the greatest care. When I found a hole growing across the right sole, I traced my finger around it and wept.

For long hours, we labored in the Siemens-Schuckert factory near camp, where we made electric components for submarines. During those shifts, I made a mental list of new German words so I could learn to react without delay. They forced us to sing on the march to and from work. As we rounded the lake, my voice would grow hoarse with false cheer, and I sometimes caught myself cursing all those people Theo and I had sheltered, all the news we'd spread with our crystal radios— What had it amounted to? Half the Jews we'd helped were probably dead, and we'd become prisoners ourselves. I was inmate 21522. But I was determined not to be worn down, not to transform into one of the skeletons that moved through the camp like the living dead. And so I clung to Theo's memory with all my strength: how he'd pleaded my innocence when the Gestapo had herded us out onto our darkened street, the bells of the Westerkerk tolling overhead. How he'd clutched my hand in the detainment cell, pressed my wedding band to his lips, his palms still blotched with grease from the radio. I thought of all the dreams we'd stockpiled throughout the war: of baking three-layered cakes again and picnicking along the Amstel River in new clothes, of me traveling with the orchestra to perform in Paris, of his history papers being published in journals as far off as New York. Of starting a family.

I promised myself I would do whatever it took to make it through the war alive.

My chance came on a cool morning near the end of June. At four o'clock, the reveille sirens woke us. An SS officer with a clipboard walked down the rows with a female guard. With a cleft chin and sagging neck, he appeared even older than my father, the type of man I'd expect to see bundled up by the fireplace in a café back in Amsterdam, smoking a pipe and complaining about the persistent rain. Whenever this officer passed a woman with light hair and fair skin, he stopped to look her up and down. Some, he pulled aside. When he got to me, he asked where I was from and when I told him, he reached out to cup my breast, rubbing his thumb over my nipple. "Good shape," he remarked.

He noted my number on his clipboard and ordered me to join the others. Attractive girls, all of them. Despite their pale, bruised skin, they looked young and healthier than the rest of the inmates. All of them had their hair. Most wore black triangles for "asocial" behavior—sexual deviants, alcoholics, prostitutes, troublemakers. Some wore the "criminal" green; a few others, red, like I did.

We huddled together but broke into rows of five as the officer approached. I pinched my cheeks to draw some color into them. How many times had I seen it before: women pulled out of the line, never to return? He surveyed us with a wry smile. "Consider yourselves lucky. I'm going to offer you a rare opportunity, a chance to serve the *Führer*, to help promote the efficiency and operations of camps across the Third Reich."

He paused to glance at the guard and suddenly I was sure he intended to make us *Blockovas*—block supervisors. A despicable function. Twice, the *Blockova* in our block had demanded my bread ration because she claimed I was too pretty, that I needed to learn that things wouldn't always be handed to me. Other *Blockovas* beat women or assigned extra labor. We hated even those who did nothing but follow the rules, because they had the power to hurt us on a whim.

"Strip."

At that, I unbuttoned my shift. Goose pimples flared across my chest as it fell at my feet. Some women tried to cover themselves, but I knew well enough to keep my hands at my sides. The officer circled us, removing a shadow of a girl with a spine that stuck out like a string of beads, and two women with misshapen breasts. He ordered them back to the work *Kommandos* before returning to position in front of us. "I want sixteen volunteers to service the prisoners at our new bordellos. We need some ripe, willing young women."

It took me a moment to understand what he meant. My skin started to prickle, bringing flashes of an Amsterdam alley: low necklines and tawdry earrings, drunken soldiers stumbling out of doorways, smears of cherry lipstick on their chins.

"Through the *Führer*'s generosity, you'll receive fresh food and a quarter of your earnings, and you will be released from the camp after six months of service." He grinned, letting that remark dangle.

I touched my hand to my side, yearning for the reassuring weight of my wedding band, which the *moffen* had confiscated upon my arrival. A pain hit my stomach, as if someone had reached in and pressed down on my gut. Six months, could it be? The girls around me shifted their weight. Perhaps their own stomachs were growling, their minds clouding with visions of hot dinners, of comfortable trains with dining cars headed away from Germany.

"Who is willing to service the Reich?"

At first, nobody moved. Eyes remained cast to the ground. The only sounds were the distant steps of marching prisoners.

"Think about it," he said. "Quarters with proper beds and hot running water."

A crow cawed, drawing my gaze upward. The bird sailed high above the compound, a dark speck against the dark sky. It swept past us, beyond the electrified confines of the camp, and disappeared.

A girl stepped forward. A green delinquent triangle marked the uniform at her feet. Her hair was the color of butter, and she wore a certain confidence, like she'd spent years weaving her way up through the German underworld. I wondered what had brought her here, if she'd been accused of theft or maybe assault.

The officer nodded and turned to us. One by one, girls hesitantly offered themselves. Some looked as young as twenty, others twenty-six or twenty-seven. Only two had brown hair; the rest were textbook Aryans.

The officer rapped a pen against his clipboard in impatience. "If no one else volunteers, I'll select someone."

Hunger scraped at my insides. I pictured a plate of fresh fruit and even a slice of meat, imagined being granted my freedom, but I considered that the officer might be lying. He watched us without any emotion. Yet if he'd wanted to, he could have driven into camp and carted us all away without a word of explanation.

Two days earlier, on the way to the factory, I'd passed a group of women digging ditches, the roughest work of all. One stood knee-deep in water and mud, wincing as she heaved the shovel over her shoulder. She'd rolled up her sleeves to reveal a fierce rash, a clear sign of typhus. In a few days, she would be dead, her body fed to the greedy fires of the crematorium.

A heated room, a hot shower. Away from the scourge of lice and vermin, a chance to maybe feel human again.

"Where are you sending them, sir?" The woman beside me shook as if she couldn't believe she'd dared speak up.

Without a glance in her direction, he swatted away the question. "To my men's camp, Buchenwald."

That name. One that had taken seed in the transit camp at Vught, as I'd spotted Theo's back retreating into the cattle car. A rumor passed on in whispers, as we wives and mothers, sisters and daughters watched through our tears, watched our very purpose for living disappear down the rails. A name I'd also heard at Ravensbrück, but one that had never seemed like anything more than a word, a spot in my mind where I'd tucked him for safekeeping. But it was a real place, a camp with fences and a crematorium and a brothel.

Two SS men approached and stood behind the officer, leering at our nakedness. One of them winked and moved his hand to reveal the erection swelling in his trousers.

The officer cleared his throat. "Well?"

I knelt down to pick up my uniform, making sure to glance up and look that dirty *mof* straight in the eye. I felt the solid ground against my palm, dirt beneath my fingernails.

Then I stood and took a step forward.